THAI HORSE

ALSO BY WILLIAM DIEHL

Hooligans
Chameleon
Sharky's Machine

William Diehl

GUILD PUBLISHING LONDON

To four treasured friends:

my agent, Owen Laster,
my editor, Peter Gethers,
my adviser, Buddy Harris,
and, as always, to the love of my life, Virginia

BOOK
ONE

Some men go skimming over the years of existence to sink gently into a placid grave, ignorant of life to the last, without ever having been made to see all it may contain of perfidy, of violence, and of terror.

—JOSEPH CONRAD

VIETNAM
1972

BLACK PONY DOWN

He hardly felt the hit, but he heard it. The muffled roar shook the stick slightly, and he looked out to see the end of his right wing shatter and flake away. A moment later the familiar and frightening sound of .50 caliber shells rattled the fuselage behind him as the bullets ripped the twin-engine OV-10. Suddenly the plane began to yaw, then it made a wrenching slip in the opposite direction. The plane dipped slightly toward the good wing and dropped a hundred feet. Cody was fighting the aircraft, trying to get it stable. He pressed the radio button: 'Mayday . . . Mayday . . . this is Chilidog one to Corkscrew. I'm hit and out of control. . . .'

The voice was remarkably calm, almost resigned. The only hint of trouble was in the timbre of his voice. It was shaking from the violent action of the plane, like a stereo with too much bass.

They were too low to bail out. Cody always played it like that, treetop-level stuff. 'Get down where you can see the whites of their eyes,' he would tell his men. From under the umbrella of green foliage, deadly ground fire chewed at the twin-engine assault plane. Fifty-calibers rattled the fuselage.

'Brace yourself,' he told his gunner. 'There was no response. Cody turned in the cockpit and looked back. Rossiter was slumped in the seat, his canopy riddled, his face shot away. But Cody had no time to feel sorry for the youngster, he was losing the plane. The jungle catapulted toward him. Two hundred yards in front of him was the river and on the other side of the river was freedom. He knew he'd never make it.

Before HQ could answer, the pilot was back on.

9

'This is Chilidog one . . . half mile north of checkpoint Charlie . . . I'm down to five hundred feet . . .'

The radio operator answered immediately.

'Chilidog one, can you make it across the river?'

'. . . trying . . .'

The radio operator switched bands and called Rescue. 'Rescue, this is Corkscrew. I have a Black Pony going in half mile north of checkpoint Charlie, a couple of hundred yards into Indian country . . . Do you read?'

The answer came immediately. 'Corkscrew, this is Rescue . . . we hear him . . . Got a Huey on the way . . .'

'Chilidog one, we have a Huey in the area. Can you stay aloft to the river?'

'Negative . . . I'm going in . . .'

The transmission ended suddenly.

'Shit, we're losing him,' the radio operator muttered. He turned to his assistant. 'Get the Skipper over here fast, Wicker.'

'On it,' the assistant, a ruddy-faced seaman first, snapped back and snatched up the phone.

The plane suddenly jerked again. The stick was useless. Cody was trying to get it under control with the rudder pedals, but that, too, was futile. The ship went up on its good wing and then slowly began to roll. The green jungle rushed toward him as he rolled upside down. Cody slammed the stick forward in a last attempt to get control and the plane's nose rose sharply. Its tail raked the treetops and disintegrated, and the black craft was snapped down into the green tapestry below. Cody shoved the stick forward, away from his chest, and braced himself against the instrument panel, his forearms shielding his face. He heard the plane crumpling around him, the metal screaming as the trees tore it apart. Then it all stopped – the noise, the forward thrust – everything seemed suspended in time.

Cody, hanging upside down, looked over his head and stared straight down at the ground, about twenty feet below him. The plane was a twisted wreck around him. He looked back at Rossiter, his gunner. The kid's arms hung down toward the ground.

The canopy was half off, dangling from its tracks. Cody slammed the flat of his hand into it and it toppled away into the trees. He smelled smoke.

He started talking to himself, rattling off the drill. 'Got to get out,' he said and, loosening his safety belt, tried to hang out of the plane and drop to the tree limbs. The smell of smoke grew stronger, and suddenly he was free of the plane, arcing through the air. He reached out toward a branch, felt it slap his palm and then slip away. It spun him around so his feet were now below him. Just like a bail-out, he thought as he hurtled toward the ground. Knees together and bent, roll when I hit . . .

But he hit wrong, and as he landed he heard his kneecap pop, felt the pain burn deep in the leg, coursing down to his ankle. He trapped the scream of pain between his teeth. Sweat boiled out of his skin.

He looked up. The river was twenty yards away, shimmering in the early morning sun. He got up and started hobbling frantically toward it. He knew there were bandits all around, but maybe he'd get lucky. Then overhead and behind him he heard a sizzling sound and a moment later the dull *thumpf* as the gas tanks went. Heat from the explosion wafted down over him, but he kept hopping toward the river, dragging his ruined leg behind him. He didn't look back. Then he heard the familiar *chump, chump, chump* of the chopper, off to his left, coming upriver.

Oh God, c'mon, baby, he thought.

Twenty yards to freedom.

'Corkscrew, this is Rescue one. We have the Black Pony in sight . . . .'

The Huey was suspended twenty feet above the river. In the belly, Harley Simmons, a young gunner, squinted and peered into the thick foliage, looking for signs of life. The pilot's voice crackled through the earphones.

'How about it, Simmons, anything?'

'I'm looking, Captain, I'm looking . . . .'

The explosion cut him off. It was almost like slow motion. First the shock wave of the burst rippling through the trees, then the Black Pony disintegrating, then the bright orange fireball boiling up into the sky. Seconds later the ping of bullets sang off the fuselage a few feet from Simmons's head.

'We got bandits shooting at us!' Simmons screamed into his mike.

'How about our man?' the pilot yelled back.

Then Simmons saw him; he was hobbling from under the awning of fire, heading toward the riverbank. He was almost there – twenty, thirty feet maybe. But before Simmons could say anything, another round of bullets ripped into the edge of the open hatch, tearing it up. Bits and pieces rattled off Simmons's helmet. He heard the whine of 9 mm. shells wailing inches from his ear, and fear charged deeply into him like a bolt of lightning. The plane in the forest exploded again and fire raged through the treetops.

He can't make it, Simmons said to himself as more gunfire tore at the Huey.

'I don't see nothing, Captain,' he lied. 'We got bandits chewing us up back here.'

The pilot rolled the belly of the chopper toward the forest and spun around, heading back downriver.

Simmons dropped weakly to his knees. He was shaking all over. Oh God, he thought, what have I done . . .

But he was too frightened to say it aloud. He heard the pilot's voice on the intercom: 'Corkscrew, this is Rescue one . . . We lost him . . . .'

Cody almost reached the bank when the chatter of an automatic weapon off to his right startled him. He dropped to the ground and crawled to the edge of the water. The Huey was a hundred feet away, hovering over the river.

Over here, over here! he urged silently. He started to get up, to wave at the chopper. And watched in horror as it peeled away and headed back downstream.

No, he cried to himself, No, no . . .

'I'm here,' he screamed desperately.

He stood up, determined to jump in the water and swim to the safety of the other side, at just the moment the sky erupted in fire as the plane disintegrated in flames. The heat roared down over him like a blanket. He covered his face and fell to the ground, huddled against the raging fire in the trees overhead. And as the inferno baked his back and legs he kept crawling toward the river.

Freedom was ten feet away when he gave up.

The commander burst into the radio shack, his face frozen in a scowl.

'What the hell is it, Wicker?' he snapped.

'We just lost a bird, Commander,' the radio operator answered forlornly.

The commander's shoulders sagged. He shook his head.

'Damn!' he barked. 'Who was it.'

The radioman hesitated for just a second.

'Chili one, sir, Lieutenant Cody.'

The commander closed his eyes for a moment and his jaw

12

twitched as he clenched his teeth. 'Jesus H. Christ,' he moaned. And a moment later: 'Okay, get me GHQ, Saigon. I gotta tell the Old Man we just lost his son.'

CENTRAL AMERICA
1985

LOS BOXES

The river had been broad and energetic at the beginning of the journey, but the jungle had gradually encroached on it until now, after four days, the tortured umbilicus between Madrango, the capital, and the forlorn outpost 160 miles away was a mere trickle. The ancient riverboat, scarred by years of heat and rain and piloted by a captain who could barely stay awake, chugged feebly up the last few cramped miles. Trees and ferns snapped at its gunwales and rattled its portholes. The old tub groaned as it fought the brush. The only passenger was an obese grotesque, his delicate face squinched by layers of fat, his faded blue eyes, tiny mouth and pointy nose lost in folds of flesh. He sat on a decrepit old lawn chair near the bow, knees and ankles tucked together, his chin pulled down, a white hat hugging his brow, his soft, dimpled hands clutching a white umbrella to shield him from the broiling sun. His white suit was skimpy, ill fitting and sweat-stained, and his unbuttoned shirt cuffs hung loose, for they no longer fit around his massive wrists.

His name was Randall Wilfred Pratt III, and he was with the U.S. State Department in Madrango, much to the chagrin of the embassy staff. On paper, Pratt had looked good, an honor graduate of Harvard whose father was a major contributor and leverage broker for the party in power, and a confidant of the president.

In person, Pratt III was an embarrassment to all, a closet case who came in the package, along with the donations and endorsements. Banished to the minute, unstable Central American country, he was kept discreetly out of sight and used only when some undesirable occasion arose. This job was perfect; it required no diplomacy at all.

14

For two days he had sat thus, all tucked in, waiting and watching for his first glimpse of a place so foul, so unforgiving, so terrifying by reputation, that even the judges who condemned men to its depths whispered its name. With each passing hour Pratt's anxiety grew until it was a scream waiting to happen, a scream that could not be suppressed.

The old scow burst through the trees and the place rose like a specter before them, a towering stone bastion tortured by vines, smothered with damp green moss, and choked by the forest that entrapped it. Pratt was so undone, so utterly terrified by the sight that he yelled out loud, a piercing cry that jarred the master of the boat awake and brought him immediately to his feet. Pratt quickly recovered. Turning with embarrassment, he dismissed the outburst with a wave of his chubby hand. He pulled a handkerchief from his pocket and furiously mopped his face.

My God, he thought, was Hatcher still alive? And if so, was he sane enough to be worth this trip?

HATCHER

Christian Hatcher had been there for three years, two months and twenty-seven days – 1,183 days, to be exact. Nobody in Los Boxes knew his real name, which was not uncommon; nobody in Los Boxes knew anybody's real name. To be sentenced here was to be sentenced to oblivion.

There was no escape from Los Boxes. It loomed like an apparition from the jungle floor, encircled by two hundred miles of steamy jungle as deadly as it was verdant, an emerald paradise whose green canopy concealed a floor crawling with venomous snakes, jaguars and wild hogs, pocked with quicksand bogs, and teeming with vines that grew so fast in the hot, fertile forest that a man could be strangled by them as he slept. There were no paths here; the jungle devoured them in hours.

Centuries-old vines entwined the crumbling citadel and seemed to hold it together. Inside, there were 212 rooms carved from dirt and stone, each ten feet square and eight feet high, and each lit by a single bulb, the electricity supplied by an aged and unreliable generator. The barred windows were hardly more than slivers in the wall, barely wide enough for a man to get through. The only adversary here was nature. Nobody could remember why this fortress had been built, but it had served as a political prison for more than a century, surviving one feeble government after another. In Madrango its name was whispered in fear.

There were no records of names or arrival dates. A new inmate was simply assigned a box and its number became his identity.

Three years, two months and twenty-seven days ago, Hatcher had become no. 127.

The rules of Los Boxes were simple: You did your work, you never spoke to another prisoner. That was it.

Nobody refused to work, it was the only way to get outside, where there was fresh air and exercise. Those who did refuse, out of obstinacy or rebellion, were locked away in their box and forgotten.

If one prisoner spoke to another, the guards simply cut out his tongue.

There were no second chances here; Los Boxes was ferociously expedient.

The guards – there were only six – had once been inmates themselves. When the *federales* quit or went mad or died from belly worms, they were replaced with inmates. The inmate guards were no better or worse than the regulars. And although they were armed, they used weapons only to protect themselves or to shoot occasional predators.

Escape? To escape was to die. Those who tried to were never pursued. The guards chuckled and waited, and when the fugitives realized the futility of escape and returned, they were put back in their box, fed twice a day, and forgotten.

In the beginning there had been incredible frustration. Like a poet without paper or an orator without a voice, Hatcher had no way to express his rage. Only that ruthless, sleepless inquisitor called conscience kept him company. Unable to escape from a constant evaluation of his deeds, his anger turned inward, and as the months turned to years the specifics of his arrest and the politics behind it merged into philosophical abstractions.

Had he betrayed a trust? Had cynicism robbed him of all sense of value? Was this the price for intolerance, for the arrogance of pride? The cross-examination was endless. He went to sleep with the questions on his lips and awoke with no answers, for even his memories had convoluted into fiction.

His calendar scratched out on earthen walls, Hatcher's clock was a shadow flitting across the floor. Only a dream of freedom kept him alive, and after three years that had dwindled to a mere flicker of hope, hardly enough to inspire escape.

At first, Hatcher seriously considered escape. He had survived five months in the steamy backwaters of Laos and Cambodia and walked out to tell about it, had led two crewmen out of the southern jungles of Madrango when his planeload of arms had crashed, although one had died of snakebite just before they got out.

So memories helped to stave off madness – memories and the dream of escape. There was no rush. He would take his time. He studied his prison carefully until he knew the layout. He memorized every niche and crack in the walls, studied the jungle paths and made elaborate escape plans, which he drew on the dirt walls and floors of his box so he could revise them. The cell window was easy. Time and erosion had crumbled the wall around the bars. A little work with sticks he could smuggle back to his box could work it loose. From outside he carefully studied the face of the prison. It was old and rotten. Climbing the sheer wall to the top of the citadel would be a breeze. He had learned that lesson well from Cirillo.

It was a day he would never forget and he played and replayed it in his mind.

Hatcher had clung to the rock as if it were a magnet while the wind tore at his clothes and pulled at his bleeding fingers. If he could have, he would have dug a hole in that rock and crawled in. He was seventeen years old and petrified.

It was not a mountain – no way you could have called it a mountain. It was a spear, a slender spear a hundred feet high with a flat top and sheer sides, snuggled against the foothills of the Green Mountains, three hours from Boston. And what had started out as a warm clear-skyed September day had suddenly turned ugly.

Cirillo was ten feet above him, inching like a spider up the face of the cliff. Cirillo had no equipment. No rope. No ax. Just a canteen and a small bag of resin, which he had attached to the back of his belt. Free climbing, he called it, and the only way to start was to do it.

Before starting, Cirillo had stood looking up the rock face.

'This looks good,' he said. 'Not too high for a beginner.'

'You talkin' about *me* goin' up that?' Hatcher had said with an edge of panic in his voice.

'Gotta start somewhere.'

'I don't gotta start anywhere,' he answered.

'That's right,' answered Cirillo, 'it takes a little guts.'

He had laid another resin bag at the base of the cliff.

Then Cirillo ran his fingers across the perpendicular face of it until he found a small fissure. He dipped his fingers in the resin bag, blew the excess resin off them, and started feeling his way up, clambering hand over hand, foot over foot, looking like a giant crab as he went up the cliff by his fingertips and toe tips, using cracks and ridges to haul himself up. The kid watched in awe.

'You're nuts,' the kid said.

'Uh-huh.'

'What happens if you run out of cracks?'

'You fall.'

'Great, just great!' Hatcher said.

Cirillo kept going, his muscular arms bulging as he worked his way laboriously up the cliff. Hatcher watched, began to feel embarrassed. He walked close to the cliff and ran his hands tentatively over its surface, feeling its ridges, cracks and tiny ledges. Finally he picked up the bag of resin, attached it to his belt and, copying Cirillo, started painfully up the wall.

'Don't be in a hurry and don't look down,' Cirillo said quietly. 'The ground ain't goin' anyplace.'

Hatcher had started up, his fingertips aching, his toes aching, his stomach aching. An hour later he was forty feet up the side, hugging the spear like a found child hugging its mother.

Cirillo was near the dead end, the ledge at the top of the cliff that projected out over his head.

'I can't go any farther,' Hatcher's wobbly voice yelled. 'Can't find anything to get hold of.'

'To your left, kid,' Cirillo yelled back. 'A little farther . . . up a coupla inches . . . there!'

Hatcher's bleeding fingers found a split in the rocks barely deep enough to get a fingernail in.

'Not enough,' he yelled back, still hugging, his eyes closed.

'It was good enough for me,' yelled Cirillo, 'and my fingers're twice the size of yours.'

Hatcher dug his fingers in, scraped dirt out of the tiny ledge, made a crevice deep enough to slowly pull himself up another six inches. Fear was bile in his throat.

That's when it had started getting darker. The clouds blew in on a cold, biting wind that carried with it the dampness of rain.

The wind picked up, battering him. He could feel his fingers trembling.

18

'It's turning bad, kid,' Cirillo yelled. 'Pick it up, keep movin'.'

'Can't . . .'

'Bullshit. Get your ass in gear or you're gonna be nuthin' but a puddle.'

'Shit,' was all Hatcher could manage. His fingertips were raw and bleeding and his toes ached as they had never ached before. His arms trembled with exertion. Sweat stung his eyes and tickled the corners of his mouth.

He was hanging on for dear life. The first drops of rain had begun to pelt Cirillo's face and panic began to gnaw at him, too. But he couldn't let the kid know that.

Cirillo was at the overhang. He reached up and slowly crawled the fingers of one hand toward the edge, stretching out as far as he could until he very cautiously reached around the edge and felt for a finger hold. His aching fingertips found a small trench. He dug at it, making sure it would hold him, then pushed himself up and out and swung free of the face of the wall. He hung there by one arm, staring down at the kid, who clung to the wall, pressing against it like a piece of moss.

Cirillo switched hands. Hanging with his right arm, he extended his left toward the kid.

'C'mon, another six feet, I gotcha.'

Hatcher inched his way up, snatching a peek at Cirillo and then closing his eyes and feeling for another finger hold. Finally his head bumped the overhang. No place else to go.

'Grab my hand, kid,' Cirillo said.

Hatcher looked at him through terror-stricken eyes, stared at the fingertips wiggling an invitation to him.

'Trust me,' Cirillo said.

The kid had never trusted anyone before. He started to look back toward the ground.

'*Don't* – look down,' Cirillo said quietly but sternly, and the kid closed his eyes and clung on for dear life.

'Gimme your hand, kid,' Cirillo ordered. Hatcher reached out very slowly, stretching toward the cop's bulging arm. He felt Cirillo's callused fingertips, felt his hand slide across his palm, felt the powerful fingers enclose his wrist.

'Okay,' said Cirillo, 'swing free.'

'What!'

'Do it now, I can't hang on here forever.'

The kid closed his eyes, swallowed, and freed his other hand. He was hanging in midair with nothing below him but space. Cirillo gritted his teeth and slowly lifted the kid's dead weight.

'Okay,' Cirillo whispered, 'hang around my neck.'

Hatcher reached up and wrapped his arms around Cirillo's thick, bulging neck as the cop chinned himself on the ledge.

'God Almighty,' he whispered as Cirillo hauled himself over the lip of the ledge and rolled to safety. Hatcher lay on his face, his breath blowing little billows of dirt away from his mouth. His heart was beating so hard his teeth hurt. Then suddenly he started laughing hysterically.

'Damn,' he said, 'we're alive! We're a-fuckin' live!'

He had confronted and cheated death, a new and seductive experience for him.

'I did it!' the kid yelled at the forest and it echoed back: ' . . . I did it!'

'Just remember, kid,' Cirillo said. 'Ya can't quit in this life. Quit and yer dead. Ya take a job, ya do it. Ya don't hold back nothin', ya put it all on the line. Ya don't leave yourself any outs.'

Hatcher turned to Cirillo. 'Let's do another one,' he said eagerly.

And Cirillo had smiled.

'We still gotta go back down,' he answered quietly.

Yes, Hatcher thought, these old walls would be a piece of cake. Getting through the jungle, that was the tough part.

Then the rains came. The face of the prison became a slimy river of muck. The rainy days became rainy weeks and then months. With each passing day, climbing the wall became more treacherous. He drew rough maps on the floor, trying to remember directions and distances from the trip upriver. And finally he accepted the reality that without weapons or even a compass, without maps or any knowledge of the area, escape was suicidal. As the rains continued, the challenge slowly faded.

And so he imposed upon himself a daily regimen: calisthenics to keep his muscles from atrophying; mental exercises to keep from going mad, although gradually madness and sanity became one.

To postpone insanity, he thought about the women he had known. Sometimes names eluded him and he associated them with events in his life. He tried to reconstruct his first high school romance – what was her name, Haley? He remembered touching her the first time, in the backseat darkness of Cirillo's Chevy, groping, feeling her soft down and feeling her rise to his touch, moving his hand to her breasts, those soft buds just

20

beginning to bloom. He was terrified, she was impassioned. But after the first time, their fervor approached insanity. They did it everywhere, in the darkness of the balcony of the town's only movie house, rolled in blankets in the green Massachusetts forest, and once, late in the afternoon, in the girls' locker room at the high school, abandoned for the day, the tin rattle of the locker door providing rhythmic cadence as they stood against it, thrashing in the agony of youthful passion.

Then he had gone off to the academy and she had fallen madly in love with the high school wrestling champ.

The loss of his innocence haunted his fevered memory as his mind wandered freely in time, back to the alleys of Boston, where Cirillo had nabbed him. Hatcher was a tough, crafty street orphan, and Cirillo a just-as-tough cop who had taken him in hand and changed his life forever. It had been Cirillo who had forced him to go to high school, challenged him not only to climb walls but to show his best, and finally arranged the appointment to Annapolis, where Harry Sloan had discovered him. Sloan. Hatcher's torment was that he could no longer imagine life without that treacherous intrusion, could not remember the precise moment when he had traded truth for expediency, had traded light and beauty for the shadows of the shadow warrior, and in his desolation, Hatcher, like many men and women in less desperate conditions, futilely cried out to relive that moment and change his destiny.

At first, hate was all Hatcher had. Sitting in his box at night, he would imagine every conceivable kind of torture he could inflict on Harry Sloan. But as time passed he began to look elsewhere, to shift the blame to someone else. But in the end it always came back to the same thing. Sloan had betrayed him, had set him up and condemned him to a living death.

Cirillo had been Hatcher's salvation, Sloan his destruction.

And yet the cord was difficult to break. Sloan had been more than a friend, he had been Hatcher's mentor, had exposed Hatcher to experts in every conceivable field of lawful and unlawful endeavor, from lock-picking to murder, had taught him how to survive under the worst conditions. In a strange irony, Sloan had prepared him to survive Los Boxes.

Yes, Sloan had delivered his promises. His silver tongue promised adventure and romance, spiced with words like 'patriot' and 'duty' and 'country'. Well, there had been plenty of both. There had been a lot of good times. Tokyo, Singapore, Manila.

21

Hong Kong and Bangkok.

He always thought of them together, remembering Cohen and the weekends when he would fly to Hong Kong from Bangkok just to get away from the hell of the river wars for a little while.

And the special suite he had at the Peninsula in Kowloon, shared only with Daphne.

God, Daphne. What a memory. Was she still alive? Was she still as beautiful as ever? Daffy, he had called her and it fit.

There was also Sam-Sam Sam and Joe Cockroach and the Ts'e K'am Men Ti, the secret lair of the Chinese river pirates. And there was Tollie Fong, the triad assassin who had sworn a blood oath against Hatcher for killing his father, his uncle and four of his most trusted gangsters.

He could never go back to Hong Kong and Bangkok. Too many ghosts. Too many enemies. Too many unsaid good-byes.

And so Hatcher always thought of Sloan with mixed feelings. The bond between mentor and student was almost as primal as that between father and son. In his misery, his feelings toward Sloan wavered. One day he thought of Sloan with affection, the next he damned him to hell.

What he eventually learned was that there was no precise moment when his values changed. When he met Sloan he was young and impressionable, easily charmed by Sloan's omnipresent smile, and seduced by his soft-spoken promises. It was what Sloan did best, spinning images of mysterious worlds with that silver tongue of his. In the end, Hatcher had to accept the responsibility for what he was and where he was, a house of his own making.

Life in Los Boxes became Hatcher's penance.

Then one night he heard a scratching on the wall. He thought it was a roach or perhaps a rat until a small stick punched through the wall, augered for a moment, and was withdrawn.

'Psst.'

Hatcher leaned over and put his ear close to the tiny hole.

And heard a voice, an ancient voice, hoarse with disuse.

'One twenty-seven?' the voice said.

126

Hatcher would not answer, could not answer. Paranoia and fear prevented any response. Suppose it was a guard, testing him? He would not risk having his tongue ripped out. He leaned against the wall, his ear against the pinpoint, listening.

Again the hoarse whisper: 'One twenty-seven?'

His mouth was dry with suspicion. He sat for a moment, then he coughed.

'Ah, very good, very clever,' the voice whispered in Spanish. 'I am one twenty-six. I knew your predecessor for many years. He was a journalist in my country. A famous journalist. Green berries and belly worms got him.'

My God, to hear a voice, a friendly voice, was like a postponement of his madness, and finally Hatcher asked himself, What good is a tongue, anyhow, if you don't use it?

'I am here,' he whispered back, and immediately, reflexively, stuffed his fist in his mouth.

'Ah,' whispered 126. 'Salvation.'

'I am Hatcher, what is your name?'

'Immaterial, immaterial,' 126 said in flawless English. 'There is no parole from here, no pardon, no escape. I am one twenty-six. I will be one twenty-six for eternity. You are one twenty-seven.'

'How long have you been here?'

'Since God created cockroaches.'

'Why are you here?'

'A lie for the convenience of the state.'

'And I, too,' said Hatcher.

'To give such a lie relevance is to perpetuate it. Why I am here, why you are here, that is no longer material. By now even the courts have forgotten us. And if nobody else cares, what matter is it to ourselves? It is, quite simply, a lie.'

'It helps me to think about it. It gives me a sticking place.'

'There is no vindication in hatred. Besides, we are all products of our own devils.'

'I'm not sure I agree with that. My devil had a silver tongue.'

'Ah yes,' answered 126. 'Show me a devil who doesn't. Forget hatred, it will drive you mad.'

'If something else doesn't first.'

And so in the ensuing months and years, Hatcher had decided that if he ever saw Sloan again, perhaps he could forgive him. Forgive but never trust him again. He knew Sloan very well,

well enough to know that Sloan would betray him again if he thought it was expedient.

'Did you kill?' 126 asked one day.
'Yes, but it was my duty.'
'Many crimes are committed in the name of duty.'
'I suppose you're right,' Hatcher said.
'Listen, when one shares the secret of murder, then one is guilty of murder.'
'What's that got to do with anything?'
'Sometimes we can excuse anything in the name of patriotism and so an outcast can only find redemption by claiming to be a patriot. Are you a patriot, one twenty-seven?'
'I don't remember. Yes. I think I was.'
'Well, you are certainly an outcast.'
'Yes, that's a fact.'
'Then it stands to reason that you are probably *not* a patriot. But it's all relative. I am here because I thought I was a patriot. Then I discovered one man's patriot is another man's traitor. . . . What I thought was an act of patriotism turned out to be an act of murder.'
'I can understand that,' Hatcher replied.
'Then you have had the experience.'
'Yes.'
'Yes, of course. You see what I mean. Righteous indignation comes much easier to the patriot than it does to the felon.'

Hatcher's lessons came hard. He forgot that in the hell of Los Boxes the rules never changed. One day, he had been working at the edge of the jungle, preparing one of the endless vegetable gardens that surrounded the citadel, when a wild boar had suddenly lunged from the underbrush and charged him. It was enormous, a hulking, stinking beast with curved tusks and insane eyes, snorting and hooking as it ran toward Hatcher.

Hatcher took its first charge with the hoe, smacking it on the snout, but the beast merely backed off a few yards and charged again. Hatcher screamed for the guards as he parried tusk with hoe. The large tusks could easily have torn out his stomach, opened up a leg, ripped away his throat.

A guard appeared nearby but made no attempt to shoot the beast. He stood fifty feet away, laughing.

'Shoot it,' Hatcher screamed, and the guard instantly reacted.

'*¡Silencio!*' the guard demanded.

The boar attacked again. This time Hatcher swung the hoe in a wide arc and buried the blade in the boar's thick neck. The hoe handle splintered and broke. The boar, roaring in pain, backed off, and began to circle.

'For Christ's sake, shoot the son of a bitch!' Hatcher screamed as he backed away.

'*¡Silencio!*' the guard ordered, running toward him.

The boar wheeled, snorting crazily, pawed the ground and came at him again. Hatcher was defenseless. He scrambled to his feet and started to run. Then he heard a shot and the boar's scream of pain. Another guard across the field lowered his rifle.

Hatcher turned and saw the boar lying on its side ten feet away, its short legs pawing the air, its head jerking back and forth in the spasms of death.

Hatcher's sigh of relief was shattered by the first guard's gun butt as it smashed into his throat. He reeled back, clutching his neck, feeling the mangled veins and muscles as blood surged into his mouth. He fell to his knees gagging.

The guard leaned over him.

'*Silencio,*' he repeated, then turned and walked away.

That night, 126 had told him, 'You are lucky you still have your tongue.'

'I hate that bastard,' Hatcher's tortured voice answered. 'I'll kill him if I ever get the chance.'

'No, don't think about that,' 126 had answered. 'Hate comes easy here and hate kills the spirit. You must learn to love. Something – a woman, your country, anything. Without love, life is meaningless. To be in love means to laugh, to cry, to feel without touching. Without feelings, one twenty-seven, you are a robot.'

It was true, Hatcher thought, and yet for a good part of his life, hate had sustained him.

'Why is talk prohibited, one twenty-six?' Hatcher whispered feebly.

'Talk is the seed of revolt.'

'Ah, that makes sense.'

'In a very primitive way, everything here makes sense, one twenty-seven.'

'What did you do on the outside?' Hatcher's shattered voice asked.

'I was a teacher. A mentor. Did you have a mentor?'

Hatcher thought for a moment. 'I had two,' he answered.
'Ah, and what did they teach you?'
'One taught me the meaning of honor,' said Hatcher.
'And the other?'
'He taught me to ignore it.'

One twenty-six had grown old in Los Boxes and would die there.
In a moment of insanity he had tried to run, but two days in the
jungle was all he could bear. Now he was trapped forever in box 126,
and to hold on to his sanity he philosophized endlessly.
'Talk is fertilizer for the brain,' he told Hatcher. 'If there is no one
else to talk to, talk to yourself.'

There was also practical advice:
'If it is so important to you, scratch your name and your age
in the wall so you don't lose your identity. Just remember no
one else cares. To everyone else, you are one twenty-seven.
Forget what's happening outside the walls, it's no longer of any
consequence. This place is your reality. To survive, all that
matters is reality.'
'Why bother,' asked Hatcher.
'Because hope is the key to heaven,' 126 answered.

He became Hatcher's tutor. Every day when Hatcher returned
from the fields around Los Boxes, there were new lessons to be
learned.
'When you are outside, don't eat green berries. The green ones
will kill you.'
And: 'Masturbate every day, it will keep your emotions alive.'
And: 'Forget the politics of your agony. Politicians are vermin in
the soul. They sway with the winds and keep you angry, and anger
becomes madness, and madness is the step before death.'
And: 'Don't waste your time on thoughts of vengeance.
Vengeance is depressing. It requires action, and action is the enemy
of thought and the friend of illusion. Here illusion leads to
madness.'
'Ah . . . that is tough to do.'
'It will get easier. Better to forgive your enemies than to invite
madness.'

'What do you fear most, one twenty-seven?'
Hatcher gave it some thought.
'Cowardice,' he said finally.

26

'Then as long as you're alive, you have nothing to fear. Only cowards kill themselves to escape this place.'

And: 'If you get sick, cure yourself. Otherwise they will kill you to keep whatever you have from spreading. There is no doctor here.'

And: 'Do not lose your sense of humor. Humor feeds the soul. If the soul starves, so does the conscience, and your conscience is your only true companion.'

And: 'Do not eat the pork. It is cooked badly. It will put worms in your belly.'

'Thank you, one twenty-six.'

'For what?'

'I'm learning.'

'I am a teacher. It is a joy for me.'

Then there were the Mushroom People.

At first Hatcher thought 126 was merely having one of his mad days. They all had mad days.

'Look for the blossoms,' 126 had told him shortly before he died. 'The big ones that grow in the shade under the tall trees. Chop them and mix them with a meal, never straight. The Mushroom People are friendly, but if you eat the blossoms straight, they get out of hand.'

Hatcher had no idea what 126 was raving about.

'Time to say good-bye.'

'No!'

'I've been here twelve years, old friend. It has been two years since I saw the sun or breathed fresh air. Enough is enough. Besides, my heart is worn out. It skips every other beat.'

'But I need you,' Hatcher implored.

'Nevertheless . . .' He paused. 'I will miss you, one twenty-seven.'

'Not half as much as I'll miss you.'

One twenty-six laughed. 'Good. You have not lost your sense of humor.'

He first spotted them while chopping out a new area for a garden. Large, bright yellow mushrooms, half a foot in diameter, glowing like jewels in the thick, dank shadows. He picked one, chopped it up, and stuffed it in the pockets of his cotton shirt. That night he sprinkled the pieces on the tin plate of vegetables that was shoved

27

through the slot at the bottom of his cell door. Their taste, a musky, cardboard flavor, overpowered other tastes.

He lay on his pallet and stared at the ceiling, wondering why 126 had told him about the blossoms. Perhaps they provided some necessary vitamin or mineral that would keep his bones from turning to sand.

A dervish mist appeared in the corner of his box, brightening the shadows with soft light, and then, what began as a shimmering aura took shape in flesh and blood, standing in the corner as if awaiting orders.

'Who are you? What do you want?' he whispered fearfully.

But the Mushroom People never answered, never spoke. They simply kept him company, and as he learned to trust them he addressed them as he would visitors, describing his daily monotony.

Sometimes he danced with them, spun and twirled an insane Irish jig in his earthen crypt. He made love to the women and sparred with the men. With 126 gone, the Mushroom People became his only friends.

There were days when Hatcher was lucid; there were days when he spent hours in the company of the Mushroom People, dancing, singing, making love, recounting whatever fragments of history he could remember or make up. He told them jokes to keep his sense of humor alive, sang songs to them because music fed the soul.

When he discovered the Mushroom People, Hatcher no longer needed 126. And if the thin line between sanity and madness be judged by what's in the mind, Hatcher was indeed mad during his years in Los Boxes. It would be two more years before he recovered enough from the brutal, dehumanizing experience to admit to himself that there was no hole in his cell wall, and no 126 on the other side talking to him. It would be two years before Hatcher admitted that 126 was his own conscience.

MADRANGO

The boat came once a month, bringing supplies as well as whiskey and whores for the guards. Its doleful horn announced its arrival with three bleats as it neared the last crook in the river. There was no outside work when the boat came. When the horn sounded, the prisoners were quickly herded back into the boxes. They were not allowed to see the women, although those on the southern side of the citadel could sometimes catch a glimpse of them through the narrow slits in their cells. The boat always stayed three days and then left. A few of the men always went crazy. Like dogs in heat, they lay in their boxes and bayed in agony.

Hatcher was on the north side of the structure. He had not laid eyes on a female since the day he arrived. But when the wind was right he could smell their perfume, the musk of their sex, even the bitter odor of the alcohol, and he would summon the Mushroom People and stay mad for the whole three days.

This time the boat came just before dusk. The men were already inside and dinner was being doled out when the foghorn moaned upriver. Hatcher was confused. He immediately checked the primitive calendar scratched on the wall. It had been only sixteen days since the last visit. Maybe they were going to come every other week, give the guards an extra ration of sex and booze. Maybe they were bringing someone special in, some big shot.

Hatcher, who was eating, slipped a rock away from one wall and reached behind it, pulling out a small bag of magic mushrooms. He broke one of them into small pieces and sprinkled them on what was left of his meager meal. He chewed the rubbery bits well, knowing that the easier they were to digest, the faster and better he would react.

When he finished, he lit a cigar made of crumbled palm leaves stuffed in bamboo shoots. The acrid smoke burned his nose and lungs. He lay back and waited for the Mushroom People. Outside thunder rumbled across the sky and he could hear the first drops of rain splatting against the wall outside his window slit. A cool breeze seeped through the narrow gash in the wall, soothing him. The drab earth colors of his box began to change, growing brighter, and he closed his eyes as patterns took shape and danced on the back of his eyelids. He began to chuckle softly to himself and his stomach began to tickle deep inside.

They were coming. He could almost hear them sneaking down the narrow corridors toward his cell, and he wondered which of the Mushroom People would be visiting him tonight. Not that it really mattered, he loved them all – passionately. They had never seemed more real. He could hear them outside his cell, hear the door groan open. One of them kicked the bottom of his foot. He giggled with anticipation.

'One twenty-seven,' a thick, guttural voice said in Spanish.

29

The Mushroom People had never spoken to him before. He opened one eye and peered out cautiously. A guard was standing over him.

'Come,' the guard said. He reached down, pulled Hatcher to his feet, and led him out of the door. A cold wind, damp with rain, sighed down the stairwell and moaned through the corridors. Hatcher knew better than to ask where the guard was taking him. But the mushrooms were working on him. Colored light patterns blazed around him like shooting stars. He tried to keep steady, but he kept lurching against the wall as they climbed the stairs. On the top level they stopped, and the guard beat on the door. It swung open. Bright lights scorched his eyes and he reeled back, blinking. He squinted and stared up to the top of the second stairwell. Haloed in shimmering bright lights was an enormous hulk of a man, a mastodon in a white suit clutching a briefcase to his chest with both hands. The garish white light turned red, then yellow, then broke into shards like broken bits of colored glass.

'Mr. Hatcher,' the apparition in white said, 'I've come to take you home.'

Hatcher fell against the wall and leaned there for a moment, then slid down into a crouch and began to howl like a hyena.

'He hasn't said a single damn word since we took him out of that pigsty hellhole,' Pratt said to the captain. 'Just lies down there staring at the ceiling.'

The captain, who was standing above him in the thatched wheelhouse, peering intently through the driving rain, shrugged. 'Hey, what you expect, señor? He doesn't spoke to another human being for three years. You want him to jump up and down, sing the "Star-Sprinkled Banana" or somping?'

'You filthy illiterate,' Pratt snapped, 'it's the "Star-Spangled Banner".'

The captain laughed. 'Okay, *amigo*, Star-Spangled Banana, whatever you say. That guy, he's loco as a jumping bean, at least, watchacall, maybe more so.'

'Christ, whoever told you you could speak English?' Pratt shook his head and poured another stiff scotch. He had taken off his jacket and pulled his tie down. Rain seeped through cracks in the bulkhead and dripped on the table. Sweat turned his white shirt and pants gray. A crazy man staring at the ceiling, an illiterate seaman with green teeth and breath like a jackal's, and a rainstorm that would probably sink the filthy scow before they got to the main river. This was it for him. When he got back he was going to call

30

Father and get the hell out of Madrango. Screw the service, screw the State Department, screw Hatcher and Los Boxes and this rotten, leaky crap of a tub. He knocked off the glass of scotch and poured another.

'Did Sloan send you?' a tormented voice growled behind Pratt. He jumped and twisted in his chair. Hatcher, standing shirtless in the doorway leading below, was a living wraith, his green eyes flicking insanely within sunken black circles, his arms as skinny as broomsticks, his matted, filthy hair tumbling down around his shoulders, his thick, gnarled beard covering most of his bone-ribbed chest. Dirt etched the furrows in his forehead.

Pratt stared at him speechlessly.

'Did Sloan send you?' Hatcher growled again in his deep, harsh whisper.

'As I t-t-told you, uh, I'm from the embassy in Madrango,' Pratt stammered. 'The ambassador arranged f-f-for . . .'

'Did Sloan send you?'

'Well, I believe perhaps Mr. Sloan did have something to do with the arrangements. He—'

'Shower?' Hatcher's frazzled voice demanded.

'Shower?' Pratt echoed, raising his eyebrows with the question.

'The pump she broke, señor,' the captain answered.

'The pump she broke, the pump she broke,' Pratt aped.

Hatcher turned and went out on deck.

'She's the wind bad blowing, señor,' the captain called after him.

'Jesus,' Pratt snapped and followed Hatcher. He stood in the hatchway and watched the ex-inmate crawl out on deck and lie on his back with his mouth open as the rain poured down on him.

'He says to watch the wind,' Pratt yelled. 'We wouldn't want to lose you now, not after all this, would we?'

Hatcher didn't answer. Spread-eagled on the deck, he fell sound asleep as the wind and rain laced his emaciated body. Finally the captain lashed down the wheel and crawled out after him, put a slack line around his waist and tied the other end to the rail.

'You keep a look on him,' he said to Pratt when he returned to the wheelhouse.

The next day was clear and bright with a northeast wind.

'Stop the boat,' Hatcher's tortured voice ordered the captain, who pulled back the throttle and shoved the scow in reverse. In the stern, the engines boiled up the river.

31

'What the hell's going on?' Pratt demanded.

Hatcher didn't answer. He peeled off his ragged pants and jumped naked into the river.

'Jesus, there's alligators all over the place,' Pratt babbled. He cupped his hands and yelled to Hatcher as he surfaced. 'There's alligators in this river, Mr. Hatcher.' Hatcher rolled over on his back and floated. Pratt sat on the dilapidated lawn chair and held his head in his hands. 'That's all I need,' he muttered to himself. '"Where's Hatcher?" "Oh, I'm dreadfully sorry, sir, an alligator ate him."'

Ten minutes later Hatcher scrambled back on board. Pratt handed him a terrycloth towel. The United States crest was embroidered in one corner. Hatcher stared at it for a moment or two, then began toweling off.

'I brought some fresh clothes for you. They're below,' Pratt said. 'Although they may be a size or so too large.'

Hatcher finished and, throwing the towel over his shoulder, stood naked in front of Pratt, waiting.

'Oh, yes,' Pratt said, jumping up as fast as a man so fat can jump. 'I'll just get those clothes. There's, uh, also a razor and a toothbrush, toothpaste. Some, uh . . . uh . . . cologne . . .'

The pants were two sizes too large and the shirt sleeves dangled around his knuckles, but they were cotton and they felt cool and clean. Hatcher stared at himself in the mirror. He had not seen his own face for more than three years. Now clean-shaven, with his hair scissored back to the bottom of his neck and combed, he could have looked worse. His cheeks and eyes were hollow and he was thirty pounds underweight, but it could be worse. He could be dead. He could be sharing heavenly mushrooms with 126. He rolled the sleeves up above his elbows and went back on deck.

'Well, I must say, you look A-one, sir, just A-one,' Pratt said.

'Smoke?' Hatcher rasped.

Pratt fumbled in his briefcase.

'Yes, sir, yes, sir, right here.' He handed Hatcher a pack of Dunhills. 'Your brand, I believe.'

'It is?' Hatcher said, staring at the package. He turned it over a couple of times before he figured out how to peel the wrapper off. He lit one up, took a deep drag, and almost coughed to death. His face turned purple and he gasped for breath.

'Hands over your head!' Pratt shrieked and held Hatcher's arms up. He stopped coughing finally and sat down on the gunwale. He looked at the cigarette for a moment and threw it overboard.

'We have some fresh fruit, excellent cheese, wine, uh, sliced chicken and roast beef. Also there's some beer and Coca-Cola down in the fridge,' Pratt said and, laughing nervously, added, 'It's a regular old cruise ship.'

Hatcher stared almost quizzically at Pratt and kept staring until the fat man began to feel uncomfortable, then he said, 'Coca-Cola. Yeah.'

'How did Sloan arrange my pardon?' Hatcher's ruined voice asked.

'Well, uh, it's not exactly a pardon –'

'What do you mean?' he whispered menacingly.

'You see, Mr. Hatcher, Madrango is going through a rather traumatic upheaval right now. There was a military coup and the new president, his name is Garazzo –'

'Garazzo! He sent me up there.'

'Oh, that's right. You see, there was a democratic election just after you, uh, went away, and Garazzo and his people were, uh, displaced by Venzio. But then, four weeks ago, Garazzo, uh, pulled off this, uh, coup and he's president again. Anyway, he arranged for your escape.'

'Escape?' Hatcher's green eyes glittered dangerously.

'It's just a formality,' Pratt said hurriedly. 'They won't try to extradite you or anything like that. I mean, nobody's even going to know you're out, know what I mean?'

'Where's Sloan?'

'You'll see him when you get to Washington.'

'Washington?'

'Right. We're going to hustle you right on out of the country, yes siree. . . . He's, uh, dying to see you.'

Hatcher stared at him again. He was intrigued by the man's face, by the layers of fat that seemed to reduce his features to miniatures. A little face peering out of a big, fat head.

'How'd you get mixed up in this?' he growled to Pratt.

'I'm a career diplomat,' Pratt said, trying to sound proud of it.

'Some things never change,' Hatcher whispered.

They could see pillars of black smoke rising from the city when they were still twenty miles away.

'It's got a fires!' the captain said, pointing upriver.

'It's got a fires,' Pratt mimicked, shaking his head. He stood up and looked over the bow, toward the capital city. 'My God, there must have been a counterattack on the city,' Pratt wailed. 'The whole place is burning up.'

33

'What do we do now?' Hatcher snarled anxiously.

'I'll try to radio the embassy,' Pratt said and disappeared below. Hatcher kept watching the towers of black smoke as they got closer to the city. He could hear explosions and gunfire. When Pratt returned, he was smiling.

'They're going to send a chopper to the pier. It's in friendly hands,' he said excitedly. 'They'll fly us straight into the embassy.'

'Why're you doing all this for me?' Hatcher demanded.

'I, uh, I really don't know, sir. They didn't tell me that. They just said to go down with the papers, bribe the warden, and bring you back. If you want to know the truth, Mr. Hatcher, they don't ever tell me anything.'

'I drop you off and scramming,' the captain yelled to them.

'Yeah, right,' Pratt said. 'You scramming. Know what they told me? The captain speaks perfect English, that's what they told me. See what I mean?'

As they neared the pier they saw the chopper, a four-passenger job, sweep over the warehouses along the edge of the river and hover over the bank, churning up the water below it. Pratt stood up and waved to them. The captain guided the scow along the pier and bumped it gently. So he couldn't speak English, Hatcher thought. He sure knows how to run a boat.

'You go now, good luck, señors,' he yelled.

Pratt scrambled to get up on the railing, and as he did, a shell exploded a hundred yards away, tearing out the corner of a building. A naked woman ran down the street with her hair burning. A jeep squatted on flat tires, burning furiously, the charred body of the driver still sitting behind the wheel. Pratt stopped, his face bulging with horror.

'Let's go,' Hatcher yelled, and pushed him onto the dock. The boat roared back into the middle of the river.

'My God, look at this, it's horrible, horrible. . . .' Pratt whined as the chopper swept over and settled down twenty feet away. Hatcher ran to open the hatchway. A young marine, who looked scared to death, helped him scramble aboard. Behind him, Pratt waddled across the dock towards the chopper. The pilot, a captain, looked at him in horror. 'Christ, we can't take him, we're overloaded already,' the pilot yelled. 'Close the hatch, Corporal.'

'Sir,' the corporal yelled back and slid the door shut.

Stranded on the dock, Pratt screamed as he saw the hatch slide shut. 'No, no, you can't leave me here,' he screamed, beating on the side of the helicopter. It shuddered and lifted off as he slammed his fist over and over against the side. Then the wind began to buffet him, he was showered with dust, stinging his eyes, and the chopper lifted off. Pratt fell to his knees, his hands covering his head, and began to sob uncontrollably.

Hatcher and the young marine stared down at the huge man and watched as he grew smaller and smaller. Another explosion erupted behind him and part of the dock disintegrated, but Pratt did not move. He knelt like a Buddha, cowering with fear, unable to move.

'It's madness,' the young marine cried out and Hatcher began to laugh for the first time. He had been a companion to madness for so long it all seemed perfectly normal to him.

BANGKOK
SIX MONTHS LATER

MALAY CROSSING

From the air the dark blue Mercedes could be seen slowly moving through the crowded streets of Bangkok. It appeared to have no particular destination. It drove at a crawl, slowing down as it passed the mouth of each alley as it zigzagged the streets, until it finally stopped.

The alley was narrow and teeming with people. Although it was early in the day, music blared from a nightclub nearby adding to the cacophony of people talking and horns blowing and the din of the large, crowded city.

A bulky Chinese got out of the Mercedes and headed into the alley. He had a florid face seamed down one side by a long, thin scar. He threaded his way through the steady stream of people to a tiny, pitifully scrawny woman wearing a turban. She was huddled over a baby. She was barefoot, with dirt ingrained in her callused feet, and her sunken cheeks and hollow eyes told the whole story. A young woman, one of thousands of prostitutes, known as *e-san*, who was a Laotian from northeast Thailand whose father had sold her into prostitution at the age of twelve, had a child and now, unable to cope, was slowly starving to death. There were hundreds like her. Dozens of unwanted babies were born every week.

The driver of the Mercedes, a lean, short man in a gray business suit, leaned on the fender, smoking, and watched his partner talking to the small woman with the child. The big scar-faced man leaned over and spoke quietly with his hands folded in front of him. The woman shook her head. The man took out a thick wad of bills, held them close to his body, and counted out several, but the woman continued to shake her head.

36

He counted out a few more, folded the bills and, holding them between his two middle fingers, pointed them toward her. She hesitated but still shook her head. The man with the scar slipped his hand into his suit pocket and took out a packet of white powder. He folded it among the bills that he put in her hand.

The car driver watched as the big man took the child and walked back up the alley. The driver held the door open for him.

The gleaming point of the needle dipped into the dab of rich, green paint. The client was a powerfully built Chinese in his mid- to late-thirties. When the tattoo needle pierced the skin of his arm, he did not flinch or blink. He was naked from the waist up and was sitting in an ornate antique chair. He stared straight ahead without emotion. His arm was outstretched with the forearm facing up. Kneeling on a ruby-red pillow, an elderly Chinese leaned over the young man's arm, etching his work of art into the young man's forearm. He did not use the newer, electric-type tattooing needle but instead did it the old way, tapping the drawing into the skin with deft, quick strokes. He worked quickly but with great care, etching into the skin a thin green dagger with a purple snake entwining the blade, its yellow head peering around the handle.

When the old man finished the job, he leaned back and appraised his work. Satisfied, he nodded to his client and the younger man finally looked down at the dagger. It was a work of art, beautifully executed and conveying a sense of menace. A hint of a smile cracked the young man's inscrutable expression. He stood and walked across the room to a large gilt-framed mirror and stood in front of it, glaring coldly at his reflection. There was only a hint of self-adulation on his face. He turned to the old artist.

'Magnificent', he said and bowed to the tattooist, who returned the honor. He put on a ceremonial robe of scarlet and yellow brocade and went into the adjoining room, which was stunningly decorated with Chinese antiques, objets d'art, and Oriental rugs. Beyond the room, through large windows, the city of Macao lay at the feet of the house.

An elderly man in his seventies was standing by a large tank of marine fish, crushing flakes and dropping them into the tank. He stopped as the young man entered the room, brushed his hands, and studied the tattoo for several moments before nodding his approval. 'Another work of art,' he said.

He bowed his thanks to the old tattooist, who responded in

kind and left. The old man was head of a powerful Chinese clan known as the White Palms, which controlled the Chiu Chao triads, the fourteen most powerful underworld gangs in the world. But a stroke had left him lame and shaken his memory a bit, so he had decided to step down. The young man, whose name was Tollie Fong, would on that night become the new *san wong*, the hill chief, as the leader of the triad was known.

'It is quite a day,' the old man said, tending his fish. 'Your father would be very proud of you, as I am. I can think of no one who deserves to become *san wong* of the White Palm Triad more than you.'

They were standing beside a saltwater aquarium, a big one, a hundred gallons. The old man crumbled brine shrimp in his fingers, and sprinkled it in the tank. 'Now I can spend my time playing with my fish.'

Beautiful rainbow-colored fish drifted in and out of the coral on the bottom. The most dominant was a cobalt-blue angel, about the size of a dollar pancake, with a long snout.

'For fifty years we have been the most feared of the triads. Now it is more important than ever to be undisputed,' the old man went on.

As the shrimp pieces sank, the other fish swarmed around them. The blue angel attacked them, ramming and dispersing them and then swooping and darting about the tank, gobbling up the small bits as they sank toward the tank floor. The angel cleared the area and circled lazily, snapping up the bits of shrimp floating down through the tank.

'Never show weakness to anyone –' The old man sprinkled some fish food in his hand and held it down into the tank. The angel circled cautiously for a moment and then darted in, grabbed a bit of food and backed off. Through the water, Tollie Fong could see the tattoo on the old *san wong*'s forearm. It was identical with his own, put there, in fact, by the same artist when they both were much younger men.

'– not to your family, your wife, your brother, not to me – but most of all, never to your enemies. Well, enough of that. While the old man was performing his magic on your arm, your man in Bangkok called. I took the liberty of accepting the message, since you could not be disturbed.'

'Ah, good. What did he say?' Fong said eagerly.

'He said the garden is planted. The harvest will be tonight.'

38

Twenty miles east of Kangar near Padang Besar, the railroad crossing from Thailand into Malaysia, Father Kilhanney drove the pickup truck cautiously along the crumbling back road. He was only a mile or so from the border station and the rain had come suddenly, as it always did in southern Thailand. Lightning streaked the sky, and palm fronds, urged by the wind, snatched at the windshield. Kilhanney felt sorry for the women in the back. There was no tarp covering the bed, and the eighteen laborers were huddled together against the storm. Kilhanney wasn't sure exactly what was going on and he didn't want to know. His job was to meet a private plane at Songkhla and drive eighteen laborers to the Thai-Malaysia border.

The road wound down past the guard station, coursed back through the jungle for thirty miles to the main road, then north up the Thai peninsula to Bangkok. The border station was little more than a customs house with two guards.

Before dawn, eighteen women, twelve carrying their babies in slings on their back, would walk across the invisible line that divided Thailand and Malaysia. With their work permits they would earn ten dollars a day as laborers on the rubber plantations or as domestic help for the moneyed aristocracy. Across the isolated border another truck waited to transport them to their jobs. It was a daily occurrence, nothing out of the ordinary.

Except that these were not ordinary babies. They were all barely six months old. All had been bought on the streets of Bangkok a few hours earlier. All had been murdered just before the plane took off for Hao Yai airport.

Kilhanney did not know about the dead cargo he was carrying. The women had seemed uncommonly quiet when he picked them up, but he thought it was probably the weather.

He pulled the truck up at the border crossing and jumped out. The rain had slacked off for a few moments and was falling only in a light, steady drizzle, but lightning still ripped the sky and snapped at the thick jungle surrounding them.

Kilhanney got out, went to the back of the truck and lowered the tailgate. He helped the women out, particularly the ones with their babies on their backs. The women scurried along a muddy path toward the guard station with their work permits ready.

Two guards huddled in the small outpost to keep out of the rain. Kilhanney got back in the truck and watched as the women approached the border guards. The rest was routine. The Malaysian guards were friendly and flirted with the women.

As one of the women started past the guard her child's arm

dropped out of the sling and dangled loosely. She hurried on, unaware that the child was slipping and its head had come out of the sling. As she passed the guard he stopped her and, smiling, reached out to put the baby back. But as he touched it he froze. The baby was ice-cold. The woman panicked and ran, and the child toppled out of the sling into the guard's arms.

The guard holding the baby in the rain screamed to the other guard, 'This baby is dead! Stop her,' as the woman ran back toward the pickup.

Then all the women with babies began to run. The second guard checked the child on another woman's back. He stood in the rain holding another dead child. 'This one is dead, also!' he yelled back.

The women scrambled. They started to run back toward the pickup, and the guards fired several shots in the air to stop them. Kilhanney freaked out. He slammed the pickup in gear, and with tires digging into the mushy road, he drove off.

Kilhanney drove like a madman, the heavy pickup skittering along the slippery back road. The truck roared through the savage storm with Kilhanney frantically peering through the rain-swept windshield. Fear had turned his mouth to ashes.

'Oh God,' he kept repeating over and over again. Then suddenly the road in front of him exploded in white light, a bolt of lightning seared the sky in front of him and shattered one of the towering trees. The blaze of light temporarily blinded Kilhanney. He wiped his eyes and then the road seemed to vanish and there was only the jungle in front of him. He spun the wheel. The truck's tires slithered in loose gravel and crumbling pavement and water. The truck plunged sideways into the jungle and snapped to a crunching stop against an embankment.

Kilhanney was dazed. The windshield was shattered. He groped for the door handle, pulled it up, and as the door swung open he toppled into a soggy ditch. The cold rain brought him around. He sat up for a moment, then scrambled up the slippery side of the gully and plunged headlong into the jungle.

He ran frantically through the jungle as tree branches and bamboo snapped at him, tore at his clothes, stung his face. Lightning turned the jungle into a strobed nightmare. Vines the size of boa constrictors curled out of the ground and strangled the big mangrove trees. Another jagged bolt of lightning streaked overhead. In its eerie blue-white light, Kilhanney saw a giant stone Buddha, eroded by time and weather, glowering through the ferns at him, its face and body shrouded by the relentless growth. Kilhanney fell back against a tree with a scream. Then with his heart smashing at his ribs, he raced on through the storm.

The place looked like the set of a Western movie, a big, sprawling room with tables and chairs scattered helter-skelter and splashes of sawdust on the floor. Green shaded lights hung from the ceiling like upside-down funnels. The room was low-ceilinged and darkness-cooled and smelled of old beer and onions. Slowly whirring ceiling fans kept the air moving. It was a place that seemed lost in time.

At the far end of the room an aged and battle-scarred oak bar stretched the width of the room. It was a magnificent bar with a brass footrail and several spittoons scattered along its length. Above it, a beveled mirror also spread across the full width of the saloon, and at its center, engraved in arched, foot-high letters, was the name 'Tom Skoohanie' and under it, arched in the opposite direction to complete the circle, 'The Galway Roost, 1877'.

Above the mirror, a mangy, moth-eaten bison's head glared balefully through a single marble eye – the other was covered with a black patch. Near the center of the mirror there was a single large-caliber bullet hole.

One wall of the saloon was covered with old, yellowing daguerreotypes and drawings of famous cowboys, Indians and bandits: a family portrait of Jesse and Frank James in black bowlers and their Sunday best; the Doolin boys shackled and lined up in front of a prison wagon but smiling as if they hadn't a care in the world; Wild Bill Hickok stretched out dead on a poker table with the back-shooter Jack Dance standing behind the table holding Hickok's last hand, aces and eights and a three of diamonds; Pat Garrett standing over a dead buffalo, his Sharp's rifle cradled in his arms; Geronimo kneeling Indian fashion, his rifle across his knees; a defiantly staring Crazy Horse.

In a corner near the bar, a Wurlitzer juke box in mint condition was murmuring the Beach Boys' 'Surfin'.' On the opposite side of the room and raised two steps above floor level was a smaller room shielded by a curtain of twinkling glass beads. Several people were playing cards at one of two tables in the alcove while at the other end two men were shooting pool on a table covered with red felt. At the end of this secluded room, in an overstuffed chair flanked by a floor lamp with a fringed shade, sat a portly gentleman in a white suit, his hair a wisp of white, his

41

double chin bulging over a white shirt and black tie. There was a small table in front of him containing a large strongbox and a bottle of red wine. The man was reading. As he reached the end of the page he dipped a finger in a glass of wine he was holding in one hand, licked the wine off the finger, and turned the page with it.

A tall, lean man with a white handlebar mustache sat at the end of the bar nearest him chatting quietly with a tall, elegant black man in a black T-shirt covered by a suede vest, blue jeans, cowboy boots and a cowboy hat big enough to take a bath in. A red, yellow and green parrot feather was stuck in its band. The butt of a large pistol peeked from under the tall man's jacket, and as he spoke he continually cast glances at the portly man in the white suit. The only other person in the main room had long blond hair and sat hunched over the bar.

A phone rang somewhere in the back room, a muffled anachronism. The bartender went through a door, was gone for a few seconds and then reappeared. He wiggled a finger toward the tall man, who went behind the bar and, as he entered the rear office, took out a pistol the size of a cannon and handed it to the bartender. He entered the office and closed the door behind him.

A few minutes later he returned. His face was stern and angry, the muscles at the corners of his jaw twitching.

'I gotta leave,' he told the bartender. 'Tell the Honorable to close up the bank until I get back.'

'What is it?'

'Kilhanney killed himself,' he said simply and stalked out of the bar. As he stepped outside he left the past and was suddenly enveloped by the night life of the Patpong nightclub section that was in full swing. Music and chatter filled the night. The tall man motioned to a *tuk-tuk*, one of the three-wheel motor vehicles that seem to dominate the choked traffic of Bangkok. The little Thai driver started up the tiny vehicle and pulled up to the tall man.

'Sam Peng,' he said quietly as he entered the cramped two-seater. 'Just off Tri Phet Road.'

The little two-seater pulled down a deserted alley in Yawaraj, the Chinese section of Bangkok, and slowed to a stop. From the shadows a stooped Chinese scurried from a doorway and got in beside the tall man.

'What happened?' the Oriental's voice whispered.

'The way I get it, four nights ago Kilhanney took the

42

overnight train south and drove a bunch of women laborers to the border crossing near Kangar. A dozen of the women were carrying babies. The babies had all been suffocated, and each of the bodies was stuffed with three kilos of China White.'

The Oriental man hissed softly but said nothing.

The tall man shrugged. 'Baby killers,' he said. 'But ingenious. Hell, you can buy a child on the streets of Bangkok for fifty dollars. Done every day in the week.'

'How did this happen?'

'Wol Pot.'

'Damn! *Damn*, why did he keep this from you?'

'I don't know. He told Max that Wol Pot leaned on him to do the run. He didn't know about the babies. Max says Padre thought he could make the run and come back and forget it, but the thing with the babies blew his mind. By the time he got to Max's place he was a raving maniac. This morning he went over to the beach, swam out into the surf, and didn't come back. His body washed up an hour ago.'

The two men sat without speaking for a block or two. Finally the Chinese spoke.

'I wonder how much Wol Pot has told them?'

'I'd say as little as possible. What the hell, we're his ace in the hole.'

'The little weasel should have been killed a long time ago.'

'Well, you know what I say,' said the tall man. 'Better late than never. Maybe we can set it up so they'll take out Wol Pot for us.'

'How do you propose to do that?'

'*Thai Horse,*' said the tall man.

AMERICA
THE PRESENT

BIRD

In Interpol's highly classified files, known as the Holy Ghost Entry and available only to those with first- and second-level clearance, the flier – he, she or them – was known simply by the code name Bird. The reports were deeply classified because none of the authorities in Europe or America wanted the press to get wind of the moniker. In particular, they didn't want Bird – or the press – to know they had linked the Paris and Chicago jobs.

The Bird knew it anyway. He was flying at that very moment, seven feet above the floor of the French Impressionists room of the International Salon of Art.

Outside on Sixty-fourth Street life went on. Monday night: wives or husbands hurried home to their husbands or wives – from work, from their lovers, from a movie matinée, a business meeting or a quick drink on the way home.

The custodian of the Salon had left early, so the night watchman had cheated a little and locked up at five to six. In the last hour there had been only one customer, a strange fellow with a thick red beard, who was huddled in a bright yellow slicker. Apparently he had left the museum unnoticed. At least, that's what the watchman thought.

But the Bird had not left. He had hidden himself in a hallway broom closet and waited while the watchman followed his usual procedure: he had locked up, turned on the alarms and electric eyes, punched out the digital combination that controlled the floor sensors, checked the eight screens that monitored each of the museum's rooms. Then he sat down to watch Dan Rather and eat one of the two sandwiches his wife always prepared for him. Tonight it was his favorite, chicken salad with a slice of

44

pineapple dressed with hot mustard. He could get lost in chicken salad, pineapple and hot mustard.

The Bird waited until the watchman was just that, totally engrossed in his sandwich and the CBS News. He left the closet, walked ten feet down the hall to the small room containing the electric terminal boxes, and jumped the trigger switches for the window alarms and electric eyes. He ignored the floor sensor. It was too complex to bother with, and besides, it wouldn't be a problem. He never went near the floor.

The Bird's pulse raced as he made his way up to the roof. He loved the challenge. Working the air, he called it, and the tougher the job, the faster his pulse raced. The score didn't matter nearly as much as doing it. He had stashed his kit on the roof two days earlier, presenting his forged fire inspector credentials to the day security man and then casually checking out the whole building without being disturbed. He had hidden his operating kit – a large black nylon bag filled with what he called 'the necessities' – inside the air-conditioning vent. This one was a cakewalk, almost too easy. Security was not that tough and the watchman would never suspect that the museum would be hit so soon after closing.

He pulled off the beard and slicker and stuffed them in the bag, blackened his face, then picked the lock on the skylight over the French Impressionists room. Attaching a large, aluminium vise to the sill, he threaded a thousand-pound-test nylon rope through the rings in the vise and the rings in his thick harness, and rappeled down.

Now he was flying seven feet above the floor, close to the south wall so the TV monitor could not see him, his lifeline attached to his waist. Using his head as a fulcrum, spinning around, sometimes hanging head down, sometimes feet down, the Bird was a living Peter Pan surrounded by Monets and Manets, Cassatts and Signacs, Gauguins, Van Goghs, Sisleys, Cézannes and Renoirs. *Beautiful*, thought the Bird. *Who else works in such an atmosphere of creative splendor?*

But as he swung in a leisurely arc, enjoying the wondrous works that covered the walls, his eyes suddenly fell on a bench in the center of the room. On the bench lay a cat.

The Bird froze. The ions in the air froze. Everything froze but the cat, who slept peacefully.

If that cat jumps, the Bird thought, the floor sensors will knock the old watchman into the middle of Canarsie. He swung on the end of his line for several seconds watching the cat, a big

45

gray-striped feline. He had to move slowly and quietly and hope he did not wake it up.

The Bird slowly moved his head back and forth, swinging himself until he could almost touch the wall. He reached into his kit, took out two pressure clamps, then swung against the wall and quietly fixed the two suction cups to it, using them to stabilize himself.

He used a small pressure wrench to pry open each of the frames, lifted a Monet, a Cézanne and a Renoir and slid them out, carefully covered each with a sheet of tissue, rolled them tightly, and put them in the tube slung over his shoulder, which he strapped tightly to his back so it would not swing free. He released the suction cups and swung back in the air, free of the wall, his head hanging down toward the floor.

The cat rolled over on its back, stretched, opened its eyes and stared up at the biggest bird it had ever seen in its life.

The Bird stared back.

The cat's eyes widened. It jumped to its feet. Its back arced and it spat up at him.

Don't jump, thought the Bird, please, don't jump.

The cat jumped on the floor.

The floor sensors set off an alarm beside the monitor screen in the office. The watchman, startled by the buzzing noise, stared at the monitor, but the cat was standing directly under it and the watchman could not see it on the screen. The room appeared empty.

'Damn,' the old man muttered under his breath. Loosening his revolver in the holster, he walked down the hall and stood for a moment outside the open archway leading into the large room, then took out his gun and, holding it in both hands, jumped into the room TV style. The cat streaked past him and ran down the hall.

'Damn you,' the watchman yelled.

The watchman holstered his weapon, took a few steps into the room and stood for a moment with his hands on his hips.

The Bird dangled directly over his head, a foot away.

'You little son of a bitch, gonna give me a heart attack,' the watchman said aloud. 'That's the second time this week you scared the piss outa me.'

The Bird held his breath. If the watchman looked up, they would literally be eye to eye. But he didn't. He gave the room a cursory once-over and went back down the hall, calling, 'Kitty, kitty.'

46

The Bird sighed with relief. He was well named. He hated cats.

SLOAN

It was four-twenty-eight when Stenhauser left the twenty-eighth-floor offices of Everest Insurance on East Fifty-seventh Street, took the elevator to the second floor, walked down one flight and left by the west-side fire door.

Sloan was in a coffee shop on Fifty-seventh between Second and Third avenues. It was a perfect location for him. Through its glass window, he could see three sides of the Everest building. The fourth, the back side, led to a blind alley that emptied on Third Avenue. No matter what route Stenhauser took, Sloan could spot him. Sloan took out his small black book and made a notation, as he had been doing for the last three days. Then he followed the little man.

Stenhauser's name had been filed discreetly in Sloan's computer for two years. Until three days ago he had no idea what Fred Stenhauser looked like or anything else about him other than his profession. It wasn't necessary before now. The names in Sloan's file were like savings accounts, and Sloan was big on savings accounts, on keeping something for a rainy day. He was also a neurotically patient man. Sloan was never in a rush, he could wait forever. Or at least until he was ready. Now he was ready to cash in one of the accounts, the one with Fred Stenhauser's name on it.

Stenhauser was an easy mark. He was as precise as Sloan was patient. He always left his office a little before four-thirty. He always stopped for a single martini at Bill's Safari Bar on Fifty-sixth Street. He was always home by six and by six-ten was back on the street with his yappy little dog.

Life, to Stenhauser, was a ritual. He wore double-breasted glen plaid suits, with a sweater under the jacket, and a paisley tie. Every day. He had his hair trimmed every Tuesday morning at eight-thirty at the St. Regis Barber Shop, ate the same breakfast at the same coffee shop on Fifty-seventh Street every morning, always read the paper, the *Wall Street Journal,* from the back forward, always went to Cape Cod on his vacation. Everything Stenhauser did he always did.

Even Stenhauser's one little eccentricity was predictable, for while he followed this ritual day in and day out, he rarely left his office by the same door or took the same route to Bill's or took the same route from Bill's to his brownstone on Seventy-fourth Street. It was as if he were playing a game, as if someone were constantly following him and his gambit was to evade them. Sloan loved the irony of it. Now someone was following Stenhauser and he didn't even know it.

On this day, Stenhauser, a short, slender man in his mid-thirties with heavy-lidded eyes like a frog's, went east to Second Avenue, south to Fifty-sixth Street, then turned right and walked two blocks to Bill's Safari Bar. He walked briskly, always looking at the ground in front of him, as if he were afraid he would step on something.

Sloan had decided to brace him in Bill's. The bar was never too crowded, which was the main reason Stenhauser took his evening-cap there. And while the decor was a little heavy on ferns and stuffed animal heads, it was small and quiet, and the bartender made a perfect martini.

When Stenhauser turned off Second Avenue onto Fifty-sixth, Sloan crossed the street and picked up his pace. He passed Stenhauser, waited until the short man neared Bill's, and entered it a few seconds ahead of him, killing time until Stenhauser had hung up his coat and found a place at the bar. Sloan sat down next to him. Stenhauser ignored him, reading a copy of *Art World* while the bartender concocted a perfect martini. He put it in front of Stenhauser, then turned to Sloan. 'What'll it be?'

'A light draft,' Sloan said. He looked over at Stenhauser. 'You prefer Bombay gin over Beefeater's, I see,' he said for starters.

Stenhauser, staring at him from under his heavy lids, appeared somewhat annoyed. 'It's the bartender's option,' he said in a nasal voice that was almost a whine. 'Frankly, I doubt that I could tell the difference between the two.'

'But you do prefer a rather wet martini.'

'Let's just say I don't like straight gin,' Stenhauser said absently while leafing through his magazine.

'I couldn't help noticing that you're interested in art,' Sloan persisted.

Stenhauser tapped the magazine cover with a nervous finger. 'Business and pleasure,' he said curtly.

'No kidding,' Sloan said. 'What's your line?'

'My line, if you want to call it that, is insurance.'

'Life insurance, corporate –'

'Actually I'm a claims adjuster,' Stenhauser said, turning his attention back to the magazine.

'No kidding,' Sloan said enthusiastically. 'How does that tie in with the art world?'

The little man placed the magazine back on the bar and sighed. 'I'm a specialist,' he said. 'I specialize in recovering stolen art works.'

'Hey, that sounds interesting. And profitable, right?' He winked at Stenhauser.

'Well, I'm not ready to retire yet, if that's what you mean.'

'Not yet,' Sloan said, taking a sip of beer and not looking at him.

Stenhauser's eyes narrowed. The man was beginning to annoy him. It was almost as if he were prying. Stenhauser studied him. His face was weathered and leathery, he had a small scar under his right eye, his body was square, like a box, and muscular. His charcoal-black hair was clipped in a severe crew cut, and his sport coat seemed almost too tight. An outdoor man, Stenhauser figured. A hunter rather than a fisherman. He had the burly look of a hunter; fishermen were more aesthetic. Probably did weight-lifting every day. A big sport fan and a beer drinker. Not too bright, thought Stenhauser.

'And what's your business, Mr. uh . . .' Stenhauser began.

'Sloan. Harry Sloan. I'm a snoop.'

'A detective?'

'No, just a snoop,' Sloan said, drawing him in, slowly weaving a shimmery web for his fly.

Stenhauser chuckled. 'That's good. That's very funny,' he said. 'That's what gossip magazines are all about, right? I suppose we're all a bit nosy.'

Sloan leaned over toward Stenhauser and said, very confidentially, 'Yeah, but nothing like I am. I stop' – he held two fingers a quarter of an inch apart – 'about that far short of voyeurism.'

Stenhauser looked surprised. 'Well most people wouldn't admit it,' he said, taking another sip of his martini.

'I like to study people,' said Sloan. 'I feel I'm a very good judge of character.'

'Is that right.'

'Take you, for instance. I'll bet you're a very precise man.'

'Precise, huh.' Stenhauser thought about that for a few moments. 'I suppose that's true. It pays to be precise in my business.'

'I'm sure it does. Can't afford a slipup.' Sloan leaned closer to him. 'Do you deal with the criminal element?' he asked, adding more sheen to the web.

'That's what I do,' the little man said proudly. 'I realise I don't look very imposing, but I speak their language. I can be very tough when need be.'

'I can tell,' Sloan said.

'You can, huh?'

'Absolutely. I'll bet you're one helluva negotiator.' It was Sloan's oldest trick, working the mark's vanity. It never failed.

Stenhauser somewhat arrogantly wiggled his head back and forth a couple of times but did not comment. He's hooked, Sloan thought.

'I do a little writing,' Sloan said. 'I'd like to talk about some of your cases, the tough ones. Might be something in it for me.'

'Uh, well, I, that's very flattering but, uh, most of my work is highly confidential.'

'I don't mean real names. Just, you know, some inside stuff. The more you know, the more authentic the work is.'

'I suppose so. Well, perhaps some other time. I have to leave in a few minutes.'

'Look, why don't we just talk on the way up to Seventy-fourth Street,' Sloan said, smiling as he sipped his beer.

Stenhauser stared at him with surprise for a fraction of a second. 'How did you . . . I'm not going home,' he said quickly. 'I've got tickets for the theater.'

'That's a shame. Your dog's gonna bust a kidney.'

Stenhauser leaned over close to Sloan, and said between clenched teeth, 'What the hell are you up to, anyway?'

'Hatcher.'

'Hatcher?'

Sloan nodded. 'Hatcher.'

'Is that supposed to mean something to me?'

'Christian Hatcher, Mr. Stenhauser. I just want him, that's all. An address, a phone number. I'll vanish from your life like that.' He snapped his fingers.

'I think you oughta just' – he snapped his fingers, too – 'vanish like that anyway, whoever the hell you are.'

'No matter what happens, the game's over, Mr. Stenhauser. It's not going to work anymore – the art scam, I mean, and I know you know what I'm referring to. Now, I just want to talk to Hatcher, that's all. No big hassle. Hell, we're old friends. I once helped him out of a bad scrape.'

'Is that a fact.'

50

'Yes.'

'Listen, I don't know any Hatcher, but if I did know a Hatcher, I wouldn't tell you so much as his middle name. I wouldn't tell you his shoe size, I wouldn't tell you his – I wouldn't tell you a damn thing about him. I don't like you. I don't like your style, or your crazy talk. Is that clear?'

Sloan nodded earnestly. He wiggled a finger under Stenhauser's nose.

'You're going to be obstinate, I can tell,' he said as slowly, as patiently as always, still smiling. 'And that's too bad.'

'Really?'

'Really. Obstinacy will buy you about – oh, I don't know – at least ten years. Plus they'll take every dime you've got, which I'd say is plenty at this point.'

'I don't know what the hell you're talking about, Mr. . . . Sloan, was it?'

Sloan nodded. 'Listen, why don't we just walk up to Seventy-fourth Street together. Maybe I can clarify all this for you. Nobody will pay any attention to us, and you've got to go up there to let your dog whiz anyway, theater or no theater. And in case you need more convincing, we could even chat about Paris, Chicago – New York.'

They sat there, trying to stare each other down. It was Stenhauser who lowered his eyes first.

'What the hell,' he said in almost a whisper. 'If you promise not to mug me on the way, maybe it'll get you off my case.'

Outside, a brisk spring wind was blowing across town. They walked over to Madison Avenue and headed north. Stenhauser said nothing. He looked at the ground while he walked and his hands were jammed deep in his coat pockets.

'You know, maybe I've been a little hard on you,' Sloan said, his smile broadening. 'Maybe Hatch changed his name. Maybe you know him by another name.'

Stenhauser said nothing. He walked briskly, still staring a foot or two in front of each step.

'He used the same technique in all three jobs. I know his style. Down through the ceiling on a wire, pressure sensitizers on the walls when he lifts the paintings. He never goes near the floor, no worries about electric eyes, floor feelers, that kind of thing. And the son of a bitch always leaves a little something behind to help the police along. Old Hatch hasn't changed a bit. He used the same technique hitting the Russian embassy for me in London.'

Stenhauser looked up sharply, staring at Sloan as they walked.

'Also the Iranian embassy in Washington, before the hostage thing. Always leaves something. One of the sensitizers, the wire, something. It's magician stuff – misdirection, because he always jumps the alarm system but he never leaves the jumper behind, you know why?'

Stenhauser's pace began to quicken.

'Because to jump the system requires inside knowledge. In both my cases, Hatcher had an inside man, but he didn't want to blow their cover, so he leaves a little something behind. Now, here he is pulling the same old stunt. Hell, I was on to him from the first job, the thing in Paris. What a score!' Sloan laughed appreciatively.

Stenhauser stopped. He jabbed a finger at Sloan. 'You're crazy, you know that? I don't know who you are or what your game is, but you're stuffed full of shit.'

'I haven't gotten to the good stuff yet. See, here's the way I figure it works. Let's say somebody lifts a Picasso from a museum. The museum doesn't want a million bucks' insurance money, they want the work. They want it before it winds up on some Arab's yacht over in the Mediterranean. So they make a deal. The insurance company pays fifteen percent, no questions asked. It costs the insurance company a hundred fifty grand on a million-dollar policy, the museum gets its goods back, and the thief walks with a clean bill of health.'

Stenhauser was not a brave man. All he did was provide information and make deals. It had never occurred to him that he and the Bird would be caught. Now fear began to nibble at his insides.

'There's nothing illegal about what I do, Sloan,' he said defensively. 'I make deals, sure. But it's perfectly legitimate. It saves the taxpayers money because the police aren't involved. It saves the insurance company money. The victims get their things back. Everybody ends up happy.'

Bluffing, and not very well, Sloan thought, chuckling to himself. Still smiling, he shook his head. 'I couldn't care less,' he said with a shrug. 'But let me give you a new scenario. A thief hits the Louvre and walks off with twelve million dollars' worth of goods. The fixer steps in, quietly gets the word around, makes a deal. The insurance company gets stiffed for one point eight mill, but saves ten point two mill in the long haul, and the museum gets its paintings back. Now, just supposing we had a real smart man working for the insurance company. And supposing he approaches this flier and says, "Look, pal, I can give you advance information on where art's gonna be, when it's vulnerable, the security systems, I'll set up the buy, and we just split the pie up two ways.'" Sloan paused. 'Neat, isn't it?'

'I know where you're heading with this, and I'm telling you right here and now you're nuts,' said Stenhauser vehemently.

Sloan kept talking, slowly, quietly, as if Stenhauser had never uttered a word. 'I figure the two of you have split almost four million dollars over the last two years, Stenhauser. You're not only going to have cops all over the world crawling up your ass, you're gonna have the IRS sitting in your lap every time you take a load off. All I have to do is tell them what you've been up to. Whether they can prove it or not, they'll make life so miserable for you –'

Who is this man? Stenhauser wondered. He had never before entertained even the remotest thought of murder – of any form of bodily harm to anyone else – but now, walking up Madison Avenue, he found the blackest kind of ideas buzzing in his head.

'I know what you're thinking,' Sloan said, as if reading Stenhauser's mind. 'Forget it. You don't have the guts or talent for it.'

Stenhauser's mouth dried up.

Sloan shook his head. 'There's no reason for all this anxiety,' he said. 'I don't want to make life miserable for you. I want Hatcher.'

'And I keep telling you –'

Sloan cut him off. His eyes grew cold, lost their expression, but the smile remained. Stenhauser suddenly felt a chill creep over him.

'Get off it, little man,' Sloan said very quietly. 'You're going to tell me what I want to know – now – or I'm going to come down on you so hard you'll think it's raining bricks. Think about it. You're out of business anyway. Do you want to keep what you've got, smile all the way to the bank, or do you want a lot of grief?'

Stenhauser looked up and down the street. He hunched deeper into his coat and stared at Sloan's feet. 'He'll kill me,' Stenhauser whispered.

'No way.'

'You don't –'

'Know him?' Sloan finished the sentence. 'I was in business with the man when you were still taking the SATs.'

Stenhauser turned away from Sloan. He strolled to the curb and looked up at the gold lights on Trump Tower. He had dreamed of owning an apartment there, a million-dollar layout with all the trimmings, and now this stranger, whom he'd never seen until half an hour ago, was stealing the dream. Anger roiled up inside him, but Stenhauser was smart enough to know there was nothing he could do about it. Sloan had him and was squeezing.

'I don't know where he is,' Stenhauser said finally. 'I've never laid eyes on him. Didn't even know his name until you brought it up. I get in touch through a dead drop, a relay phone.'

Sloan, smiling, walked over to him and patted him on the shoulder.

'That'll be just fine,' he said.

'Who the hell are you, anyway?' Stenhauser asked bitterly. 'What's in this for you?'

'That's none of your fucking business,' Sloan answered as slowly and methodically as ever.

GINIA

He lay on the floor with his chin resting on the backs of his hands, watching a bright yellow flame-tail tang darting in and out of the coral, its snout pecking for food. A moment later, she swam into frame, trailing bubbles from her tanks, her long black hair waving behind her.

She was as naked as the fish she was chasing.

Her hard, perfectly rounded buttocks ground together as she scissor-kicked her long, muscular legs, and glided over and around the small coral cluster, chasing the tang. She had an astounding figure and the tiny white triangles, where her bikini had blocked the sun, made her tawny figure even more alluring.

An absolutely stunning creature.

He studied every rippling muscle in her body, every square inch of tanned skin, knowing she knew he was watching and was enjoying his voyeurism just as much as he was. He felt himself begin to tighten, felt his pulse tapping in his forehead.

The six-foot glass square mounted in the floor was what really had sold him on the yacht. It was hidden beneath the plush Oriental carpet in the main cabin. With the push of a button, a panel in the hull slid back and four powerful floodlights mounted on each corner of the window switched on. The result was a spectacular undersea panorama.

She was holding a plastic tube about two feet long, which looked like a large syringe four or five inches in diameter with a plunger on one end. She was behind the tang, extending the tube slowly toward it, then she suddenly drew back the plunger and the suction pulled the tang into the tube where a mesh valve trapped it. The fish darted up and down the tube, confused by the almost invisible plastic sides that entrapped it. She turned toward the window and proudly flexed her muscles.

'Nicely done,' he said aloud in a harsh, rasping voice that was almost a whisper. He leaned up on one elbow and crooked a finger toward her, inviting her closer, and she swam up close to the window, rolled on her back and spread her legs, tantalizing him. He leaned down and pressed his lips against the window and she moved slowly through the water, rising up against it, pressing first her breasts, then her stomach, then her thighs, against it, and he opened his mouth slightly, flicking his tongue against the inch-thick window, and she began to slowly wiggle, taunting him as he moved his head over her breasts, down to her hard, flat stomach and then down farther, to the matted hair that was pressed on inch away from his mouth. Then she was gone.

He lay there, watching the fish darting in and out of the coral cluster, thinking about Ginia. He was lucky. She was bright, beautiful, and sensuous. They had been lovers for almost a year.

It had been Cirillo who found this island. And it was to Cirillo and his wife, Millie, that Hatcher had come after Los Boxes. He had walked away from Sloan's rescuers, hitchhiked from Miami and arrived at Cirillo's door in the middle of the night, a gaunt, hollow-eyed replica of himself, wet to the knees from stumbling through the marsh. The Cirillos had asked no questions; they simply had nursed him back to health, providing the care and understanding necessary to heal his shattered mind and body.

The years after Los Boxes had been almost as traumatic as the experience itself. His emotions had become so armored, so distrusting and involuted, that he had spent the first months alone, wandering the bases of his past, looking for someplace to sink a root, something to hook him to reality. The closest he had come was a boat, but there were no roots in the sea. For a year he had indulged himself, cruised the Caribbean, lain in the sun, gorged on good food and wine, read constantly, and made love to women of every possible persuasion – white women, black women, red women, married women, unmarried women, smart women, dumb women, old women and young women.

Ultimately he had returned to the island. Hatcher had learned to love the place; to love the marsh that insulated the island from the rest of the world, and the island itself, so teeming with new life that it had rekindled his own spirit after Los Boxes. It had become his first real home. The isolated corner of the world was a perfect refuge for him.

There had been rumors about him, this strange, quiet man with the shattered voice and the haunted eyes, who sat night after night in Murphy's Tavern, nursing brandy. That he was a doper on parole, that he was a doper who had never been caught, that he was a narc looking for dopers on the isolated island, that he had served twenty years for murdering a faithless wife. All fictions written with whiskied tongues by the women he ignored and the men whose women were attracted to him.

He laughed at the stories, flattered by a status that had become mysterious and legendary, and gradually the islanders had accepted him, attracted by his sense of humor, his independence and a sense of loyalty to fellow islanders that was revealed slowly and without fanfare. He was one of them now and the stories had been put aside. Like many others who had escaped a checkered past and sought refuge in the small waffle of land two miles off the coast of Georgia, his past remained a mystery.

Ginia had her eye on him for a couple of months before he finally moved on her. She asked no questions, nor did he, although he knew she was a native of the island, had graduated from the Wharton School with honors, had been one of the most respected brokers on Wall Street, married a wealthy attorney and then, on her thirtieth birthday, had chucked it all and returned to the island and set up a small brokerage firm. That was all Murphy talk, and he never asked her anything about it, just as she never questioned him. It was as if they had no past, only their future.

It was two months before he asked her to dinner, a dinner he cooked and served a mile offshore, anchored over what since had become their favorite reef. They sat on the floor and ate dinner and watched the sea creatures at play through the glass bottom and drank a lot of wine, and when she finally left the boat two days later, she knew nothing more about him than she had known when she came on board – except for his taste in furniture, clothes and art, all of which were impeccable – not what he did for a living or where he came from or what he had done before he came to the island or whether he had ever married, had children, was wanted by the police or was dying of an incurable disease. Now, nine months later, she still didn't

56

know. And she didn't care. He was a tender lover, an experimenter, considerate, unhurried, aware of her wants, unthreatened, funny, and she responded in the same way. Sex had remained a joy rather than a task. He never showed anger, never judged anyone, and he treated her with uncommon respect. That was good enough for her.

It was around noon when the Lear jet whistled over the island, banking sharply to the east, circling out over the Atlantic and sweeping back over the island a second time.

Sloan studied the island as the pilot circled it. It was shaped like the island of Manhattan, but there the similarity ended. Ten miles long and barely two miles wide, it was little more than a thin strip of hard land surrounded on three sides by a sprawling marsh and on the east by the Atlantic Ocean.

A tiny village squatted at the southern point of the island, its fishing pier pointing a hundred yards out into the ocean like a finger pointing toward Florida. A whitewashed old lighthouse seemed to guard the three-block-square shopping area, which was surrounded by moss-laden oak trees that hid most of the inland houses populating the south end. Weathered old homes of tabby and wood lined the ocean like sentinels, defying the unpredictable Atlantic.

On its leeward side was a shopping center and a handsome new redwood marina, where several large yachts were moored among the smaller sailboats and fishing boats. A small jetport was located just north of the village, and north of it the upper half of the island was heavily forested and uninhabited. You could walk the inhabited part of the island in an hour, thought Sloan.

A tall man slender as a reed and wearing a battered captain's hat pulled up in the fuel truck as the Lear howled to a stop near the low-slung terminal.

'Anyplace to get some good home cooking?' Sloan asked, climbing out of the plane.

The man, who seemed to be on about a ten-second delay, stared at him and then said, 'Might try Birdie's over in the village.'

'Can I get a cab?'

He thought about that for another ten seconds.

'No cab out here.'

'How can I get over there?'

'Well,' the man in the peaked cap said after some thought, 'you can walk, takes ten or fifteen minutes.' Another delay. 'Or you can rent a car inside.'

57

'Actually I'm looking for a friend of mine. Maybe you know him – Christian Hatcher?'

After half a minute: 'Wouldn't know.'

'Birdie's you say?'

'Uh-huh.'

It was a beautiful day, the temperature in the eighties and a cool breeze hustling through the trees from the beach.

'We'll walk.'

The island, a quaint bit of Americana worthy of a Rockwell painting, had changed little in twenty years. Its charm lured the big cruise ships from Miami and Charleston. They came once or twice a week, tied up at the pier and spent the night. The cruisers, as its passengers were called by locals, ambled down the fishing pier and checked out Tim's gift store, pored over Nancy's used books, stocked up on T-shirts and stuffed animals at the Island Hop, got the latest magazines and paperbacks at Doc Bryant's drugstore, had a drink at Murphy's Tavern or home-made ice cream at Clifton's and then wandered off the Main Drag – the only drag, since the village was a single street a mere three blocks long – and did some sightseeing. In that short main stretch, the cruisers could eat home cooking at Birdie's, hamburgers at the Big T, barbecue at the Rib Shack or seafood at Mallory's before returning to their ship for the night. By the next morning they were gone.

As Sloan stood looking over the minuscule hamlet, his smile broadened. This is it? he thought. This is what he calls home.

He would be casual and cautious in asking questions. He walked down to the city pier, where the locals were crabbing and fishing or taking in the sun, watching the shrimp boats come and go and the big brown pelicans dive-bombing for lunch.

Roland Smith, who regarded himself as the unofficial mayor of the island, appeared at the pier each morning dressed in sports jacket and tie with a fresh flower in his lapel to do his rounds. He petted dogs, babbled over babies, flirted with all females over sixteen, and slowly worked his way up to a niche of a restaurant called the Bowrider to have breakfast and trade gossip with the locals. He was never without a smile and spent his days simply being pleasant. He had come to the island ten years ago on vacation with his wife, who had dropped dead on the beach of a heart attack. Smith, a window dresser for a New York department store, had sent a letter to his boss announcing his retirement and never left.

Sloan watched Roland stroll the pier and its nearby park,

58

smiling and chatting. Sloan knew a talker when he saw one. He wandered to the edge of the park and sat on a bench until Smith ambled by.

'Morning,' Smith said with a smile. 'Lovely day, isn't it?'

'Perfect,' said Sloan, matching the smile.

'I do love this island,' Smith said, which was his standard greeting to tourists.

'It's beautiful,' Sloan agreed.

'You vacationing here?' Smith asked innocently.

'Well, kind of. Actually I'm looking for an old friend of mine. We were army buddies. But I lost his address and I can't find him in the phone book.'

'Maybe he moved,' offered the putative mayor.

'Perhaps you know him. Chris Hatcher? I just thought I'd surprise him.'

'Maybe he doesn't like surprises,' Smith said pleasantly, his grin fading only slightly. He nodded, and strolled away.

Sloan wandered in and out of the shops, striking up conversations in his easy, smiling way, finally getting around to the big question. Nobody said, 'I don't know him' or 'I never heard of him'; they simply generalized the question into oblivion with answers like 'Lots of folks on this old island' or 'Where did you say you were from?'

Typical small town, thought Sloan, everybody on the island was as closemouthed as they were pleasant. But Sloan was gifted with infinite patience. Hatcher was on this island somewhere. *Some*body on this island had to know Hatcher, it was just a matter of time before somebody owned up.

Sloan went into Birdie's. It was a pleasant, unintrusive restaurant, which smelled of fresh vegetables and seafood, its fare listed on a large blackboard on the wall. He found a table next to a group of men who looked as if they belonged.

When he had first come to the island, Hatcher had chosen to become a recluse, avoiding people and living a solitary life on his boat. His only friend was Cirillo. But gradually he became close to these people. They were nonjudgmental, warm, and simply supportive of one another. Like Hatcher, they had escaped to the island, leaving behind bad memories or shattered careers or the abuses of Establishment phonies.

All the men at the adjoining table were Hatcher's friends. One was an enormous Santa Claus of a man with white hair and a thick white beard whom the others called Bear. Then there was a slender, quiet man, his gray-white beard tickling his chest, who was reading a paperback novel as he ate, and another gentle-faced man who was jotting lines of poetry in a tattered notebook. Sloan listened to their choppy conversation, hoping for clues. He got none, although it was obvious they were islanders. The reader's name was Bob Hill. He had been a thoroughbred horse trainer, a circus clown, a schoolteacher, and he now owned his own shrimp boat. The poet, whose name was Frank, worked as a night clerk in one of the mainland motels and spent his days on the beach, writing poetry. Bear was an architect. The fourth man at the table, trim and weathered, whom they called Judge, had fallen from the bench in disfavor, a victim of the bottle. He was now the maître d' at the island's premier hotel and had not had a drink in fourteen years.

'Haven't had food this good since I left home,' Sloan said pleasantly.

'That's the truth,' Bear answered. 'And almost as cheap.'

They chatted amiably back and forth during the meal. Finally Sloan popped the question and was greeted with the same vague response.

'Probably end up here eating sooner or later,' said Bear. 'Everybody does.'

Sloan was undaunted. Hatcher had no listing in the city directory or phone book. No auto registration. But since he lived on this island and he was ex-Navy and he loved the sea, it seemed reasonable that Hatcher had a boat. The process of elimination ultimately led Sloan to the marina.

By this time everybody in the village knew he was looking for Hatcher.

He tried to strike up a conversation with Cap Fendig, who operated the marina itself. Fendig's roots were dug deep in the black soil of the island. His father and grandfather and great-grandfather were the harbor pilots who captained the big cargo vessels from the ocean through the sound to the state docks on the mainland.

'Actually I'm looking for an old friend of mine, Chris Hatcher. We were in the Army together.'

'That a fact.'

'He's big on sailing. Thought perhaps he might have a boat down here.'

'Well, this would be the place to keep a boat.'

Fendig moved up the pier.

'Name's Chris Hatcher,' Sloan called after him.

'Wasn't born here. Lived here all my life, nobody by that name was born on this island.'

'No, he would have moved here about a year and a half ago.'

'Oh.'

End of discussion.

Sloan changed his tack. He approached a kid working the gas pumps.

'What time's Chris Hatcher due back?' he asked pleasantly.

'Never know,' the kid answered.

Bingo.

'Does he live on the boat?'

'I wouldn't know,' the kid answered and vanished into the small pumping station.

Sloan went back up to the marina, got a beer, and went back down to the pier and waited.

The sharp bleat of a boat's horn snapped Hatcher back to reality.

'Oh God,' he groaned. He got up, arranging the bulge in his skimpy bathing suit as best he could and went topside; he peered cautiously over the bulkhead.

A shrimp boat called the *Breeze-E* was idling nearby, its engines muttering as it rocked gently in the calm sea. Its captain, a tall, leathery stringbean of a man with a neatly trimmed gray-white beard, was standing in the stern. He cupped his mouth with his hands and yelled, 'This fella's wandering all over the island asking after you. Been to Birdie's, Po Stephens. Murphy's. The marina. Even tried to pry information out of old Roland.'

'What'd he want?' Hatcher yelled back in the harsh voice that was part growl, part whisper.

'Said he was an old friend of yours from the Army.'

Hatcher shook his head. 'What's he look like?'

'Big guy, built like a lobster pot, real broad in the shoulder. Looks to be in his late forties. Real friendly sort.'

'Talks real soft and smiles all the time. Little scar on his cheek?' He drew an imaginary line from his eye to the corner of his mouth.

'That's him. Friend of yours?'

'I wouldn't say that. What'd you tell him?'

'Not a damn thing.'

'Thanks, Bob.'

'Anytime. Fishing?'

61

'Kinda.'

'See ya.'

Bob Hill waved, returned to the bridge and shoved the throttles, veering out towards the open sea. Hatcher heard a sound behind him and, turning, saw Ginia looking at him over the rail.

'What was that all about?' she asked.

'Bob Hill. Says somebody's asking about me in town. You know how islanders are, they get a little overly protective sometimes.'

'I think that's nice,' she said, jumping over the rail from the Jacob's ladder, grabbing a towel off a chair and wrapping it around her like a sarong. 'It's nice to know your friends care that much about you.'

'Uh-huh. Let's see that tang.'

She reached back over the railing, retrieved the tube and handed it to him. He held it up close, studying the fish.

'Big guy,' he said.

'Just look at that tail. Do we keep him?'

'Absolutely.'

He took the tube below to the main salon, where the six other fish they had caught that morning were still circling and exploring the hundred-gallon aquarium. He stood over the tank, turned a knob opening the valve in the tube, and the yellow fish swam out and immediately began staking out his territory amid the coral and sea grass in the floor of the tank.

'Beautiful,' she said from behind him. Her arms slithered around his waist. 'Swimming makes me horny,' she said, close to his ear.

Without turning he reached behind him and moved his hands under the towel and up the insides of her thighs. She leaned back a trifle, giving his hands more room to move, and slid her hands under the band of his skimpy swimsuit, feeling him rise to her touch. She slipped his trunks over his hips and let them drop to the floor, freeing him.

'And everything makes you horny,' she said.

He turned and pulled the towel loose and, sliding his hands gently down her back and over the soft mounds of her cheeks, drew her to him.

'You got a cold rear end,' he growled in her ear.

'But a warm heart.'

She stood on her toes, spreading her legs a little more, and stepped into him, her thick hair surrounding him, and wrapped her lips around one of his nipples and began sucking.

'Been a while,' his peculiar whisper-voice answered.

62

'Right,' she chuckled. 'At least two hours.'

She leaned over and whispered in his ear, 'Put it on automatic pilot,' then took his hand and drew him back toward the master stateroom.

OLD TIMES

She was a real beauty, sleek and uncommonly low in the water that looked more like a racing craft than a yacht, with her squat cockpit, the long, trim bow jutting fifty feet in front of the windscreen, the four 750 hp fuel-injected engines rumbling in the stern. The long, slender profile concealed a large main salon, a master bedroom with a king-size bed, ample quarters for two other guests and a galley fit for a cordon bleu chef.

Sloan saw only the exterior, but he could not suppress a soft whistle as the boat sliced silently through the water toward him.

The hardest emotions to control, 126 had once warned Hatcher, would be love and hate. Hatcher had loved Harry Sloan as he would have loved his own brother and hated him as he would his deadliest enemy. Now, as he approached the dock and saw Sloan for the first time in seven years, he was overwhelmed with mixed emotions.

The bond between mentor and student is as hard to break as the one between father and son; 126 had told him that, and it was true.

He wanted to get even with Sloan for betraying him, and yet part of him was glad to see the son of a bitch. Rage began to grow in him as the boat neared the dock. Rage at Sloan. Rage at himself for not hating the man more than he did. The hardest thing to forgive was not the three years in Los Boxes – it was that Sloan had betrayed him.

What the hell was he doing here?

He turned to Ginia.

'See the big guy standing by the slip house?' he said.

'Uh-huh.'

'He's the guy who's looking for me.'

'Friend or foe?' she asked breezily.

'Jump off as soon as we tie up, okay? We've got some talking to do.'

'The old screw-and-run trick, huh?'

63

'Yeah.' He kissed her on the cheek. 'I'll call you later. Catch the bowline for me.'

'Sure. Dinner?'

'Maybe.'

She leaned over and kissed him hard on the mouth. 'Remember that, just in case you feel like playing soldier-boy with your pal.'

'He's no pal.'

Sloan watched Hatcher ease the big boat into its slip, watched Ginia jump on the dock and hook up the front line, then turn and blow him a kiss, watched her walk up the pier toward the setting sun, which silhouetted her long legs through a thin white cotton skirt. Sloan ambled down the pier and stood below the bridge, looking up at him.

'Been a while, Hatch,' Sloan said around his perpetual smile.

He looks great, Sloan thought. Tanned, filled out, got a lot more hair than I do. Hell, he's better-looking than he ever was.

Hatcher glared back at him and said nothing.

'Permission to come aboard, Captain?' Sloan asked with a laugh. When Hatcher didn't answer, Sloan clambered on board anyway.

Pushy as ever, Hatcher thought.

Sloan held his hand out toward Hatcher, who ignored it. Instead Hatcher turned abruptly and went below. Sloan stood for a moment, made a fist and blew nervously into it, then decided to follow him.

He was surprised at how large the main cabin was and how elegant. The walls were paneled with bronze mirrors and teak, the designer furniture was gray and plush, an Oriental rug covered the floor. A pedestal table large enough to seat eight divided the main cabin from the forward staterooms. Sloan could not suppress another low whistle, which Hatcher ignored as he went to the bar, poured himself a glass of red wine and sat down. He didn't offer Sloan anything, and the burly man finally sat down facing him.

'You look great, Chris. Never better,' he said.

What balls, Hatcher thought, although he still said nothing.

'You've got a lot of funny friends,' Sloan said. 'None of them'll admit they know you.' He chuckled. Hatcher just stared at him.

'It's good to see you again,' Sloan said, trying to sound sincere.

No answer. Just get on with it, Hatcher said to himself. His

64

face clouded up, but he still didn't speak. Sloan sighed and watched Hatcher take a sip of wine. His mouth was getting dry. Hell, thought Sloan, I may as well get straight to it.

'Here I went to all that trouble to spring you down in Madrango and you don't even show up in Washington to thank me.'

Be grateful I didn't kill you, Hatcher thought, but he still didn't speak.

Sloan made a fist and held it in front of his lips, blowing gently into it. Smiling, he said slowly, 'I've got to admit I was a little nervous coming down here. I figured there was as good a chance as not you'd try to put me away. And I can understand that, Hatch, I really can. But, you know, why throw all this away just to get even, right?'

Hatcher said nothing. But the yellow flecks in his green eyes danced like charged ions.

'You know the boys in intelligence still talk about you,' Sloan rambled on. 'I told them you were the best in the business, I mean any job, laddie, *any* job. Nobody believed me until you vanished at that refueling stop in Miami. Nothing but the clothes on your back. No money, no ID, nothing, and you're gone. I gotta give it to you, that was beautifully done. Three years in that place, you didn't lose your edge.'

Hatcher said nothing.

Sloan stood up and wandered around the cabin, looking at things, checking them out, still speaking in that smooth, oily voice of his.

'Took me sixteen months to get a line on you. I didn't have the outfit out shaking the bushes or anything like that, y'know, just keeping my eyes and ears open.'

You talk too much, Hatcher thought. You always talked too much.

Hatcher took another sip of wine, staring over the rim of the glass at Sloan.

'You've really stirred them up,' Sloan chattered on. 'Know what Interpol calls you? The Bird. Shit, the best flier in the business, I always knew that. Of course, I never said anything to anybody. None of my business. Anyway, I gotta hand it to you, you're a real trend setter.'

Hatcher didn't bite. He kept staring at Sloan. Sloan put his briefcase in his lap, unlocked it and flipped it open. From where Hatcher was sitting he could not see inside the case, but he knew exactly how it was laid out. File folders, all neatly labeled and stacked. A comprehensive airline schedule. Sloan's little black book, the bible that kept him in business. And in the top of the case in special pockets, two handguns, a .357 Python and a 9 mm. H&K. Speed loaders and magazines in pockets between the two pieces.

Sloan would never change. If it worked for him, it stayed in. Sloan took out a newspaper clipping.

'Listen to this, this was in *The Times* last Sunday. "The international art theft market is second only to narcotics in the world market." According to this piece, Hatch, art thefts have doubled since 1981. There were four hundred ninety-three cases last year alone. Four thousand one hundred fifty pieces of art got lifted.'

Still no comment.

'The Paris job was what put me on to you,' Sloan said, his smile broadening as though he was proud of it. 'Then when you hit that gallery in Chicago and Stenhauser was the fixer in that one, too, I put it together. The New York trick put the icing on the cake.'

Still no response. Hatcher took another sip of wine and continued to stare. He was remembering what 126 had said once about vengeance. It's depressing, is what he said, and a waste of time. One thing Hatcher had learned to respect in Los Boxes was time.

'That Paris job was inspired, better than the thing we did in London that time,' Sloan went on.

He paused for a moment. Hatcher said nothing.

'Some haul, man. That one Monet was worth over three mill. Five pieces, twelve million. I didn't know you knew that much about rare paintings, old pal.'

No answer.

'I guess Stenhauser tipped you on what to grab, right?'

No answer.

'Anyway, you were right up front with that Paris job, kind of set the pace for what's been going on. I'll give you a hand for your style, too. I figure you've only done the three jobs.'

He paused and shrugged. 'And who got hurt? The insurance companies, right?' Sloan chuckled. He held out his hands, palms up, like a magician about to perform sleight of hand. 'Who gives a big damn, they probably screwed a lot of little people out of twenty times what you took 'em for.'

Still no comment. Sloan sighed and looked up at the ceiling. He was getting annoyed. 'You've changed, Hatcher. You were

66

always good for an argument – about anything. You used to be quite the talker.'

Hatcher stood up suddenly, took three long steps across the room and hit Sloan with a fast, hard jab straight to the corner of the jaw. The big man flew backward out of his chair, landed on his neck and rolled over against the bulkhead.

'God damn,' he snapped. He wiped blood from the corner of his mouth and looked up sharply as Hatcher leaned over him.

'I have this thing about wasting words,' Hatcher whispered.

'Jesus,' Sloan cracked, 'what happened to your voice?'

Hatcher didn't answer. He rinsed out his wineglass, slid it into an overhead wine rack and locked it down. Then he went topside. Sloan got up slowly, massaging his jaw. He went to the refrigerator, opened it and took out a light beer. He popped the top off, took a deep drink and then held the cold can against his jaw. Then the four big engines coughed to life and the boat began to move. Sloan rushed to the top. Hatcher was backing the 48-footer away from the dock.

'What the hell're you doing?' he demanded, but Hatcher didn't answer. He swung the boat around in a tight arc and headed back out to sea, cruising slowly through the sound, and then as the boat broke out into the open sea he eased the throttles forward and the engines changed their voices, their basso tones keeping rhythm to the slap of the ocean as the small yacht picked up speed and began bounding from whitecap to whitecap.

Sloan caressed his jaw with the cold beer can. 'You didn't forget how to hit,' he said. His smile slowly returned. 'What the hell, I guess I had it coming.'

Hatcher turned around and stood nose to nose with Sloan.

'Is this a shakedown, Harry?' his harsh voice asked.

Sloan looked shocked. 'C'mon!'

'Then what're you doing here? Don't tell me you came to apologize, I'll deck you again.'

'You know me, Hatch. I, uh, tuck info away for a rainy day. I always figure sooner or later . . .' He let the sentence dangle.

'Yeah?'

'So now is later.'

'You set me up, you son of a bitch.'

Sloan shrugged. 'You do what you have to do.'

'To protect a drunken bum.'

'Shit, it was all politics there. We were just trying to save the country is all.'

'From what – rats and cockroaches?' Hatcher rasped.

67

Sloan shrugged with a grin. 'From the Commies, who else?'

'And I happened to be expendable.'

'The whole thing went sour,' Sloan went on in his sincere voice. 'You were supposed to be in the prison in Madrango. Then the country blew up before I could get back to get you. Next thing I know, they moved you to Los Boxes. So it was a bad call, I'll give you that,' Sloan said.

'A bad call!' the ruined voice whispered.

'I brought you in when I could, laddie,' Sloan said.

Hatcher moved the throttles forward a little more. The engines got throatier, the bow lifted a little more.

'What happened to the little fat guy?' Hatcher said finally.

'Pratt? Ah, the rebels held him for a couple of months. He lost forty pounds and quit the State Department.'

'I wonder who's better off.'

'He got you out, didn't he?'

Hatcher growled between clenched teeth: 'Our beloved ambassador, Craig, murders a woman and child with his Mercedes, I take the fall, go to Los Boxes, and two months later the government goes down the toilet and Craig is out on his ass anyway. Beautiful.'

'Hatch, you've been in the business long enough to know how fast things change. What the hell, I didn't forget you. Did I forget you?'

'Three years?'

'The timing wasn't right.'

Hatcher shook his head. 'When they passed out heart, Harry, you were in the asshole line. What the hell do you want?' Hatcher's voice rasped.

'I've got a job to do. A job nobody can hack like you can.'

Hatcher looked astounded. 'Fuck off,' he snarled.

'Listen to me –'

'Our slate's clean.'

'I don't quite see it that way.'

'I don't give a damn how you see it.'

'I got your pal, Stenhauser, by the gonies,' Sloan said softly but with menace. 'I squeeze him, you're looking to do about twenty years' hard time.'

'You always did dream big.'

'Look who's talking.'

'I don't dream,' Hatcher snapped, 'I do it.'

Smiling, Sloan leaned over and said softly, 'Chicago, Paris, New York . . . I'm not dreaming, pal. Let me play it out for you. They'll hit you one, two, three, back to back, nothing concurrent. Three major felonies, three different cities, three different courts, and France is real touchy about its art works. I figure you'll do at least fifteen years. And they'll take everything you've got. So they won't find the kiwash you got stashed in Panama or Grand Cayman or Switzerland' – he smiled his most insincere smile – 'but they'll get your boat and everything that shows.' He winked.

Hatcher stared at him for a moment.

'I think I'll just call that hand,' Hatcher said flatly.

'Maybe you better call Stenhauser first.'

'What'd you do, Sloan, kneecap the poor little bastard?'

'I just tightened his suspenders a little bit. He hasn't got your class. He folds easy.'

'As easy as blackmail comes to you?'

Sloan's anger was beginning to rise, but he controlled himself. The smile stayed, the soft tone, the sincerity. 'Okay, okay. I got off on the wrong foot. Look, you do this little thing for me, you'll never see me again. I'm history. You're forgetting, I taught you everything you know, Hatch. I'll forget all about –'

Hatcher suddenly twisted the wheel sharply to the right, then spun it back the other way. The boat started to go into a tight turn, then just as quickly switched into the opposite direction. Sloan was thrown backward. He hit the bulkhead. The beer can flew out of his hand and was swept away in the wind, then the boat yawed in the other direction and he lurched forward, scrambling for his balance and falling to his knees in front of the cabin hatch. Hatcher pulled the throttles back and then jammed them forward, and the defenseless Sloan, once again caught off-balance, vaulted headfirst into the cabin and flipped halfway over, landing on the back of his neck. He scrambled to get his feet under him and started to get up, but the boat turned sharply again and he flew forward and slammed into one of the bronze wall panels. His breath burst out of him as the mirror shattered from the force of the collision. Sloan fell to the floor as shards of the shattered mirror tinkled about him.

Topside, Hatcher pulled the throttles all the way back. The boat died in the water, and he jumped off the captain's chair and bounded the steps to the cabin. Sloan was on his knees, scrambling across the floor to his briefcase.

Hatcher moved fast, and, grabbing the briefcase, pulled out the .357. He tossed the case aside. File folders spilled out and their contents splashed all over the floor.

'Damn it –' Sloan began, and then felt cold steel under his nose. Hatcher stood over him with a Magnum pistol pressed against Sloan's upper lip.

'You taught me everything you know, all right,' his flinty voice snarled. 'Trouble is, Harry, you stopped learning and I didn't. Blackmail me, you son of a bitch.'

'You got it all wrong!' Sloan said, his smile finally vanishing. 'Just hear me out.'

Hatcher shook his head – Sloan never quit. 'Your ace in the hole is that fast mouth of yours. You could coax the devil into a cold shower. You lace it all up with your favorite words. Duty, patriotism – hell, you sell patriotism like Professor Wizard sells snake oil.'

'What's the matter with patriotism?'

Hatcher ignored the question. 'The trouble with you, Harry, is you do lousy math. One time, two and two equals four. Next time, it equals seven or twelve or eighty-two or whatever you want it to equal. Damn it, do you think you can frame me twice in the same lifetime?'

'Just listen for a –'

'Shut up,' Hatcher snarled, his eyes flashing.

Sloan thought to himself, If I can get past the next minute or two, I'm okay. It had been a calculated risk, facing up to Hatcher. So Sloan shut up. He leaned back in the chair and Hatcher stepped back a couple of steps, holding the gun at arm's length, pointed between Sloan's eyes. Then Sloan's smile returned. The hands went out, away from his sides again. 'I was hoping we could have a friendly talk.'

'Christ,' Hatcher snorted. 'You are something else.'

'Will you listen to me? Give me ten minutes of your time and I'm out of here forever –'

Hatcher cut him off. His harsh whisper took on a new edge. 'There was a time, Harry, when the only thing that kept me going, the *only* thing, was fantasizing about this moment. That's what kept me alive, imagining what it would be like to have you in the squeeze. Right now you're a trigger finger away from eternity.'

The smile faded a little but was still there. 'Okay, so what's stopping you?' Sloan said boldly.

Hatcher ignored the question. 'You'll be out of here forever, all right. I can stash you in the coral, the fish'll nibble you to bits before you have time to float up. Nobody'll ever know what happened to you.'

70

'You could do that, but you're not going to,' Sloan said, confidently shaking his head.

'I've done worse to better than you. Hell, you ought to know, I was working for you.'

'You think I don't know you're nursing a hard-on two miles long?' Sloan said, and for a moment there was almost a touch of sadness in his voice. 'Look around. Did I come in here with the whole brigade at my back? Did I come in waving around a lot of iron? Hell, no.'

Sloan had spent his life studying faces, learning to recognize the slightest nuances: the vague shift in a muscle, the almost imperceptible twitch of an eyelid, the slightest tightening of the mouth, the subtle shift of focus in the eyes. They were all signals to him that in an instant something had changed. Then it was like having a fish on a line. Time to reel in. Hatcher was good about concealing his emotions, but it was there, Sloan sensed it. I've got him, he thought. We're past the real touchy part. He leaned toward Hatcher and his eyes glittered as he put in the fix. 'I'm here on a mission of mercy, pal.'

And Hatcher thought, Shit, here it comes. Now he's got that tongue of his going full speed, now he's on the con.

'Let's stop horsing each other around, okay?' Sloan said. 'So you're tough and I'm tough, we don't have to prove that to each other anymore. I know you, Hatch. I know you know I'm not here to get a tan, so you've got to be real curious. Why don't you put that thing down and listen to me before you do something real crazy?'

Hatcher sighed. He leaned his gun arm on his leg. The pistol dangled loosely in his hand, pointed at the deck somewhere between Sloan's feet.

'Okay, let's hear the part about the mission of mercy,' he snickered. 'That ought to be a classic.'

CODY

Sloan gathered up his file folders from the deck and put them back in order. He dropped one in Hatcher's lap.

'Read this,' he said.

It was the service record of Lieutenant Murphy Roger Cody,

71

USN. Murph Cody. Hatcher hadn't heard that name since Cody died in Vietnam a long time ago.

'What's this all about?' Hatcher asked. 'Cody's been history for fifteen years.'

'Fourteen actually.'

'Fourteen, fifteen, what's the difference.'

'Read the file, then we'll talk.'

Hatcher leafed through the 0–1 file. There was nothing out of the ordinary about the record. It began when Cody entered the U.S. Naval Academy in 1962, and ended abruptly when his twin-engine OV-10 crashed and burned while flying a routine search-and-destroy mission near Binh Thuy in the Mekong Delta, April 13, 1972. Cody had been assigned to Light Attack Squadron 6, Naval Riverine Patrol Forces, and had gone 'in-country' in July 1971, nine months before he was lost. There were two commendations for outstanding service and a recommendation for the Navy Cross, which had been approved and awarded posthumously.

Supplementary reports included a tape of the debriefing interrogation of two of Cody's wingmen and the gunner of an SAR Huey crew that had tried to rescue Cody and his radioman; a confidential report by the MIA commission dated January 1978, confirming that no trace of Cody had been found; a tape of the review board and the official certification of death in 1979; and another commission report filed when the crash site was located in 1981, reporting that charred bones had been found on-site but were unidentifiable – they could have been the remains of either Cody or his crewman, Gunner's Mate John Rossiter, or parts of both.

The only mention of Cody's father was on the service form under 'next of kin.' It said merely, 'William John Cody, General, U.S. Army.' Not *the* Buffalo Bill Cody, commander of all the field forces in Vietnam. A typical bureaucratic understatement.

There were two photographs, a drab black-and-white that was Cody's last official Navy photo and a five-by-seven color shot of him with his wife and two small children in front of a Christmas tree. The date on the back was Christmas, 1971, his last Christmas home. There were also some news clippings, including the announcement in the San Francisco *Chronicle* that Cody's widow, Joan, had married a rear admiral two years after Cody was officially declared dead. Cold, hard facts and not too many of them.

Hatcher studied the two photographs. He remembered Cody

as being tall and hard with a quick laugh, a man who loved a good time almost as much as he loved the ladies.

The photographs prodded Hatcher's memory, but twenty years had dulled it. Hazy incidents flirted with his brain – the good times, oddly, seemed the most vague – then there were other incidents, juxtaposed visions of Murph Cody, that were crystal clear. In one, Cody was the brutish sophomore, a hulking shape in the boxing ring, pummeling his opponent relentlessly, driving a youngster into the ropes, slamming punches in a flurry to the chest and face of the kid until Hatcher and another member of the team jumped in the ring and pulled him off. In the other, Cody was the penitent, showing up at the hospital later that evening, apologizing in tears for hurting the young freshman, who had two broken ribs and a shattered cheekbone, and sitting beside him all night.

He remembered, too, his own fear as a freshman of Cody, who had a reputation among the new frogs as a mean hazer.

'When did you meet him?' Sloan asked.

Hatcher thought for a moment as memories bombarded him. Opaque memories like the shape of a room but not the furnishings in it and faces without voices. Then slowly the memories began to materialize as his mind sorted through fragments of his life.

'The first day at Annapolis,' he answered. 'I'll never forget it. . . .'

August 1963. A bright, hot day. Hatcher and a half-dozen other frogs were lined up ramrod-straight, their backs flat against the wall in the dormitory hallway. It was their first day at Annapolis, and they were all confused and scared. Two upperclassmen had them braced and were giving them their first introduction to the cruelties inflicted on a frog, a new freshman at the academy.

The worse of the two was a burly midshipman with a permanent sneer named Snyder. Snyder hated all lowerclassmen. Because he had almost busted out himself, he had no tolerance for them.

The other second-year man merely watched. He was tall, muscular and handsome despite features that were triangular and hawkish and made him appear older than he was. He stood at parade rest, never taking his eyes off Hatcher.

'Look at these maggots,' Snyder said, stalking the line of frightened young midshipmen. 'Look around you, maggots. By this time next year only two of you will be left.'

He stood in front of Hatcher. 'You're the juvenile, huh. How did a delinquent like you get into Annapolis?'

Hatcher stared straight ahead, not knowing what to answer.

73

Snyder's face was an inch from Hatcher's. 'What's the matter, maggot, can't you talk?' he yelled.

'Yes, sir!' the terrified Hatcher answered.

'Are you a maggot?'

'Yes, sir!'

'Are you lower than dog shit?'

'Yes, sir!'

'I can't hear you!'

'Yes, *sir*!'

'Awright, clear the hall!' Snyder yelled. 'Move it, move it, move it. On the double!' And he laughed as they all scrambled to their rooms.

A minute later the tall cadet appeared at the door to Hatcher's room.

'Everybody clear out but Hatcher,' he snapped and the room emptied. Hatcher stood as erect as a statue in his new uniform, his chin tucked against his clavicle. Cody stood very near him but did not look at him; he stared out the window at the courtyard as he spoke. 'My name's Murphy Cody. You call me *Mister* Cody.'

'Yes, sir.'

'I hear you're a street kid. Is that right, maggot?'

'Well, sir, I . . .'

'Yes or no!'

'Yes, sir!'

'I hear you were a Golden Gloves champion in Boston. That correct?'

'Yes, sir.'

Cody looked him over. 'Middleweight?'

'Yes, sir.'

'You don't look like you could break wind, maggot,' Cody said and walked out of the room.

Thanksgiving, 1963. A cold, harsh-wind day. 'Hit the wall, maggot,' Snyder bellowed as Hatcher was leaving the mess hall and the underclassman assumed the position.

A dozen frogs had already fallen before the relentless hazing of Snyder, Cody and other midshipmen. Yet Hatcher felt that in a funny way Cody was watching out for him. Hatcher had surprised them all. While other freshmen broke under the rigorous schedule and hazing, Hatcher seemed to get stronger as the months went by. By winter he knew he would get by that crucial first year if Snyder didn't force a confrontation.

74

Snyder had other plans.

'Hatcher's mine,' Snyder bragged openly. 'I'll break him. He'll be gone before Christmas.'

He braced Hatcher constantly, in the lowerclassman's shower, in the yard, in the halls, his comments always insulting and humiliating. Eventually it started to get to Hatcher.

Now he was at it again.

'The academy is for men, maggot,' Snyder snarled. 'You're not a man, you're what we used to call a J.D. back where I come from. You know what a J.D. is, maggot?'

'Yes, sir.'

'I'm going to make it my business to run you off. You're history. You don't deserve to be an officer in this man's Navy.'

Hatcher didn't say anything.

'You want to be an officer, maggot?'

'Yes, sir.'

'Well, that's a joke. You don't even have a mother and a father, isn't that a fact?'

Hatcher didn't answer. He could feel the blood rising to his face.

'I asked you a question, maggot.'

Still no answer.

Snyder moved so close his breath was hot against Hatcher's face.

'You know what they call someone who doesn't have a mother and a father, maggot?'

Hatcher stared straight ahead. He fought to keep himself from trembling with rage.

'Say the word,' Snyder demanded.

'Maybe he doesn't know the word, Snyder,' Cody's voice said. Hatcher was staring straight ahead; and Snyder moved out of the way and suddenly Cody was staring at him.

'Maybe he never got that far in school,' Cody said.

'Is that right, maggot?' Snyder snapped.

'Well, maggot, is that right?' Cody repeated.

'Yes, sir,' Hatcher said.

Snyder leaned over to Cody and said softly, 'He's mine, Cody. He'll be Boston dog meat by Christmas.' He chuckled and moved on.

'You almost lost it there, maggot,' Cody said sharply. 'I was watching you. Now, you listen up. Everybody figured you'd be history by now, but you fooled us all. So don't lose it now. Snyder's trying to provoke you, and if he does, you're gone. You took it this long, just keep taking it. Couple more months and you're a second-year man and nobody can mess with you anymore.'

'What's he got against me, sir?'

'He's an elitist. He doesn't think you fit the profile.'

'Do you, sir?'

'It doesn't make any damn difference what anybody thinks, it's what you think. And we never had this talk,' Cody snapped and walked away.

'You and Murph Cody were pretty close for a time, weren't you?'

Hatcher was drawn back to the present by Sloan's question. He stared at him for several seconds and then said, 'Yes . . . we were at Annapolis together. I didn't see much of him after we graduated. He went in the air service and I went into intelligence. Why? Why the interest in Cody?'

'You know how it is. The general never has gotten over his death. I guess he just wants to put it all in perspective.'

Hatcher's eyes narrowed. Sloan was lying to him and he knew it. But it wasn't Sloan's tone of voice or expression that gave him away.

'Don't bullshit me, Harry. You didn't track me down and then come all the way here to chat about Murph Cody. You think I got stupid since I saw you last?'

Sloan held up his hands in a gesture of apology. The smile got broader when he was in trouble. 'Hey. Please. Stick with me for a couple of minutes more, okay?'

Hatcher relaxed. He was curious and had nothing to lose by going along with the game, whatever the game was.

'Well, that's a long time ago,' Hatcher went on. 'Annapolis was – 1963 to '67. I was in his wedding. That was . . .'

''Sixty-nine,' Sloan said. He pointed to the records. 'It's in the file.'

'Then I didn't see him again after I joined the brigade.'

'Why?'

Hatcher paused for a moment. 'We had a falling-out,' he said. 'Anyway, Cody was tough at first. Big on hazing. It was – like paying dues to him. Cody was very big on paying dues. Maybe it had something to do with being Buffalo Bill's son.'

'How so?' Sloan pressed on.

'Well, you know, Polo had to measure up. As I remember, the general wouldn't put up with any slack in the line.'

76

'He played polo?'

'Did I call him Polo?' Hatcher replied, surprised. 'Jesus. I didn't even think about it, just came out. Polo's a nickname, short for Polaroid. Cody had a photographic memory, could remember anything – faces, names, math formulas, you name it. Everybody from the old gang at the academy called him that.'

He paused again as new images came back. 'Look, he was a good guy, very loyal, liked to raise a little hell –'

Hatcher looked back down at the family Christmas photograph. Somehow the man in the Christmas picture seemed smaller and sadder than the Cody he remembered. And then Hatcher remembered the Christmas holidays that first year.

'– and loved the ladies.'

Christmas, 1963. There was a light snow, just enough to call it a White Christmas and make being away from the Cirillos for the first time a painful experience. Hatcher was huddled against the wind, walking across the yard with his head down. Broke and with no place to go, he was spending the Christmas holidays at the academy along with perhaps a dozen other midshipmen. As he was crossing the chilly yard he heard yelling and what sounded like furniture being overturned.

My God, Hatcher thought, two of the guys are going at it. He ran into the sophomore dorm and up to the second floor. The furor was coming from Cody's room.

The room was a shambles. Books, papers and clothes were strewn all over the floor. Cody was in a rage, stumbling around the room, yelling obscenities, tears in his eyes. He picked up his desk chair and, turning to the window, swung it back with both hands. Hatcher leaped into the room and grabbed the chair. Cody turned on him, his face red with drunken fury. 'Wha' the hell're you doin', maggot!'

'Shit, sir, you're going to be in a lot of trouble. The OD's bound to hear you.'

'Up the OD's dick, maggot.'

Hatcher looked out the window. The OD was charging across the yard through the snow toward the dormitory.

'Oh shit!' Hatcher said.

He put the chair back and rushed around the room, straightening it up, stacking up papers and arranging them on the corner of the desk. He threw the clothes in the closet and closed the door.

'What d'you think you're doin', maggot?' Cody demanded.

'The OD's on his way over here,' Hatcher said. 'If he catches you drunk in your room, you're gone, sir.'

'S'be it,' Cody replied drunkenly. 'Teach 'em all.'

'All who, sir?'

'Min' your own business.'

'Yes, sir.'

Hatcher heard the front door of the dorm open and close.

'He's on his way up here,' Hatcher said in a panic.

'Who're we talkin 'bout?'

'The fucking OD, sir.'

'Up the OD's –' Hatcher grabbed Cody and steered him toward the bathroom. 'What the hell're –'

Hatcher shoved him in the bathroom and turned on the shower. He went back in the room and pulled the door shut. Then he went to Cody's closet and got out a pair of shoes and a shoeshine kit. He could hear the officer of the day approaching the room. He started frantically shining the shoes as the OD pounded on the door.

'Mr. Cody?'

Hatcher opened the door.

'What're you doing in here, maggot?' the OD demanded, staring at Hatcher.

Hatcher held up a shoe and a rag.

'Doing Mr Cody's shoes, sir.'

'Where's Cody?' the OD demanded, brushing past Hatcher and entering the room. From behind him, Hatcher looked down at the foot of the bed. A capped bottle of vodka was sitting on the floor. Hatcher moved as cautiously as he could to the foot of the bed and dropped the shoe, waiting until it hit the floor and at the same moment kicking the bottle under the bed.

The OD whirled and Hatcher popped to attention. 'Sorry, sir,' he stammered. 'I dropped the shoe.'

At that moment the door opened and Cody's dripping head peered around its edge. He had a towel wrapped around his shoulders.

'What's going on?' he asked sternly.

'Sounded like a riot in here, Cody,' the OD answered.

'The radio,' Cody said. 'I turned it off. Get back on those shoes, maggot.' He slammed the bathroom door shut.

'Yes, sir!'

The OD stalked out of the room. 'Just keep it down,' he said as he left.

Cody came out of the bathroom. The towel was still wrapped

around his shoulders and his hair was dripping wet. Water had splashed on his tunic. He walked into the room and looked around, got down on his hands and knees and reached under the bed to get the bottle of vodka. He sat on the floor, leaning on the bed, uncapped the bottle and started to laugh.

'That was very quick thinkin', maggot, very resourceful, 'ndeed. Have a drink.'

'I don't think –'

'S'down and have a damn drink, maggot,' Cody said with a flourish and held the bottle toward him. Hatcher sat beside him on the floor, took a swig, and shuddered.

'You're a real case, maggot,' Cody said, almost sneering. 'I been watching you. You got a funny kinda attitude. What d'you call that, street ethics?'

'I suppose so.'

'You suppose so, *what?*'

'Sir.'

'Right.' He took another swig and handed the bottle back to Hatcher. 'M'old man's a soldier's soldier, maggot. E'body loves Buff'lo Bill Cody.'

'Yes, sir.'

'Well, shit,' Cody said with a vague wave of his arm. He stared down at the vodka bottle. 'Think I'll ever make adm'ral, maggot?'

Hatcher took another swallow of vodka and handed it back to Cody. 'Is that what you want to be, sir?'

'Isn't that what this's all about? This is the U.S. Naval Aca'emy, maggot. We're all suppos' t'be admirals before we retire, didn't y'know that. Isn't that why you're here? You jus' tryin' to get recest – respect – respectable?' He chuckled at the tongue twister and passed back the bottle.

Hatcher took another swig of the vodka. The room was beginning to tilt a little.

'I like the ocean,' he said finally, handing the bottle back to Cody.

'I like the ocean,' Cody repeated with a snicker. 'Jesus, he came to Annapolis because he likes the friggin' ocean. Well, maggot, which ocean d'you like best?'

Hatcher chuckled. 'I like 'em all, long's they're wet.'

Cody laughed. 'Tha's very funny. But 's indiscriminent. You're indiscriminent, maggot. Got t'be discriminating, 's part of – 's what we're doing here, becoming elit – elit-isss.'

'Elit-isss, yessir.'

Their laughter progressed toward a laughing jag.

'Elit-isss-t,' Cody said through his laughter.

'Elit-isss-t,' Hatcher replied.

'Why'd you do this for me, maggot. I been giving you an awful lot of shit. Was it because I gave you that advice 'bout Snyder?'

'Maybe.'

'F'r the record, I wasn't doing you any favors, Hatcher, I'm an opportunis', prob'ly the wors' snob of the bunch. Next year I'm capt'n of the boxing team and right now Snyder's our only middle-weight and Snyder's got a glass jaw. A good, hard shot and 's ass is planted. I want a winning team, maggot, and I need a good middleweight for that, so I gotta keep you around until spring tryouts, see what kinda stuff you got.'

'Well,' Hatcher said with a shrug, ''s good a reason as any.' And then after a pause he added, 'But it'd take more than you and Snyder to get rid of me.'

Cody looked at him with surprise, and then, leaning back against the bed with the bottle perched on his knee, he nodded. 'Y'know somp'n, I think you're right,' he said and passed the bottle back. 'What the hell're you doin' here, maggot? Why aren't you back in Boston?'

'I couldn't afford it. Besides, the only people I really want to see are out West skiing.'

'No kidd'n. Me too, maggot, got n'place to go. M' old man's in the Far East somewhere and Mrs Cody's on a Caribbean cruise. Wha' the hell's the diff'rence, anyway. Just 'nother day, right?'

He took a deep swig and handed the bottle to Hatcher.

'Mostly, though, it's because m' lady fair – sweet, adorable Cassie – decided to marry a lawyer. Can you believe that, she's marrying one of those fuckin' blood suckers. She decided she didn' wanna be a sailor's wife.'

'Well, you can't really blame her for that.'

'Maybe you're right,' he said. 'Also she didn' wanna wait three more years to legalize her favorite sport.' Cody giggled and held the vodka bottle up in a toast. 'To past sport with Cassie.'

He took a swig and handed it back to Hatcher.

'I know how it is,' said Hatcher. 'My girl dropped me for a *wrestler*. Talk about humiliating. No neck and solid muscle from the balls of his feet to the top of his head.' He held up the bottle. 'Here's to stupidity.'

'What're you gonna do New Year's Eve, maggot?'

'Nothing.'

'Ever seen Times Square on New Year's Eve?'

'Mr. Cody, I don't have the price of a bus ticket to the showers.'

'Well, money is not one of my problems. It's on me, jus' don't ever tell anybody that Cody and the maggot Hatcher spent the weekend together.' He winked and laughed and took a swig. 'We'll stay in a fancy hotel, order up room service, maybe even fin' a coupla lonely ladies. And at midnight, we'll go down 'mong the heathen hordes.' Cody held up the bottle. 'To the heathen hordes.'

And so Midshipman Murph Cody and maggot Christian Hatcher went off to New York for New Year's.

From the moment they got on the bus it was Murph and Hatch, and finding lonely ladies was not a problem – selection was the problem. The bars were crowded, there were parties in the rooms that overflowed into the halls and parties in the streets. There was an epidemic of brotherly love. And occasionally when opportunity presented itself in the form of two lonely ladies, Hatcher and Cody would vote, holding the fingers of one hand behind their backs and then flashing them. If the total number of fingers for each was more than seven, they would make a move. They scored before dark.

The girls were roommates. Helen, who was with Murph, was an assistant photo editor for a news magazine. Hatcher's date, Linda, was an usher at one of the Broadway theaters. Both were eights. And both slept in the same room, so there was the added sense of excitement that came with trying not to be too demonstrative with another couple a few feet away.

Two in the morning and the sharp, intrusive ring of the telephone. Helen took the call. 'Hi Mom, Happy New – What? . . . Oh, no! When? . . . Oh God, Momma, I'll be there as soon as I can. Yes, yes . . .' She cradled the phone and sat on the edge of the bed, shaking and crying, and Cody sat up and put a blanket around her shoulders.

'What happened?' he asked.

'My brother . . . was in an automobile . . . automobile . . . wreck. I've got to go straight to the hospital. They don't think . . . don't think . . .'

'C'mon, get dressed. I'll take you.'

'It's way out in Queens.'

'Hey, get dressed. I don't care where it is, you can't go alone.'

Cody was a true gentleman. His macho bravado had vanished when they met the girls, replaced by a tenderness that astounded Hatcher. Now Cody organized the trek to the hospital quickly,

81

and when they were gone Hatcher and Linda lay side by side in the bed, the news of the wreck somehow making sex – even touching – seem self-indulgent and frivolous. They lay there for a long time, Hatcher dozing off, then waking, then dozing off again. The sky was turning gray when the doorbell rang.

Linda sat bolt upright in bed.

'My God, who could that be?' she whispered. Hatcher scrambled to the door and peered through the peephole.

'It's Murph,' he said and opened the door.

Cody stood there with his hat under his arm.

'Just thought you'd like to know that Fred – that's Helen's brother – is gonna make it.'

'Hey, that's great,' Hatcher said.

'I didn't know the phone number, that's why I didn't call.'

'Hey, right, we're glad to get the news.'

'Uh . . .'

'Yeah?'

'I don't feel like going back to the hotel alone,' he said quietly.

Linda, huddled in a bathrobe, appeared in the doorway beside Hatcher.

'C'mon,' she said, drawing Cody into the apartment. Hatcher and Linda got back in bed and watched Cody strip to his shorts, and as he sat on the edge of the bed taking off his socks, Linda looked at Hatcher and turned back to Cody and said, 'Hey, sailor, come on over here, this bed's warm already.'

Cody smiled and looked at Hatcher, who motioned him over; he crossed the room and slid in beside Linda. And Hatcher and Murphy each put an arm around her and they all fell back to sleep.

Hatcher, in remembering that night, thought, My God, was life ever really that simple and innocent? Had friendship and love ever been closer together than on that night?

Then the next morning they were back on the bus, and suddenly Hatcher was 'maggot' again and it was as if the trip had never happened.

Spring 1964. There was still a chill in the air but fifty miles away in Washington the Japanese apple trees were in bloom and tourists were crowding the malls and parks shooting pictures, and at the academy Hatcher was double-timing across the yard thinking, Two more months, only two more months, and this shit will be over.

The now familiar voice cried, 'Maggot!'

82

Hatcher stopped immediately, chin in, eyes boring straight ahead. Cody stood behind him.

'Tryouts at the gym, three tomorrow. Be there.'

'Yes, *sir!*'

Hatcher got to the gym early and worked the fast bag for fifteen minutes, loosening up, enjoying the familiar arena smell of alcohol and Ben Gay. Then Snyder showed up, cocky as always.

Cody, still a few weeks from being captain of the team, was acting referee. When they called for the middleweights, Cody made sure Hatcher and Snyder were paired off against each other.

'Three rounds,' he said. 'Winner makes the team, loser goes to the bone pile. Break clean when I tell you to, no rabbit punching. Shake and come out fighting.'

He checked Snyder's gloves, patted him on the shoulder, then crossed to Hatcher's corner and, leaning over, checking the laces, said very softly, 'I told you he's got a glass jaw. He also has a left uppercut like a torpedo. He'll try to infight and tag you with the left. Box him two rounds to slow him up, move in and keep on top of the left so he can't throw it. One good shot anywhere from the point to the ear and you'll plant him.'

It was sound advice. Hatcher played to Snyder's left, constantly jabbing and moving, crowding the left so Snyder couldn't break it loose. Twice he took good solid shots and shook them off, countering quickly with combinations of his own. He was faster than Snyder and, he quickly knew, smarter. Snyder was a flat-footed fighter, a plodder, stalking his opponent while looking for a shot. Hatcher didn't give it to him. Then Snyder made a move. He jogged in, threw the right and then brought the left up hard. Hatcher took it on his shoulder and there, right in front of his eyes and wide open, was Snyder's flat, ugly jaw. Hatcher fired a hard, straight right cross over Snyder's shoulder, right into the jaw just under the ear. He felt the power of the punch telescope up his arm to his shoulder, saw Snyder's eyes roam wildly out of control, saw his legs turn to jelly. Snyder turned halfway around and fell straight to the deck.

Cody walked across the ring and stared down at Snyder's limp form for a moment, then nodded to Hatcher. 'Welcome to the team,' he said with a grin.

Graduation day, 1964. Outside Hatcher's room, there seemed to be a constant scurrying of feet as the midshipmen rushed to and fro across the yard getting ready for the dress parade. Hatcher was setting his cap when Cody appeared in the doorway, that stern hawk face glowing.

'All right, you're still maggots until after the parade. Every-body out but Hatcher.'

Hatcher's roommates vaulted out of the room. Hatcher stood at sharp attention in front of Cody, but for the first time he stared straight at the upperclassman, a practice forbidden the first-year frogs.

'Maggot, do you know what a floogie bird is?' demanded Cody.

'No, sir.'

'A floogie bird is a curious bird that flies in ever-decreasing concentric circles until it disappears up its own asshole, from which vantage point it slings shit at its adversaries. That's what a floogie bird is, maggot. Well, mister, you had a tough time, but by God nothing could bend you. You are now a floogie bird, my friend, and you can start slinging shit at your adversaries.'

'Yes *sir*!'

Cody took a bottle of vodka from under his tunic. A big grin spread across the stern hawk face. He handed the bottle to Hatcher. 'You first, Mr. Hatcher. Welcome aboard,' he said. And for the next two years he and Hatcher would be inseparable teammates and friends.

'. . . anyway, Cody was a year ahead of me,' Hatcher said to Sloan. 'He went straight into the Navy Air Corps when he graduated. I went into intelligence. We didn't see each other after that, but we kept in touch. Then in 1969 he asked me to be an usher in his wedding.'

'Very fancy, I hear.'

'Very high society D.C. affair, typical Washington bash. Congressmen, senators, admirals, generals, TV big shots, they were all there.'

'What was his wife like?' Sloan asked.

'The model of icy perfection, a gorgeous woman, perfectly groomed. Had all the assets – proper schooling, proper back-ground, proper, proper, proper.'

'And you disliked her.'

'No, I think she disliked us. His old school pals were too rowdy. Her father was an admiral, you know the type.' Hatcher thought back to the day, a collage of uniforms and chatty people. 'I think Polo was unhappy about the marriage.'

'What makes you think so?'

'I don't know. Seems like he was awfully – cynical that day. More like the old Cody from hazing days at the academy. I don't know why he should have been. At that point Cody had done everything right. Graduated from the academy, breezed through flight training, married an admiral's daughter.'

'Like he was filling in the blanks of an outline,' Sloan said.

'Exactly. I don't know how the hell he got in the Brown River Navy.'

'He volunteered.'

'No kidding? Gung ho to the last.'

'His father-in-law tried to block it, but from what I understand, Cody was insistent,' Sloan added.

'That was really garbage work,' Hatcher said.

'Whatever,' Sloan said with a shrug. 'And you never saw him again after the wedding?'

'Once. At San Diego Air Base. I was there doing a security check and he was stationed on the base.'

'Must have been just before you joined the brigade.'

'Yeah. I had already announced I was retiring my commission. . . . We had kind of a run-in.'

'About what?'

'Does it matter?'

'I suppose not.'

'I never saw him again after that. And I sure as hell can't see him now.'

'Don't be too sure,' Sloan said and his grin became mischievous.

'What do you mean?' Hatcher's harsh whisper asked.

'Supposing I told you that I got information that Murph Cody is alive.'

'Where? Is he a prisoner?'

'He's free as a bad cold. Bangkok.'

A little shock went through Hatcher when he heard the word. Bangkok. A place he had packed and put away forever. 'What kind of information?'

'I trust it.'

'That doesn't answer the question. How reliable is this source?'

'A small-time Thai politician. He wants a free trip to the States and a work visa. According to our information, Cody's marked, so he's on the run.'

'Marked by who?'

'The White Palms,' Sloan said.

'That's a Macao outfit. What would they be doing in Bangkok?' asked Hatcher.

'It's the source. And you've been away a long time. The damn triads are everywhere now.'

'What's this guy's game – opium?'

'We're not sure. We suspect he was a courier for the White Palms. But we haven't really dug into it for obvious reasons.'

'What *obvious* reasons?' Hatcher whispered, although he knew the answer already.

If Murphy Cody was alive in Bangkok and had remained silent for all these years, there had to be a reason. And if military intelligence didn't know the reason, it didn't look good for Cody.

'Don't play dumb,' Sloan said. 'What the hell's he doing in Thailand? I mean if he's alive, why hasn't he surfaced?'

Hatcher could think of a lot of reasons, none of them good.

'Maybe he's got amnesia,' he finally offered.

'Yeah, maybe I'm Doris Day, too,' Sloan answered.

'It's a possibility. He could have amnesia.'

There was also the possibility that Cody had been a collaborator, or a defector, or a deserter, or that he was involved in drugs, murder, white slavery or any of a dozen other crimes Hatcher could think of.

Sloan obviously had the same things in mind. He said, 'I can't think of a good way for this to turn out, if it's true. There's desertion, to start with. If he wasn't killed, he still belongs to the U.S. Navy, heart and soul.'

'Question is, why did he go underground in the first place?' Hatcher said. 'What I mean is, if he wasn't killed and he wasn't in Hanoi, where the hell was he?'

'Well, wherever it was, the Navy was convinced he was KIA.'

'Maybe that was his out.'

'Or his trap.'

Hatcher nodded slowly. 'Or his trap. So what's this got to do with me?'

'Nobody knows Thailand like you do, Hatch. You know the good guys *and* the bad guys, and you've worked both sides of the stream. I can't let military intelligence handle this, everybody in the Pentagon'll know about it in an hour. It has to be unofficial. If Cody's alive and mixed up in something – improper, there's the old man's reputation to consider.'

'Improper,' Hatcher growled with a chuckle. 'Very delicate, Harry.'

'You get the point,' Sloan continued. 'We need somebody who knows the territory and can keep his mouth shut. And nobody I know is better at keeping quiet than you, old buddy. Besides, you were a damn good investigator in your day, if I do say so myself.'

'My day's not over, and don't call me your old buddy. And who the hell's we?'

'Half a dozen of Buffalo Bill's old staff. Look, this Thai, his name is Wol Pot, brought the trade-out to the embassy in Bangkok. Luckily, the IO there is one of Cody's old exec officers, Lew Porter.'

'Windy Porter?'

'Yeah, you remember him?'

'Vaguely.'

'He interviewed Pot. Right away he sizes up the situation, puts Pot on hold and calls me. I round up a couple of the old-timers from S-town, we kick it around. Finally we had to take it to the Old Man.'

'Why?' Hatcher rasped.

Sloan stared hard into his eyes. 'Because Buffalo Bill's dying of cancer, Hatch. He won't last the year.'

That stopped Hatcher cold. He had a hard time picturing General Buffalo Bill Cody with some insidious worm eating up his insides.

'We all love the Old Man, okay?' Sloan said, and his voice turned husky. He stopped for a moment and swallowed hard before he went on. 'He asked us the favor. If his kid's alive, he'd like to see him once before he dies.'

'What if he's in trouble?'

'That's why I need you, Hatch,' Sloan said, his voice still shaky. 'If he's in deep shit, Porter can't handle it. He's a burned-out old trooper. Point is, the general will meet Cody somewhere – anywhere – Hawaii, Tokyo, Sydney. Wherever Murphy wants to meet him. Nobody needs to know it ever happened.'

'A trip like that would probably kill the Old Man,' Hatcher said.

'His quality time's running out anyway,' Sloan said with resignation. 'The thing is, it has to be handled with satin and lace by somebody who knows the score, who can roll with it, no matter how it might go, convince the kid we're not out to dump on him, we just want to give the Old Man one last gift.'

'He's hardly a kid,' Hatcher said. 'He'd be – forty-two now,' he said, adding a year to his own age.

'Go to Thailand and find him, if he's there,' said Sloan matter-of-factly. 'Or put the old man's mind to rest.'

'Prove he's dead,' Hatcher rasped.

'Yeah. One way or another.'

Hatcher laughed hard at that.

'Navy's been chasing down leads on Cody for fourteen years,' he said, 'and you want me to go to Bangkok, which has fifty million people, and turn him up, just like that.'

'Nobody's been looking for Cody. As far as the Navy's concerned he's dead meat. But you, hell, laddie, you're the best I ever had.'

'Can the shit, Harry.'

'You got the edge, Hatch,' said Sloan. 'We'll give you Wol Pot. We'll give you Windy. You know Cody. You know the territory. And you can keep your mouth shut no matter what happens. You proved that in Madrango. All I want you to do is go over there, find Cody and set up the meet. Or tell me he's dead. Hell, you'll even have Flitcraft at your disposal.'

'Flitcraft's still on the roster, huh?'

'He's my number one.'

Hatcher poured himself another glass of wine and fiddled with the file for a few moments.

'You know I can't go back there,' he said finally.

'C'mon, that was, what? Eight, ten years ago?'

'Wouldn't matter if it was fifty.'

'You get in a bind, I'll give you all the backup you need. I've still got a few heavy hitters over there.'

'What's the deal with this Thai, what's his name again?'

'Wol Pot. Look, I don't care what you do to the little slope. If he gives you any shit, break his legs, hang him on the rack, pull out his fingernails. I don't care.'

'Same old Harry.'

'It's his story, make him prove it.'

'That's not what I mean. Does he get his visa?'

'If he delivers, I suppose I can arrange something.'

'It's got to be straighter than that. If he turns him up, I've got to know what kind of deal I can give him.'

'If he turns him up, we'll provide protection and get him out of Thailand.'

'You're sure?'

'Why do you care?'

'If I make a promise I want it kept.'

'Done. You'll do the job, then?'

Hatcher stared at him for several seconds. He put the .357 on a table.

'The price will be $236,600.'

'What!'

'That's two hundred dollars a day for every day I was in that rat hole.'

'Get real, man.'

'That's as real as it gets, Harry.'

'Where am I going to get that kind of money?'

'Hey, this is Hatch, remember? You got private-sector accounts all over the world. Panama, Switzerland, the Bahamas. So maybe you'll have to scrimp somewhere else. Tough shit.'

'You're a rich man, Hatch.'

'Punitive damages. The price is $236,600, non-negotiable. Take it or leave it.'

Sloan's grin broadened as big as it could get. His eyes began to twinkle again. 'It's more than that, isn't it? I can see it in your eyes, pal. You miss the edge. You miss the old adrenaline pumping. Life's too easy. Hell, when you're hooked, you're hooked forever.'

Part of what Sloan said was true. But it wasn't that razzle-dazzle feeling one gets running the edge that was sucking Hatcher back to the old life, back to places he'd sworn never to go back to, to people he never thought he'd see again, to work again for Sloan, a man he once thought he was going to kill. It was Cody, a man who had once been more of a friend than Sloan had ever been because Cody had always been honest with him.

'I'll take the jaunt because of Murph Cody and the old man, period. It has nothing to do with you and me. If Cody's there, I'll find him. If he's not, I'll let you know. And if you ever come back here again, I'll feed you to the fish.'

Sloan leaned over closer to him, the old teeth sparkling, the gray eyes twinkling.

'You know, I think you're serious,' he said.

Hatcher smiled back without mirth.

'Keep thinking it,' he said. 'Your life may depend on it.'

PREPARATIONS

It was dusk when Ginia, responding to Hatcher's call, returned to the boat carrying a wicker picnic basket. She opened it and took out the contents while Hatcher took the boat out through the sound and into the open sea, sticking close to the shore.

'Fettuccine with fresh vegetables from Birdie's, homemade clam chowder, cold shrimp and hush puppies from the Crab Trap,' she said. 'How soon do you want to eat?'

'Now. I'm starving.'

'What happened to your army buddy?'

He leaned over and kissed her on the throat. 'Gone,' Hatcher growled and the subject was dropped. She knew better than to ask 'Gone where?' If he wanted her to know he would tell her. Obviously he didn't. She was delighted that the stranger had left and Hatcher was hers for the evening.

She went below, selected a bottle of vintage red wine from the liquor cabinet and opened it to let it breathe. She heated the food in the oven and set the table. Then she turned on the radio, keeping the volume low.

'Hey,' she yelled up to him, 'you want to put this thing on automatic pilot and come eat?'

'Done,' came the hoarse answer. She heard the engines die out and the anchor splash in the water, and a moment later he appeared in the salon.

'I decided to anchor for a while. We're right off Sapelo Island,' he said, dipping his fingers into the fettuccine and tasting it.

'Mind your manners,' she snapped.

'Delicious,' he said and poured each of them a glass of the red. They clinked their glasses in a silent toast. He leaned over and kissed her very lightly, tasting the dry, musky wine on her lips.

'Thank you,' she whispered. Then, making small talk, she asked, 'How long have you known Jimmy Cirillo?'

'A long time.'

'Where did you meet him?'

'In an alley in Boston.'

'An alley?'

'Yeah. I was breaking into a store and he was a cop.'

'Are you kidding me?'

'Nope.' Hatcher leaned back and realized he was about to give away some family secrets. He felt comfortable doing it.

'My old man was an architect, and not a very good one. Blew his brains out in the shower of the Boston Men's Club one afternoon. I was ten at the time. Three years later my mother ran off with, uh, hell, I don't even know, never saw the man. Anyway, I hit the bricks. By the time I was fifteen I was one of the best cat burglars in Boston.'

'Why, Hatch, I had no idea,' she said in amazement.

'That's just the tip of the iceberg,' Hatcher said with a smile.

'Well, what did Jimmy do to you when he caught you?' Ginia probed.

'He took off his badge and his gun belt, put them carefully on the sidewalk, and beat my ass to a bloody pulp.'

Ginia broke up – she put her hands over her mouth and giggled into them.

'And that's not all. He got me a job; actually he got me three jobs, and I walked out on all three. So one night he grabs me, shoves me in this alley, off comes the badge and gun belt and he gives it to me again. Then he says, "I'm gonna keep whippin' your ass until you hold a job and stop boosting my beat." And that was the beginning of a beautiful friendship.'

'He made you what you are today,' she said with mock pride.

'Yeah,' Hatcher said and then added rather solemnly, 'but the guy on the dock had a hand in it too.'

'What did he catch you doing?'

'Going for admiral.'

'Huh?'

'That's another story.'

They ate the rest of the dinner in silence. Hatcher was not one to talk and eat, but she sensed something impending. She knew he was going before he said it.

'I have to leave for a while.'

'Uh-huh, and just what does that mean, Hatcher, "a while"? A week, a month, ten years?' She asked it lightheartedly.

He smiled and reached over and laid the palm of his hand softly on her cheek. 'Longer than a week, hopefully less than a month,' he answered.

'Can I do anything for you?'

'Call John Rogers at the bank and tell him I had to leave in a hurry. I've prepared a power of attorney for you so you can handle my market and bank accounts. If I should need money for any reason, shift funds at the bank into my drawing account.'

'You trust me that much?' she asked, surprised.

He smiled at her.'Implicitly,' he answered.

'When are you leaving?'

'In the morning.'

She smiled at him, but she was already beginning to feel the longing that went with his absences. 'Then let's not waste time,' she said. 'You can sleep on the plane.'

He took her hand as she stood up and drew her close to him. He slowly unbuttoned her white button-down shirt, let it fall open, slipped his hands around her hips and drew her closer,

91

kissing her hard stomach. Then loosening her belt and zipping down the fly, he slid her jeans off. He wrapped his arms tighter around her, his hands slipping under her buttocks, lifting her up slightly so that his thumbs slid under the edge of her panties, and began caressing her lightly with both thumbs, felt her tighten, felt her wetness as he gently probed while he moved his head lower, felt the hair under her panties, began to nibble very lightly while his hot breath caressed her. He spread his fingers up and drew down her panties and buried his face in her hair, smelling her sex, tasting her, felt her hands pressing his head harder into her. She stood on her toes, her head fell back and she sat on the edge of the table and put one leg over his shoulder. Her breath came faster, her muscles tightened, she began to move in tight little circles.

She had this wonderfully erotic habit that drove Hatcher crazy. As she neared her climax she began to count, low, almost under her breath, gasping between the numbers: 'One . . . two . . . three . . . f-four . . . uh, oh-oh, m'God . . . five, six, seven . . . uh-huh . . . uh-huh . . . eight-nine-t-ten . . . my God, *oh*!'

Her back arched and she jammed herself against his mouth and held herself taut for ten or twelve seconds and then, gasping, she relaxed, collapsed forward and, wrapping both hands around his head, drew him up to her, searching for his mouth and, finding it, began kissing him ravenously.

He picked her up and carried her back to the king-size bed in the sleeping cabin, laid her gently on the bed and stripped while he kissed her. Then he slid into bed beside her, drawing her tightly to him, and she felt him hard against her. She slipped one leg over his hip and pulled him to her, moving up until he entered her smoothly and without effort.

'Oh God,' he whispered as she surrounded him, tightening her muscles, sucking him in deeper and deeper and deeper.

Still out of breath, she whispered, 'A month, huh?' and he whispered back, equally out of breath, 'Maybe . . . just . . . a couple of weeks . . .'

She lay on her side, dozing. Hatcher moved easily off the bed, pulled a down quilt over her and began to pack. There had been a time when Hatcher's Gurkha bag was always packed and ready to go – two suits, a casual jacket and slacks, half a dozen shirts, a couple of ties, an extra pair of shoes and his underwear and toilet articles. Basics. No frills. And he quickly fell back into the routine of preparing for the trip.

The mental checklist was still in his head: Check out his

credentials, review his finances, select the right equipment, and pack everything into two pieces of luggage, his suit bag and an aluminum case, which he always hand-carried.

While Ginia slept he slid back a panel in the bulkhead over the head of the bed, opened a safe built into the wall and took out a small strongbox. He carried it back to the main cabin and checked the contents. He took out a $50,000 letter of credit from his bank, $20,000 in traveler's checks and $10,000 in cash. He never used credit cards, too easy to trace. He also took out two passports, one his valid U.S. passport, the other a forged French passport. Both identified him as a free-lance television journalist and cameraman. Then he returned the box to its hiding place.

On the way back to the main salon, he got a medium-size aluminum Halliburton case from the closet and carried it forward. Then he got down on his hands and knees and crawled through a hatch under the stairs leading to the cockpit and into a tight compartment below the afterdeck. A waterproof chest was built into the hull. When Hatcher opened it, a light turned on automatically. Inside was a small arsenal: two .357 pistols, an H&K 9 mm. pistol, an M-16, a 9 mm. Uzi submachine gun. There were several loaded magazines for each weapon. There were also four ten-foot reels of extension cord, which was actually C-4 plastique. One weapon was wrapped in a green Hefty bag. Hatcher took the bag, two reels of C-4, closed and locked the compartment, and went back to the main cabin.

He spread a blanket on the dining room table, took the weapon out of the Hefty bag and laid it on the blanket. It was an Aug, an Austrian automatic assault rifle that broke down into three simple components: the barrel, which was sixteen inches long; the tubular sight, which was capable of instant target acquisition; and the stock and trigger mechanism, which were high-impact plastic and rustproof. The weapon was totally waterproof. All other weapons, with which Hatcher was familiar – the M-16, Uzi and Mac 10 – were vulnerable to moisture in the barrel and would explode if water got in them. But not the Aug. It literally could be fired while coming out of the water.

His memory began to stir again, a common ailment since Los Boxes. He called it an ailment because he had learned early from Sloan that memory had value for one thing only – reference. But

93

now, staring down at the Aug, he remembered the first time he ever used the gun.

Sloan had sent a slick upriver to the Boston drop, a hook in the Chu River near a small village. The chopper picked up Hatcher and flew him back to a forward base in the Mekong Delta. Sloan was waiting for him in a hooch he had commandeered for the night.

'I've got a problem,' Sloan said over a glass of gin. 'We have a Southern papa-san working for us, name of Di Tran. He's a good slope. Charlie killed his wife, mother, two small kids. So he's got plenty to get even for. He's been working behind the lines for us, six, seven months. Very reliable information.'

He paused for a moment, flattening his hands on the desk. 'He knew the odds, it wasn't like he didn't know the odds,' Sloan said, his fingers splayed out. He stared at them for several seconds before he went on. 'He contacted the Swing Man about a week ago and asked for a drop. We met him and he passed us this tape.'

He put the tape in the cassette deck and pushed the play button. The man's voice was high and tinny, laced with fear: 'I have just this yesterday receive information that an American is sell information to the ARV. He has given up the names of three Vietnamese agents working in the North for Shadow Brigade. One of the names is mine. I am feared it will take them very shortly to break through my real name. I must warn my two friends of their danger before I run. Please arrange meeting for us at the Boston drop in two days. Wednesday. Sunset. If two hours passed, you may think we have been taken. This American was paid ten thousand dollars for each name. He is promise to sell them more. His name is Norgling. *Joi gin*, my friends.'

Hatcher looked up sharply when he heard the name Norgling. 'Do you know who this Norgling is?'

Sloan nodded. 'He's talking about Chick Norgling!' Sloan said. 'He's in the brigade, like you. Working with crossovers.'

'So he'd have access to that information?'

'Also codes, maps, general info bulletins – and the basic information on the brigade itself,' said Sloan. 'Now you know why we maintain individual integrity in this outfit. Norgling's just like the rest of you, he only knows his direct contacts.'

'Which means you,' Hatcher said.

Sloan nodded slowly.

'Get him off the street before he sells them anything else,' Hatcher said.

94

'I can't bust him on the basis of that,' said Sloan, nodding toward the cassette deck. 'It's his word against the voice on the tape. Without corroboration the provost marshal'll laugh at me.'

'How about this Di Tran?'

'We sent a slick in for him but he didn't show at the drop. We have to assume he's dead.'

'Then this Norgling's gonna blow your whole show.'

Sloan stared back at his hands for a few more seconds, then nodded to himself and looked up at Hatcher.

'We'll set him up. I'll arrange for him to meet you someplace. Tell him it's an operation requiring two men. When he shows up, drop him. Upriver maybe.'

'No. Too many ears on the river. We'll do it in Saigon. The Princess Hotel. I'll dust him, you dump him.'

'Fair enough.'

Seven P.M. Fourth floor of the Princess. If Norgling was paranoid, if he suspected anything, he'd show up early to throw Hatcher off-balance. Hatcher knew the game well.

Norgling arrived at a quarter to seven to find Hatcher's door open just a crack. He loosened his coat, reached under his arm and felt his pistol grip, then stepped cautiously inside.

The bedroom was empty. He heard music coming from the bathroom.

'Hello?' he called out.

'In here,' he heard Hatcher's voice answer. 'Close the door, will you?'

Norgling closed the door and approached the bathroom slowly. Hatcher was in the tub, his head resting against the back of it, taking a bubble bath. There was a bottle of red wine on the floor beside the tub and a half-empty glass. There was another glass on the sink.

Hatcher looked up and smiled. 'Norgling?'

'Right.'

'Jesse Caruthers,' Hatcher said. 'Pardon me for not standing. Grab a glass and pull up a chair.'

He could see Norgling's face relax. The muscles around his mouth loosened, his smile came easily, his whole body was at ease.

A real amateur, thought Hatcher.

As Norgling was pouring a glass of wine, Hatcher said, 'What the hell kind of man sells out three buddies for thirty thousand dollars?'

Norgling reacted immediately. He dropped the bottle and

glass and reached for his gun. As he did, Hatcher swung his right arm out of the tub. The Aug was in his hand, firing as it came out of the water, soap suds twirling off the barrel as bullets stitched a line from Norgling's belly to his chest and then made a tight little spiral. Nine shots in less than a second – nine hits, four in the heart. Norgling's body slapped against the tile wall and the air wheezed out of his lungs. His knees collapsed. He fell straight down, landing in a squat on the shattered wine bottle, and toppled to his side.

Hatcher was out of the tub before Norgling was all the way down. He opened the towel closet and pulled out the green body bag he had stashed there earlier, grabbed Norgling by the hair, lifted his body back to a sitting position and slid the bag over his head. He then let him fall backward, pulled the bag down the rest of the way and zipped it up. He slid it to the corner of the bathroom, put on his slippers, cleaned up the broken glass and mopped up the wine with a towel, which he washed off in the tub. Then he went to the phone and punched out a number.

When the voice on the other end answered, Hatcher said, 'Come get him!' and hung up.

That was one of the few times Hatcher knew who his victim was and why he was executing him. Usually it was blind obedience. 'Do it,' Sloan would say and Hatcher did it. Not only did it, accepted it, believed in it. But now, looking back, Hatcher realized he could have been used. Perhaps Norgling was just a fugazi, a screw-up, and they needed to get rid of him, and they could have dummied up the tape, and . . .

And perhaps it was 126, whispering in his ear, stirring thoughts that Hatcher had never stirred, never wanted to stir, before.

He flipped the dials of the combination lock on the Halliburton case and opened it. Inside was a thick sheet of Styrofoam cut to fit snugly into the case. Fitted into that were a half-inch video camera, two battery packs, a 400 mm. and a 200 mm. telephoto lens, a shoulder mount for the camera, four blank VHS tapes and several extension cords, carefully coiled and tied with plastic ties.

All were dummies.

Hatcher cleaned the gun thoroughly, then quickly broke it down into its three sections. He slid the barrel into the specially designed tubular hinge of the case and twisted a small screw cap on the end of the hinge. He popped open the dummy video camera, placed the trigger housing inside it and snapped it shut.

Then he unscrewed the lens from the 400 mm. telephoto and slid the gun inside it. The two plastic magazines, each capable of holding thirty rounds, fit inside the two hollow batteries for the dummy video camera. He also had a short barrel, four inches long, which converted the weapon into a pistol. He secreted the short barrel in the 200 mm. lens. All the equipment fit easily into the case, which weighed less than twenty pounds.

The case also had a fake lining with a pocket, attached with Velcro to the inside of the lid. He peeled it back and put his money, letters and the fake passport into the waterproof pocket. Hatcher replaced the phony lining and dropped several file folders in the pocket, then closed the case and spun the dials on the five-digit combination lock.

Broken down into its three parts and secreted in the attaché case, the Aug defied any detection device. Assembled, it was one of the most lethal and versatile weapons in existence, a killing machine without recoil or noise. The loudest sound the gun made was the trigger clicking. It was accurate to 450 yards. It was the only weapon Hatcher carried. The ammunition was available anywhere in the world, no problem.

He went back in the bedroom, swiftly packed the Gurkha bag, zipped it up and took it back to the living room. Then he returned to the bedroom.

Ginia was still sleeping. He stared down at her.

The past was tapping his shoulder. What the Chinese called the *ch'uang tzu-chi*, the window to oneself, was open.

What ghosts were waiting back there to wring his soul? Hatcher had thought Hong Kong and Bangkok were history. Upriver and the lair of the Ts'e K'am Men Ti. The White Palm Gang and the Chiu Chaos. Tollie Fong, Sam-Sam Sam and White Powder Mama. Fat Lady Lau's, Cohen.

Bangkok.

And Daphne.

Names he had tried to forget and couldn't.

He had tried to put them away, but they were all his yesterdays, the sum of his life.

Sloan had returned like the devil crawling up out of Hades, extending a long, bony finger to him, beckoning him back to the dark places that even 126 did not talk about, places seeded with hatred and death.

Going back really didn't have much to do with Sloan, or with the names he'd dredged up – Buffalo Bill or Murph Cody. It was time to go back, time to close out some unfinished chapters in his life. Time to pay the fiddler.

He sat down on the bed and began to rub Ginia's back. She stirred and rolled over on her stomach. He got some moisturizer and began to massage her. For a moment the thought occurred to him that he was going to miss her, and the thought annoyed him because missing was like remembering. Hatcher had never missed anyone before in his life. It didn't fit the pattern. It could be distracting, and that could be dangerous, screw up the old clicks, pull you out of the shadows into sunlight, where he knew he didn't belong.

'Attachments can be fatal,' Sloan had said once. 'They put your mind in the wrong place at the wrong time.'

Funny how often 126 and Sloan disagreed. What was it old 126 used to say? A man who has forgotten how to cry is dead inside.

He dismissed the thought, kneading his fingers into her shoulders and then up to her neck, moving along her arms to her finger-tips and stretching each one, massaging it with cream, then back to her sides and down to her hips. She groaned very faintly and spread her legs slightly. He put one leg between hers, pulled her down against it and, leaning forward into her, started to massage her neck again.

'Hurry home,' she whispered.

CIRILLO

Hatcher waited near the marina parking lot, listening to the night birds courting one another in the darkness, their melodies echoing across the broad, flat marsh. It was past midnight and the causeway leading to the mainland was almost deserted. Five miles away on the other side of the marsh, the lights of Brunswick twinkled like fireflies. He had one more task to finish before he left on his journey. He had said his good-bye to Ginia and now he waited in the dark, the briefcase sitting beside his leg.

A pair of headlights appeared far down the causeway and gradually grew larger as a car approached the docks. It turned off the narrow two-lane blacktop that connected the island with the rest of the world. The tan-and-brown police car, its tires crunching on the oyster-shell drive, stopped beside Hatcher. The door swung open.

Hatcher peered in at the beefy police officer in the brown uniform, a gold lieutenant's bar twinkling on the open collar of his starched shirt. Jim Cirillo was a muscular man, deeply tanned, his black hair salted gray by time and sun. Powerful hands rested casually on top of the steering wheel.

'You lookin' to get busted for loitering?' his deep voice drawled.

'Yeah,' Hatcher answered with a grin. He got in beside the cop. Cirillo dropped the stick into drive and wheeled out of the lot, turning back across the drawbridge and onto the island. Tall oak trees with Spanish moss hanging from their limbs like gray icicles arched the narrow roads. This was Cirillo's time. He was a night person who preferred to sleep and fish in the daytime. They drove in silence for a few minutes.

'Sloan found me,' Hatcher finally croaked.

'So? You don't owe him,' Cirillo answered with a shrug.

'That's right,' Hatcher answered.

'If anything, he owes you.'

'Yeah.'

And Hatcher thought to himself, I owe you a lot, Jimmy. Cirillo had been surrogate father, friend, teacher and confidant, had even arranged his appointment to Annapolis.

A small mule deer hardly any bigger than a Great Dane darted across the road in front of them and dashed off into the woods.

'Sloan wants me to do a job for him,' Hatcher said.

'No kidding,' Cirillo snorted, slowing the car and shining his spotlight in the window of a tiny bait shack. Satisfied that the place was secure, Cirillo drove on.

'I'm going to have to do it, Jimmy,' Hatcher whispered in his strange cracked voice.

Cirillo drove for a few moments, then said, 'Okay.'

'It hasn't got anything to do with Sloan,' Hatcher went on.

'Okay.'

'A classmate of mine at Annapolis was supposedly killed in Nam in 1973. Apparently he's turned up alive in Bangkok. It's a touchy situation.'

'And you're the only one that can find him?'

'I'm the only one who knows the subject – and who Sloan trusts.'

'And do you trust him?'

'Never again.'

'You believe this story?'

'Enough to find out.'

'Lot of devils over there waiting to be dredged up,' Cirillo said quietly.

'Yeah,' Hatcher answered.

'Is that part of it, Hatch?'

They drove quietly. Hatcher thought about the question and said, 'That's part of it. Been off the wire too long, too.'

'A real seductive lady, danger is.'

'Yeah. Well you're the one who introduced me to her.'

Driving through the overhanging moss, Cirillo was remembering that day on the mountain. 'You looked pretty good that day,' he said. 'To tell you the truth, I never thought you'd do it. That was the day I decided you might turn into something.'

From Cirillo, Hatcher had learned a sense of obligation and duty, a simple code of honour, but a code easily exploited by a man like Sloan. The irony was that Cirillo had joined the Boston SWAT Squad at almost the same time Sloan had proselytized Hatcher. Like flies, both men were drawn into a web of violence that would shape their lives for years to come. Now both had come to this island to break the patterns.

Hatcher broke into both men's silent reverie. 'I need to check out the Aug, make sure it's A-l.'

'You need an Aug to look for a guy in Bangkok?' Cirillo said, obviously surprised.

'I've got a lot of enemies between here and Bangkok.'

'So make your peace with them.'

'It's a nice thought,' Hatcher said. 'There's only one way to make peace with some of these people.'

'Then I guess you'll have to do that, too,' said Cirillo.

'I hope not,' Hatcher said. 'You'll keep an eye on the boat?'

'I got the key. Any way I can reach you?'

Hatcher thought for a moment. 'The Oriental Hotel in Bangkok. Just leave a message for me.'

'Right.' Cirillo paused and added, 'You're not a little too rusty for this kind of stuff, are you, kid?'

Hatcher thought for a few moments and shook his head.

'I don't think so,' he said.

BUFFALO BILL

It was raining in Washington, a steady spattering downpour from a cold leaden sky that etched teardrops down the black polished face of the memorial. The rain collected in the shallow letters chiseled into the stone, overflowed and dribbled erratically down to the floor of the chevron scar in Constitution Gardens. There, memories of the fallen had been placed: a purple heart, a vase of daisies, the tattered photograph of a perfectly restored '56 Chevy, a now soggy worn teddy bear.

The rotton weather had not discouraged visitors. There were dozens, standing like statues staring at the vast granite slab, searching, discovering, reaching out, and touching the names of daughters, sons, lovers, fathers, husbands, best friends or college pals, saying good-bye as the sky wept with them.

Hatcher knew a lot of names on that solemn roster. He had fought but not served in Vietnam; a civilian, he had done jobs so dirty even the military would not sanction or talk about them. There were no medals or commendations, not even any records kept, for the kind of work he had done, but he had been there, done his work, and watched friends and enemies die in every inhumane, ugly, loathsome, unspeakable way human beings can leave this earth.

Hatcher had never seen the monument before, had never wanted to see it. But now, looking down through the rain, he was awed by its simple eloquence. It stirred in him, for the first time, the thought that he might have returned to the World with the same scars, the same guilt and confusion, as everybody else who fought in Nam. In that particular operation he had been labeled a mercenary, and mercenaries do not share glory, do not march in parades or have holidays named after them. For them there is only winning or losing – or more simply defined – living or dying.

But here there was no politics, no arguing the endless, unresolved yeas and nays of that faraway war; there was simply an open grave and the good-bye list of a conflict that probably would be nothing more than a footnote in history books a hundred years hence – a paragraph without resolution. History deals fleetingly with events it cannot explain.

He would never have recognized the old warrior had it not been for the four stars on his shoulder. Buffalo Bill Cody was still ramrod-straight, but ten years and the worms gnawing at his insides had devoured his body, leaving behind a craggy, hollow-eyed sliver of a man with pain written in every crevice of his face. The tailored trench coat that accentuated his bony frame was a further reminder that even legends are mortal.

But a legend he was. While other military big shots were destroyed by the scandal of Nam, Cody had emerged with his

101

reputation unscathed. A hero and a soldier's general who somehow maintained a sense of dignity in the middle of chaos, Cody had become the acceptable military figure of the Vietnam war. Shy, almost self-deprecating, he avoided the spotlight and was admired by left, right and center, an ordinary man who had sacrificed a son to the conflict and who seemed to bring a sense of sanity to an otherwise totally insane endeavor. He was like the nation's favorite uncle, over there watching out for the kids. Now he stood, between a hunched-over man in combat fatigues and a woman with a teenage boy, looking at the list. Nobody paid any attention to him. The place was like that. It made commoners of everyone.

'He looks a hundred and ten,' Hatcher croaked.

'He might as well be,' Sloan answered. 'He'll be lucky if he lasts six months.'

'Do we have to stand out here in the rain?' Hatcher asked.

'He'll be through in a minute. The ritual never changes.'

Hatcher huddled down deeper in his raincoat, watched the general, and inwardly marveled at Sloan's remarkable ability at the big con. Yesterday Hatcher had considered killing him. Today Hatcher was standing in the rain, seven hundred miles from home, actually considering doing a job he didn't need, didn't want and didn't believe in. A hundred years ago, thought Hatcher, Sloan would have been hawking elixirs from the back of a wagon or selling shares in the Brooklyn Bridge. Now he sold dirty tricks with fictions of adventure and patriotism, seducing wide-eyed young men and women into the shadow wars, to become assassins, saboteurs, gunrunners, second-story men, safe crackers, even mercenaries, all for the glory of flag and country. Hatcher had met Sloan in the time of his innocence and had bought the lie.

The general finished his ritual and started back toward the street. Hatcher and Sloan watched Buffalo Bill slowly mount the steps, leaning heavily on a cane but avoiding the help of his assistant, a young major who had West Point inscribed in every move.

'He doesn't know anything about the money,' Sloan said, half under his breath. 'That's between you and me.'

'Does he know anything about me?' Hatcher asked.

'Yes.'

'And he approves?'

'He trusts my judgement.'

Hatcher chuckled. 'How long has he known you?'

The general's arrival ended the exchange. Up close, he looked even sicker than from a distance. His color was gray, and his eyes were watery and lifeless and had lost the fire that had once touched

102

even his photographs with electricity. But he still stood erect, and if he was in pain, he didn't show it.

'Glad you made it, Harry,' he said and then turned to Hatcher. 'You must be Christian Hatcher. It's a pleasure meeting you.' He switched his cane to his left hand and offered Hatcher a bony but hearty handshake.

'My pleasure, General,' Hatcher said.

'You served well in the Far East,' Cody said. 'Sloan kept me up on you.'

'Thank you, sir.'

The old warrior seemed shocked when he heard Hatcher's ruined voice. 'Let's get out of the rain shall we?' he said, quickly covering his surprise. His aide held the rear door open and they got in the limousine. Hatcher sat in the jump seat, facing Sloan and Cody. The old man shuddered from the effects of the cold and rain, and the aide wrapped a blanket around his legs.

'Thanks, Jerry,' Cody said, and the aide closed the door, leaving the three men alone in the backseat.

'Don't have enough meat left on these old bones to stave off the cold,' Cody said with embarrassment, then hurried on: 'Well, sir, Colonel Sloan tells me he's filled you in on our problem.'

Hatcher nodded.

'What do you think?'

Hatcher said, 'Our best bet is the Thai, Wol Pot. If he's telling the truth and Murph is alive, I can find him.'

'You sound pretty positive,' said Cody.

'I qualified it – *if* your son's alive.'

The general nodded. 'And what do your instincts tell you about that?'

Hatcher shook his head. 'Nothing yet. The files are pretty bleak.'

'Yes, not much to go on. Sorry.'

'There may be a few leads in there,' Hatcher said.

'You understand the need for discretion,' Cody said, and it was a statement rather than a question. Hatcher nodded again. 'Also,' he went on, 'there is some urgency in the matter.'

'Yes, sir,' Hatcher said.

'You two were pretty close at the academy, as I recall.'

Hatcher nodded again. 'We were on the boxing team together. He graduated a year ahead of me.' He paused for a moment, and added, 'He was okay, General. A stand-up guy.'

'Good. I feel a little more comfortable knowing you knew him – and liked him.'

'You and I met once before,' Hatcher whispered suddenly, 'at Murph's wedding.'

The general peered hard at Hatcher, but there was no recognition in his bleak stare. 'That was a long time ago. I'm afraid my memory isn't what it used to be.'

'Hell, mine isn't anything to write home about, either.'

The general looked at Sloan for a moment, then back at Hatcher. 'May I ask you a personal question?'

'Sure,' Hatcher said.

'Why did you accept this mission?'

Hatcher wasn't sure how to answer. He thought for a moment, then said, 'A friend of mine once asked me if I was a patriot. At the time I said I wasn't sure. Now maybe I can find out.'

'There's nothing patriotic about this job,' the general said forlornly.

'I'd like to think there is,' Hatcher said.

Cody smiled – a fey, faraway memory of a smile tinged with sadness. 'That's a kind thing to say, Mr. Hatcher. Thank you.'

The old general focused his watery eyes on Hatcher and stared hard at the tall man for several seconds to make sure he phrased his next question properly. 'I understand you left the brigade and returned to the private sector,' the general said.

'Yes, sir.'

'Too bad,' he said. 'You were a good soldier, Hatcher.'

'Thank you, sir.'

'Mind telling me why you quit?'

Sloan cast a sideways glance at Hatcher, but the tall man ignored it.

'I was losing my edge, General,' Hatcher lied.

Cody stared at him for several seconds.

'Well, let's hope you have it back,' Cody finally said with a wry smile.

'Yes, sir.'

Cody turned to Sloan. 'Looks like you found us a good man, Harry – as usual.'

'Thank you, sir,' Sloan said, obviously pleased. 'Then we're on?'

Buffalo Bill Cody looked at Hatcher and repeated the question, 'Well, sir, are we on?'

Hatcher nodded. 'We're on,' his tortured voice answered.

FRAGMENTS

The place was like no other museum in the world. It was called MARS, an acronym for the Museum and Archaeological Regional Storage Facility, and it was in a plain one-story building forty miles south of Washington in a small village in Maryland. It took Hatcher an hour and a half to drive down there in his rented Chevy.

The curator was a young man, perhaps forty, although it was hard to tell, and he was jacketed in blue, like an intern. Sandy-haired, bearded and soft-spoken, he was a man whose task was reflected in an obvious sadness of spirit, for there was about the place a sense of longing and hurt and disquietude. He handed Hatcher a pair of white cotton gloves.

'We wear these to prevent any further deterioration of the articles,' he told Hatcher, pointing vaguely in the direction of a plastic bag that held two small identical seashells attached to a simple note: 'I love you, Charley.'

'They're cataloged by position, the panel nearest where they were left,' he said, leading Hatcher down a long row of gray metal floor-to-ceiling shelves.

Many of those who came to the Vietnam wall seemed compelled by heart or conscience to put something down, to leave a piece of themselves behind. These oddities of the heart, like relics of a history yet to be written, were gathered up each day and carried by rangers of the Park Service to the warehouse, where they were sorted, cataloged and stored. Like the fragments of the shattered lives it recorded, the collection was disparate: heartbreaking, humorous, touching, and determined entirely by emotion – by the love of a child for the father she never knew, the anguish of a lonely parent, by a lover left alone at night, and the guilt of the buddy who survived. Frustration, sorrow, pride, anger, all were here, in a plain storage room on uniform shelves of gray metal. Here was the pain of the living.

The pieces lay encased in plastic bags, and unexplained. Baseballs. Maps. Flags. Many, many flags, the most inspiring

105

– and abused – symbol of the war. Hatcher passed one and saw the note scribbled across a white stripe: 'From Kenny, the son-in-law you never met.'

Notes ('My friends, I pray that our children will never have to go to war but if they do, I pray they will go with all the courage and dignity that you did'). Letters, some still sealed. Poems ('To my father, killed two months before I was born').

Toy airplane models, helmets, military patches, medals, high school dance programs and college yearbooks, C rations, combat boots, a roll of GI toilet paper, a six-pack of Miller's, a copper POW-MIA bracelet dated 1973, photographs of automobiles and homes, children never seen, fathers never known. Fragments.

'Were you in Nam?' Hatcher asked, following the ranger down the rows of memorabilia.

'Yep,' came the answer with a finality that precluded further questions.

It was easy to find specific articles because of the simple code they had devised to catalog these small treasures left behind by relatives, lovers and friends. The man stopped, leaned forward and checked a code number.

'This is his row. It would be in here, if there's anything,' he said and moved away to leave Hatcher to his investigation. On the shelf was a worn and dirty teddy bear and beside it a Louisville Slugger with a crack in it and a photograph of a cocky-looking teenage couple standing beside a bright-red vintage Thunderbird. There was a withered stem of a corsage with a white ribbon still attached and a wedding ring sewn to the ribbon of a Purple Heart.

Then he found two notes.

The first one was addressed to: 'Our father, Lt. Murphy Cody, U.S.N. From your loving children, Keith and Sharon.' It was attached to a photo of two teenagers who looked sad beyond their years.

Beside it was a second note. It read simply: 'Thanks for everything, Polo. And thank God for Thai Horse. Jaimie.' It was attached to a green beret. There was nothing else.

Polo.

That's what this Jaimie called him, Polo. So the nickname had stayed with Cody. Funny, thought Hatcher, I never thought he liked it. But it proved one thing to him. The note was left for Murphy Cody. That couldn't be a coincidence.

Was it a good-bye note from someone who knew he was dead?

Or was it a thank-you note from someone who knew Murphy Cody was alive?

106

And there was the reference to the Thai Horse. To Hatcher that meant only one thing – Thailand heroin. China White.

Did Cody provide heroin to his men? Were he and this Jaimie in some kind of smuggling ring together? Was this some kind of coded message? Hatcher unconsciously shook his head. He didn't want to believe that. And yet, what else could it mean? Could there be some other answer?

The side trip had raised more questions than it answered.

'No way to track back on this Jaimie, right?' Hatcher's hoarse voice asked.

The caretaker shook his head. 'That's none of our business,' he said simply.

Hatcher checked the beret. Inside the lining were the initials 'J.S.' Nothing more. Hatcher took out a small notebook and wrote down all the information, such as it was. There was one more piece of data. The beret and note had been recorded fourteen months earlier, on July fourth.

There was nothing else. Whatever the legacy of Murphy Cody, it seemed to end here, with this brief epitaph.

'Okay,' he said to the caretaker. 'Thanks.'

'Yep.'

Hatcher looked around the room one more time, at the baseball mitts and tattered kites and flowers.

He thought of something Conrad had written: ' . . . an unselfish belief in an idea – something you can set up, and bow down before, and offer a sacrifice to. . . .'

And he thought of all the restless heroes represented here, butchered and buried or lost in an alien place in a war most did not understand but did not question either, deprived of their hopes and dreams in that awesome sacrifice that crown and country seem determined to demand of every generation. Ordinary men who became extraordinary in death. The cold breath of ghosts chilled the back of Hatcher's neck and he could not get out of there fast enough.

MONTANA

Hatcher disappeared that night with his briefcase full of twenties and the Murphy file, leaving Sloan waiting alone for

107

him in the Occidental Restaurant. Sloan was on his third scotch when the bells went off in his head: *The son of a bitch isn't gonna show up.* A quick call confirmed his fears. Hatcher had checked out of his hotel two hours before. Just like him! And it angered Sloan because he should have known Hatcher would duck out on him. The first way Hatcher's anger at Sloan would manifest would be for Hatcher to cut loose, flaunt his free-lance status, and show Sloan who was boss.

Well, thought Sloan, we'll see about that.

'Will you be ordering soon, Colonel?' the maître d' asked after he hung up.

'Cancel,' Sloan snapped. He slipped him a five and headed out into the rainy night. Knowing Hatcher, Sloan knew it could be weeks before he heard from him again. He went back to his office and tracked down Zabriski. Zabriski could find anybody. Besides, he was sure Hatcher was traveling under his own name. Hell, he hadn't changed it so far. Besides, Hatcher wasn't dodging Sloan, he was ignoring him. Sloan would get a line on him, just to show the son of a bitch.

The next morning he had his report.

'He flew into Billings, Montana, on an Eastern flight last night, stayed at the Palace Hotel, checked out early this morning and caught a local feeder to Shelby,' Zabriski reported.

'Montana! What the hell could he be doing in Montana?'

'I dunno, sir. But that's where he went.'

'Where the hell's Shelby?'

'About two giant steps south of the Canadian border,' the agent answered. 'There's nothing there, Colonel, it's been snowed under for three months. It's where God lost his snowshoes.'

Montana? Sloan pulled out the Murphy file and went back over it, reading every line, looking for some reference to Shelby, Montana. But he found nothing. Well, hell, Sloan thought, where can he go from Shelby? He assigned Zabriski to take the next flight to Billings, wait for Hatcher to show up and follow him.

'And, Zabriski, this guy's slippery, got it? He's got tricks you haven't heard of yet.'

'Do we bust him?' Zabriski asked.

'Hell, no, he hasn't done anything wrong,' Sloan said. 'I just want to know what the hell he's up to.'

Maybe, thought Sloan, he's doing a double-back. Maybe he's checking *me* out. The risk in hiring Hatcher was that he was too clever. If Hatcher turned into a loose cannon, he could be very dangerous. After Los Boxes, it was much too early in the game to trust Hatcher.

The twin-engined De Havilland snaked its way through the narrow lane the blowers had trenched through the snow. On either side of the plane, high-piled snowbanks loomed above the fuselage, snow that had been collecting for months. The airport terminal was a small one-story building almost hidden in the white drifts. There was a hangar nearby, barely peeking over the snow, with a tattered windsock flapping straight out from its warped pole in the subfreezing wind. That was all there was to the airport. Hatcher's boots squeaked and his breath left trails of steam in his wake as he hurried across the snow-packed tarmac toward the warmth of the tiny terminal, which was barely the size of a large living room.

On one side of the room was an airline counter operated by a skinny young man who looked half asleep; facing it on the other side of the room was a food-dispensing machine and a combination taxi and rental car service, both operated by the same person, a grizzled man in need of a shave, wearing a fur cap and three layers of wool shirts. The arrival of the flight hardly stirred much activity in the terminal. There were only two other passengers on the small feeder line.

Hatcher drew a cup of coffee from the machine and waited until one of the passengers had gone through the drill of renting a car. When he left, Hatcher approached the fur-capped old man, who was leaning over the rental form, completing it with a stub of a pencil.

'How long's it take to get to Cut Bank?' Hatcher's frazzled voice asked.

The old man kept working on his form. 'Depends.'

'On what?'

'Time a year. Summertime, takes about forty-five minutes.'

'Well, how about in the winter, like right now, for instance?'

'Two hours, if you know the road.'

'Know how far it is up to the government hay station?' Hatcher growled.

The old fellow kept writing and said, still without looking up, 'Thirty-seven miles, more or less, most of it uphill. You ain't used to driving in snow, forget it. They won't even find you until spring.'

109

'You the cabdriver, too?'

'Yep.'

'How much to run me up there?'

'Son, you make it sound like a bike ride in the park,' he said, still concentrating on the form.

Hatcher slid a hundred-dollar bill under his nose. 'There's another one just like that when we get back,' he said in his chafing whisper. 'I shouldn't be up there more than an hour.'

The old fellow stared down at Ben Franklin's cryptic grin for a few moments, then looked up. 'You must be a government fella,' he said.

'You want a biography, it'll cost you that Ben Franklin,' Hatcher's frazzled voice answered as he nodded toward the hundred.

'Nuff said,' the old man said, folding the bill and tucking it in one of his shirt pockets. 'Last plane back to Billings is at four.' He looked at his watch. 'Gives us six hours.'

'How about Spokane?'

'One flight a day. Two-thirty.'

'Let's aim for that,' Hatcher said in his grating voice.

'Uh-huh,' the old fellow said and stuck out his hand. 'Name's Rufus Eskew.'

'Chris,' Hatcher said, shaking a hand tormented with calluses.

'Better do something about that cold,' Rufus said, reaching under the counter for his keys.

The chopper swept in low over the meadow, scrambling the deer that had already sniffed out the first batch of hay it had dropped. Simmons stood in the open hatch layered in heavy clothing, his face protected by a scarf against the frigid wind that blasted down on him and his partner from the chopper blades overhead. His eyes peered out from behind sunglasses between the scarf and the wool hat that was pulled down hard over his ears. His thick black eyebrows were caked with frost. He held on to the heavy lifeline over the side hatch and waited until the pilot whipped the chopper around.

Below them, the herd bounded about erratically, except for one magnificent stag who stood his ground, testing the air with his quivering nostrils, watching as the helicopter lowered over the frosted meadow that was trapped between two mountain peaks.

110

'Lookit that arrogant son-bitch,' Simmons yelled to his partner in the waist of the chopper. 'That's one gorgeous buck.'

They were twenty feet above the drifted lea when Simmons put both feet against the two-hundred-pound bale and kicked and pushed it out the door. He watched it tumble down, end over end, smack the ground and burst in a shower of snow and hay.

'Come and get it, little darlin's,' he yelled down at the herd, which had been trapped by a sudden snowstorm and was facing starvation. On the other side, Eddie, his kick-boss, launched the last of the bales. He turned to Simmons and shot a thumb toward the roof of the plane. Simmons heard his voice over the intercom: 'Okay, bombs away. Let's go get some hot coffee.'

'I hear that and that's a roger and good-damn-news,' the pilot answered.

Simmons and Eddie closed the hatch doors and sat in front of the feeble heaters. The air that blew out of the two vents was warm air only by comparison with the outside wind. Simmons took out a pint of Canadian Club, pulled down his scarf and took a long swig from the bottle. He wiped the mouth off with his gloved hand and gave the bottle to Eddie, then shook all over as if he'd been struck by lightning. 'Who-eeee! That'll get us home,' he cried out, then pulled the scarf back up over his face, put away the bottle when Eddie had taken his turn, and wrapped his arms around himself. He would sleep for the twenty minutes it took to get to the station.

The pilot's voice came over the intercom: 'I just got a call from base. There's a guy waitin' there to see you, Harley.'

Simmons perked up. Now, who in hell would come out to the base to see him in this weather? he wondered.

'What's his name?' Simmons asked the pilot.

'Didn't ask.'

Simmons worried about it all the way back. He had problems with paranoia anyway. If Lee back at the base didn't know who it was, then who the hell was it? He was out of the chopper and running toward the office while the chopper blades were still spinning. Who *was* this guy, anyway?

Simmons knew Rufus Eskew, so it had to be the other guy. He was standing over the floor heater, drinking coffee from a cup he held with both hands – six, six one, dark hair

111

streaked with gray, built like a boxer. Lookit that tan, Simmons thought. That guy's from someplace south. L.A. or Florida. He was wearing a black turtleneck sweater, tan corduroy pants tucked into fleece-lined boots and a heavy fleece jacket. And sunglasses. L.A., Simmons decided. Then he took off the glasses and Simmons was staring into the coldest gray eyes he'd ever seen.

Washington, Simmons said to himself.

'Mr. Simmons, my name's Hatcher,' his grinding whisper said.

Jesus, Simmons thought, listen to that. The guy whispers.

'Let's go someplace and talk for a minute. This is kind of personal,' Hatcher suggested.

Personal? Personal? What the hell could be personal. He didn't owe a dollar. His alimony was paid up. Even his jeep was paid for.

'You got twenty minutes to warm your asses,' the pilot said as the rest of the crew piled into the shack behind him. 'They're loading us up again.'

'We can go in the director's office,' Simmons said. 'He's down in Helena for a couple days.'

He led Hatcher into a small room with a desk that was barren except for the phone. The room contained the desk, an old-fashioned glass-front bookcase with several government publications scattered in it, and a hat tree. The calendar on the wall was from the Haygood Seed and Feed Company in Shelby. Hatcher looked around the office and thought, The director is either incredibly well organized or incredibly underworked. He sat down on the corner of the desk.

'Grab a chair,' he said.

Simmons sat. He looked scared to death.

'What's goin' on?' he asked.

'I'm with the MIA Commission. We're wrapping up the Cody case,' Hatcher said.

'Oh Jesus, I knew it. I knew it was that. Damn it, how many times I got to go through that thing? I been outa the fuckin' Army for almost fifteen years and they been wrappin' up the Cody case ever since.'

Hatcher was shocked at Simmons's reaction. But it was also revealing. It was as if Simmons's worst fear had risen up and grabbed him by the throat. Hatcher knew the signs and at that moment knew his hunch was correct. All he had to do was keep pressing. Simmons was looking to crack.

'It's just a routine thing,' Hatcher said. 'No reason to get crazy on me.'

'I been out here for ten years,' Simmons said. 'Trying to forget all that. I don't need . . .' He didn't finish the sentence.

'Just a few loose ends,' said Hatcher. 'Won't take but a minute.'

'Anyway, I heard Cody was officially dead.'

'That's correct.'

'Then what the hell . . .'

'What it is, there are one or two things we need to clarify.'

'I can't remember that far back, man,' Simmons said. 'That's fifteen years ago. I saw a lot of people die in Nam. They all just kind of run together.'

'This was the wing leader, Cody. His father was commanding general of the whole theater. I'm sure you remember that one, Simmons.'

Simmons started to get angry, but it was a defensive kind of anger. 'Look, Mr. whatever-your-name-is,' Simmons snapped. 'I don't remember. I don't want to remember. I've spent fifteen *years* trying to forget all that.'

'All what?'

'Everything that happened over there. Twelve months in my life that I want to . . . try to make believe never happened. It's hard enough. . . . Anyway, they all looked alike that far away.'

'Who?'

'The flyboys that went down.'

'How far away?'

'Across the river. You know, we were flying Hueys in Sea-Air Rescue. When you're doin' SAR, you're never just . . . right on top of them.'

'Yeah, that's one of the things I wanted to run by you,' Hatcher said, taking a file folder out of his briefcase and flipping through it. He let the comment hang, watching Simmons get edgier. A lot of guilt here, he thought, this guy is fragile, he's broken and the pieces haven't fallen yet. He waited a little longer, then whispered, 'What it is, we got a little discrepancy in the reports.'

'Discrepancy?'

'Yeah, just a little thing. In your debriefing just after the incident you said that the plane hit the trees and blew up immediately. Wait a minute, here it is. "We were about half

113

a mile away and he went in upside down and the whole forest seemed to explode. I don't see how anybody could have survived."'

Simmons nodded. 'That's right,' he said.

'But in this transcription of the review-board tape in 1981 you say you were close enough to feel the heat when it blew and you could *see* that nobody got out. Then you started taking heavy ground fire and had to abandon the rescue attempt.'

'Happened all the time. So?'

'So which is right? Were you close enough to feel the heat or half a mile away when he augered in?'

He turned away from Hatcher and started toward the door. 'I gotta get going. Deer to feed.'

'You've still got fifteen minutes,' Hatcher whispered softly. He decided to fire long shot. 'Look, Simmons,' his voice rasped, 'I don't give a damn whether you lied to the review board. I just want to know the truth now. You tell me, it stops right here.'

Simmons turned abruptly, his face reddening with anger. 'What the hell would I have to lie about?'

'The debriefing officer noted in his report back in '72 that you were scared. In fact, he wrote that you were stuttering. It was all over and you were back on the ground, but you were still that scared.'

'I was three weeks in-country, man,' Simmons said brusquely. 'That was only my third trip out. Sure, I was scared. I was scared the last day I was over there, too. I was nineteen. I was scared all the time.'

'Being scared isn't being a coward,' Hatcher said softly.

'Coward? That what you think?'

Hatcher shook his head. 'That's not what I think. But maybe it's what *you* think.'

Simmons kneaded his wool cap in his hands and shook his head. 'You just never get away from it. Damn Vietnam, *God* damn Vietnam,' he cried out with such passion that it surprised Hatcher. He felt sorry for Simmons but not sorry enough to stop.

'You swear to me you didn't see anyone coming away from that plane, and I'm gone,' Hatcher whispered. 'But if you lie, I'll know it.'

'Such a long time ago . . .'

'You weren't under oath, Simmons. So maybe you made a mistake . . .'

'I'm not under oath now.'

'Simmons, is it possible that Cody escaped from that plane?'

114

'Anything's possible.'

'What do you think?'

A voice from outside yelled, 'Five minutes, Simmons.'

'Right away,' Simmons yelled back. He looked back at Hatcher. 'Why are they checking into this again, anyhow. It's all over?'

'There's a chance Cody could be in an MIA camp in Cambodia,' Hatcher lied. 'Before we make a stink about it, I've got to be sure he didn't die that day.'

'It's all in the reports. I told them all of it. They were always going down. It was a suicide outfit, everybody knew that.'

'You mean Cody's outfit?'

'He was crazy, man. First thing I heard when I joined the SAR, "You're Cody's backup," they'd say, "you're gonna stay busy. Better keep your head down. . . ."'

The vision began flashing in Simmons's head. He rubbed his eyes, but it persisted, as it always did. The figure limping frantically toward the river's edge, waving futilely at him, then the explosion, the great awning of fire spreading out over the treetops. And still the pilot kept coming, waving, a specter silhouetted against fire until the image burned out in Simmons's head.

'Maybe . . .' Simmons said.

'Maybe what, Simmons? Maybe Cody didn't die, that what you're saying?' Hatcher knew he had Simmons going, could almost feel his pain. That was part of it, knowing when they were going to break, keeping the squeeze on.

'I never said he died,' Simmons cried, 'I never said that at all. He could of got outa there without me seeing him. They were shooting at us, there was a lot of fire. . . .'

'Bullets come close, did they?'

'They were chewing the Huey up three feet from my face.'

'So it was time to split, right?'

Simmons turned away from him. Outside, the familiar whine of the chopper could be heard as the pilot cranked it up.

'I gotta go.'

'Then I'll wait until you get back.'

'Jesus, what the hell do you want me to tell you?'

'The truth.'

Simmons slammed the heel of his hand against the doorjamb.

'Damn it! Damn it all. Damn you.'

'Been eating at you, has it?'

Simmons didn't answer.

'Look at it this way, if you did see somebody running away from the plane that day, maybe we can still find him.'

Simmons moaned, 'I still get nightmares. Nothing's worked for me. My wife left me. . . . It all turned to pig shit.'

'Maybe this'll help clear up those dreams,' Hatcher suggested, but Simmons shook his head.

'So you came up here to forget it?'

Simmons nodded mutely.

'And it didn't work.'

Tears suddenly flooded Simmons's eyes. He tried to blink them back, but they slowly drew streaks down his face.

'I keep thinking, maybe we coulda got him outa there, but they were shooting us to pieces, so I told them . . . "Let's get outa here, I don't see anybody" and God *damn* it . . . started tearing me up before we even got back to the base and it never stops and I can't stand to . . . can't . . . talk about it, see people I knew over there, I was just scared, man, that's all.'

'So Cody got out of the plane,' Hatcher said bluntly.

Simmons was weeping softly and he was trying not to show it. He leaned against the window, watching the chopper stir snow clouds as it warmed up. Simmons took a deep breath and sighed.

'One of 'em did,' he said finally.

'They think they found some of the gunner's remains at the site,' Hatcher said, 'But they never found Cody.'

Simmons faced Hatcher, his face twisted with grief. 'What the hell happened to him?' he asked, his voice quivering with guilt.

Hatcher shrugged and shook his head.

'If you ever find out –' Simmons started, and the voice from the plane yelled again, 'Simmons, what the hell're you doin'? We got work to do.'

'I'll let you know,' Hatcher said. 'There's one other thing. Does Thai Horse mean anything to you?'

'You mean heroin?'

'That's all it means?'

'That's all it means to me.'

'Thanks. You better get going,' Hatcher said.

As Simmons walked toward the office door Hatcher stood

116

up and touched his arm. 'Listen to me for a minute,' he said. 'What happened in-country, that doesn't count over here. You forget that. That was another life. What you did? That could happen to anybody. And if you did cost Cody his life, you probably saved the lives of the pilot, copilot and you. Three for one, that's a fair enough trade.'

'I've thought of that,' Simmons said. 'It doesn't help.'

'Conscience can be a terrible companion,' Hatcher whispered.

'That doesn't help either,' Simmons said bitterly.

He pulled his cap down tight over his head and left the room. Hatcher watched through the window as Simmons ran through the snow toward the chopper. He thought to himself, Okay, so Cody could have gotten out. And if he could've gotten out, he could still be alive and that means he's not dead for sure.

So where's he been for fifteen years?

'You lost him? You *lost* him,' Sloan said softly but firmly. 'How can you lose anybody in – What was the name of that place again?'

'Shelby,' Zabriski answered. 'He didn't come back to Billings, Colonel. He took a feeder into Spokane and from there to Seattle, then he caught a flight into L.A.'

'Where are you now?'

'L.A. International. He's going out in the morning.'

'Where?'

'San Diego.'

'San Diego! What the –' Sloan hesitated for a moment, then: 'Wait a minute. I'm putting you on hold, just hang on.'

Sloan punched the hold button, and turned to one of four computer operators who worked in his tiny headquarters.

'Holloway, I need a current location on two Navy men. Lieutenant Commander Ralph Schwartz and Commander Hugh Fraser. And I got a man holding on long distance.' Sloan spelled the two names.

'Gimme a minute, sir,' Holloway said. Sloan drummed his desk nervously and leafed through the copy of the Murphy file while Holloway typed questions into his computer. Sloan's operational headquarters was three rooms in a small office building four blocks from the White House. There was a small waiting room manned by his secretary, the main terminal room, which had four computer terminals connected to

117

a network of phones and satellites, and Sloan's private office, which did not contain a single personal item of any kind.

It took less than two minutes for the sergeant to get the answers.

'Coming up now, sir,' the sergeant said. 'Fraser retired eighteen months ago, Colonel. He's VP of a small charter airline in Seattle. No current civilian address on tap. On the other one . . . uh, here we go. Ralph Schwartz: he's full commander now, sir, director of flight instruction at NAS San Diego.'

'That'll do it, Sergeant, thanks,' Sloan said and switched back to Zabriski in L.A. 'Okay, I got it worked out. Cancel the surveillance and come back in.'

'Cancel the surveillance?' the agent asked, surprised.

'Cancel it,' Sloan said and hung up. He started to laugh. *That son of a bitch*, he thought, *he's playing games with me, showing me he still has the stuff*. The whisper man had made no attempt to cover his tracks, he just wanted to see how long it would take to catch up with him. Sloan looked at his watch. It was 7 P.M., 4 P.M. on the coast. Hatcher had covered a lot of ground in twenty-four hours.

Another computer operator interrupted his thoughts.

'We have a computer call coming in, Colonel.'

'Who from?'

'M base.'

The caller was using a computer modem to make the call. It was a method for securing the telephone line on risk calls. The computer screen in front of the operator scrolled out several questions requiring responses.

Code number:

Daily code:

Operation code:

Level clearance:

Call target code name:

Your code name:

Your clearance number:

Voice check:

An incorrect response anywhere along the line would result in an instant disconnect and a freeze on the calling number so it could be traced. Numbers and names appeared across the screen as the caller answered the questions.

'He's cleared the voice check,' the operator said.

'Put the call on the green box,' Sloan ordered and went

into his office. He closed the door and unlocked a drawer in his desk. It contained a phone with a device that scrambled transmission both ways and then unscrambled them on a one-to-one line. There were two small lights on top of the box. A green light assured Sloan that the line remained clear. If the other light, which was red, lit up, the call was immediately terminated.

Sloan answered the phone.

'This is Moon Racer,' he said.

'This is Hound Dog, sir. We're having problems.'

'It's all right, Hedritch, we've got a virgin line.'

'Our boy is giving us fits, Colonel.'

'Same old problem?'

'Yes, sir. It's okay as long as we keep him on the lake, security's a breeze. But he's determined to hit the night spots. I told him it was impossible and I won't repeat what he told me.'

Sloan chuckled. 'I can imagine, I brought the man out, remember. Those tropical types are all alike. Hot blood and all that.'

'His hot blood is going to be all over the floor if he's not careful. Do I have the authority to stop him?'

'Negative. He's a guest of the United States, not a prisoner. Our job is to protect him, tough as that may be.'

'He wants to go to a disco called Split Personality, to a costume party. We couldn't secure the place if we had the whole Israeli Army helping us.'

'When?'

'Day after tomorrow.'

Sloan thought for a moment.

'All right, we'll just have to take our chances. Don't let anybody know you're coming. Get there about eleven o'clock, tell the manager who you are. Locate in a spot that's inconspicuous. That's the best you can do.'

'It's gonna be hairy, sir.'

'It always is, Hedritch.'

'Yes, sir.'

Sloan hung up. He took a long Havana cigar from his desk drawer, took it out of its protective tube and drew it back and forth under his nose several times, smelling its rich tobacco. Then he lit it and picked up the green phone again. He punched out a number.

'Yes?' a voice answered after the first ring.

119

'This is Moon Racer. Is the man available?'

'Yes, sir.'

A moment later a voice asked, 'Moon Racer?'

'Yes,' Sloan replied.

'Are you smoking, Moon Racer?'

'Yes. Do you know what I'm smoking?'

'La Fiera.'

'Good. I've got the mark for you.'

'Is it the troublesome one we have discussed?'

'Yes. Campon will be at a place called the Split Personality in Atlanta, Georgia, eleven P.M. day after tomorrow.'

'That would be Wednesday.'

'Right. Is there a problem?'

'No problem. Enjoy your smoke.'

'I intend to.'

Sloan hung up, closed the drawer and locked it. Then he picked up his regular phone.

'Get me on the next flight to San Diego,' he said.

WATER BABIES

Windy Porter sat at his customary table in the corner of Queen's Pub watching a dozen Thais trying to launch a *chula*. The enormous kite was at least six feet long and the team was having a problem getting it aloft. On the other end of Sanam Luang Park, several *pakpao* kite fighters already had their small one-man kites in the air and were yelling good-natured insults at the team.

When the big dragon kite finally caught the wind and spiraled up into the air, one of the *pakpao* charged, zigzagging toward the big kite, trying to pass it and get to the *chula's* end of the field and win the match. The *chula* was difficult to maneuver, but its team was expert and they cut across the path of the *pakpao*, snared its string with their line, and brought the smaller kite augering to the ground. There was a great deal of cheering and now it was the *chula's* turn for insults, and the young man with the *pakpao* gathered up his wounded flyer and went back to his end of the field in humiliation. Another *pakpao*, whose kite was purple with a blazing red tail, reeled his bird in tight and got ready for the run.

'A red on the *pakpao*,' Porter said to Gus, the bartender, and slapped a red hundred-baht note on the table.

'Yer covered,' the Cockney bartender replied, accepting the five-dollar bet.

The new fellow, who was short and muscular, started running toward the *chula* team, then let the kite run its string, up, up, almost a hundred feet, and began his drive toward the imaginary goal, moving like a good quarterback breaking field, pulling the purple diamond down, maneuvering it away from the long *chula* string, then letting it out as he dodged under the threatening dragon kite. He was very good, outsmarting the team players and dipping his kite under the big dragon just as they were about to collide, hauling it in for a second and then letting it glide back up so that it brushed the larger kite for a moment before he ran on to win the match.

'Way to go, sport,' Porter yelled gleefully. He turned to the bartender and added, with smug satisfaction, 'Just take it off my tab, Gus.'

Porter loved the kite fights. He left his post every day at four-thirty, walking a mile across Bangkok's crowded streets rather than fight the noisy traffic jams, to Queen's, where he sat in the same corner table with a clear view of Sanam Luang Park and the gleaming spire of the Golden Mount atop Wat Sakhet. Porter had been stationed in Bangkok since the end of the Vietnam war, and he loved the ancient beauty of the city and particularly the Thai people, whose prevailing attitude was *Mai pen rai*, 'Never mind.' He had been a close friend of Buffalo Bill Cody's for many years, a once proper Bostonian who had, on a summer day in 1968, suddenly chucked his executive job in one of the city's larger banks, accepted Cody's offer of a commission and a spot on Buffalo Bill's Nam staff and gone off to find a purpose for his life in a place most men feared and wanted to avoid.

It was an amazing turnabout, for Porter not only quit but burned his bridges, telling the president of the bank what to do with his job and where to take it once he did it, and giving his wife who was equally appalled by his sudden decision, a variation of the same message. After ten years in the stultifying atmosphere of Back Bay and his debasing daily bank chores, which consisted mostly of disapproving loans and foreclosing on unfortunates, Saigon had been a breath of spring air to Porter. The general had even arranged an assignment for him as intelligence adviser in the embassy at Bangkok when the war fizzled out. Porter's last visit to the States had been ten years ago.

Although he was pushing fifty, Porter kept trim on the squash courts, had grown a monumental mustache, which he waxed

121

every day, and had learned the language and customs of Thailand. He had become, for all practical purposes, a native. He also adored the Old Man and considered his assignment – to keep a loose tag on Wol Pot – a privileged responsibility.

Porter was not trained in intelligence work and surveillance, but he had managed to keep up with the Thai informant, although he was getting nervous. Wol Pot had moved twice since he had first discussed the Murphy Cody affair with him. He was obviously jumpy and afraid of something. Could the Thai be stinging them? If so, how did he know about Murph Cody? Why pick him? And why had Wol Pot refused Porter's offer of protective custody in the embassy? It was obvious the man trusted no one.

He watched the fights until the shimmering fireball of the sun sank slowly behind the Golden Mount, first silhouetting the gleaming gold spire, then etching it against the scarlet sky, and finally surrendering the bell-shaped landmark to darkness. Night began to settle over Bangkok, the lights blazed on, the tourists trekked out of their hotels in pursuit of evening joys, and Windy Porter left Queen's and hurried another few blocks across town to a park called Bho Fhat across from the Sakhet temple, there to begin his nightly vigil on his customary bench, a bench well hidden by jasmine bushes.

There was no question in Porter's mind that Wol Pot was terrified of *something*. After the initial contact, he had turned rabbit. At first, he had followed a loose routine. Porter had followed him once to a junk on the river, to his nightly forays along the klongs, and the strip joints on Patpong Road and particularly to Yawaraj, the Chinese section. The little bastard was addicted to hot Chinese food. Then two days earlier Pot left his rooms and disappeared. Porter had panicked. The little weasel was the only person he knew who might lead them to Murph Cody, if Cody was alive. He had put out the word – all over Thailand – to his informants, his contacts, his friends, and had run down a few leads, which had fizzled out.

Then Porter had lucked out. A priest, a friend of Porter's for many years, heard that Porter was looking for this man, Wol Pot.

'It is probably nothing,' he said, 'but a man, no longer a youth, has joined the Wat Sakhet, and has been seen to leave the grounds every night.'

Strange behavior, since the discipline at the monastery was quite rigid though purely voluntary.

122

'When did he enter the monastery?' Porter asked.

'Only two days ago. That is why his conduct seems strange,' the priest answered.

'*Khob khun krap*,' Porter said, thanking the priest. 'May I ask you not to discipline him until I check him out?'

The priest agreed. It was a long shot, Porter thought, but certainly a clever deception if it was Wol Pot. Porter was familiar with the demands made upon neophyte monks of Theravada Buddhism. One of the most familiar sights in Thailand was the hundreds of saffron-robed *Naen* with their shaven heads wandering the streets and meditating in the city's hundreds of wats, the monasteries or temples that were the most common structures in the country. When he first came to Bangkok, Porter had found the monks an annoyance; they reminded him of the Hare Krishnas who had turned most of the airports in the United States into a bizarre distortion of the wats. But while he did not pretend to understand the mysteries of Eastern religion, he had gradually come to accept and respect these dedicated men.

During the rainy season of late summer and early fall, the ranks of these monasteries were swelled by thousands of young men. It was a tradition for them to enter the wats, sometimes for two weeks, sometimes for six months, and learn the virtues of an ascetic life free of material possessions. While there, they were obligated to adhere to 227 strict rules, abstaining from lying, idle talk, and indulgence in sex, intoxicants, luxuries and frivolous amusements. Their only possessions were the familiar saffron robe and a brass alms bowl, with which they begged the two meals a day allowed by the order. Their stay was a matter of personal dedication, nothing prevented them from leaving whenever they wished. But while they were pledged to the order, they had to adhere to its demands. At night they prayed in the wat and went to bed with the sunset, arising before dawn to go on the street with their brass bowls to seek their first meal of the day.

Since the wats were open to everyone and monks were free to travel from one to another, it was an ingenious place to hide, particularly now when so many were in the order.

That night Porter had stationed himself across from the temple with its great golden dome and waited. Sure enough, just after sunset he saw the yellow-robed monk slip out of the temple. Porter followed the little man, who trotted about a mile to Hua Lamphong, the main train station, where he

123

kept clothes in a locker. He changed in the rest room. When he emerged, dressed in a Western suit, Porter recognized him immediately as Wol Pot. The Thai took a cab and doubled back to Yawaraj, Chinese Town, where he ate dinner in a small nondescript restaurant in the old section. Having satisfied his hunger, he strolled down to Klong Phadung, one of the many canals that branch off the Mae Nam Chao Phraya, the main river that defines the western edge of the city, and there Pot negotiated a price with a tiny teenage prostitute, one of many 'water babies' who sold their wares from *hang yao*, long tail boats discreetly covered by bamboo sheds. Pot spent an hour with the young woman, then returned to the train station, switched back to his robe, and was back at the monastery by midnight.

It was a ritual with Pot, one that bored Porter, although he followed Pot every night, leaving only when the Thai was safely back in his hiding place.

Porter was a little irritated on this night, for he had hoped to turn over his nightly vigil to the new man, Hatcher. He wasn't sure he could trust Hatcher. He was Sloan's man, and Porter never liked Sloan, never liked the shadow wars he fought, breaking all the rules and operating outside what Porter felt were proper military parameters. But it was Sloan's game now, and since Hatcher had not shown yet, Porter had to continue the loose surveillance himself, making sure Pot didn't slip away into the night and vanish again, this time for good.

If Pot was coming out, he would leave the Buddhist monastery soon after the sun died. Porter lit a British 555 cigarette and waited.

The street was quiet. There was very little traffic, and the din of the city was a like a murder in Porter's ears. An elderly woman scurried up to the spirit house adjacent to the Wat Sakhet, placed a wreath of jasmine in front of the prayer station, stuck several sticks of incense in the ground and lit them. Then she clasped her hands together and swayed back and forth for several minutes, invoking the generosity of the spirits. Porter wondered what she was asking for. A healthy new grandchild? A good crop of poppies? A winning lottery ticket?

His thoughts were interrupted by the appearance of Wol Pot. A door in the side of the temple opened just wide enough for Pot to slip through. Porter killed his cigarette and watched the little man as he huddled in the shadows, looking around nervously, then started off toward the station. Porter fell in behind him, keeping far enough back so Pot would not be suspicious. He was concentrating so hard on Pot, he did not notice the other two men who fell in behind the Thai.

They were Chinese, small and wiry, dressed in the stark black shirt and pants that many Chinese affect. They followed Pot to the train station, where he changed into civilian clothes, and from there to the edge of the Yawaraj. Pot got out of the cab and strolled down cluttered Worachak Road, one of Chinese Town's main thoroughfares. As he turned and headed down into the noisy, cramped alleys of Chinese Town, the two Chinese split up, each taking one side of the street. Pot strolled down through the twisting, neon-lit alleys while the two worked both sides of the street behind him. It wasn't until Pot entered a tiny restaurant in an alley off Bowrong Street that the pair realized that Porter also was tailing Wol Pot.

One of the Chinese was in his early twenties with long blow-dried hair and a trace of a mustache. The other was older, his face scarred and angry. A sharp cut separated his right eyebrow, and the eye below it was partially closed by the same old wound. He was the leader, and it was he who spotted Porter. He had seen the husky American in front of the train station and now he saw him again, getting out of the cab just behind Pot. He nudged his partner and nodded toward the other side of the street, where Porter was checking the restaurant while mock window-shopping. When Pot was seated, Porter entered a small noodle shop across the street from the restaurant, found a seat near the front window, and ordered something to eat while he kept an eye on the Thai.

The two Chinese became as interested in Porter as they were in Pot. They decided to split up again, the younger one following the American while Split-eye stayed with the Thai. They had just begun following Wol Pot that day and were not familiar with his nightly habits. But Split-eye had little respect for him. Pot had successfully eluded them and found a perfect hiding place, then blown it all by going into Chinatown to eat, the most likely place in the city for him to be recognized. Now it looked as if the American had also blown Pot's cover. The Thai was smart, but he also appeared to be stupidly reckless.

125

When Pot left the restaurant, he started a small parade. Split-eye, Porter and the young Chinese all hailed cabs and followed him.

Pot walked along the crowded bank of the canal, ignoring the flower women and floating trinket shops, checking out the young girls in the big tail boats, flirting, joking, negotiating. He obviously enjoyed bartering for sex.

I like it, thought Split-eye. What they needed was a *hang yao*. It would be a perfect setup for the hit. All they had to do was distract the American.

'We must create a diversion,' Split-eye told his young partner. 'I will get a *yao*. After the Thai has started his business, pick the American's pocket. But do not be too good. The American must feel it. Start a commotion and keep him arguing until I finish the Thai. When that distracts him, come to the boat. We will leave by the river.'

Split-eye hurried through the crowds along the canal bank until he found a small river taxi that was free. The driver, wrinkled beyond his years, was sitting in the back nibbling on a piece of chicken. Split-eye climbed into the boat and told the oarsman to take him to the other side of the klong. He sat in the rear seat of the long, slender craft as it glided out into the dark canal. When they were alone in the darkness of the canal, Split-eye drew a dagger and struck the oarsman just below his ribs on the left side. It was a perfect hit. The oarsman's eyes bulged, his mouth gaped but not a sound came out, and he slumped straight down on the seat. The knife had gone up under the ribs into his heart. The Chinese grabbed the back of the dead oarsman's shirt, stretched him facedown on the floor of the boat and threw a blanket over him. Then he turned the boat back toward shore, searching the crowded bank for Wol Pot.

Pot strolled through the crowds, continuing his lighthearted bartering. The boats were tied three and four deep along the bank of the klong and there was a great deal of yelling and bargaining between the water babies and the tourists and locals on shore. Then Pot spotted the young beauty. She was less eager than the rest. Her *hang yao* was separated from the pier by two others. She stood with her legs slightly spread on the back of the boat, her arms crossed over her chest, staring defiantly at the tourists and locals who crowded the canal bank. Her white cotton pants hugged her thighs, and she turned slightly so he could see her firm buttocks outlined by the flimsy cotton.

Pot was entranced. Ah, he thought, she is not only beautiful, she has spirit. This could be an interesting encounter.

126

He took out a red hundred-baht note and held it over his head. She saw him, squinted her eyes as she focused on the bill, then shook her head. Pot was surprised, having thought his offer was a generous one. He took out a five-hundred-baht purple and held it up. The girl pondered, then held her hands apart, palms facing, and slowly closed them. Pot thought for a moment, then held up both the purple and the red. She nodded. The deal was struck.

Windy Porter watched Wol Pot cross the two boats to the *hang yao* of his newly acquired 'water baby'. They stood on the deck for a moment, talking back and forth, until finally the girl took the two bills and led Pot into the thatched cabin in the rear of the boat.

If he was true to form, Pot would be in there for about half an hour. At first Porter paid little attention to the *hang yao* that slid through the water and bumped gently against one of the other two boats. The oarsman walked swiftly down the length of his boat and tied it to the first. He went aboard the *hang yao* he was tied to and started talking to the prostitute who operated it. Some money changed hands. Porter became suspicious. The oarsman was nodding toward Pot's floating brothel. Porter sensed something was wrong. He brushed rudely past a young Chinese who was walking toward him, clambered down onto the boat, and started after the oarsman. The young Chinese, startled by how quickly he had moved, stared for a moment before following him.

Inside the small thatched covering on the boat, the young prostitute had begun her seduction. She had taken off Pot's shirt and pants and then stripped off her own blouse. Her almond breasts brushed his chest, teasing him, then she reached down and began to stroke him, to bring him to life. She placed a hand on his chest and gently forced him to lie down on a straw mattress on the deck. Pot was lost in ecstasy, unaware of the drama being played out twenty feet away. He did not feel the *hang yao* rock slightly as Split-eye cautiously started to come aboard.

Porter jogged across the first boat as Split-eye began to board Pot's *hang yao*.

'Hey!' Porter yelled, rushing up behind him. The man turned. His ruined eye dodged crazily in its socket. His hand flashed under his sleeve and Porter saw the gleam of a dagger in his hand as the Chinese lunged toward him.

'Jesus!' Porter yelled. As the Chinese made his thrust Porter sidestepped and felt the blade nick his shirt; he grabbed the man's wrist and twisted it outward. Split-eye was thrown off-balance. The knife spun out of his hand and, as he turned sideways, he tripped over the gunwale and lunged backward into the river.

An instant later Porter felt a stabbing pain as a cold sliver of steel invaded him, slicing deep into the small of his back. He turned and was face-to-face with the young Chinese. The youth's arm arced again, but Porter spun away and the knife slashed his side. Behind him, Split-eye rose out of the river. His hands wrapped around the gunwale of the *hang yao* and he pulled himself out of the water with one lunge, stepped into the boat and grabbed his stiletto off the deck.

Porter was too busy to feel or hear anything. He slammed an enormous fist into the young Chinese's face, felt his nose shatter, heard his muffled cry of pain. He brought his knee up sharply into the man's groin, and the assailant jackknifed and fell on his knees. Behind him, Split-eye very deliberately and with no particular haste stuck the point of his dagger in the base of Porter's neck, severed the nerve to his brain and paralyzed him.

Porter turned, stricken, and stared blankly at Split-eye, his arms dropped to his sides and dangled uselessly there. Split-eye struck again, bringing the dagger up in a short, hard arc, and burying it to the hilt in Porter's side. The big man felt very little. He was aware that something was inside him, aware that it was coursing upward deep into his chest. Then his heart collapsed and his eyes rolled up. Split-eye pulled the knife out and slammed into the big American, knocking him sideways into the river.

Pot heard the commotion, felt the *hang yao* begin to rock, heard a woman scream, then another. He was struck suddenly with fear, like an electric shock flashing through every nerve. He jumped up, scrambled for his pants, then heard a tremendous splash. He crawled on his hands and knees and peered out of the thatched room in time to see the young Chinese stab Porter, watched in horror as Split-eye rose out of the river, attacked the big man and knocked him over the side. Split-eye turned toward Wol Pot, his good eye glittering with evil.

Pot was struck with terror. He twisted, rolled over the side of the *hang yao* in his shorts, and dropped into the black water.

Onshore, the shock of the brief, violent drama was wearing off, but there was still a great deal of shouting. Split-eye knew the Thai had escaped him again. He grabbed his young partner by the shirt front, shoved him into the *hang yao* he had commandeered, and turned back to the young whore. He shoved her into the seclusion of the thatched cabin and held the point of the blade to her throat.

'Where does he live?' his voice hissed.

She shook her head but was too frightened to speak.

'Where do I find Thai Horse?' he demanded.

'Who?' she stammered.

The assassin could tell she knew nothing.

'Speak to the police and I will come back and carve your face until you look like a grandmother,' he said and, jumping into the *hang yao*, raced off into the darkness.

HOOCHGIRL

Hatcher was watching from the observation room as the Navy fighters streaked like silver dragonflies over the Pacific Ocean and landed at the NAS. An F-16 banked sharply into its final approach, caught the morning sun on its gleaming surface for an instant, then leveled off, its wheels dropping and locking in place a few seconds before the big fighter's tires screeched on the runway.

The bullet-shaped plane glided smoothly to its hardstand and stopped, and the pilot emerged from the cockpit. He was a diminutive man, tiny in every way – short, skinny and small-boned – who seemed dwarfed by the helmet, the parachute harness, the Mae West, even his crew chief, who loomed over him like a giant. The pilot came down the ladder and spoke with the chief for a few minutes, then walked around the perimeter of the fighter, pointing here and there. Quite a difference from Cody's other wingman, Hugh Fraser, whom Hatcher had interviewed the night before in Seattle. The pilot seemed to make up for his size with kinetic bursts of energy while the chief strolled along behind him, taking half as many steps, looking bored and nodding constant agreement with whatever the pilot was telling him.

Hatcher knew it would be another ten or fifteen minutes before the flier was through with the postflight check. He left a message with the officer in charge of the flight line and walked a block down the neatly mowed and trimmed street to the Officers' Club. Inside, he stood at the doorway to the club room. He had been in this room once before, eighteen years ago. As far as he could remember, it had not changed a bit. Even the tables appeared to be in the same place. The oak-paneled room gleamed and smelled of lemon polish and floor wax. The walls were lined with photographs of men who had served there and gone on to other places: fresh, clean-cut, neatly trimmed, eager young men in dress whites, smiling innocently for eternity. The Navy never changed. Part of the allure of the service was a sense of security in knowing that even the furniture polish was a tradition. For Hatcher there was sadness in this room, which in a few hours would come alive with the ring of raised glasses and toasts and songs to the glory of the corps.

He walked around the empty dance floor, his shoes making hollow clacking sounds on the hardwood floors. It was ironic that the ghost of Murph Cody had brought him back to this place, to this very room where a friendship that had endured hardship and mockery, good times and bad, and had been bonded by promises of loyalty and respect had ended so rudely. In this very room Cody had terminated that comradeship as finally as a bullet to the heart terminates life.

Hatcher had come to the party filled with anticipation and excitement. He had not seen Murph since his friend's marriage almost a year earlier. He arrived expecting a rowdy reunion.

Instead, he was humiliated and disgraced by the unpredictable Cody in a manner that in other times would have called for a gloved slap across the face and satisfaction with a choice of weapons at dawn. Hatcher would never forget the cold sneer, the harshness of the words, spoken loud enough to stop every conversation in the room. Cody had handed Hatcher a glass of champagne, and holding it up in what was to become a mock toast, he said, 'Here's to a maggot who is still a maggot. Here's to a maggot who was fed and clothed and housed by the service and taught by her and who now has turned his back on her. Here's to a maggot I once called friend who's running out because there's a war on. Here's to a coward.' And had poured his glass of wine on the bar and turned and walked away. Pledged to the secrecy of the Shadow Brigade, Hatcher had no response. Every eye in the room had followed Cody out the door.

A harsh memory for a room where heroes normally frolicked.

'I'm Commander Schwartz, you looking – for me?'

130

Hatcher turned to face the pilot. In person, Schwartz seemed even smaller than he had from a distance. He spoke very quickly and with a peculiar kind of staccato rhythm, pausing in the wrong places and accenting his words on the wrong syllables, like a man avoiding a chronic stutter. His helmet and goggles had left ridges under his eyes and his short-cropped hair was matted like an ink-blot to his skull. He did not look like the head of flight training at one of the Navy's major bases. He looked more like a college whiz kid.

'Commander Hatcher,' Hatcher lied, offering his hand, 'Navy Review Board.'

'What did – I do now?' Schwartz asked with a relaxed grin. He struck Hatcher as just the opposite of Simmons. Other than being an apparent case of permanent hypertension, Schwartz didn't seem to have a care in the world.

'We're just wrapping up some hangnails,' Hatcher whispered. 'You know how the Navy is.'

'After eighteen years I ought to,' Schwartz answered. 'Can we do this over a sandwich? I'm starving.'

After they had ordered hamburgers and beer, Schwartz asked 'This about An Khe, Hanoi or Cody?'

'That's quite a selection,' Hatcher growled.

'I was shot down near An Khe,' Schwartz said, 'I was a prisoner for almost four years in Hanoi, and I was one of Cody's wingmen. I've been asked a lot about all three.'

'This is about Cody,' Hatcher whispered.

'Look,' the little man said, 'I know you're not with the board. Hugh Fraser called me last night. He checked Washington right after you talked to him. Far as the Navy's concerned, the Cody affair is closed. They never heard of you.'

Before Hatcher could say anything, Schwartz held up his hand. 'I don't see there's any security involved here,' he said. 'Anything I could tell you is in the record anyway. What's this all about?'

Hatcher decided to tell Schwartz just enough to keep him interested and talking.

'I'd like you to keep part of this confidential,' Hatcher said, stalling a little to get his thoughts regrouped.

'That depends,' Schwartz said warily.

'You know his father was General Cody?'

'Of course.'

'Cody's dying of cancer. It's not public knowledge at this point and he'd like to keep it that way until it leaks to the media.'

'How much time does he have?' Schwartz asked, obviously stunned and genuinely sorry at hearing the news.

'Maybe six months.'

'Shit!'

'The thing is, the old man's never been satisfied that Cody was killed,' Hatcher croaked. 'So they asked me to do one last check, just for the old man. I worked intelligence for him in Nam.'

'What is it you want to know?' he asked.

'I'm kind of interested in the man. Did you like Cody?' Hatcher asked.

Whereas Harley Simmons and Hugh Fraser had been reluctant to talk, Hatcher couldn't stop Schwartz. The little man babbled away as though Hatcher had pushed his talk button.

'Sure, I like him okay,' Schwartz started, then he paused a moment, rethinking the question. 'Well, look, it wasn't a question of did you *like* him, Murph wasn't the buddy-buddy type, y'know. He was, uh . . .'

'Standoffish?' Hatcher offered.

'Standoffish. That's good,' Schwartz said.

'When I talked to Hugh Fraser, he gave me the idea Cody was some kind of suicidal war lover leading his men to certain death.'

'See, Fraser was always a pretty bitter guy,' said Schwartz. 'His accident didn't help any.'

'What happened, exactly?' Hatcher asked.

'He was making his approach to the *Forrestal*, flamed out on his final, had to ditch. Broke his back. That's a real irony, y'know, all he ever wanted was carrier duty. Glamour city.'

'Yeah, but the Cody thing was long before that.'

'Y'see, Fraser was a jet jockey, he dreamed the carrier dream,' said Schwartz. 'The Brown Water Navy definitely wasn't his idea of big-time war duty.'

'Brown Water Navy?' Hatcher asked. It was a term with which he was not familiar.

'That's what they called our outfit,' Schwartz explained. 'We were the only inland squadron in the Navy. We were there mostly to support the Riverine Patrol Forces, covering river convoys, that kind of diddy-bopping shit, but what we really did was support ground movements. It was rotten duty. I suppose there's an element of truth in what Fraser says. We had big losses. But suicidal? Never. That's bullshit.' Schwartz thought for a minute then went on, 'I'll tell you, it

132

was like he didn't want to get too close to anybody, Cody I mean. No favorites. What we were doing, that was the worst, and Cody's outfit had – a reputation for doing the meanest jobs and working the longest hours. Nobody wanted to go to his outfit.'

'Did you fear going there?'

'Yeah, sure. But it was, uh, because of the unexpected, so much talk, y'know. Apprehension.'

'Okay.'

'Anyway, Murph really pushed hard, man, like seven days a week, day, night, around the clock, bad weather, night stuff, you name it. He was like, uh, crazy to get the war over with. Don't get me wrong, he went out there just like everybody else. I'd guess Murph flew more individual sorties than any other man in the outfit.'

Hatcher's mind wandered back to the night before and his meeting in Seattle with Hugh Fraser, Cody's other wingman, who had quite a different impression of Cody. At first, Fraser had refused to talk to Hatcher. His crash had left him a pitiful cripple. He walked in a crouch, like an old man, and breath spray could not hide the sickening, end-of-the-day smell of vodka, nor could Visine wash away the broken blood vessels in his eyes. Because Fraser had refused to take Hatcher's calls, Hatcher had waited for him in the parking lot of one of the small satellite buildings clustered around Seattle-Tacoma International where Fraser was vice president of a small charter airline. Hatcher felt sorry for the man. He had obviously aged considerably since his accident. He was vitriolic, like a grouchy old man, and in the conversation that was occasionally interrupted by one of the big commercial jets taking off, he lashed out with each question.

'Would you like to hear what Fraser had to say?' Hatcher asked Schwartz. He took a small recorder from his pocket and pressed the play button.

Fraser: I'm a busy man. You have five minutes.

Hatcher: I just want to talk a little about Murph –

Fraser: Who'd you say you were with?

Hatcher: Navy Review Board. We –

Fraser: God damn Navy.

Hatcher: – just want to close this thing out once and for all.

Fraser: So what can I tell you that you don't know already?

133

Hatcher: You saw Cody go down, isn't that – ?

Fraser: I told you boys all this before.

Hatcher: One more time for the wrap-up.

Fraser: (Sighing) I was flying off his port side, half a mile behind him. I heard his Mayday and saw him barrel-roll in.

Hatcher: Any chance he got out?

Fraser: (Skeptically) C'mon. He set half the Mekong Delta on fire.

Hatcher: I got one report says he may – (there was a pause while a jet roared over) have got out of the plane and made a run for –

Fraser: Whoever told you that's crazy.

Hatcher: How would you rate him? As an officer, I mean.

Fraser: First-class asshole trying to impress his old man. He loved war, a typical career officer. He ate it up with a spoon. He didn't give a damn what happened to his men.

Hatcher: Oh . . . (the rest of the comment was obscured by another jet)

Fraser: (partially inaudible) . . . Army brat. Annapolis man, big-shot father. Never drank with the guys, never hung out. He had this hoochgirl, a real beauty. You know, perfect skin, perfect teeth, those limpid eyes you could take a swim in. She waited on him like a slave. When he wasn't flying, he was laid up with this hoochgirl balling all day.

Hatcher: Well, hoochgirls were a dime a –

Fraser: This one was a real piece, I'll tell you that. Couldn't have been more than fifteen, sixteen. Eyes for him, nobody else. He treated that stinking slope like she was his wife, like family for Chrissake. God damn Nam hoochgirl.

Hatcher: What happened to her?

Fraser: When he bought it, everybody in the outfit moved on her – but she wasn't having any. Next day, she was gone. Vanished. Like Puff the fucking Magic Dragon. (Pause) Listen, the son of a bitch got more men killed than the Vietcong.

Hatcher: You mean doing his job?

Fraser: There's doing it and there's doing it. He was a maniac, you ask me. 'Get it in the gutter, get it in the gutter!' he'd scream. Christ, we were . . . (Another pause while a jet took off) flying down tunnels as it was. Lost

134

half our planes to ground fire. Shit, we blitzed some Charlie, burned some boats, whacked out some villages. Next day they were right back. Like stepping in a puddle, you take your foot out and never know it was there. All those guys gone for that.'

Hatcher: C'mon, nobody goes into combat expecting room service and the Holiday Inn.

Fraser: He was like all those military academy grunts. All they care about is looking good on the record so they'll be sure to make admiral before they retire. Listen, do you think you'd be here now if Cody wasn't a general's son.

Hatcher: (Pause) No.

Hatcher snapped the machine off.

'Well, hell, we were all crazy as loons after a few weeks on the line with him,' Schwartz said. 'I mean, we were dragging the gutter every time out. I used to come back with tree limbs stuck in my wings. But Cody didn't like it, Hugh's wrong, Murph wasn't any war lover, quite the opposite. It ate him up, sending all those guys out there day after day. He knew most of us were jet pilots who hated fighting a ground war in those old De Havillands. They were just . . . twin-engine crates loaded down with hardware – Gatlings, a twenty mike-mike in the nose, four fifty-caliber machine guns, cluster bombs. But we flat tore up the fucking Mekong Delta. Trouble was, everybody had a bullet with his name on it. We were flying so much, sooner or later it had to be your turn. Our losses were running sixty, sixty-five percent, about – a third of them MIA or POW. You can understand why Cody's outfit wasn't considered Shangri-la by the flyboys.'

A steward brought their lunch and Schwartz attacked his hamburger with animal fervor.

'God was good to me in one respect,' he said, his mouth half full, 'I don't grow any taller when I eat a lot, but I don't get any fatter either.' He took another bite. 'What happened to Fraser, it gets to me a little. I'll tell you something, I may have done four years' hard time but I'm lucky.'

'That's a generous attitude,' Hatcher whispered hoarsely.

'Reality,' Schwartz said.

'What happened the day Cody bought the farm?' Hatcher's grinding voice asked.

Schwartz didn't have to think about it, the scene was still fresh in his mind after all the years. It had been raining that

135

morning and Cody was jumpy. There were reports of Charlie activity upriver and the infantry was asking for help. As soon as the weather lifted, Cody called a scramble. They went off so fast, Cody had to give them the coordinates of the ground action after they were airborne. They had made two passes, dropping cluster bombs along the river's edge, then suddenly he heard Cody's 'Mayday!'

At first Cody didn't seem to be in trouble. His De H. was a half mile in front of Schwartz. Then Schwartz saw the plane begin to weave. Its one wing dipped and began to crumble. He's taken an RFG or some kind of rocket, Schwartz thought, and then: My God, he's going in, as he watched the cumbersome plane begin to dive toward the green blanket below. Schwartz dipped his nose and began raking the woods in front of Cody's plane, blasting a path with twenty millimeters and fifty calibers. Jesus, Schwartz thought, all he needs is about five hundred yards and he's got the river and, on the other side, friendly country. Come on, come on, Schwartz repeated to himself as he continued to riddle the forest in front of the stricken plane. Then the scratchy voice over the radio, ' . . . I'm going in . . .' and suddenly the plane rolled over like a large animal dying, and almost flopped into the trees. The green carpet streaked beneath Schwartz, and as he pulled over the shattered wreck of the De Havilland and swept out over the river, he saw an SAR Huey below him heading toward the crash site, then the jungle seemed to erupt. A geyser of fire shot up from the wreckage and he felt the wave of the explosion wash over him. He banked sharply trying to circle back, then heard the voice of the Huey pilot, 'Corkscrew, this is Rescue one . . . We lost him. . . .'

' . . . Anyway, I overflew him and started to peel around and I saw this SAR Huey coming up the river and then the plane blew,' Schwartz said, finishing his story.

'How long after he crashed?' Hatcher asked.

'Long enough for me to maybe do a one eighty.'

'Long enough for him to maybe get out?' Hatcher whispered.

'Murph?'

'Yeah.'

Schwartz shrugged. 'Sure, I guess so. I disagree with Fraser – the notion Cody may have gotten out of the plane isn't crazy.'

136

Hatcher nibbled at his soup, then asked, 'How did his girlfriend take it?' he whispered.

'Inscrutably, the way hoochgirls always did. Hugh's a little off-base there, too. The bottom line is, Cody didn't like Fraser. Or maybe he sensed Fraser didn't like him. Whatever, Fraser was never invited to join Cody.'

'And the rest of you were?'

Schwartz nodded. 'Hell, I'd go over there every once in a while, she'd cook up dinner for a couple of us. Viet shit, it was great.'

'Does the expression "Thai Horse" mean anything to you?' Hatcher asked.

'You mean heroin?'

'Does it mean anything else to you?'

'Nope. What's that got to –'

'Did Cody have a drug problem?'

Schwartz looked shocked. 'You gotta be kidding. Murph Cody? Cody didn't even smoke. Where are you going with this?'

'No place, just touching all the bases.'

The question about Thai Horse and dope had upset Schwartz, made him suddenly wary.

Hatcher quickly changed the subject. 'Tell me more about the girl.'

Schwartz hesitated, still suspicious, but his obvious respect for Cody won over. He began to relax again. 'Y'know, in a funny kind of way I think maybe Murph was in love with Pai.'

'Pai?'

'Yeah. I think what it was, he was kinda proud of her, was showing her off.'

He sat strangely quiet for a minute or two, sipping his beer, then he said, 'You know, I went down three weeks later. Just – north of Binh Thuy. The first four, five months I was a prisoner, we were in transit camps. They just, like, y'know, moved us around a lot. Then finally they took us to Hanoi. Anyway, I heard rumors about this camp over in Laos. It was like a mobile unit, y'know, and they supposedly had a big shot over there.'

'What kind of big shot?'

'That's it, a big shot. I heard everything from Westmoreland to Bob Hope. You know how rumors are. Anyway, until they took us north, I heard about this camp all the time.

137

They called it, uh, Huie-kui, the spirit camp, I guess because it – seemed to disappear all the time.'

'It wasn't uncommon for them to move their camps around.'

'I know. It never occurred to me before, I always assumed he was dead, but maybe the celebrity was Murph.'

'Do me a favor, will you, Commander? Keep this under your hat. If Cody is alive, give me a chance to find him.'

Schwartz stared hard at Hatcher and then slowly nodded. 'He deserves that.'

Hatcher's thoughts went back to the hoochgirl. 'Did you like his girl?' Hatcher asked.

'Are you kidding? She made Natalie Wood look like Porky Pig.' Schwartz paused for a minute and then said, 'Would you like to see her? I got a picture of her in my scrapbook.'

On the way to the airport, Hatcher's pulse began racing, his nerves humming. Forty-eight hours before, the whole notion that Murph Cody was still alive had seemed like a big joke to Hatcher. Now there was a question in his mind. When Hatcher was studying criminal detection, Sloan, his mentor, had once said, 'Don't ever trust written reports. When it's in writing, people tend to make themselves look good.'

It had cost him forty-eight hours to run that theory, but he was glad he had. He thought about the three men he had interviewed, each with a different view of Cody, each affected in a different way by his own role in the events of that fateful day when Murphy Cody had disappeared.

To Schwartz, Cody was a hero doing a dirty job; to Fraser, a war-loving madman; to Simmons, a haunting ghost whose cold fist squeezed Simmons's heart. To Fraser, escape from the flaming wreckage of Cody's plane was impossible; to Schwartz, it was a toss-up; to Simmons, it was a reality.

And, too, there was Schwartz's report of this ghost camp, Huie-kui. Could that be the reason Cody had never turned up? Had he been a prisoner for all those years? And if so, how did he get out?

There was one other thing that gnawed at Hatcher's brain. If Murphy Cody had died, where had Wol Pot, the Thai, come up with his name? Wol Pot had a lot of questions to answer.

There was only one thing on which Fraser and Schwartz

seemed to agree – that Pai, Cody's hoochgirl, was special. Looking at the photograph Schwartz had given him, Hatcher had to agree. It was a colour photograph, dog-eared and faded. In the picture, Cody was standing in front of his thatched hooch, his arm around a small, almond-colored beauty, her chin down, staring mystically up at the camera. She looked almost childlike. But while her body was the body of a young girl, her eyes seemed to reflect some inner knowledge that was far beyond her years. Hatcher stared at those eyes, felt them connect, could almost see them blink. He put the photograph back in his wallet.

He looked at his watch. In twelve hours he would be in Bangkok. He hoped Windy Porter would have a lot of answers for him. He had no way of knowing that at almost that same moment Windy Porter was dying in the dark waters of the Phadung Klong, four thousand miles away.

BOOK
TWO

A good man who thinks he's in the right and keeps on a-comin' is hard to bring down.

—*A TEXAS RANGER*

STORK

The stork's legs were four feet long from its knees to the soles of its feet. It bobbed through the crowd and every move was perfect. The four-foot stilts lifted the surreal bird a foot above the rest of the bizarre crowd, which it stalked, chin out, butt out, butt in, chin in, a rainbow-hued spray of feathers sprinkled with glitter bursting from its yellow bustle, its face painted white, its lips exaggerated and bright yellow, vertical blue streaks painted from its forehead through its eyes all the way down to its chin, a wig of bright blue feathers sweeping straight back from its forehead, its body encased in a yellow feathered body stocking. There was no way to tell whether the person encased in the costume was male or female.

Surrounding it was an eerie assortment of other surreal creatures, their heads jogging in waves to the Eurythmics' 'Would I Lie to You Baby,' which thundered from a dozen monster speakers. Spinning spears of flashing strobe lights augered down from the ceiling. Below the clear lucite dance floor, a six-foot Mako shark circled in its tank, agitated by the beat.

The Annual Critter Ball had attracted its biggest crowd yet to Split Personality – known as the Split – Atlanta's environment club, a fancy name for a disco. In the balcony, Spears and Hedritch surveyed the crowd dubiously. In a roomful of bizarre people, they stood out by the very nature of their normalcy, dressed as they were in dark blue suits, even though they had taken off their ties and opened their shirt collars.

'Christ, this is absolutely insane,' said Spears, the taller of the two, a six-footer, blond and square-jawed, with the look of a forty-year-old surfer. Hedritch was five foot nine with balding dark hair, a neck the size of a tire and big ears. Very big ears.

'Let's call it off,' Hedrich said, looking around the supercharged dance floor. 'We don't need this shit.'

'You don't call off Campon and you know it,' Spears replied. 'He does whatever the hell he wants.'

'This goes way beyond a security risk,' Hedritch snapped nervously.

'So what's new? Let's give him the bad news. Maybe he'll take our advice for a change.'

'Yeah, sure he will,' Hedritch answered.

They turned and went back through the crowd to the balcony entrance. The stork's eyes, glittering, watched them all the way.

Outside, the line waiting for entry through the magic portals of the club snaked halfway around the block. The black stretch limo sat in front of the door. Spears and Hedritch got in the backseat; the sweet smell of marijuana permeated the interior. General Héctor Campon was leaning in the corner dressed in full military regalia, three rows of ribbons twinkling from the breast of the dark blue uniform, the joint glowing between his finger-tips. His dark glasses swung slowly toward the two men.

'Well?' his Spanish-accented voice asked.

'Bad news,' said Hedritch. 'The place is wall-to-wall crazies in costume. You can't hear a word. The stage and dance floor are back-lit with strobes.'

'A security nightmare,' Spears added.

'Ridiculous,' Campon answered, sitting up, 'you *caballeros* need to grow bigger *cojones*.'

Spears mimed the words to himself. He had heard the line often enough. Big balls was Campon's answer to every crisis.

'General,' he said, 'this is the worst yet. You go in there, we can't guarantee anything.'

'Your job is to protect me, not bore me with your problems,' he snapped. 'Driver! The door.'

Six men had been guarding Campon since he escaped from Madalena three months earlier. Spears and Hedritch headed the third team that had worked the trick. Three weeks in Fort Lauderdale and Campon was bored. Two weeks in St Louis and he was bored. He had lasted a month and a half in Chicago, and now for two weeks he had been living in a houseboat on Lake Lanier, fifty miles north of Atlanta. Actually it was just as well; moving around like that made it harder to get a fix on him. The security force of ten comprised Campon's four bodyguards and the Americans. What was needed to guard a reckless bastard like General Campon was a small army.

'Six men to cover the insanity inside,' Spears mumbled as they followed Campon out of the car to where he stood like a ramrod, waiting for his entourage to get in position. He was over six feet tall, making him an easy target, and with the medals on his chest there was no way to miss him.

Campon was hotter than boiling water. The president was browbeating everyone in Congress to approve a $50 million appropriation to back Campon's planned overthrow of the leftist

144

government that had deposed him. Campon was biding his time, lobbying influential friends with phone calls by day, raising hell every night, while his army, or what was left of it, was cooling its heels across the border in a neighboring country. To throw off his enemies, the Feds had leaked lies to the press: that the general was supposed to be in the Bahamas; that he had moved on to Canada; that he was hiding out on a ranch in the Far West.

At times Spears and Hedritch felt like Campon's pimps, rounding up women, checking their backgrounds, paying for his sex and for secrecy. But this behavior, appearing in public this way, was a violation of all the rules.

So, what else was new? Hedritch ordered two of his men to go in ahead and work the stage at the back of the dance floor. The other two he sent to the balcony. Spears looked around the shopping center, checking the rooftops, while Hedritch checked out the line. Hell, thought Spears, if they want to get him, they're going to get him. But they were sure they had not been followed, and that reduced the odds a little. They moved to the door.

'Names?' asked the king of the portals.

'Campon,' the general said.

The doorman's finger ran down the list and stopped. 'Yes, sir, General,' he said, unsnapping the red cord.

Spears looked at Hedritch with panic as the entourage moved into the club.

'Did he make a reservation?' Hedritch asked incredulously.

'Yes, sir, yesterday,' the doorman answered.

'Shit!' he snapped as they rushed after the general. They caught up with him as Campon was about to enter the main room, a sprawling semicircle of tables crowding up to the dance floor.

'General, at least go upstairs, please,' pleaded Hedritch. 'You can see better from up there and we can cruise the room a lot easier.'

'The action's down here,' Campon answered curtly, following his four beefy men into the club. Spears and Hedritch trotted along behind him, looking frantically, futilely, around the club as the deposed dictator walked to the edge of the dance floor where he stood watching the madness. He was a stationary target.

'Shit city,' Spears yelled in Hedritch's ear, 'keep your head on a swivel.'

The general's gaze swept the dance floor, stopping once on a woman dressed like a giraffe with her bosom swelling over the top of her striped costume. Beyond her, on the far side of the floor, the yellow stork jerked weirdly through the crowd, blurred by the flashing lights. It raised its yellow-feathered wings and turned in a slow circle, bobbing to the beat of the music. Campon laughed and applauded the stork, although it was hard to see it because of the lights flashing in his face.

The stork's alert eyes checked the general's entourage, the two men in the balcony, the two men behind it on the stage, as it turned slowly, making a 360-degree survey of the club. The stork was so bizarre, so visible, the security men ignored it.

Campon clapped his hands again and chuckled gleefully at the spectacle. It was the last sound he ever uttered.

Well concealed amid the feathered wings attached to its arms, the stork held a silenced mini-Uzi. Only a foot long and weighing six pounds, the submachine gun held a thirty-two-round clip and was equipped with a plastic cup to catch the casings. The stork was an expert. It squeezed off three three-round bursts, watching in the slow-motion flashes of the strobes as the rounds splattered into their target. Campon's head jerked forward as the first three rounds exploded in his chest; his arms swung out in front of him and then he arched backward as two more rounds ripped into his head. The third struck a waiter behind him in the spine and took down two of the bodyguards.

Spears and Hedritch were caught totally by surprise as Campon seemed suddenly to have a seizure. The music continued to thunder. One of the bodyguards spun around and fell against Hedritch.

Oh my God, it's happening! Hedritch thought.

The stork swung its feathered arms in a slow arc and sent another burst into the crowd. A young woman and her date spun around as the bullets ripped them. She screamed. Somebody else joined the scream. Nobody was aware yet of what was happening. Then suddenly the woman yelled, 'I'm shot!'

Pandemonium.

The second attack created more confusion in the room.

The security men had no idea where the shots were coming from. They saw the young couple fifty feet away go down. The girl started screaming. Campon was on the floor on his back staring up into the darkness above. Guns appeared in the security men's hands. Hedritch dropped over Campon, felt his throat for a pulse. The screams swept the room like a hurricane blowing through. There was a rush for the door. A table went

146

down. Glasses broke. Panic seemed to explode like a bomb in the room.

The men on the stage jumped into the crowd and raced toward the general's group. In the balcony the other two men stared down at the figure of the general. In the confusion nobody could tell where the shots came from.

The stork sat down on the stage, pulled off the stilts and whirled behind one of the big speakers. It snapped the back open, dropped stilts and gun into the speaker casing and snapped it shut, then dashed through a nearby fire door. It led to a catacomb of tunnels below the dance floor. As the stork bolted down the stairs, it pulled off the wig and stripped off the wings. It ran to a small door that led to a room full of electrical equipment. The stork jumped inside, still undressing. It peeled off the yellow body stocking, grabbed a garbage bag secreted behind an electrical panel and began stuffing the feathers into it. In seconds the stork was transformed into a young man in jeans and a blue T-shirt. He took a towel soaked in cold cream from the garbage bag and wiped his face clean. Then he rushed down the labyrinth of corridors and back up another set of stairs. When he reached the top, he opened the door a crack and looked into the kitchen. The employees were crowded at the end of the large stainless steel room, peering into the main room.

'My God,' one of the cooks said, 'somebody's been shot!'

The assassin slipped into the kitchen, stuffed the garbage bag into a large can, slipped a dolly under it and wheeled it out the back door. The chaos had not spread outside yet. He shoved the garbage can among a dozen others, took a quick look at his watch, and walked off into the darkness.

Three and a half minutes. Not bad.

THE HIT

The big, stocky black guy turned off Suriwong Road and headed through Patpong toward Tombstone. At nightfall the city of Bangkok was transformed, as if by some perverse genie, from a frantic, crowded, noisy business hub into a blazing neon jungle. Topless tigresses stalked the jungle, performing in nightclubs, whorehouses, massage parlors and storefronts. Promising everything and delivering a great deal of what it promised, the frenetic section known as Patpong exemplified the attitude, catering, in a bizarre distortion of American rowdiness, to European and U.S. tourists. Patpong was for the *farang*, the foreigners, who flocked to the area every night seeking out the legendary sexy naughtiness of Bangkok as part of their 'Thailand experience.'

Except for an occasional 'Hey,' the big man ignored the pimps, barkers and ladies. Most of them knew him anyway. He passed Jack's American Star and the San Francisco Bar, where topless go-go dancers performed special 'shows,' and turned down a side street, away from the neon glare, the bellowing loudspeakers and the hawkers. It was not a dim street, but it was more Phoenix than New Orleans. Were it not for the signs printed in both English and Thai and the nature of the buildings themselves with their characteristic Thai architecture, this section called Tombstone might have been mistaken for a street in any Western American town. The only thing missing was dirt streets and hitching posts. In fact one establishment did have a hitching post on the edge of the sidewalk.

There was a store that featured traditional Western clothing, including Tony Lama boots and Stetson hats; a restaurant called Yosemite Sam's, whose menu consisted of barbecue, Brunswick stew and ribs; the Stagecoach Deli, which, although more West Side New York than Western, had swinging doors and an imitation Tiffany window. It might be argued that Langtry's Music Hall, with its naked Thai and Chinese dancers, was more Patpong than Tombstone, but it too catered to the Western motif that dominated the street. There were old posters of Lillie Langtry and Eddie Foy beside the color glossies of its star attractions. The entrance was straight out of a John Ford movie.

Across the street was Pike's Peak, an ice cream parlor whose decor was perhaps more turn-of-the-century than Western, and the Roundup, a twenty-four-hour corral-styled cafeteria specializing in coffee, doughnuts and eggs. The tiny hundred-seat movie house that was next on the block was called the Palace and played old double features, everything from classics to B flicks from the thirties, four shows a day, and changed programs every Tuesday and Friday.

And there was the Longhorn, as Western as a bar could get. It sported the one hitching post on the street. A rowdy Texan had once tied his rental car to the post and, hours later and several drinks drunker, had forgotten and driven off, taking the front of the place with him. Sweets Wilkie, the proprietor, had settled for a thousand dollars and repaired it himself for $346.

On this night Wilkie was in heaven, his gold tooth glittering from the corner of a broad smile. The jukebox was booming 'Bad Moon Rising,' by Creedence Clearwater, and the place was jammed to the walls, mostly by some of the five hundred or so expatriate Americans who lived in the city. Few tourists found their way down the Tombstone back street, and if they did, the Longhorn was hardly what they were looking for.

The burly black man, whose inner-tube-size arms strained the sleeves of a blinding Hawaiian shirt, strolled through the noisy Longhorn, nodded to Wilkie, went up the two steps and through the glass-bead curtain into the private sector of the bar known as the Hole in the Wall, a section reserved for regulars. The Honorable was sitting in his personal easy chair, reading the *Wall Street Journal*. On the table beside him was a bottle of wine and a rack of poker chips.

Two men were shooting eight ball, and beyond them six men were seated around a poker table playing five card stud under the glare of a green shade. The black man didn't have to check out the players; he knew who they would be. Gallagher, Eddie Riker, Potter, Johnny Prophett, Wonderboy and Wyatt Earp. A strange-looking crew, particularly Wonderboy, who looked like a mime. His face was divided by a thin red line that ran from his hairline down his forehead and the bridge of his nose to his chin. His face was painted black on the left side and white on the right.

The black man pulled up a chair and sat down next to a tall, lean man in a flat-brimmed Stetson. He had white hair and a white handlebar mustache, and wore a black Western shirt, jeans and a tattersall vest, which concealed the .357 Cobra that he called his Buntline Special under his arm.

'Decided who's on the roster, Mr. Earp?' he asked quietly, studying the cards on the table.

'Early and me for starters. Haven't decided who the third man'll be yet,' Earp answered.

'You ain't discriminating, are you?' the black man asked with half a grin.

'You went last time, Corkscrew,' he said.

'Shit, I'm the best you got and you know it,' Corkscrew answered with a touch of arrogance.

'Yeah, I know,' Earp answered, repeating a line he heard at least once a week from Corkscrew. *"'I once had every pimp in De-troit right there.'"* He pressed his thumb down on the table.

"'But this ain't Detroit,'" Corkscrew answered with a smile, incanting Earp's customary reply.

149

'Next time I'll scratch you in,' Earp promised, turning over his hole card, which, added to the pair on the table, gave him trips and the pot.

Earp looked at his gold Rolex. Nine o'clock. Thirty minutes until show time.

He looked around the table, making his final decision. For the most part, a tough bunch. All of them had suffered their share of grief in Vietnam.

'Take my seat,' he said and got up.

'What you got?' Corkscrew asked.

Earp counted his chips with one hand. 'Three hundred,' he said.

'I owe ya,' Corkscrew said, slipping into his chair.

Earp had planned this operation carefully, as he always did, and he was feeling comfortable about the whole thing. Keep the team small and run the show fast, that was his motto. It had worked for him for years. He moved away from the orb of light into the shadows, checking out the regulars, also as he always did.

The man who had been sitting next to him was Max Early, who was wearing a light tan safari jacket, which hung open. He had no shirt under it and his trim body, like his hard-angled face, was well tanned – a man who worked in the sun. Unlike the others, who wore their hair trimmed short, Early's auburn locks tumbled from under a weathered and sagging safari hat down to his shoulders. Early stood quietly when Earp got up. 'I'm out,' was all he said, gathering up his chips.

Earp knew all their stories by heart.

Max and the big kid, Noel, and Jimmy, who had a problem with acne, were sitting in the jungle staring down at the hole while the rest of the patrol was shaking out the grass nearby. It looked as if it was abandoned. There were no fresh footprints and Jimmy had been lying on the damp ground with his ear to the hole for ten minutes and didn't hear a sound.

'So whose turn is it?' said Noel, the big hunk of a kid from Oklahoma. Typical Army, picking a man who weighed 270 pounds to be a tunnel rat when he could hardly get his leg down the hole.

'I went last time,' said Jimmy, the skinny kid from San Berdoo.

Early was the oldest. He was twenty-six and he felt ninety and he had this feeling that he was responsible for the other two.

'Shit, I'll go down,' he sighed. 'Ain't been anybody down this

hole for a week or two. Look there, there's spider webs over the entrance.'

'You know these gooks,' said Noel. 'Lay down in there for weeks, they can.'

'Uh-huh,' said Early, slapping a fresh clip in his M-16 and charging it and checking the K-Bar in his boot and the clip in his .45. He hated dusting these tunnels, hated it more than anything else about the war, but it had to get done and the sooner the better, so why waste time. He tied his hair back with a bandana and quietly slid over the edge of the tunnel headfirst and slithered down into the black pit. He lay, holding his breath, listening. He didn't smell them and he didn't hear any breathing. It's okay, he thought, Charlie left this one behind. He started through headfirst with his knife between his teeth and his M-16 probing the darkness. These tunnels could go forever, sometimes twisting and turning for a mile or two. He hated the darkness and the damp, musty feeling, but he didn't want to use his light yet, not until he was sure the tunnel was abandoned.

Damn, what's an outdoorsman from Utah doing in this piss-hole, he thought.

Then he heard the first faint sound.

A scratching sound.

Then a squeak.

Then a flapping.

And then suddenly the tunnel was alive with squealing, flapping, biting, hungry bats, dozens of them, surrounding him in the darkness.

Early screamed a scream of pure terror. He started firing. He emptied his rifle, heard the bullets thumping into the earth as the bats kept coming, started to back up, slashing the darkness with his knife, clawing for his pistol. The screeching creatures were all around him, and his scream was endless and ear-piercing as he thrashed in the darkness. Pulling himself up against the side of the tunnel, he emptied his .45 into the blackness around him, firing blindly. He clawed out another clip as he backed through the tight confines of the tomb toward the entrance. He was disoriented in the dark and his hands were shaking. There were bats in his hair, biting his cheeks. He slammed another clip in the .45 and emptied it. Then he pulled out the flashlight and began sweeping it around the tunnel, hoping the light would scare them off. Finally he could feel the cool draft from the opening sweeping past him and he reached back to get a grip on the edge of the shaft; his hand touched something soft and wet and at first he

151

thought it was mud. He twisted around and flashed the light back. The big kid, Noel, was hanging upside down, his arms resting on the floor of the tunnel. His face was mush. Blood bubbled out of the gaping bullet hole under his eye and poured out of his nose and mouth.

'Oh God, oh Jesus!' Early screamed as the bats continued to assault him and flew past him and attacked the dead soldier's bleeding face. And Early, still screaming, clawed frantically past his fallen comrade, gasping for the fresh air that rushed down the shaft, knowing deep down that in his panic he had just killed his own buddy. . . .

Eddie Riker, who would very humbly tell you that he was the best slick pilot in the whole damn Vietnam war, was the next man at the table.

They sent a light colonel in from Saigon to interrogate Riker. The first thing Riker noticed was that the colonel didn't sweat. A hundred degrees in the shade with the humidity running about 98 and his shirt was still starched. Dry as the Sahara. Riker was wearing khaki shorts and a T-shirt and was soaking wet. The colonel came to the barracks where Riker was under house arrest. An arrogant little man impressed with his own importance, carrying an alligator briefcase and a little stack of files. He spoke in a monotone and never looked Riker in the eye. He stared down at the report the whole time, tapping his pencil slowly on the table while Riker told him the story. Riker knew the type, just another scummy lawyer sitting out the war in Saigon.

'You are charged with criminal assault on an officer,' the colonel said.

'I know it,' Riker said.

'I'd like to hear your version of this,' the colonel said, leafing through the report in front of him. The pencil went tap, tap, tap. Riker knew whatever he said would go right past the colonel. To people like this, combat was running out of toilet paper in the middle of the night.

'Okay,' Riker said. 'First of all, you got to understand I'm the hottest damn slick pilot in the outfit. We been evacuating wounded along the DMZ in Song Ngan for five months now. It's about thirty minutes by air from here. A real shit situation. A lot of action and heavy casualties. I been doin' six, seven runs a day, which puts a lot on the Huey. I tell you this so you understand, with that kind of schedule, maintenance is critical.

'Anyway we inherit this lousy little fig-leaf major – a real fugazi, man – in charge of maintenance. Short-sticker, y'know, had about two months to go, sat around carving notches in this piece of wood keepin' track of his time. All he cared about, gettin' out of here. And we're losin' choppers left and right, maintenance was so shit-ass bad. The other mornin' I'm dropping down to pick up a bunch of wounded kids and all of a sudden I don't have any power. I'm at maybe ninety, a hundred feet, all of a sudden my slick drops like a fucking body bag. I hit, the Huey rolls over, the blades shower off. A dozen kids are chopped liver. Ever seen a human being after a chopper blade works 'em over?'

The colonel sighed but didn't look up. He turned away, staring out the window.

'Just stick to the facts, Lieutenant,' he said.

'These are the facts, Colonel. A dozen kids down there waiting for salvation and I fell in and butchered them.'

Riker paused long enough to light a cigarette.

'Me? I end up with a bruise on my neck and a headache. They fly me back here to base and all the way back I'm thinkin', That son of a bitch, all he's gotta do is keep the slicks up to snuff and he can't do anything but carve notches in his Goddamn stick. That's his whole fuckin' job. It really ate me. When I got back, I went straight to that little short-sticker and I took his stick and I rammed it where the sun don't shine and then I broke it off and I whipped the shit out of him with the rest of it. I whipped that sorry bastard till he looked like a bowl of ravioli. I was gonna shoot his ass off, but I didn't. I just whacked him. Then I called the provost marshal and they put me under house arrest and that's the whole story.'

'That's all you have to say?' the colonel asked.

'What else is there?' Riker answered.

'You have no remorse?' the colonel said with surprise.

'Remorse?' Riker said after a moment's thought. 'Yeah, I got remorse. I think now I should have killed that worthless shit. God knows how many body bags he filled.'

The colonel looked up at him for the first time. He looked angry. 'I'm recommending that you be arraigned for criminal assault,' he said. 'You'll be assigned an attorney. You'll also be returned to Saigon for incarceration.'

'So what else is new,' Riker said with a shrug.

The colonel flipped the file folder shut and meticulously arranged things in his case and stood up and brushed some lint off his sharply creased trousers.

'You have a bad attitude problem,' the colonel snapped.

'No, Colonel, what I got is a bad maintenance officer.'

The colonel stalked out of the barracks.

Riker watched him priss across the yard and get in his jeep and drive off. He stood there and he thought, What the hell, this is a waste. The hottest slick pilot in Nam and I'm playing solitaire in a fuckin' Quonset hut and kids are out there dyin'. So he walked out and grabbed a chopper that was warming up and went back to work. . . .

Gallagher sat next, the man who walked with this funny hitch like limping with both legs, as if his feet hurt all the time. That was because they did. A land mine had driven the floor of his jeep up to his armpits. And beside him was Johnny Prophett, who had been nominated for a Pulitzer Prize, but he stayed in Nam too long. Burned out at twenty-five, he had turned to heroin to ease the pain of losing his golden touch.

Prophett was sitting beside the road, scratching out some notes on a legal pad he kept stuffed in his canvas shoulder bag. His back hurt and his throat was choked with dust. It hadn't rained for days, and the roads were brick-hard and beginning to crack into jagged seams. He had lost the war two days before, twenty or so miles away, awakening in the morning after a night of white-powder hallucinations to find the outfit he had tied up with gone. Nothing left behind but the usual: empty cans and shell casings; ashed remnants of fires; tattered socks and tank tops too worn out to bother with. It was always the same when they moved out, like a gypsy carnival that had packed up in the night and moved to another town.

He had run out of horse and was already beginning to feel the agonies of withdrawal. The stomach pains, the itching, the headache, the dry mouth. His hand was shaking so badly he could hardly write. Besides, it all sounded the same. He hardly heard the jeep until it was almost on top of him, and he jumped, startled, and then scrambled to his feet and stuck out his thumb. It reminded him of the day he had hitchhiked to Woodstock, or tried to. By the time he got there the music was a memory.

The dust-coated jeep whizzed by, then skidded to a stop, throwing out pounds of dirt and dust.

'You oughta be careful,' Gallagher said, a Cincinnati-flat accent, 'I almost creamed ya.'

Prophett limped over to the shotgun seat. 'How about a ride?'

154

'Sure, hop in,' said Gallagher, grinding the gears into low. 'Where you headed?'

'I lost track of the war,' said Prophett, rubbing his arms.

'Shit, you're goin' in the wrong direction. Action's back there,' Gallagher said, jabbing his thumb over his shoulder.

'Where you headed?'

'Thought I'd jog cross-country to Camranh,' Gallagher said.

'What's your gig?' asked Prophett.

'Run a coupla service clubs down in S-town.'

'Sounds real tough.'

'It's a living. You a reporter?'

'Uh-huh.'

'I know a few TV guys down country. Keep them happy, know what I mean?'

'Right,' said Prophett, huddling down in the seat, hoping the shakes wouldn't get too bad. At least he could score there, maybe catch a Huey ride back up to the line. He draped a foot over the side of the jeep. 'Camranh sounds fine t'me.'

'I'd watch that,' said Gallagher. 'This road's fulla cracks. Hate to lose control with you hanging that leg over the side like –'

The words were hardly out of his mouth when they hit the land mine. Gallagher didn't even hear the explosion; all he felt was the ungodly pain in the bottom of his feet, as if he had been hit with a baseball bat by Hank Aaron, and he was tossing head over heels in the air, trying to grab on to something, anything, only there was nothing to grab on to. He landed in a soggy ditch twenty feet away with a thunk that sounded like someone smacking a pumpkin with a board. The air hissed out of him. He rolled over on his back, out of the gooey mess, and stared up at the sky and thought, Jesus, Mary and Joseph, be kind to me. Don't let me die here.

On the other side of the road the shattered jeep lay upside down, its wheels still spinning around, its undercarriage blown away. Prophett lay on his side, staring dumbly at his leg, which was trapped under the wreckage. He had forgotten withdrawal, the pain in his leg was so great. He slid up to a sitting position and pushed halfheartedly on the side of the vehicle, as if he thought it might just topple back upright. Then he passed out. . . .

Then there was Wonderboy, rock star turned marine. He had left most of his face in the Mekong Delta.

Harswain was a short, lean stick of a man with a bushy

155

mustache and hair like a porcupine's and he still carried his swagger stick from the days when he was a DI at Parris Island. He sat on a log and drew little nothing doodles in the dirt with it.

'You'll know when it's coming, pretty boy,' he said to Wonderboy. 'That round with your name etched into it. You'll know it. It'll come sighin' 'cross the field and it'll spit in yer eye a second afore it eats up yer brain.'

He laughed.

Wonderboy felt a cold chill on the back of his neck. Fear nested in his chest and squeezed his lungs and he was out of breath. It was time for some relief. On the line for seventy-seven days. No break. Out of the first sixty that had gone up,' there were fourteen left. He listened to Harswain and he thought about that bullet.

That was when Charlie hit. There was chaos – everybody running around, scrambling to get behind something, grabbing for weapons. Mail coming in. Harswain yelling at them as usual.

'Get below his horizon,' he was yelling and Wonderboy was snaking across the ground on his belly, crowding a downed tree and suddenly it was being chewed up a foot away and he cowered down behind it and got his piece ready and then he did a John Wayne, twisting, rising, throwing his rifle across the log, popping half a dozen caps at the jungle.

That was when he saw the bullet, or thought he saw it, that lead slug augering through the air toward him as if in slow motion, spinning white-hot like an angry wasp, an ugly stub of lead whistling through the air.

He fell on his back with his eyes squeezed tight shut and waited, listening to more lead ripping the tree over his head, and then he dropped his gun and scrambled on his hands and knees away, toward the jungle, sobbing with fear, listening to Harswain's scream, 'Come back here, you lily-livered little freak, you. Damn you,' heard him fire a burst toward his back and saw it chew the ground up around his feet but he didn't stop. He stood up and kept running until he couldn't run anymore. He fell on his hands and knees and threw up.

He heard the flamethrower nearby, felt the backlash of heat from it and peered through the jungle grass. The kid was twenty feet away, burning everything in front of him.

Perfect cover, thought Wonderboy, scrambling in behind him.

Then somebody yelled, 'Incoming!' and he heard the sigh of the mortar falling down from the sky, and he pulled into a tight little curl like a slug in a garden. It was a direct hit on the tank, and the flamethrower and the kid erupted in a giant splash of fire that

*swept over him and a moment before he passed out he felt the skin
on his face begin to melt. . . .*

Finally there was Corkscrew and Potter. Now, there was a
pair. Corkscrew and his brother, Hammer, had once run most of
the class hookers in MoTown from the backseat of a gold-tinted
stretch Lincoln, while Potter had scratched out a living on an
Arkansas farm where the earth was so poor 'the ants climbed
trees to fuck,' as he delicately put it. They had come out of the
war closer than twins.

*They had been holding the hill in Dang Pang for two days
against a bunch of VC that seemed to be everywhere.*
*On the morning of the third day Potter crawled around the top
of the hill and checked pulses. The rest of his men were dead.
Mortars had taken down most of the trees and rain had filled the
shell holes with stagnant water. Baby mosquitoes popped from
their eggs and skimmed along the surface of the smelly ditches.
Now there were three of them. Potter, the poor Arkansas dirt
farmer, and Corkscrew and his brother, Hammer, a couple of
fast-living Detroit pimps who got caught in the draft. Dogface
infantry soldiers all, with about as much in common as a banana
and a glass of gin.*
*Potter crawled back to the small bunker he had fashioned from
fallen trees and dirt.*
*'We're outa everything,' Corkscrew told Potter and Hammer.
'Outa ammo, outa food, outa water,' he said.*
*'Outa luck,' Potter groaned, clutching his stomach. 'I gotta
have a drink, Corkscrew.'*
*Corkscrew said, 'You got a stomach full of shrapnel, man, if you
drink, you'll die.'*
'I'm dead anyway,' Potter answered.
*'Bullshit,' snapped Corkscrew. Hammer had said nothing.
Corkscrew reached over and shook his brother to wake him up,
and Hammer rolled over and toppled facedown in the muck at
the bottom of a ditch.*
*'Ham!' Potter yelled. He jumped down and lifted Hammer up
and dragged him back to the top of the ditch. But Hammer's body
was cold and his eyes were sightless.*
*'Oh God damn, God damn you all,' Corkscrew screamed
angrily. 'You motherfuckers, come on up here. You want something, you fuckin' apes, come and get it. . . .'*
When the relief column came up the hill, Corkscrew was

157

standing over the wounded Potter and his dead brother holding
his empty M-16 by the barrel, waiting for the VC. . . .

Yeah, thought Earp, they'd all do in a pinch, but tonight Riker
will do. He nodded to the man in the safari hat.
'Checking out,' Riker said. He took off his hat with 'Home
Sweet Home' embroidered across the crown in gold and swept
his chips into it. He was wearing khaki cotton tennis shorts and a
red tank top, his chest hair curling over its neckline, and while
his thick black hair was turning gray and he sometimes wore
gold-rimmed reading glasses, his deeply tanned arms and shoulders had the smooth muscles of a man who kept himself in top
physical shape. He walked across the room and cashed in his
chips to the portly man they all called the Honorable.
A thin, hollow-eyed Johnny Prophett got up from the poker
table and urged Earp into a dark corner of the alcove. 'Let me go
on this one, Wyatt, please?'
'C'mon, look at you. Your hands are shaking so bad you could
mix a martini without moving your arm.'
'A cup of coffee, a quickie . . .'
'Johnny, some other time, okay? I'm being straight up with
you. If I take you on this, you could get us all killed. Maybe next
time, okay . . .'
'I pull my own,' Prophett mumbled, looking down at his feet.
'Sure, you do,' Earp said and slapped him on the shoulder.
Earp, Riker and Early left the alcove, passing behind the bar
and entering Wilkie's private office. He ignored them. The office
looked like an indoor junkyard. Old newspapers, bills, file
folders, and magazines were piled on the desk, chairs, on the
floor, and were stuffed in an old-fashioned file cabinet shoved in
one corner.
'Sweets has every piece of paper he ever got in his life,' said
Early, shaking his head sadly as he surveyed the oppressively
cluttered office.
'That he has,' Earp answered. He opened a drawer in the desk,
put his .357 in it and took out a 9 mm. pistol with a silencer
attached. He popped the clip and checked it. Full.
The phone rang, a muffled announcement from under a stack
somewhere. Riker found it and handed the receiver to Earp.
'Earp. Yeah . . . excellent, excellent! Okay, we're on. Be real
careful. Good luck.'
He hung up the phone and rubbed his hands together very
slowly.

'We're in luck. She got there ahead of him. He checked in ten minutes ago and she managed to get the connecting room.'

'So it's a go, then,' said Early.

'Yep,' said Earp.

'Sounds like a stroll down the lane to me,' said Riker.

'Could be,' Earp said with raised eyebrows. 'Let's go, we got ten minutes.'

Prophett, too, left the alcove and walked across the bar to the men's room. He sat down in a stall and took a small plastic box from his pocket. It contained a hypodermic needle, a candle, a spoon and a packet of heroin. With shaking hands he lit the candle and set it on the toilet-paper holder, then tapped some of the powder in the spoon and cooked it over the flame until it was a clear bubbling fluid, dipped the tip of the spike in the fluid, his fingers squeezing the bulb on the end of it, forcing out the air, sucking in the fluid. He flexed his fist. The needle flirted with a vein, nicked it, then slipped deeply into it. Prophett flinched slightly, took a deep breath and shuddered. A look of contentment crossed his face. He closed his eyes and smiled.

The Dusit Thani was a short walk away, but they took Riker's pickup truck and parked at the rear. Riker got out but stayed close by. Early and Earp went to room 429. She was waiting.

'We'll give you about five minutes so you can find out the size of the load,' Earp said. 'Nervous?'

She shook her head.

'Good girl. Let's do it, then.'

She left the room, took the stairs to the third floor and took the elevator back up, just in case he was watching or listening for it. She knocked on the door of 427 and it was opened almost immediately by a large Chinese with a livid scar down one side of his face.

'Mrs Giu?'

She nodded, and he stepped back as she entered the room, then quickly checked the hall before closing the door. He was surprised. The woman was beautiful – tiny, erect, almost regal in her bearing. She was wearing an emerald-green silk evening dress and white gloves. Her pearl earrings looked expensive. She certainly did not fit the profile of a drug courier.

'I am Mr. Sen,' he said. 'Passport?'

She took the small leather-bound booklet from her purse and gave it to him. He checked it closely, looking for signs of a forgery, but couldn't detect any. If it got past him, it would get past customs.

The passport identified her as Mrs. Victor Giu, a widow, twenty-nine years old, born in Bangkok. She had done her share of traveling, mostly to Malaya, India, Hong Kong and the Philippines.

'I see by your passport you are a dancer,' he said.

'Yes. The steamer trunk is for my costumes.'

Sen smiled thinly. 'Very good,' he said. 'A clever stroke, the trunk. It holds three times what a normal suitcase carries. You understand what you are to do?'

'Yes. I check the four cases through to Seattle. After I pass through customs, a limousine will be waiting to pick me up. Once the bags are loaded in the car, I will be paid the rest of my money and be free to go.'

'Yes. Really quite simple.'

He took an envelope from a dresser drawer and gave it to her.

'Here is your round-trip ticket and two thousand seven hundred ninety-five dollars. That's five hundred dollars for expenses and half the fee.'

Mrs. Giu quickly calculated the weight.

'Not bad for a few hours' work,' Sen said.

'You forget the risk,' she said, moving toward the door that connected the two rooms.

'There are no problems,' Sen said. He was attracted to the elegant widow and began bragging. He picked up one of the suitcases, put it on the bed and opened it, explaining that the walls were lined with cakes of pressed heroin wrapped in thin sheets of aluminium foil soaked in coffee. The coffee shielded the odor from dope-sniffing dogs. The pockets in the suitcases and several of the drawers in the steamer trunk contained small bags of sachet, which concealed the smell of the coffee from inspectors. As he described the carriers, Mrs. Giu leaned back against the connecting door and unlocked it, then moved across the room to the foot of the bed, keeping Sen's attention away from the door.

'We have not lost a shipment in six months,' Sen said. 'Nothing to worry about.'

His back was to the door connecting the room next door. As he spoke, the door swung open and Earp stepped quickly into the room. Sen heard the sound and then, in the dresser mirror, saw Earp behind him. He reached for the gun in his belt and twisted around at the same time, dropping to his knees.

Earp, ten feet away, was standing with his feet slightly apart and his gun at arm's length. He fired his first shot. The pistol

160

made a flat sound like someone slamming a door. As Sen pulled his own gun Earp's bullet hit Sen just above the left eye, snapping his head back. He fell against the bed.

A blinding pain seared through Sen's head. His hands and feet went numb, and the salty taste of blood flooded his mouth. The room swirled crazily. He saw his gun tumble from his hand and, looking up into the end of the silencer and behind it, saw the tall man with the white mustache standing over him. The gun thunked again and he saw the room explode into hundreds of blinding colors and then it turned black.

As Sen's body seemed to collapse into itself and sagged forward, Riker rushed into the bathroom, grabbed several washcloths and some towels and, dashing back, slammed the washcloths against Sen's bleeding wounds. It was all over in twenty seconds.

Earp turned the steamer trunk on its back and opened it.

'It's gonna be a tight fit,' Earp said.

'This guy's got to weigh two hundred pounds,' Riker said as with great effort he and Earp lifted the dead man's body and forced it into the trunk. Sen lay on his side with his knees jammed against his chest and his head down on his chest. They forced the door shut, locked it and lifted the trunk by one end and set it upright.

'We'll send over four messengers for it,' Earp answered.

Mrs. Giu took the elevator to the lobby, walked out of the hotel empty-handed and got in a *tuk-tuk* that was waiting nearby.

Two minutes later Earp and Riker left the hotel by the rear door after having checked both rooms. They walked down the fire stairs and threw the suitcases in the truck.

'How much?' Early asked.

As they drove off into the night, Earp settled down, smiling, and said, 'Thirty-seven keys.'

HONG KONG

Hatcher loved the Orient. He had spent years there before Sloan sent him to Central America, years on the back rivers, rubbing elbows with the Ts'e K'am Men Ti, the river pirates who operated south from Shanghai and east from Thailand into the

Macao Runs of Hong Kong. He knew them all. Joe Cockroach, half Chinese, half Malaysian, who had a flawless British accent and wore tailored raw-silk suits when he did business in the backwaters of the Jungsian River. Harry Tsin, who had a degree from UCLA and a peg leg from a Japanese prison camp. Sam-Sam Sam, a psychopath who controlled the river, demanded tribute from all who did business on it, and skinned anyone who double-crossed him and hung the skin on the side of his boat as an example.

And Cohen, the white Tsu Fi.

As the 747 swept over the bay and banked into Kai Tak airport he felt a surge of excitement. Not that Hong Kong was a particular favorite – it was too crowded, too noisy, too full of itself. But this was where everything in the Orient began, where the money changers squatted on the doorstep of China, and riches flowed back and forth like the tides. The first red glow of dawn streaked the horizon as they swept in low from the south. Shaukiwan, the floating city of junks, sampans and snakeboats, slid silently below them, then Hong Kong island and the bay, and finally Kowloon peninsula, facing a harbor fat with cargo ships from all over the world. Junks and sampans surrounded them like pups nuzzling a bitch hound.

Hatcher had old friends here – and old enemies, too, but he never thought about them. Don't ever look back, Sloan had told him in the beginning. Bad for the old clicks. Clicks, that's what Sloan called instinct.

It was 5 A.M., only two hours before his nonstop left for Bangkok, hardly time to get into trouble. He would eat at a small restaurant he liked a few miles from the airport and be off again.

As he left the plane his plans were suddenly changed. The first thing he heard when he entered the terminal was the page.

'Attention, arriving passenger Hatcher, please contact Pan American information as soon as possible. . . .'

He went to the Pan Am counter near the gate.

'I'm Hatcher,' he told a handsome, very erect Asian woman. 'You paged me.'

'Take the phone right there,' she said pleasantly, pointing to a house phone on the end of the counter. The operator was just as pleasant. 'You have a message to call this number collect in Washington, D.C., and ask for Sergeant Flitcraft,' she said, and dictated the number. Hatcher repeated the number, then found a pay phone and made the call.

162

'OSI, Sergeant Flitcraft,' a crisp voice on the other end answered. He quickly accepted the call. 'Mr. Hatcher?'

'Yes,' Hatcher whispered.

'Would you mind giving me your old Navy serial number, sir?'

'Not at all,' Hatcher's voice rasped. 'N3146021.'

'Very good, sir. You also cleared the voice print. Colonel Sloan says to wait in Hong Kong for him. He's a few hours behind you. You have adjoining rooms at the Peninsula Hotel, he'll meet you there at about ten hundred hours, give or take.'

'That's it?'

'That's it, sir.'

'Thanks, Sergeant,' Hatcher said and hung up. Damn, he thought, Sloan was really riding tight herd on this one. What the hell could all this be about?

To Hatcher, the Peninsula Hotel defined Hong Kong. It stood like a beacon on the tip of Kowloon, facing the Star Ferry that carried passengers to the Central District on Hong Kong island. Rolls-Royce limos for the guests lined up at the door in front of rickshas. The desk manager was a short, sleek Oriental in a dark double-breasted suit; the ancient concierge wore a traditional silk brocaded *cheongsam*. In a corner of the lobby a blond woman who looked Swedish played Chinese melodies on a Swiss harp for those who came in late or rose early. It was truly where East and West came together and was one of the finest hotels in the world. Guests were treated like royalty.

It was raining when he got to his room. The bellhop hung up his suit bag, turned on the ceiling fan and the television, vanished for a minute or two and returned with a bucket of ice.

'*Mm goi,*' Hatcher said, thanking him and tucking a Hong Kong five in his hand.

When the bellman was gone, Hatcher flicked off the TV, opened the sliding door and went out on the balcony. He had slept little for the past three days, and he let the rain-cooled breeze refresh him as he watched the rising sun chase the storm across the bay. It had already passed over the island, leaving behind a glittering jewel of skyscrapers and glass towers below the towering peak of Victoria Mountain.

He ordered breakfast and had the waiter set up the table on his balcony. While he ate he watched the riverboats moving in and out of the harbor, the Star Ferry streaking toward the island, the Peak Tram gliding up the side of the mountain.

He began to doze. Jet lag was catching up to him, and for reasons he did not immediately understand, Hatcher's mind slipped back to a dark night ten years before. To the tram rising up in darkness, through the banyan trees, past the rich houses. The dark figure of Harline waiting at the top, a cigarette glowing between his smiling lips. Hatcher leading him around to the cliffs of the overlook and Harline holding out his hand eagerly, almost salivating, his effete British accent in the darkness – 'Good to do business with people you can trust, chum' – and Hatcher dropping the envelope, leaning down to pick it up, grabbing the Britisher around the knees as if he were tackling him, vaulting the slender man backward, down into four hundred feet of emptiness, his terrified scream fading into the darkness.

Hatcher jerked awake and sat staring out at Victoria Peak. Ten years. Where in hell did that come from? Yesterday was history, you never looked back, never thought back, never went back unless the job required it, and when it did, you dealt with it with the old clicks, your subconscious providing whatever background was necessary to stay alive. Now, suddenly, here it was, hunched on the rim of the alpha zone, dogging him. Suddenly he found himself wondering for what purpose he had killed Harline. Sloan had never told him and he had not asked.

'It's a sanction. You're a soldier doing what soldiers do. Soldiers don't ask.' Sloan had said that the first time he ever asked why. And now, for the first time since he met Sloan, Hatcher thought, A soldier without uniform, without identification, without credentials or identity. What the hell kind of soldier was that? And now here he was, back again, and the doubts about Sloan gnawed at him.

Out on the island, black-eared kites, who had rushed to the sanctuary of the trees to escape the rain, spread their two-foot wings and soared over the island. For centuries they had shared the lofty aerie with rich taipans, the business rulers whose homes dotted the precipitous face of the mountain like small forts. Below them spread the Central District, the business heart of Hong Kong, where Chinese gangsters cavorted with British bankers and taipans, where dynasties were created and empires won and lost, gold was king, and where the binding ethic was money.

An island founded by smugglers and pirates, thought Hatcher. The only thing that changes here is time.

And thinking of pirates, Hatcher's mind slipped again, this time to Cohen, and another memory crowded his brain. This time it was a happy one.

Thinking of Cohen made Hatcher feel good, for Rob Cohen was one of those characters who made the Orient the Orient, a man of mystery, an American expatriate who had become a Hong Kong legend. Hatcher was one of the few people who knew the whole scenario. They were close and trusting friends, though they had neither seen nor talked to each other for several years.

Ten years before, when they first met, Cohen was known as king of the Macao Runs, and an unlikely king he was, buying contraband merchandise with the skill of a Rothschild and smuggling boatloads past the Hong Kong customs several times a week with the adroitness of a Chinese warlord.

By then Cohen was known as the white Tsu Fi of the river, although it was a while before Hatcher understood what that meant. All Hatcher knew was if you wanted to know the back-room secrets of Hong Kong, this short, wiry Jew with the Boston accent and the scraggly beard, who wore Chinese clothes, spoke three different dialects, had a lock on the river trade, and had become one of Hong Kong's most mysterious and feared characters, was your man.

Before they met, Hatcher had heard many stories about Cohen – rumors, tall tales, lies – all slanderous, and all, to one extent or another true. But the real truth was far stranger than any fiction Cohen's detractors and enemies could have invented. Through the years as Cohen and Hatcher progressed from being cautious adversaries to becoming close friends, Hatcher grew to trust the legendary schemer. And in time he had gradually pieced the story together.

Back in 1975, Cohen's office was a dismal, dusty, two-room closet over an acupuncture parlor on crowded Cat Street, which was just a small anteroom with two uncomfortable chairs. And it was hot. There was no air conditioning and the ceiling fan looked as if it had been out of order since the second dynasty.

'Mr. Hatcher? Come on in,' Cohen said in an accent that was part Boston, part British and part singsong Chinese.

To see him, Hatcher had to squint through dancing motes of dust spotlighted by the sun that streamed through the windows. Cohen was sitting in a straight-backed chair framed by the sunlight. Then, suddenly, Hatcher remembered him.

'We've met before,' he said, extending his hand.

'Right,' Cohen said, returning a hearty handshake, 'two years ago, up the Beijiang in Chin Chin land.'

165

'Sam-Sam Sam and his crew,' Hatcher said with a nod.

And Cohen laughed and nodded. 'Right, a true shit if there ever was one. He'll steal your eyeballs and screw your French poodle while you're holding the leash. You've got a good memory there, *gwai-lo.*'

'Yours ain't too bad either.'

'Jesus,' Cohen said with a grin, 'ain't it great to talk American. It's the only thing I miss. These guys out here? They don't know shit about the vernacular.'

Their meeting two years earlier had been a brief one. At the time, Hatcher had written off the brazen man as just another quick-buck river rat not long for this world, an easy mistake to make because on that night Cohen was making his first trip into what he called Chin Chin land – China.

For three years Hatcher had worked the back rivers from Thailand east through the deltas and terraced plains of Cambodia and north through Laos, Vietnam and China to the Macao Runs of Hong Kong. He knew the Irrawaddy, the Mekong, and the Yalu Jiang rivers and their backwaters, knew the towns and was accepted – or ignored – by the villagers, who considered him a soldier of fortune without flag or loyalty. He dodged the Red patrols in Vietnam by hiding in the daytime and traveling at night, and by speaking Russian when he was stopped. He got by on audacity and because his role was mostly benign. He was there to get information, not to cause trouble, and he gathered his information by observing rather than asking questions.

It was to learn their secret ways, their routes, their sources, their pick-up points and, mostly, their tie-in to the Saigon black market that had brought Hatcher to their meeting place in 1973. They called themselves the Ts'e K'am Men Ti, the Secret Gatekeepers. There he occasionally did business with them to bolster his credibility. On the pretense of selling guns, he continued to build his file of informants and river operators and their connection to the Hong Kong underworld. He was known as *gli Occhi di Sassi*, the Man With Stone Eyes, a nickname given him by one of the most trusted men on his team, a onetime mafioso enforcer named Tony Bagglio.

Standing in the dusty office, Hatcher remembered quite clearly his first sight of Cohen materializing out of the fog, a strange-looking creature in a silk *cheongsam* and with a long, straggly beard standing in the bow of a snakeboat – with only one other man, a hard-looking Chinese at the tiller – gliding quietly up one of the jungle-cramped offshoots of the Beijiang River, forty or so miles north of Macao.

I'll be damned, Hatcher had thought to himself, what the hell's this Chinese rabbi doing up here?

He soon found out.

COHEN: 1973

Cohen, too, remembered that night.

And he, too, had thought to himself as he cruised through the heavy fog in the long, slender snakeboat: What the hell is a nice Jewish boy from Westchester with a DBA from Harvard Business School doing here?

The barge had appeared so suddenly it startled Cohen. It was a floating department store, stacked high with crates of cameras, television sets, china dishes and forbidden icons, bolts of Thai silk and Indian madras. Heavy tarps were strapped over the stacks to keep them dry.

Han, Cohen's bodyguard and helmsman, throttled back and eased the snakeboat toward the barge. Cohen could feel his heart thundering in his throat and wrists. His mouth was dry.

Standing on the foredeck of the barge was the ugliest, meanest-looking human being he had ever seen. He was shorter than Cohen, perhaps five six, an Oriental built like a crate, his bulging arms covered with tattoos. He had no hair on the right side of his head. In its place was a mottled burn scar, which extended from a disfigured lump of ear halfway to the crown of his head. He combed the rest of his long black hair away from the scar so it swept over the top of his head and showered down the left side almost to his shoulder. He wore a gun belt and an ornate hand-made holster, designed to hold an Uzi machine gun, which was tied to his thigh Western style. His three front teeth were gold. One of them, according to rumor, had belonged to an unfortunate English businessman who thought he could bypass the unwritten and unsaid laws of the river and deal directly with the Ts'e K'am Men Ti.

This was Sam-Sam Sam, the *Do Wong*, the Prince of the Knife, a one-man Teamsters Union. Nothing happened on the river unless Sam-Sam Sam said okay. The booty stacked behind him was all tribute, collected from others who wanted to do business with the taipans.

Cohen's mouth got drier.

Behind Sam-Sam Sam there were at least twenty other men, all wearing the black shirts, shin-length hauki pants, and red headbands of the Khmer Rouge, all armed with Uzis, AK-47s, M-16s and .357 Pythons. They looked as if they expected an invasion. Behind them were the women, all young, all probably cold-blooded, dressed the same, with knives and pistols stuck in their red sashes.

All of the weapons seemed to be pointed at Cohen's stomach.

Leaning against a stack of crates was a white man, his uncut black hair covering his ears and sweeping almost to his shoulders. He was tall, handsome in a scruffy, unshaven way, and was wearing khaki cotton pants and shirt. A blue windbreaker was tied around his waist by the sleeves; a 9 mm. H&K automatic dangled under his arm in a shoulder holster; his wide-brimmed safari hat was faded and limp from sun and rain. He had his hands in his pockets and was grinning. No, thought Cohen, not grinning, the son of a bitch is leering.

'They look like Khmer Rouge,' Cohen whispered to Han.

'Disguise,' whispered his boatman, who was supposed to act as a bodyguard. 'Nobody bother them this way.'

Cohen quickly appraised the situation. He became temporarily paranoid, afraid they would hear his heart pounding. The odds were about thirty to two and there was no future in any kind of confrontation. Cohen immediately made his move.

'I'll go over alone,' Cohen said.

'Not good. They don't know you,' answered Han.

'I have this,' said Cohen, opening his hand. In his palm lay a Queen Victoria twenty-dollar gold piece. 'Stand up in full view so they don't get nervous. If there is trouble, the two of us aren't going to last long anyhow.'

He stood on the point of the bow as the motorboat idled up to the barge and opened his *cheongsam* wide to show he was unarmed, then stepped cautiously onto the barge.

'I didn't come here to fight,' he said in Chinese to the ugly one. 'I came here to make us all rich.'

The ugly man glared at him.

'I'm Cohen,' Cohen said.

The ugly man still glared at him.

Cohen made his way to the stacks of contraband goods, threading his way through the men and women, and flipped a corner of a bolt of Thai silk, felt it, and nodded.

'Good stuff,' he said, then turned to the ugly man. 'This is what I want.' He held up his fingers and counted. 'I want cameras from Japan, good brands. I want stereos, Sony and Panasonic. I want Thai silk – not cheap – good stuff, like this, and madras from India.' He flipped the corner back on the bolt. 'I'll buy green jade, no white – and don't try to dye it on me, I can see right through that. Statues, idols, stuff like that from China, I'll give you good price on all that, as much as you can bring down from Chin Chin land or over from Thailand.'

The ugly man stood with his hands on his hips, a cigar clenched in his teeth. Its tip glowed in the dark. Okay, thought Cohen, he's got to show his balls here, push me around a little.

'Who the hell you think you are?' Ugly said.

'I told you, I'm Cohen.'

The ugly man looked around at his men and they all laughed. There was some jabber between them and then the ugly man turned back to Cohen and said, 'They think I ought to skin you alive and hang you to the side of my boat.'

Cohen threw his wallet on the table. 'Kill me, all you get is ten Hong Kong dollars. I don't think you got to be the *do wong* by being stupid.'

The white man whistled low through his teeth and shook his head very slowly.

The ugly man's eyes flamed. He bit down hard on his cigar and his hand dropped over the stock of the Uzi.

'You say I am stupid, *gwai-lo*, that what you say?'

'No no, I say I *don't* think you are stupid. If you were stupid you'd skin me for ten dollars. Instead, I'll make you fat.'

'I am fat already,' the ugly man said proudly.

'One is never too fat.'

'You have a fast tongue.'

'A man wouldn't last long up here with a slow one.'

The ugly man liked that. He threw back his head, laughed heartily, and his men relaxed.

'So how do you pay?' the ugly man asked.

'Hong Kong paper. You want American dollars or gold, you won't do as well.'

'And why should I do business with you?' the pirate asked.

Cohen held up the gold coin between a thumb and forefinger. He twisted it in the beam of one of the lights. The coin twinkled in his hand. Sam-Sam walked very close and inspected the coin.

'You come from the Tsu Fi?' the ugly one asked.

Cohen nodded. 'I talk for the Tsu Fi. I got lots of dollars and there's plenty more. None of that tea-and-crumpets shit like dealing with the British. You deal with me, it's down and dirty,

169

everybody makes a pound, no bullshit, no waste of time. And the big reason is I'll take delivery upriver. I'll make the Macao run myself and worry about customs. All you got to do is get the goods to me.'

The white man shifted slightly and said in English, 'You got the balls of a Brahma bull.'

'How did you know I speak the language?' Cohen asked.

'Boston accent.'

'You got a good ear. Cohen's the name.'

'Hatcher,' the man in khaki said in a flat, no-nonsense voice. It was not unfriendly, it was a voice that said, simply, Don't mess with me. They shook hands. Hatcher had cold eyes that gave away nothing, and his smile came with an effort. Not a man to stand on the wrong side of, thought Cohen. Hatcher – Remember that name.

'You're not part of this bunch, surely,' Cohen said.

'Naw, just trying to make a buck like yourself.'

'How do you think I'm doing?'

'Sam-Sam hasn't cut your throat yet, that's a good sign. What's that you showed him?'

'Little down payment,' Cohen said and winked.

'Where's the rest of your swag?' Hatcher asked.

'Downriver a ways,' Cohen whispered. 'Ten men and a chest of paper. I don't like to show my hole card until the bets are all in.'

The ugly man had a short conference with several of his men, then came over to Cohen.

'I'm Sam-Sam Sam, *do wong* of the Ts'e K'am Men Ti. You tell me what you want, you tell me how we make deal, okay, you and me do business, nobody else.'

Cohen smiled and winked at Hatcher.

'Let's do some dealing,' he said to the ugly one.

That had been two years before their meeting in the dismal office on Cat Street. Cohen had come a long way by then, had become the Tsu Fi, the master conniver of the island. And in the next few years he and Hatcher became allies, each feeding information and assistance to the other, ultimately learning to trust each other as friends.

Hatcher stared across the bay at the sprawling houses almost hidden by trees near the peak of Victoria Mountain.

Cohen's lair.

My God, Hatcher wondered, *is the little guy still alive?*

170

ch'uang tzu-chi

As he sat staring across the bay, his eyes occasionally drooping with exhaustion, Hatcher suddenly began to feel a vague sense of malaise. The old clicks were at work. Perhaps it was coming back to the East, the sudden flood of memories invoked by the past. The Far Easterners had a strong premonitory sense; they believed not only in reincarnation but in visions. Hatcher had never bought the concepts, and yet at times in the past his clicks, or instincts or memories or whatever they might be called, had warned him of danger.

Now his clicks suddenly began racing overtime.

Sloan was on his way to Hong Kong. There was more to that than just a friendly visit to check in with Hatcher.

He had been too tired for it to register before, but now, relaxing half asleep on the balcony overlooking the harbor, he had an overwhelming sense that something had gone wrong. What other reason would Sloan have for coming to Hong Kong?

Westerners might call it memory, introspection, instinct. The Chinese always seemed to have a more poetic way of expressing such things. The Chinese called it *ch'uang tzu-chi*, the window to oneself.

Sloan had always said that to indulge in *ch'uang tzu-chi* was suicidal, that memories were weapons that attacked the mind, dulled the senses. They were distractions, misdirections, a deadly indulgence. Sloan was right, but only within the context of his own reality, for without the window there was nothing to draw on.

In Los Boxes, all Hatcher had was *ch'uang tzu-chi*. At first Hatcher had found the indulgence almost impossible, like drinking from an empty cup. But with the help of 126 he had reconstructed that part of the past that gave him pleasure. Moments of discovery; a taste of new wine, a brush of warm lips, the touch of another body, the urgency of orgasm; brief moments when love was a word away and pleasure seemed infinite and he had momentarily escaped the passion of death; moments he could reach out and touch again in the misery of his cell. Eventually they gave him life.

Hatcher now tried to shrug them away, however. He decided to take a quick nap. It would be four hours before Sloan arrived, and in four hours Hatcher could take the edge off his jet lag. He went back into the room, stripped and lay flat on his back on the floor, staring up at the ceiling fan and the whirling shadows above it.

Lying on the floor, waiting for sleep to come rather than trying to induce it, Hatcher was rushed back in time by the slatted shutters that threw striped shadows on the wall, back to Los Boxes, to a time when he had embraced *ch'uang tzu-chi* and, with it, a facsimile of sanity. He had become addicted, and after Los Boxes had fought to free himself of the habit, a kind of cold-turkey repudiation of past and pleasure.

Now as he lay on the floor that window opened again, and there, beyond its ghostly sill, was the image of the first moment he saw Ginia: a soft red dawn spreading over the flat marsh, setting the shimmering water afire for an instant.

His first reaction was physical. She was standing on the marina dock near a sailboat, wearing a pair of brief shorts and a bikini top, and he was stunned by the perfection of her body, so stunned that he stopped loading his boat and stared without realizing it. Then he looked up and saw she was staring back at him with eyes so brown they were almost black.

'If you take everything off me, I'll get arrested for indecent exposure,' she said with a hint of a smile.

Her companion, a flaccid rich boy recovering from a hangover, his character as shaky as his hands, was unfurling the main sheet. He looked up and said, 'What'd you say?'

'Not a thing, my dear,' she purred, and when he turned back to his chore, she stared back at Hatcher. Hatcher walked directly to her side, looked down at her, and shook his head very slowly. 'Life is just too damn short,' Hatcher's ruined voice whispered.

She was mesmerized by the shattered sound of his voice, and she smiled, then laughed, then nodded. 'Oh, how true.'

Hatcher pointed to the wobbly youth struggling with his mainsail.

'Roger,' she said softly.

Hatcher turned toward him and said as loudly as he could, 'Roger?'

Roger looked up, steadying himself by grasping the mast.

'Roger, you'll be happy to know that you can go home,' Hatcher said. 'Go back to bed. The lady's coming with me.'

'Who says?' the shocked Roger demanded weakly.

Hatcher looked back at her and she said, 'I says, Roger.'

What a day that had been. What a dazzling moment when she

had loosened the straps and dropped the bra, touched his face with her fingertips, leaned over and kissed his throat, when her breasts had brushed against his bare chest for the first time and he had reached up, running his fingers under her hair at the back of her neck, felt her skin grow erect under his touch and felt the goose flesh rise on his own arms and shoulders, and caressed her as she caressed him until they were both shaking with anticipation. They had postponed it for an eternity, touching, exploring, their lips flirting as they whispered to each other, until his fingers stroked her soul and their trembling became an earthquake and they could no longer push back the moment and she pressed him against her and stroked him into her and their whimpers became cries and time was suspended.

He reached out in the darkness, touched the unsettled air, tried to relive that moment, and he knew he could never, would never, overcome the addiction of *ch'uang tzu-chi*.

And now, on the edge of sleep, he realized that it was that window, slightly ajar, that had also created his uneasiness. He knew – *knew* – that something had gone sour, just as he knew that he could not ignore the friends and enemies of the past. The journey would be harder than he had imagined, he sensed that now. And for whatever dangers lay ahead, in Macao, Bangkok or upriver, the best he could hope for was to close that window for the moment.

He set the alarm clock in his head for 11 A.M., folded his hands over his chest, and started counting backward from ten. He was in a deep sleep before he got to four.

COMPLICATIONS

He awoke five minutes before eleven and lay on the floor staring at the shadows whirling on the ceiling above the fan, listening. Since Los Boxes, Hatcher's hearing was acute; he could hear a cockroach as it scratched its way across the floor. Down the hall, he heard the elevator door open and close, the sound of two people walking along the carpeted hallway, heard the door to the adjoining room open, the rustling of hangers in the closet, the muffled dialogue with the bellhop, and the door closing.

He knew Sloan very well. He would order lunch – cold cuts

and booze from room service – then take a shower before announcing his arrival. Sloan liked his booze and showers.

Hatcher waited until he heard the room service waiter come and go and the shower turn on, then got up, dressed and, using a set of hooked lock needles, picked the lock on the door between the rooms. When he entered Sloan's room, Sloan was in the shower, humming to himself.

Hatcher crossed the room and reached under the pillow, took out Sloan's .45, dropped the clip and ejected the shell in the chamber. He put the pistol back, went across the room and stood behind the bathroom door. He waited until Sloan was finished. The boxy man came out naked, toweling his hair. He strolled toward the bed, still humming some aimless tune.

Hatcher moved the door slightly so it made a creaking sound.

Sloan moved instantly, jogging slightly to his right, then switching directions before he dived for the bed.

'Too late, you're dead,' Hatcher whispered.

Sloan sighed and slid down to the floor. He turned to Hatcher. The lopsided grin that was his trademark spread across his lips. It was like the old times, an old gambit, a game they had played through the years. But Sloan did not misread it. Hatcher had learned early in the game never to let personal feelings get in the way of the job; it clouded the judgment. This was Hatcher's way of telling him that the job came first, regardless of how he felt about Sloan. It was not a sign that Hatcher had forgiven Sloan or that he trusted him. Betrayal was too high on Hatcher's list of unforgivable sins for that.

Hatcher stepped out of the shadows and threw the clip and the round on the bed. 'You're not as quick as you used to be. And how many times have I told you, you've got to stop putting your piece under the pillow. It's like putting a diamond necklace under the mattress. It's the first place anybody looks.'

Sloan reloaded his gun and replaced it under the pillow. 'Reverse psychology,' he said.

Sloan stopped drying his hair and wrapped the towel around his waist, went in the bathroom, came back and stood in the doorway, slowly brushing his short-cropped hair. 'We got a problem, laddie,' he said casually without sacrificing his smile.

'What kind of problem?'

'Somebody stuck a knife in Windy Porter the night before last,' Sloan said bluntly. 'He's dead.'

'What!'

Sloan kept talking as he walked to a room service table. The

174

room was large, with a king-size bed, rattan furniture and pastel flowered wallpaper. A vase of orchids on the dresser added more color. The balcony, furnished with white wicker, overlooked the river. A ceiling fan stirred the air, which was already getting hot and sticky.

'According to the police, he was trying to break up a fight, if you put any faith in the Bangkok police.'

'What really happened?' Hatcher's hoarse voice asked.

'I don't know. Maybe it happened the way they say it did. I assume I'll get the full story when I get over there.'

Sloan poured a cup of coffee and filled a water glass half full of scotch. He dropped a single ice cube in the glass and handed the coffee to Hatcher.

'Where was he struck?' Hatcher asked.

Sloan hesitated for a moment and, without losing his smile, said, 'The neck. Base of the skull.'

'Beautiful,' Hatcher growled. 'A classic triad hit. Breaking up a fight, my ass.'

'I don't think the White Palms are involved in this. What would their angle be?' Sloan asked, sipping his drink.

'How would I know?' Hatcher answered. 'I came over here looking for Cody, and now our only contact is dead and it looks like the triads are involved. Listen, Harry, you better not be playing games with me, I warned you back on the island . . .'

Sloan's smile broadened. 'Hey, don't be so damn paranoid. We don't know for sure it was even a triad hit. It could be just a crazy fluke.'

'In this business there's no such thing as a crazy fluke.'

'Well, there's always the exception. . . .' Sloan said, his attitude, as always, cavalier. 'One thing I am sure of, nobody but Porter knew what was going on.'

'Did they catch the killer?'

'Killers,' Sloan corrected and shook his head.

'Can we assume Porter was tailing Wol Pot when it happened?' Hatcher asked.

'Who knows,' Sloan said with a shrug. 'Maybe he lost Wol Pot. Maybe Wol Pot ditched him. Maybe he took the night off.' Sloan looked over his sideways grin. 'The way I understand it, he got stabbed trying to break up a fight between a couple of slopes and a whore on one of the klongs. But if I were guessing, I'd say, yeah, he was tailing the little bastard when it happened.'

'And Wol Pot was mixed up with the White Palm Triad.'

'That's what immigration *thinks*.'

'So the question now is, Is the Thai still alive? And still on our side?' Hatcher said. 'That is, if he was ever on our side to begin with.' He stared out at the harbor for a moment and added, 'And you called this a simple job?'

'Come on, Hatch, don't go jumping to conclusions. So we got a glitch in the program.'

'We've got a man dead, that's what we've got, and that's *all* we've got. I'd call that more than a glitch.'

'Shit,' Sloan said, 'we've been in the soup too long to let a thing like Porter's death stop us.'

'You've been in the soup,' said Hatcher. 'I was in Los Boxes.'

Sloan sighed. 'Let's keep it pleasant,' he said, still smiling, still Mr Sincerity, 'for old times' sake.'

'Old times' sake got all used up.'

'I was just doing my job.'

'You were doing what a bunch of weasels in the White House basement told you to do.'

Sloan leaned closer to Hatcher, his fingers wiggling like those of a magician about to perform a trick, his smile so constant it might have been permanently implanted on his face.

'That *is* my job,' he said with oily finality.

Though his smile never faded and his voice was quiet and level, Sloan felt suddenly uneasy. There had been a time in all the years they worked together when he didn't have to explain anything to Hatcher; when he laid out the parameters and Hatcher instinctively knew the program. Was Hatcher rejecting the whole concept of the brigade? That had not occurred to Sloan. He had assumed that Hatcher only felt betrayed.

Sloan, his eyes narrowing but the smile remaining, said quietly, 'You getting religion on me, pal? You're gonna get yourself wasted, you start worrying about the wrong things. I taught you better than that.'

'Sometimes I get a little confused about just what the hell you did teach me. Besides, it was different then, there was a war on. . . .'

Sloan threw back his head and laughed heartily.

'For Christ' sake, there's always a war on *some*place. You need a war? Shit, we got Lebanon, Israel, Iran, Nicaragua, Afghanistan. We got a whole supermarket full of wars, take your pick.' He poured himself a stiff drink of scotch and dropped an ice cube in it. 'Hell, we do what we have to do, Hatch. We got two choices on any given day – do it or don't do it. If you don't know the options going in, if you haven't made the decision, they'll get

176

you. You don't have time to figure the odds, that's the way you get dead. All you got is clicks and reflexes. And if you don't do it, they'll do it to you. Have I ever told you any different? Was there ever any question in your mind about that?'

'My whole bullshit *career* is questionable,' said Hatcher. 'I can't even tell anybody what I did in the war.'

Still chuckling, Sloan said, 'Is that it, you want to write about your war experiences?'

'That's not the point. There's sixteen, seventeen years of my life that are blotto, like they never existed.'

'You think I betrayed you, and that's clouding your judgment,' Sloan said softly. His tone had turned compassionate. Sloan had all the buttons. Push one, you got compassion. Push another, you got patriotic fervor. Push another, you got flattery. Hatcher remembered their first meeting, in a private room of the Occidental Restaurant in Washington where Sloan – as always, confident, almost fatherly – first outlined his personal gospel, describing the Shadow Brigade as a 'golden opportunity, a chance to do something for your country that's necessary, and which also offers a freedom of thought and action you don't find in other branches of the service.' No mention that this 'branch of service' had no records or that it was privately funded and did not even exist officially. Hatcher, the wet-eared kid out of the academy, all full of himself, was stroked and sweet-talked and razzle-dazzled and bought the whole package, no questions asked. That lunch had changed Hatcher's life forever.

'It was more than betrayal, Harry. Hell, you were my mentor. You got it done. You got the mission done and I looked up to you for that.' Hatcher stopped for a moment, got himself a cup of coffee. 'All those years in Los Boxes, all I thought about was you burning me for some bum in the State Department. It wasn't just doing the time. I *trusted* you, Harry, and you turned me up. And you're still doing it.'

'You're getting holy on me,' Sloan said with a chuckle and a shake of his head. 'What's your way of doing it? Take the river pirates to court for running dope to our boys in Saigon? Let our double agents dance on our graves? Compromise with the triads? Shit. Let me tell you something, pal, we learned to fight in dirty wars. And that's what we're gonna have from now on, dirty wars. Well, you don't win dirty wars with Marquis of Queensberry Rules. You kick ass and go for the body mass.'

'The way they do it in Brazil and Argentina?'

Sloan sighed. 'You know your trouble, Hatch? You're trying

177

to equate morality and warfare. Totally incompatible. If the rest of the Army had fought the war in Nam the way we fought it, we wouldn't've got our ass kicked out of there and you know it. We learned how to beat our enemies *from* our enemies. A soldier doesn't need a uniform or a fancy title, all he needs is the will to get it done. I repeat, if you don't do it, it gets done to you. That's the law according to Harry Sloan and it's kept me alive for a bloody long time and it did all right by you, too. You're just thinking too much, Hatch. How many times've I told you, consideration gets a man killed.'

'Harry, you're living proof that it's possible for a man to talk faster than he can think.'

'Well, laddie, when your ass is in the sling, you better do it before you think about it or you're history.'

But it was obvious that Hatcher's reevaluation of the brigade worried Sloan, for he slipped back to the subject. 'You do a thing and it's over,' Sloan said with a shrug. 'Why agonize over all that. You never made any moral decisions, they were made for you.'

'Maybe that's the point. Maybe I should've. Maybe this is about drawing the line.'

'Hah!' Sloan said. 'This is old Harry you're talking to, remember. You giving me ideology? Before lunch! Let me tell you something, we never did a job wasn't worth the doing. You want to get bug-eyed about methods, procedures, whatever, that's your problem. But don't belabor a beautiful morning with ideology, don't give me slogans and posters. My ideology is reality, and the reality is, it's us against them. You and me, we don't lose, pal, it's not in our vocabulary.'

'You made moral decisions, so did I. Spur-of-the-moment moves . . .'

'Exactly. Exactly!' Sloan said, interrupting him, his eyes twinkling again and the enthusiasm back in his tone. 'Spur of the moment. There aren't any moral decisions in warfare, Hatch, there's winning and losing. God and country. Beyond that, it's all superfluous.'

'We got rules, Harry.'

'Yeah, right.'

Hatcher said, 'Anyway, this isn't about God and country, as you put it. It's about you and me. Just don't ever back-stab me again. You do and I'll . . .'

'I know.' Sloan leaned over closer to him, the smile getting broader, the gray eyes still twinkling. 'You'll put me where the fish can't find me.'

There was no percentage in belaboring that subject any further. Hatcher knew he was blowing smoke at the moon. Sloan was a man impervious to insult or hurt, a man who believed what he did was right and necessary and morally justified.

'Forget it,' Hatcher said flatly, 'I didn't come here to do you any favors, anyway. I came to find Cody.'

Sloan nodded, his smile reduced to a wry grin. 'Fair enough. So what have you got so far?' he asked. 'You sure been leading my boys a merry chase.'

Before Hatcher could answer, the phone rang. Sloan glared at it.

'Now what?' he said. He crossed the room and picked it up. He talked with his back to Hatcher. His hair was still damp from the shower and beads of water twinkled on his undried back. The phone was plugged into a small black scrambler, its red light aglow.

'Sloan,' he said in his soft voice. 'S12424. Jack be nimble, Jack be . . . Okay, we're clear, I'm on the scrambler, what's the problem? What? *What!* My God, when? Damn it, Spears, he had ten people guarding him! . . . I know what I said . . . No, don't do that. I assume the media has this . . . I understand that. Uh-huh . . . uh-huh . . . No, you stick with the original story. Let the FBI handle it. . . . No, not the CIA, keep them out of it. . . . Hold on, let me think. . . .'

He turned toward Hatcher and rolled his eyes and shook his head. His face seemed to be getting redder, although he kept his voice under control.

'No pictures of Cosomil,' he said into the phone. 'Keep him under wraps right where he is. I want you to leak a story to the media that he's hiding out in . . . uh . . . Hawaii . . . No, the Big Island, Kauai's too small, yeah. . . . Right, let 'em run around there for a week or two looking for him. . . . That's fine. Thanks, Spears. If I'm temporarily out of pocket, check in with Flitcraft, he can always find me.' He slowly cradled the phone.

'Well, laddie, I got a new problem. Major, *major.* You want to hear the headline in tomorrow morning's *New York Times*? "Mandrango Iron Man Campon Assassinated in Atlanta Disco."'

Hatcher's mouth dropped open. It had been Campon's coup in Madrango that had enabled Sloan to spring Hatcher from Los Boxes. Then six months later the Communist guerrillas had retaken the capital. The revolt had been seesawing for several years.

Sloan gave Hatcher a quick account of the murder of the

179

deposed Central American dictator. 'Our people are speculating that the assassin was disguised as a stork.'

'A *stork!*' said Hatcher.

'It was a costume ball. Three other people, including an innocent woman bystander, were killed. We got two more, her date and a waiter, in serious condition in the hospital.'

'Your outfit was guarding him?'

'Uh-huh. Plus half a dozen of his own men.'

'Who was in charge over there?' Hatcher asked incredulously.

Sloan hesitated for a moment, then said, 'Spears and Hedritch.'

'*Spears and Hedritch!*'

Hatcher thought to himself, *What the hell was Joe Spears doing bodyguarding Héctor Campon?* He remembered Spears as a burned-out California surfer with rice tor brains.

'Spears, for God's sake!'

'That was our front, a personal security service.'

'How the hell did you get involved in this?'

'Because Campon was too hot for the Secret Service to handle. The taxpayers would have raised hell. So I got the job.'

'But Spears? He fried his brains twenty years ago lying around Santa Monica beach.'

'Yeah, well, he and Hedritch'll be protecting mailbags in Tomahawk, Wisconsin, for the rest of their lives.'

'If you put both their brains together you end up with a half-wit.'

'Look,' Sloan said, his face reddening. 'First I inherit this deposed *presidente* with two brigades cooling their heels on the Madrango border, waiting to go back in and chase the Commies out. He needs weapons, he needs ammo, he needs air, he needs military a.d.v.'s, he needs every fuckin' thing but the urge, so he comes up to D.C. looking for help and our leader starts calling in favors all over the Hill. He's looking for fifty million bucks for Campon and I've got to baby-sit the bastard while all this is going on. Three weeks in Fort Lauderdale, two weeks in St Louis, a month and a half in Chicago, two weeks in a houseboat fifty miles out of Atlanta. All of a sudden he's history and we got big troubles.'

'But Spears and Hedritch?'

Sloan slid open the door to the balcony of the bright, airy room and stood with his back to it, letting the breeze dry him off. He sipped his drink and stared at Hatcher. 'I had six men on this, pal. This Campon was no Boy Scout. Skipped the country with five, six mill stashed in Switzerland. A monumental hell-raiser with the morals of an alley cat. Burning up my control teams left and right. Spears and Hedritch were all I had left. But' – he pointed a finger at Hatcher – 'that's also what made him valuable. He was General Macho Man and his men idolized him, *idolized* him. And we need Madrango back, it's key to everything we've got going in Central America.'

'So how did you lose him?'

'He wouldn't stay put. He liked the night life, the ladies.' Sloan shrugged. 'It caught up with him.'

'So what's plan Baker?' Hatcher whispered casually.

Sloan looked at Hatcher suspiciously. 'Who says I've got a plan Baker?'

'You've always got a plan Baker, Harry. First thing you taught me: Always locate the back door. And Madrango's been your baby since the beginning.'

Sloan sighed. 'The back door is General Cosomil. Not as flamboyant or popular as Campon, or as young, but he's dedicated. A good tactical officer. What we've gotta do is martyrize Campon so his men'll line up behind Cosomil. Right now he's under wraps. Ferris and Joyner head that control team and they're the best I got.'

He took another sip and wiped his lips with the back of a thumb.

'You going back to Washington?'

Sloan shook his head. 'I've got it under control for now. The State Department'll step into it now. My job's to keep Cosomil alive until he can get back in there.'

'Well,' Hatcher said, 'there's always the bright side. Congress'll probably give them all the aid they need now.'

Sloan paced the room for several minutes. He stopped and did some deep-breathing exercises.

'That's not my problem,' he said finally. 'Or yours. Let's get back to our business.'

'Hell, I forgot what we were talking about,' Hatcher said.

'You were running my boys all over the lot,' Sloan said dryly.

'Just some exercises to get back in shape,' Hatcher answered.

'Turn up anything?'

'Not much.'

'You been awful busy,' Sloan said with a cock of his head.

'From the look of Buffalo Bill, I don't have a lot of time.'

'Any idea why Cody might be in hiding?'

Now, that's a strange question, thought Hatcher.

'You're way ahead of me,' he said. 'I'm still trying to find out if he's alive or not.'

'Well, what do you think?'

'If you mean have I made any earthshaking conclusions in the last seventy-two hours, the answer is no. I'm not a DA, I don't have to prove anything. At this point I'm waffling back and forth. Sometimes I think Cody's alive, sometimes I think this Wol Pot is scamming us all. It depends on the equation.'

'Well, why do you *think* he's alive?'

'I didn't say he was. I'm just not as sure he's dead as I once was.'

'Why not?'

'Little things. I've got a gunner that now admits one of the men in Cody's plane probably got out. I got an ex-POW tells me he heard about this transient prison camp and one of the prisoners was a VIP who could have been Cody – *could* have been. I got two wingmen – one thinks Cody was a crazy glory hunter, the other thinks he was the second coming. And that's about all I got. Very hazy stuff.'

'But you think there could be validity to Wol Pot's story?'

'I didn't say that. It's all part of the equation. When I figure out what X is, I'll let you know the answer.'

Sloan chuckled. 'Playing 'em close to the vest, huh? Why, if I didn't know better, I'd think you don't trust me anymore,' he said sarcastically.

'Now, why wouldn't I trust you, Harry? Your stock-in-trade is deceit. Murder and lying are your profession. And you double-crossed me. What's not to trust?'

Hatcher paused and took a swig of coffee. He had told Sloan only what he had to tell him. He had left out some things, like the note left at the Wall in Washington to Polo from Jaimie, whoever Jaimie was. And the reference to Thai Horse, which could mean only one thing to Hatcher – heroin. Ninety-nine pure China White from the Golden Triangle. But he wasn't about to throw that out yet. Sloan was far too interested in why Cody was hiding. It was setting off all kinds of danger signals in Hatcher's head. Hatcher knew exactly what Sloan was thinking at that moment. He was thinking, If Cody is into some really bad shit, it would be easy to eliminate the problem. To Sloan, termination was an easy solution for any problem. But he never said it out loud. He always left the dirty words unsaid.

Sloan threw off the towel and started getting dressed.

'We'll go into Bangkok and see what we can turn up,' he said, slipping on olive drab boxer shorts and an undershirt.

But Porter's death and the possible disappearance of Wol Pot had put a new wrinkle on the mission. Now Hatcher's mind was working in other directions, searching for options.

'I'll meet you there in a day or two,' he told Sloan. 'I've got some things I want to check out here.'

'Such as?'

'I'll let you know that when I'm through.'

Sloan started to tie his tie. There was a knock on the door.

'Christ, now what!' Sloan said.

TRIADS

A tall man, arrow-straight, with a sculptured handlebar mustache was standing in the doorway. He wore a spotless white linen suit. Hong Kong cop, thought Hatcher. He had the air.

'Colonel Sloan?' he asked. His British accent was sharp enough to hone a knife on.

'Yes?'

'Sergeant Varney, sir, Hong Kong police.' He showed his credentials.

'A pleasure,' Sloan said in his most diplomatic tone. 'Come on in, what can I do for you?'

Varney entered the room as if he were reporting to the Queen, almost sniffing the air. He smiled stiffly at Hatcher. 'And you must be Mr Hatcher,' he said, offering his hand.

'Uh-huh,' Hatcher said. They shook hands. Varney strode to the balcony door, checked the view, and turned around with his arms behind his back.

'I'm with the Commonwealth Triad Squad,' he said. When neither Sloan nor Hatcher responded, he went on. 'Things've changed a lot in the last six, seven years. I thought I might offer a hand should you need it. I happened to recognize your names when they appeared on our computer yesterday.'

'Computer?' Hatcher asked.

'We run a computer check against the airport list. Routine, y'know, try to keep tabs on who's coming and going. I was going to give you a call and then Colonel Sloan showed up, so I decided to touch in with you both.'

Hatcher said. 'That's real thoughtful, Sergeant. But our business here has nothing to do with the triads.'

183

'Yes, sir, but considering your past experience with the Silk Dragons and the White Palms, we just thought we might extend the courtesy of the force, so to speak.'

'I don't think I'll be needing it,' Hatcher said, staring at Sloan again. 'The colonel's leaving today and I plan to be out of here tomorrow or the next day.'

'Yes, sir, that's jolly good,' Varney said. He paused for a moment as if to pick the right words, stretching his neck and ruffling his shoulders. The sergeant had more ticks than a south Georgia hound. 'It's just that – I think I should advise you, sir – while you are here, you could be in considerable danger. We'd like you to know we'll extend the full courtesy of the department to you. Perhaps' – he paused another moment, pursing his lips before going on – 'you might like an escort.'

'I know the town just fine,' Hatcher's whispery voice crackled.

'Yes, yes, of course, but –'

Hatcher cut him off. 'Look, Sergeant, I never had any dealings with the White Palms, and as far as I know, the Silk Dragons are history.'

Sloan jumped in. 'That's the point, Hatch, the Silk Dragons may be history, but the White Palms kind of . . . uh . . .' Sloan stalled for a moment.

'Permit me,' Varney said. 'After White Powder Mama was assassinated, the White Palms – uh, shall we say – absorbed many of the Silk Dragon members. Rather like a merger, if you will.'

'Is that a fact,' Hatcher said, still only vaguely interested. He knew most of the history and had been battling the Silk Dragons when this Varney guy was still diddy-bopping his way around the middle school cricket pitches.

'You know about Tollie Fong?' Varney asked airily.

'Tollie Fong?' Hatcher said, raising his eyebrows, playing dumb.

'His father was Lee Fong.'

For an instant, Hatcher's mind flashed to the Singapore airport. Dusk. 1975. Twelve years ago. Yeah, he knew Lee Fong, all right.

'We thought you should know Tollie Fong is the new *san wong* of the White Palms,' Varney said with a bit of a flourish, leaning back and almost smirking. 'And,' he added with obvious satisfaction, 'Joe Lung is his Number One here in Hong Kong. They still remember. . . .'

184

So, thought Hatcher, tuning him out, it's come full circle . . .

Sweeping down from the hills on their long-haired horses, the Mongolians came. Their flowing black hair in ratty pigtails, their faces bearded and hungry, their eyes afire with opium. Cutting down or burning everything in their path: horses, cows, pigs, children, all but the women – the women were their prize of prizes. Looting and killing, the barbarians butchered the gentle Chinese in the flatlands by the sea, below the seven peaks where the seven dragons dwelt.

And the dragons, who in life had been the first seven emperors of China, angrily watching from their mountain aeries, summoned forth the leaders of the Chinese, describing to them how to fight back, telling them the tactics to use, giving them the juice.

So the taipans banded together into three-family cells, forming triangles with their farms, erecting walls between them, and hitting back from each side when the Mongols struck, and the dragons were proved right. The Chinese, in what would eventually be Hong Kong, cut the savages to shreds and sent what few were left back to Mongolia to carry the message. The barbarians never returned.

Thus, in the twelfth century, the triads were born, growing stronger for the next eight hundred years; each triad taking on its own rituals, its own passwords and secret handshakes, its own poems, legends and history, swearing allegiance to the clan, a blood oath known as the *hong mon*, growing in power until they were the ruling classes of Hong Kong and the Chinese business world. Businessmen, mostly, honored and respected.

The evil ones followed quickly, the maverick triads who grabbed the power. Calling themselves the Chiu Chao.

Growing in power also: the Silk Dragons, the White Palms, the 14K, the Thin Blade Gang, the House of Seven Hands and others, running it all, everything that was illicit and corrupt – gambling, prostitution, loan sharking, white slavery, drugs, smuggling, the black market – and running it with clear, relentless vision, so focused on cruelty and murder that they defied challenge. The mafiosi of the Orient.

The triads were eight hundred years old. The Chiu Chao was seven hundred ninety years old. It took only ten years for the corruption to start.

The evil triads divided up the underworld, each taking its own segment, and the most lucrative of them all was the drug empire

185

of the Silk Dragons, always looking to expand, seeing ahead with diabolical vision. In the late sixties a fat new market lay waiting in Vietnam, and they brought pure No. 3 China White heroin from the Golden Triangle of Thailand cross-country to Hong Kong and smuggled it into Saigon or shipped it down the Mekong River directly into Vietnam, where they sold it to American GI's for two dollars a pop to get them hooked.

White Powder Mama became the GI's soul mate, their savior, with his precious packages of dreams, their escape from misery. He created by insidious design a new market for China White in the United States, where Mexican or Turkish brown heroin had been king: using hooked American soldiers as the base, the Silk Dragons stretched across the sea to America. White Powder Mama was in reality Ma Bing Sum, the *san wong*, the 'god-father,' of the Silk Dragons. White Powder Mama and his Red Pole 'executioner,' Lee Fong, who was also his brother, were the most feared men in Hong Kong, so powerful they conscripted five members of the Hong Kong narcotics squad, who called themselves the Dragon's Breath, to control the river passages, what they called the 'long, white run.'

Spring, 1973. Enter Christian Hatcher.

They were in the back room of the officers' club in Cam Ranh Bay, which had become the busiest port in the world, the honey pot from which flowed all the men and arms to the undeclared war in Vietnam. Compared with the rest of the country, Cam Ranh was Country Club City, except when the sappers came in the middle of the night and tore things up. For Hatcher, in those days, five minutes away from Indian country was like a six-month vacation.

'Got a job for you,' Sloan said.

'Uh-huh,' Hatcher said. He had heard the line many times before.

'We've got us a big problem over here,' Sloan said.

'No kidding,' Hatcher answered with a laugh.

'I mean besides the war,' Sloan said. 'You know about the Silk Dragons?'

Hatcher nodded. 'You mean White Powder Mama?'

Sloan nodded. 'Ma Bing Sum and his bunch of dope traders.'

'They've been around forever,' replied Hatcher with a shrug. 'They're a Hong Kong police problem.'

'Not anymore. They're walking on our notes, pal,' Sloan went on. 'We have a serious narcotics problem in Nam and most of it is

186

coming downriver from the Triangle. This White Powder Mama has become a major pain in the ass. He's got five do-mommies running the rivers from Thailand. Ex-Hong Kong cops, they call themselves the Dragon's Breath. Strictly bad-ass, the bunch of them. The Buffalo wants to kick ass, teach 'em a lesson.'

'So?'

'So, you know the river. Put together two or three squads, get yourself a couple of armored riverboats, I can get you anybody you need – Crips, Seals, Berets, name it. Any bad-ass in the service is yours. I want you to take 'em all out. I want this Dragon's Breath to be history, and fast.'

'Okay,' Hatcher said casually, 'but I've got an alternative plan to suggest.'

'Shoot.'

'If we do it your way, my cover's blown.'

'Okay, how do you see it?'

'I'll take three good cutthroats, Molly McGuire, Chet Rodriguez' – he thought for a minute – 'and Bear Newton. The rest'll be Orientals. Make it look like we're just hijacking their shit. I'll run the show but keep a low pro. Hell, we'll wear masks, scare the scrotums off the do-mommies. Any other way we do it, I'm made and we wash ten years.'

'Where are you gonna get Orientals that are good enough to do that kind of work?' Sloan asked skeptically.

'That's my problem.'

'I need twenty-four men, the best cutthroats money can buy,' Hatcher told China Cohen. 'Able to take orders, no arguments. And quiet – they say a word about any of this, they lose their tongues.'

'What's the trick?' China asked.

'You don't want to know.'

Duck hunting, roaming the backwaters at night with their twenty mike-mike cannons and thermite bombs, their Uzis and K-Bar knives, hitting the hooches where the druggers slept at night, waging open warfare on the rivers against the Dragon's Breath bringing heroin down the Mekong River. In three months Hatcher's small group ambushed two dozen heroin shipments. In three months four of the five members of the Dragon's Breath felt the cold steel and hot sting of knives in their throats, died quickly and quietly, while their boats and deadly cargoes were stolen from under them, taken far upstream and burned. Only one member of the Dragon's Breath escaped Hatcher's renegades.

Two years later: Singapore airport. White Powder Mama's Number Two, the Red Pole executioner, Lee Fong, had been unsuccessfully looking for Hatcher for almost two years. Finally he had him in sight, had been tailing him for days, waiting for the right moment to kill him in the classic manner, a stiletto placed carefully at the base of the neck, cutting the nervous system and jugular at the same time — an act to save face and prove to White Powder Mama that he was still worthy to be the Silk Dragon's Number Two.

Hatcher had been on to him from the start, knew that Fong had to prove himself. A contact killing was called for, so it was easy for Hatcher to lure him on.

Hatcher went to the observation deck. It was getting dark and the platform was empty. He watched a jet take off, heard the door open behind him and swish shut, heard the footsteps moving closer. He stooped down, as if to tie his shoe. The footsteps quickened. They were directly behind him.

Hatcher twisted and stood in one swift move, burying a seven-inch stiletto under the rib cage and jamming it up into Fong's heart, staring straight into Fong's face, so close he felt the rush of the Silk Dragon executioner's dying breath on his face, and trapping Fong's hand in a steel grip until he felt the life drop out of the assassin's body.

'*Joi gin*, Fong,' he said as he dropped him.

Two weeks later, White Powder Mama was dead on the streets of Wanchai, machine-gunned coming out of a nightclub. The reign of the Silk Dragons was ended. The White Palms took over and, to show their compassion, absorbed many of the Silk Dragons' members.

One of them was Tollie Fong, Lee Fong's son. Now, twelve years later, he was the Red Pole of the White Palm Triad, and was about to become its leader. As the White Palm assassin, Tollie Fong was perhaps the most dangerous man in the world. As *san wong* his power was awesome. And his Number One in Hong Kong was Joe Lung, the last remaining member of the Dragon's Breath, the only one to escape Hatcher's guerrillas.

Both had sworn to kill Hatcher on sight.

They operated out of Macao.

188

And all Hatcher's clicks told him that if this Varney knew he was in Hong Kong, the White Palms probably did too.

'. . . hijacking their goods,' Varney was saying.

'Beg your pardon?' said Hatcher.

'I said, apparently they still hold it against you, hijacking their goods, I mean.'

The secret had been well kept. As far as Varney or Hong Kong or even Interpol knew, Hatcher had been a bad-ass who was now cooperating with the government. Hatcher knew Varney wasn't there just to offer the 'courtesy of the Crown.' He was there to size up Hatcher, decide whether he was one of the good guys or still potentially a bad guy. That was okay, too.

Sergeant Varney was smart enough to realize that Hatcher did not welcome his help or his interest. This was a dangerous man.

'I suggest you be extremely careful while you're in the colony,' Varney said, walking to the door. 'You are still high on Tollie Fong's death list. If either he or Joe Lung finds out you are in Hong Kong, they will stop at nothing to kill you. Needless to say, as a police officer I would prefer to prevent that.'

'I appreciate your interest,' Hatcher said. 'As I told you, we'll both be out of here in a day or two. I'll try to keep a low profile.'

Varney handed Hatcher his card. 'If you should need help, just call. My night number is on the back. I assure you, we will respond as quickly as possible.'

The sergeant marched stiffly to the door and left with a short bow.

Hatcher was suspicious and annoyed by the intrusion.

'I got things to do here, Harry,' Hatcher said. 'I definitely don't need this Limey ramrod crawling up my back.'

'Just don't go snooping around Macao, okay?' Sloan said.

'Don't worry about me —'

'Keep away from Tollie Fong and the triads.'

'I don't want to run into Fong and his buddies.'

'You'll end up floating in the bay. I'd hate like hell to have to explain that.'

'That's really sentimental of you.'

'You know what I mean.'

'I know exactly what you mean. And I'm not going to end up floating anywhere.'

'Start messing with the White Palms, you're as good as dead.'

'That's not the way it happened last time.'

'Don't get cocky either,' said Sloan softly. 'Tollie Fong is *the*

189

man in the White Palm Triad now and Joe Lung is his number one boy in Hong Kong. And they both have sworn to dust you. You're not in Bangkok by Saturday, I'll have the dogs out after you.'

'I'll meet you at the Imperial,' Hatcher whispered. 'The D'Jit Pochana for breakfast Saturday morning, usual time.'

'Sure.'

'One other thing. Get that whiz kid you got in the States, Flitcraft, to check his computer. See if there's anything on a Vietnam POW camp that was a floater. It moved around. I'm guessing it was a temporary holding camp near the Laotian border. It might have been called the Ghost Camp or something like that.'

'I'll see what he can turn up. I'll have him call you direct.'

'I've got his number. I'll call him.'

'All right,' Sloan said after a moment's thought. 'Just be careful.'

'I've never stopped being careful,' Hatcher answered.

Hatcher turned, went back into his room and closed the door behind him. He didn't bother to shake hands.

He stepped out on his balcony and looked across the bay at Victoria Peak and Cohen's mountaintop fortress. A lot of things had changed in the last hour. Now he knew he *had* to see Cohen.

Every man must pay for his sins, 126 had once said.

The question in Hatcher's mind was, Who was the sinner, who had been sinned against, and who was going to have to pay?

OPTIONS

Hatcher's clicks were working overtime. Sloan would have the police version of what happened and background on Wol Pot by the time Hatcher got to Bangkok, so there was no need worrying about that now. If they had lost Wol Pot, Hatcher had to take his other options. But they were risky and they were long shots. The question he asked himself was, Should he trash the project and go back to Georgia? Suddenly the Cody job had taken a bad turn. The complexities were growing. One man had been murdered and now the Hong Kong Triad Squad appeared to be involved. Varney's 'social' call had immediately fired more danger signals in Hatcher's head. This was no longer a simple trace job. It had turned lethal.

190

He formed his plan quickly, based on logic. If the Vietnam ghost camp described by Schwartz did exist, there were people upriver in Chin Chin land who would know about it. That meant he would need Cohen's help. Hatcher decided to make contact with his old friend, then wait and see if Flitcraft turned up anything interesting.

He stared up at the top of Victoria Peak, at the house he knew was Cohen's, wondering whether the years had changed him. Was he still as powerful as he had once been? Hatcher wondered. And what of Daphne?

Could he still trust any of his old friends?

He dialed a number he still remembered after all the years. A high-pitched voice answered in Chinese: *'Jo sahn.'*

'Cheap bastard,' Hatcher growled. 'Still too cheap to spring for a secretary after all these years. And that phony Chin soprano of yours doesn't fool me.'

There was a long pause, then an awed voice almost whispered, 'Christian?'

'Ah. You haven't forgotten,' Hatcher whispered in return.

'Christian!' Cohen shouted. 'Christ, I heard you were dead.'

'That's what you get for listening to rumours.'

'My God, I can't believe this. Are you here?'

'Over at the old standby.'

'What're you whispering for, you in trouble?' Cohen asked in a very confidential tone.

'It's a long story and, no, I'm not in trouble – at least not yet.'

'Get your ass over here – now! God, wait till I tell Tiana. I can't believe this, man, I can't fucking believe it! Hatcher, back from the dead!'

China Cohen's excitement seemed genuine, and Hatcher felt better after he hung up. In his heart, he believed that Cohen was still a loyal friend. But this was Hong Kong. Allegiances changed as quickly as the wind.

Joe Lung never got up before noon. He spent his evenings in Monitor's casino or doing his rounds of the various nightclubs. If the pickings were slim, he usually ended the night in one of the various whorehouses in Macao. Lung rarely got to bed before three or four in the morning, and he rarely changed the routine unless there was a job to do.

He lived in one of the new condos that were already beginning to destroy the centuries-old beauty of Macao, the tiny city at the gateway to China.

He stirred and reached over, touching the woman beside him. She was a blonde, a beauty he had picked up the night before in the Fire Duck Club. Lung liked the *gwai-lo* women, and this one was wilder than usual. She moaned and turned over on her back, still asleep, and he rolled over on his side and pressed against her, sliding his hand across the top of the silk sheet. He began to stroke her awake.

The phone began to ring. Annoyed, he turned away from the woman and gruffly answered it.

'Hatcher is here. Room 512, the Peninsula,' the voice on the other end said in Chinese.

Lung sat straight up in bed. 'No mistake?' There was urgency in his voice.

'No mistake. It is Hatcher.'

'Is he there now?'

'*Hai*, but who knows for how long.'

'*Mm goi*,' Lung said and hung up. Lung's pulse was racing. Lung long ago had given up any hope of avenging the murder of his partners by Hatcher. Then Tollie Fong had sworn to kill him, and since Fong was his boss, the possibility of revenge became more remote. He lay back on the bed and stared at the ceiling, smiling, for Tollie Fong was out of town. What a sweet surprise it would be, thought Lung, to stick the *gwai-lo* before Fong got back. Otherwise Tollie Fong would perform the execution himself.

The girl responded to his overtures. She was fascinated by the green dagger tattooed on his forearm, aroused by his muscular body, and she found his faulty attempts to speak English attractive. It was a new experience for her, making love to someone whose culture was so totally alien to hers. At first she was frightened by his gruff manner, afraid that perhaps he was into some strange Oriental sex rites and would hurt her. But it was just his manner, and it had turned out to be one of the most satisfying sexual experiences of her life. She leaned over and began to stroke the inside of his thigh. He slapped her on the rump. 'We will have again later,' he said in English. 'I do business now.'

After he had sent her back to the hotel, Lung took an ice-cold shower. He toweled off, opened a chest in the corner of the bedroom, and slid a long, narrow dagger out of its soft calfskin sheath. He tied the sheath to his left forearm, covering the tattoo, then got dressed in traditional Chinese workingman's clothes, black sateen pants and a shirt with wide sleeves. He studied himself in the mirror, shifted his gaze to the reflection of a dart board behind him on the wall.

Lung folded his arms across his chest, then whirled, lashing out his right arm, pulling the dagger and snapping it across the room. The silver blade flashed in the morning sun, hit the board dead center and stuck there, its handle quivering.

Lung smiled and uttered a tight little grunt of satisfaction. What was it the *gwai-lo* said? Practice does perfection?

Hatcher had checked his main bags through to Bangkok, so he had only an overnight bag with a change of clothes and the usual overnight necessities in it and his Halliburton case. He took both when he left the room. He went first to the wine store in the lobby of the hotel, a connoisseur's shop, and bought a bottle of wine, a Lafite Rothschild '72, that seemed to fit the occasion. When he left the hotel, he walked around the corner from the hotel and strolled up Nathan Street, window-shopping while he checked behind him in the window reflections. By the time he reached Kowloon Park four blocks away he had spotted the car.

Two men. One in the car, the other on foot. One Oriental, one Occidental. In five blocks they switched off twice. Pretty good.

Hatcher was sure these were Varney's men, and now he became even more suspicious of the Hong Kong cop. It was possible that a computer had turned up Hatcher's name. But after all these years, it did not make sense for them to be *this* interested in him. Cops throughout the world were overworked. It was highly suspect for them to be 'protecting' Hatcher without his request.

He walked across the park, doubled back down Kowloon Drive to the Star Ferry slip and boarded the ferry, standing near the stern, staring out over the bay. To Hatcher's surprise, the two men did not follow him. The man on foot got in the car; they drove off up Salisbury Road as the ferry pulled out.

They were very good, Hatcher thought to himself. By now they've alerted their people on the island. The new tail would be waiting for Hatcher when he got there. He would have to play the game again when he got to the island. He did not want Varney and the Triad Squad to know he was going to visit the Tsu Fi.

Joe Lung entered the hotel through the servants' entrance. Because of his dress, he was easily mistaken for one of the laborers that worked around the hotel. Lung went straight to the fifth floor and quickly, silently, picked the lock on Hatcher's door. He let the door glide open, standing alert as it did, then jumped inside and closed it just as silently. He entered the room cautiously, checked it thoroughly.

Hatcher was not there, nor was his luggage.

Lung stood in the middle of the room thinking. Had Hatcher left the city? Perhaps he was on the way to the airport at that moment.

Lung went to the lobby and checked the desk from the house phone. Had Mr Hatcher in 512 checked out? No, the desk answered.

The temporary setback had no visible effect on Lung. He was a patient man accustomed to setbacks. They were easily overcome. But he might have to change his plan. Obviously the job was going to require different tactics.

When the ferry docked, Hatcher strolled off and turned right, heading west on Connaught Street toward the downtown section. There was a cool breeze blowing, and he was surrounded by the sounds of Hong Kong, by music and taxi horns, laughter and ship's bells, by the rustle of banyan trees and the constant undertone of conversation.

He acted like a tourist, strolling past the nightclubs of Wanchai, where Suzie Wong had fallen in love with an American GI and died for her sin. American music blared from loudspeakers outside the doors of the clubs, and the girls wore American jeans and had had their eyes straightened.

As he got closer to the business district the crowds increased, until he had to thread his way along the street, stopping occasionally to check behind him. There were two men assigned to him again, using the same routine. By the time he reached the shabby gate that marked the beginning of notorious Cat Street he was trapped in the steamy crowd of tourists heading up the steep, winding street choked with shops, seeking bargains.

Hatcher turned into the crowded thoroughfare, moving along with the shoulder-to-shoulder crowd. He approached the acupuncture parlor where he had first met Cohen, thought about the dusty office with the uncomfortable chairs, and considered cutting through it to throw off his tail. No, he thought, too obvious.

Instead, Hatcher leaned over and bent his knees slightly, making himself shorter so that his head was below the level of the rest of the crowd. He continued to walk in that fashion for nearly

194

a city block until he came to a tiny clothing store jammed between other shops. The store was so cluttered with goods Hatcher could not see beyond the display window. He dodged quickly inside.

The tail lost Hatcher in the Cat Street crowd. Then he thought he saw Hatcher dodge into a shop. He rushed ahead, elbowing pedestrians out of the way.

The tiny store was crammed with racks of jeans and sport clothes. Shirts and blouses were stacked from floor to ceiling and shoppers stood elbow to elbow looking for bargains. Hatcher had gone straight through the store out the back door, had turned back in the narrow alley to Connaught Street and jumped in the first ricksha he saw. He leaned back in the seat, out of view.

'To the tram, and hurry,' he told the ricksha boy in Chinese. He didn't look back.

Back up Cat Street, the man following him stepped out the back door of the clothing shop and looked both ways. There was no sign of Hatcher. He pulled out his walkie-talkie and pressed the button.

'He ditched me,' he said with disgust.

The ricksha boy trotted rhythmically down Connaught Street to Garden and turned up to the entrance to the Victoria Peak Tram. Hatcher paid him and got out, looking back down the street. Just the usual traffic.

So far, so good, he thought and entered the tram.

THE WHITE TSU FI

From the balcony of his home on the side of Victoria Peak, Cohen watched the tram rise up the side of the mountain. He had seen Hatcher arrive in the ricksha and board the funicular. Cohen also scanned the street and park below to see if anyone might be following his friend. He saw nothing suspicious. But with Hatcher, one could never be sure, and now, to suddenly appear after all the years, Cohen wondered what his old friend was up to.

Cohen's mind drifted back in time, to a dark night upriver when his friendship with Hatcher had first begun to blossom.

Cohen was coming back down from the Ts'e K'am Men Ti with a load of contraband goods when a boatload of maverick river pirates had loomed up behind him and fired several warning shots

195

in the air. Cohen had only half a dozen men with him. After all, nobody, nobody, attacked the Tsu Fi, a fact that unfortunately had eluded the bunch of river scum. They ordered his two boats to heave to.

Then Cohen heard the deep roar of engines and a coal-black gunboat materialized out of the darkness. It had the profile of an American riverboat but had no markings. Standing on the bow was the white man he had seen upriver a few months earlier. He dredged the name from his memory: Hatcher. A dozen armed brigands were lined up along the rail of Hatcher's boat. Then Cohen noticed that the gunner manning the M-60 in the gun tower was wearing a shirt with Army stripes on the sleeve. A sergeant? Were these American soldiers? he had wondered. Nobody else was wearing a uniform. Hatcher wore camouflaged pants and an olive drab tank top, but so did everybody else these days. There was some conversation, and although Cohen could not hear Hatcher, whatever he said had been effective. The pirates had turned to and headed back upriver. Hatcher pulled alongside Cohen's tiny but elegant snakeboat.

'We meet again,' he said with a grin.

'So we do, mate, so we do,' said Cohen. 'And just where the hell did you come from, not that I'm complaining?'

'We've been a mile or so behind you for the last hour,' Hatcher answered. 'Then those bozos pulled out of a creek and dropped on your stern, so I figured we better check it out.'

'I owe you,' Cohen said with a bow.

'I'll remember that,' Hatcher said. 'Come aboard, I'll buy you a drink.'

The gunboat had been customized by Hatcher and his men. It was a sleek, fast-moving craft built for action and little else. It had skimpy quarters for the crew but a large, amply supplied kitchen, more guns and armor plate than a tank, and was painted coal-black. Hatcher's crew of a dozen bearded GIs was as motley as the gangsters he had just chased away. Hatcher led Cohen to his spartan quarters, a small cabin with a liquor cabinet, a desk covered with homemade river charts, and a hammock strung from the rafters. Cohen knew better than to ask his host any direct questions. Hatcher took a bottle of gin from the cabinet and poured them both a generous slug.

'Where you headed?' Cohen asked cautiously.

'Back into Hong Kong for a little R and R,' Hatcher answered.

196

Cohen's face brightened. 'Ah, I'm delighted. Now there's an area in which I am truly an expert,' he said. 'You will be my guest while you're in the colony. I insist.'

Hatcher smiled and hoisted his drink. 'Who could turn down an offer like that?' he answered. •

For the next two weeks, Cohen had entertained Hatcher like a crown prince. They had raised hell from Macao to Kowloon. A sweet time, a time to develop mutual trust and confidence. They became comrades. For Cohen a first, while for Hatcher, Cohen was his first true friend since Murph Cody. Cohen tutored his friend on the operations of the Hong Kong triads while Hatcher regularly supplied Cohen with information about the whereabouts of the British customs patrols. But what had cemented their friendship was that they genuinely liked each other. The two loners traded personal confidences and their friendship had matured in a way that endured through the years. While Cohen was the Tsu Fi and could travel the rivers with immunity from Sam-Sam Sam's interference, he always had the feeling Hatcher was somewhere nearby just in case he got into trouble.

Then, as suddenly as he had appeared on the river, Hatcher had vanished without a word. Good-byes were not Hatcher's style.

Now Cohen's pulse quickened at the prospect of seeing his friend again.

Hatcher, too, was excited at the thought of seeing the white Tsu Fi. After his first meeting with the little man, he had asked about him on his occasional forays into Hong Kong. There were vague rumors about him, but he heard nothing specific until one night when he was having a drink with a group of reporters in the Godown Bar on Connaught Street. It was a favorite hangout because of the live American Dixieland band and the generous drinks. There, a boozy ex-reporter named Charlie Rawlson perked up when Hatcher mentioned Cohen.

'I knew him when,' he said over a glass of Bombay gin and lemon juice. 'I was at Harvard with him.'

'Harvard!' said Sid Barnaby, a *Time* magazine correspondent.

'Nieman fellow,' Rawlson said with a flourish.

'Back in the late sixties,' Rawlson began. 'At the time, Cohen was kinda the campus joke. You'd see the little bugger dashin' across Harvard Square with his briefcase hugged up against his chest like he was afraid somebody would run off with it, hidin' behind this fringy little beard of his, with never a word for anyone. Had all the social grace of a friggin' water buffalo, he did. His old man was a hotshot Westchester lawyer or something. And old Cohen did his parents proud. Summa cum at Princeton, a DBA from Harvard. When he got his doctorate, every big company in the country lined up to interview him. Then they found out he was a brain without an ounce of social grace, a genius who could hardly say hello to a stranger. He was written off as a reclusive looney tune. Actually he was just shy, is what he was. Shy was invented to describe old Cohen.'

'So what happened?' Hatcher asked.

'His parents decided what he needed was a round-the-world cruise to get him back in the social world. "Time you had a little fun," his father tells him. "Find yourself a nice lady and see how the other half lives." Well, the old boy could not have conceived the limits to which Cohen would carry that bit of advice. That was the last I heard of him until about a year ago I see him waltz out of a bank on Connaught wearing a red silk *cheongsam*. He gets in a Rolls-Royce and tools off. God knows what happened in all those years in between.'

Later, Cohen had filled in the blanks for Hatcher.

On his balcony, Cohen, too, was reminiscing, remembering the first time he had ever seen Hong Kong harbor. He had hidden in his cabin all the way from San Francisco, terrified of facing all the strangers on the enormous ship. The first night in, he sneaked out on deck to take a look around and was awestruck by the towering mountain peak, the blazing lights of the city and the sampans that surrounded the big ship with the children yelling for a handout. That was when Cohen was spotted by a purser named Ringer, a seasoned and perverse hand, who genuinely felt sorry for Cohen.

'See here, sir, I'm going over to the Central District by myself – care to come along?'

Cohen, nervous but interested: 'That's the business district, isn't it?'

Ringer: 'Yes, but there are other things to see. I thought you might enjoy going to Fat Lady Lau's House of Orchids.'

Cohen: 'Is that a restaurant?'

Ringer, that rogue: 'Well, uh, I suppose you might call it that.'

Restaurant indeed. Fat Lady Lau's was perhaps the greatest whorehouse in the world and Ringer led him to it, believing he was going over to the island for egg rolls and chop suey. The

198

moment Cohen entered the double doors of Fat Lady Lau's his life changed. His sexual imagination was ignited and a new door opened for Cohen.

He smiled to himself as he remembered that night. The living room was lit by pink candles, and Chinese minstrels played somewhere out of sight. The buffet! The buffet was a succulent miracle. Every imaginable delicacy was on that table. Caviar from Black Sea sturgeon, garlicky sparrow's wings the way they do it in Canton, shark's fin and mushroom soup spiced with Chinese vinegar, slices of Peking duck served on *bao bing* and *chun juan* rolls stuffed with curried pork and squid, vegetables steamed in champagne.

And the women! Cohen was mesmerized. They were all revealed in that soft, flickering candlelight – tantalizing shadows and each one an individual, each dressed in her own manner, under the approving eye of Fat Lady.

One was wearing a naughty French nightgown, another a lacy thing with nothing under it, still another a black garter belt and corset. There was a tall Peruvian beauty wearing a high-necked Victorian blouse and not another stitch, a Nubian princess wearing a teddy as thin as air. There were women from every remote corner of the world. Eurasians and Japanese and Chinese and Thais and Egyptians and Greeks and French. There were Africans and Israelis. There was even an American Indian princess and a pair of Eskimo twins they called the Mucklucks, who always performed together in a mirrored room.

My rite of passage was a truly remarkable experience, thought Cohen with a smile.

Fat Lady Lau, who was anything but – as tall and slender as a French model, all high cheekbones and broad shoulders – was the one untouchable prize in a place where everything else was given away or for sale.

'Why do they call her Fat Lady?' Cohen asked.

Ringer replied, 'Because this, my friend, is what fat city is all about.'

Her trained eyes immediately recognized Cohen as a virgin, and she chose a rare prize for him. She left the room and returned with Tiana. Cohen relished the memory – that tiny thing, shorter than Cohen, a mere child of sixteen, wrapped in a sarong, her hair combed in a tight little bun held in place by orchids and azaleas, with black bangs brushed down over her forehead. She smiled at Cohen, the softest smile he had ever seen, then she reached out and took his hand – and led him to

199

paradise. She led him up to her room and Cohen could remember vividly every candlelit corner, the colors of the down pillows piled in one corner, the large old-fashioned tub with brass legs in the other, remembered her selecting each morsel of the delicacies set on a table and feeding it to him, mixing the tastes with such talent that simply eating was an aphrodisiac.

Then she slowly undressed him, massaging every muscle in his body before she reached up and removed the combs and flowers from her black hair and let it tumble down over her shoulders. Then she sat up, unwound the sarong and dropped it on the floor and stood there letting him admire her body before she led him to the tub, which was filled with mud so hot he could hardly bear it, then tantalizing him and then screwing him until he was close to insanity. Cohen's blood thundered through his veins as he remembered it.

Cohen never left. Never went back to the boat, or any of the boats after that. His world became Hong Kong and that Victorian mansion in Wanchai, sampling, sampling, sampling, learning to speak of love in every language and making love in every marvelously deviate way imaginable.

And then Cohen discovered something else about himself, a side of his personality that had lain dormant for twenty-seven years. He discovered that at heart he was a born scoundrel to whom a scam was far more interesting than the market or dollar fluctuations or commodities. Cohen discovered smuggling, brokering illegal gold, outwitting the customs boats to bring contraband into the colony. He also learned that in the Crown Colony, information was as valuable as goods. He and Tiana became friends as well as lovers. She taught him Chinese, he taught her English. The Oriental life-style was like a magnet to him.

It was from the Chinese that Cohen first heard about the Tsu Fi, the Old Man Who Bites Like a Dragon. The Tsu Fi dallied with the taipans of the Central District through silken puppet strings, they said. No secrets were denied him. He was feared by the most powerful of the Western robber barons. To cross the Tsu Fi, they said, was to cross the gods. In Cohen's mind, the Tsu Fi was the gatekeeper to the pantheon. Meeting him and sharing his secrets became Cohen's obsession. But the Tsu Fi was difficult and did not trust *gwai-lo* foreigners.

One night at Fat Lady Lau's, Tiana opened the door to the pantheon.

A customer who came occasionally had confided that a rich

woman had hired him to kill her husband. She knew few details except that the woman's name was the same as a flower's. Cohen checked *Toole's Guide to the Crown*, the definitive business reference book for Hong Kong. And there it was:

Hampton-Rhodes Overseas Transport, Ltd. President and Chief Executive Officer: Charles Rhodes. Originally Hampton Shipping and Transport, Ltd. Founded 1934, registry: Aberdeen. Founder, Jonathan Hampton, died: 1978. Name changed: 1979. Married: *Iris* (née Hampton), daughter of founder: 1975.

He checked with friends in the banking towers of Connaught Street and that night he asked Tiana to arrange an audience with the Tsu Fi.

'But, Robert, he will not do business with *gwai-lo*.'

'Tell him this *gwai-lo* can make him richer,' said Cohen confidently.

The plan was audacious, which was one of the reasons it had appealed to Cohen. But he knew business, that was one thing he knew very well. What a coup if this *gwai-lo* could learn the Tsu Fi's secrets.

The office of the Tsu Fi was on noisy, cluttered Cat Street over the shop of an acupuncturist. The Tsu Fi had operated out of the same two rooms since anyone could remember. The sign on the door, which was in Chinese characters, said simply, 'Wong,' and below it, 'Spices.'

Cohen was nervous, but he knew he couldn't show it. After climbing the stairs, he stood outside the door, breathing deeply, humming slowly to himself to bring his pulse down before he entered and found himself in a small anteroom no larger than a clothes closet. Through the door he could see into the Tsu Fi's office, which was not much larger. Obviously the old man did not go in for show.

The Tsu Fi sat with his back to the window behind a simple mahogany desk, which was empty except for an abacus on one side and an old-fashioned black cradle phone. A single chair sat in front of the table. Sunlight shimmered around his chair and dust hung heavily in its bright beams. There was a teak strongbox in one corner and a small table with a tea set on it in the opposite side of the room. That was it.

The Tsu Fi looked ancient, although he was erect and his eyes glittered. His skin was totally free of wrinkles and almost

201

transparent, like waxed paper holding together his delicate bones. His hair was pure white and close-cropped and he was clean-shaven. He stared at Cohen for several seconds before raising his hand and motioning him into the room with a single stroke of a forefinger. Cohen approached the table and held out his hand.

'I am Robert Cohen,' *he said in perfect mandarin.*

The Tsu Fi ignored Cohen's hand and instead held his own out at a very precise angle in the beams of sunlight that sliced through the dust. He studied the shadow on the floor.

'At least you are punctual,' *he said in a high-pitched voice and motioned Cohen to the empty chair.*

The Tsu Fi folded his hands on his desk and said, 'So?'

Cohen cleared his throat. He had practiced what he wanted to say and he leaned back, trying to be comfortable in a chair that defied comfort, and began, 'I have information I think can be useful to both of us. It has come to me that a man in business here is going to be murdered. His wife will pay for the killing.'

The old man stared at him without a flicker of a muscle, his eyes boring straight into Cohen's.

'The man is inept and lazy. He drinks too much and cheats on his wife. Her father started the business. He is dead now. The company is in deep trouble. But if this man dies, then she inherits his stock and control of the company. With him out of the way, she will be free to hire new people and reorganize. Their assets are very strong. As I see it, two things can happen. Either the company will get back on its feet, or a consortium will take it over.'

'Is there not a third possibility?' *the Tsu Fi asked.*

'You mean bankruptcy? Unlikely. This woman has her own resources. I doubt that she would go to this extreme unless she had a plan for getting the company back together.'

'What does this mean to me?' *the old man asked.*

Cohen, smiling, leaned forward. 'Us?' *he suggested.*

'I have no interest in this paper market of yours, American. It is a Westerner's game I do not play.'

'I understand it,' *Cohen said assertively.* 'Tsu Fi, if we wait until this stock dips down – say, eight points – then put, say, half a million in, the stock should rise sharply when the reorganization begins.'

'And how long would that take?'

'Six months, maybe seven.'

'And what do you think it will go to?'

202

'I estimate it should go up at least twenty points.'

The Tsu Fi's fingers raced across his abacus.

'Two, two and a half million in six months,' Cohen went on, although he realized the Tsu Fi was already ahead of him.

'I would stay on top of it every day and sell at the perfect moment,' Cohen continued.

'And what do you want?'

Cohen leaned forward, eyes aglow. 'Half the profit,' he said confidently.

The Tsu Fi glared at him. There was a minute of silence before he slowly shook his head. 'No.'

'All right, a third, then,' Cohen quickly countered. 'You make two million, I make six hundred thousand. I'll round it off. Half a million.'

'You give up a hundred thousand dollars very easily,' the Tsu Fi said.

'It is easy to give up money one does not yet have,' Cohen answered.

The Tsu Fi smiled for the first time. The gwai-lo was arrogant, but the Tsu Fi also knew about him. He was very smart. He knew this kind of business. What was more important, this Cohen had proved he knew how to use information. He could deal with the arrogance, although it would be necessary to teach him a lesson. Perhaps this Cohen could open up new doors for him, doors he had avoided in the past. The thought of a new venture stirred his blood.

'And you feel no obligation to try to prevent this execution?' the Tsu Fi asked.

'It is a family affair.' Cohen shrugged matter-of-factly. 'Besides, if I went to the police it would cause problems for my friends.'

The Tsu Fi stroked his chin, still staring unflinchingly at Cohen.

'How soon?' he asked.

'I don't know that, but when Rhodes dies, the stock will dip and we must be ready.'

'And if this paper does not turn around?'

Cohen smiled and raised his shoulders. 'Then I assume I would be in a great deal of trouble. I am prepared to take that risk.'

The Tsu Fi nodded very slowly. 'Tell me when you are ready,' he said. 'I will give you my answer then.'

'It will be too late for me to find another investor then,' Cohen said.

'You want an immediate decision?' the old man said with surprise.

'If you are not interested, Tsu Fi, I'll have to find someone else.'

The Tsu Fi stared at him again, appraising the arrogant young man.

'Then my answer is no,' the old man said.

It threw Cohen off, but he knew the old Chinese was interested in the proposition. *If I walk, will he change his mind or just dismiss the idea? he wondered. Cohen was committed. To back off now would be a sign of weakness, and he was more interested in gaining the Tsu Fi's confidence than he was in the deal itself.*

'Well, I am sorry I wasted your time, sir,' Cohen said and stood up to leave.

The Tsu Fi held his hand out into the sunbeam again and stared at the floor.

'Good-bye,' he said.

Cohen turned and went to the door and suddenly the Tsu Fi called out to him: 'Mr Cohen, your face is beginning to sag. Stop downstairs. The man's name is Ping. Tell him I said you require the needles.'

Cohen followed his advice. He sat in an old-fashioned barber's chair while the acupuncturist inserted the long, delicate needles carefully in all the secret places. Cohen felt himself relaxing. He sat for thirty minutes with his eyes closed. When Ping withdrew the needles, Cohen opened his eyes. The Tsu Fi was standing in front of him.

'Keep me informed,' he said. 'The money will be available.' And he left the room.

Cohen ran after him. 'Sir?' he called out as the Tsu Fi was going back upstairs.

The old man turned and glared down at him. Cohen took a folded paper from his pocket and held it out to the old man.

'I, uh, took the liberty of preparing a contract – just to define our arrangement,' he said.

The Tsu Fi snorted and snatched the paper out of his hand. He wheeled around. 'Come,' he snapped. Cohen followed him up the stairs.

The old man took out a match and burned the contract without reading it. His eyes glittered in the dusty sunlight. 'Now you know what paper is worth,' he said curtly. 'And never sign anything, your mark will follow you to Heaven.'

Nine days after Cohen and the Tsu Fi met, Charles Rhodes

204

was killed in an automobile accident. The stock dropped to five before Cohen decided to buy.

After an announced reorganization, it jumped, climbing to twenty-four-plus before it leveled off. The Tsu Fi was delighted, having bitten the dragon for a little over two million. Cohen hurried to the Cat Street office to collect his half million.

The Tsu Fi slid ten thousand dollars across the table.

'What's this, a down payment?' Cohen said with a laugh.

'It is fair payment for what you did,' said the Tsu Fi.

Cohen leaped to his feet, enraged. 'You're the one who told me paper wasn't worth a damn. I trusted you!'

'Another lesson,' said the old man. 'Never trust anyone.' He held his hand out to check the time.

'Put the hand down,' Cohen snapped. 'You owe me half a million dollars.'

The Tsu Fi looked up at him. 'Do you want to earn your money or do you want to yell and scream?' the old man said.

Cohen calmed down. He sat back down, staring at the old con artist.

'You have much to learn about our ways, American,' the Tsu Fi said. 'But you have talent. When you learn, half a million dollars will seem insignificant.'

Thus Cohen became the protégé of the Tsu Fi. He opened his own office, a single room on the edge of the Wanchai district with three telephones and a computer. He did all his business himself, another of the Tsu Fi's lessons ('Never share your secrets with anyone.') The Tsu Fi's advice became Cohen's bible. Then one day his mentor summoned him to the Cat Street office.

'It is time for you to go up the Macao Runs,' the Tsu Fi said. Cohen was shaken by the news. It never occurred to him the Tsu Fi would send him upriver into Chin Chin land.

'Why?' he asked.

'If it is necessary to ask, perhaps I am sending the wrong person,' the Tsu Fi said. 'You are my new negotiator. You must win these China pirates with bravado, show no fear. This is business. The price of goods. You have a taste for money, American. You are getting rich, but it will require some discomfort.'

The Tsu Fi gave him a Queen Victoria twenty-dollar gold piece.

'This says you speak for me,' he said. 'In the past my men have not done well in their negotiations. They do not trust their own thoughts and they agree too quickly. You are the nobleman of negotiators, gwai-lo, you must make new deals that are better.'

'Then we need to sweeten the pot,' Cohen suggested.

'*Sweeten the pot? What pot?*'

'*Offer them something better than the others who are doing business on the river.*'

'*And what would that be?*' asked the Tsu Fi.

'*I'm thinking,*' Cohen said.

'*Think quickly,*' said the Tsu Fi. '*You go tonight.*'

And that was the night Cohen first met Hatcher.

Cohen became the white Tsu Fi. He had his own men on the river. He was respected by the Ts'e K'am Men Ti and feared by the Hong Kong taipans. His contacts upriver in Red China were impeccable. But mostly he traded in information. Cohen was a clearinghouse for every personal and business rumor in the colony.

If there was a major problem, the taipans turned to him.

They called him China Cohen.

He loved every minute of it.

When Hatcher got to the top of the mountain, he strolled around the side of the peak to Albany Road, near the Botanical Gardens. Cohen's house stood near the edge of the peak.

He was deep in thought, but not too deep to miss the car parked far above him at the entrance to the Botanical Gardens, or the driver watching him through binoculars.

OLD TIMES, NEW TIMES

Hatcher stood in front of the large iron gates that led to Cohen's mountaintop estate. The wall that surrounded it was eight feet high. The iron grille gates had once guarded the entrance to the castle of a Chinese warlord in Shanghai. Electric eyes and an electrified wire added a modern touch to the wall, although they were not visible from the ground.

He pressed the button in the wall beside the gate, and a moment later a guard appeared, staring at him through the grille.

'*Hai?*' the guard said.

'*Ngo hai gli Occhi di Sassi,*' Hatcher answered, using the nickname, 'the Man With Stone Eyes,' by which he was known on the river.

'*Deui mju,*' the guard said. He vanished for a few moments, then returned. '*Ho,*' he said, bowing as the gates swung soundlessly open. '*Cheng nei.*'

206

The gates closed behind Hatcher, and he followed the guard down the winding road toward the house, which was hidden behind banyan and pine trees.

China Cohen had fashioned his sanctuary with taste and passion, a strange amalgam of Oriental cultures and religions, some from China, others from Thailand, Malaysia and Japan. The single-story white house sprawled at the edge of a precipice with a truly spectacular view of the harbor. The curved yellow Chinese tiles that covered the roof glittered like gold; two ferocious-looking marble temple dogs guarded the white façade of the house. On one side of the front walk was a Japanese stone garden, which had been raked with infinite care. On the other side was a garden ablaze with azaleas, roses and orchids. A six-foot long *naga*, the Thai serpent of good luck, jutted its green and yellow head from among the blossoms, flashing an evil grin that revealed rows of ivory teeth. Delicate, slender-leaved palm trees shaded the garden.

Wind chimes sang gently on either side of the gold and black lacquered doors, and delicately carved teak lintels, called *ham yon*, the 'sacred testicles,' were placed over the doorway to the main room of the house because the virility of the master was believed to be stored there.

A large bronze lion's head knocker announced his arrival. The door was opened by a small, wizened woman who looked a hundred years old and more Thai than Chinese. She was dressed simply, and she peered intently into Hatcher's eyes for a moment and then smiled and bowed. 'Welcome, Occhi di Sassi,' she said.

She stepped back and ushered him into the main room of the house, a room decorated with plush Western furniture, Oriental antiques and Turkish carpets, its French doors opening onto a sprawling balcony. Beyond it and far below was the bay, and across it, Kowloon. The room smelled of fresh flowers. Nothing about it seemed to have changed since he had last been in the house.

A moment later Tiana entered the room, dressed in floor-length silk, her hair decorated with orchids. She didn't look a day older than the last time Hatcher saw her.

'Hello, Christian,' she said in her bell-like voice.

'Look at you,' Hatcher said. 'You still look sixteen years old. Don't you believe in time?'

'I will soon be three and oh,' she said.

'Don't tell anybody, they'll never guess,' he said and handed her the bottle of wine. 'Save this for you and Cohen.'

207

'*Mm goi,*' she said, holding the bottle close to her breast. 'We will think of you when we drink it.'

'And I will sense the moment,' he answered.

She stood quietly appraising him and finally nodded. 'It is a good day for us, Christian,' she said somewhat plaintively. 'Robert used to talk about you all the time. Then we heard you were dead, and after that he never mentioned your name again. Then today! Such excitement. All those years his heart hurt because he thought you were gone. I am glad you are back, for him and for me.'

'And for me,' he said.

'You have not changed much,' she said. 'Still very dashing. I am sorry about . . . this.' She gently touched his wounded neck with her fingertips.

'Hell, it just makes me sound dangerous,' he whispered with a laugh.

'You *are* dangerous,' Tiana said quite seriously, staring straight into his eyes. Then she smiled again. 'Welcome back.' She took his face between delicate hands and kissed him ever so lightly on the lips.

'That'll bring you luck for the next twenty years,' a voice said behind him, and he turned to see China Cohen standing in the doorway.

Time had put gray in his hair and beard, added some wrinkles to his face, softened the hard lines around his eyes, but otherwise there was little change. He was wearing his customary *cheong-sam*, brocaded with gemstones, and a Thai amulet around his neck. He hurried across the room and wrapped his arms around the taller man.

'Damn, what a gift,' China said softly. 'I should've known the shmuck isn't born could take you down.'

'Close,' Hatcher whispered.

His two friends stood close by, looking him over, nodding approval, although their eyes kept straying to the mark on his neck. Hatcher touched it self-consciously and shrugged. 'An accident,' he said, reaching out and taking the brass amulet in his palm.

'Lovely,' he said. 'Thai, isn't it?'

Cohen nodded. 'It's the amulet of the ten deities, supposed to protect your front and back,' China said and then chuckled. 'One of my men took it off a dead Thai swagman. Sure didn't work for him.'

'You're going to run out of wind long before you run out of luck,' Hatcher said.

208

'I have things to do,' Tiana said and kissed Hatcher on the cheek. 'Cohen keeps me very busy minding the servants.' She giggled and faded quietly from the room.

'I hate to think what it cost you to bribe Fat Lady Lau for her,' Hatcher said.

'Not a thing. She was a gift to a very good customer,' Cohen said, grabbing Hatcher by the shoulder. 'C'mon.' He led Hatcher to the guest room, which was adjacent to the main room of the house. Hatcher had spent many nights in this room, a sprawling square decorated in yellow and black with a floor-to-ceiling window overlooking the harbor below. The headboard of the bed and the furniture were starkly simple and painted black lacquer. The sheets were yellow satin. On either side of the bed were hundred gallon saltwater tanks, alive with multicolored tropical fish, while behind the bed the entire wall was covered with a Japanese silk-screen painting of a delicate tree with fernlike leaves and tiny red blossoms. The wall facing it was mirrored. Artifacts and statues were scattered here and there.

On one of the nightstands was a two-foot-tall ivory horse, its nostrils flared, its eyes subtly hooded, standing majestically on its back legs as though leaping to heaven. A strand of black pearls was draped casually over the back of the horse.

The bathroom, which was visible through an open door to the right, was black marble with a Jacuzzi bathtub big enough to accommodate a small army, and there were fresh flowers everywhere.

'How long you staying?'

'I leave Saturday,' Hatcher said.

Cohen appeared concerned, but said nothing and simply nodded. 'C'mon,' he said, 'we'll go outside and relax.'

They went out on the balcony, sat in wicker chairs and put their feet up on the railing and leaned back, basking in the sun.

'Just like the old days,' Hatcher said.

'Better,' Cohen said. 'We're old enough to enjoy it now.'

Sung Lo, his servant and bodyguard, appeared and mixed drinks from a bar in the corner. The balcony jutted out into space on long stilts; thirty feet below it, the sharply slanted mountain was covered with ferns and bamboo grass. A large banyan tree hid the house below from their view. It was deathly quiet except for the tinkling wind chimes.

'I got one surprise for you,' Cohen said. 'Tiana and I are married.'

Hatcher was delighted. 'That's great news!' he said enthusiastically.

'Smartest move I ever made,' said Cohen. 'How about you? Ever find anybody that could take Daphne's place?'

The name momentarily triggered Hatcher's *ch'uang tzu-chi*, a brief flash of the elegant, uniquely beautiful Daphne Chien, who wore men's suits, owned a company that manufactured jeans, and was the daughter of a Malaysian beauty and a half-French, half-Chinese banker, a volatile combination.

'Hell, I try not to think about her,' Hatcher said, a white lie, for he was not ready to deal with that subject for the moment. Instead they talked about Los Boxes and past times, and they talked about the old Tsu Fi.

'He died three years ago,' Cohen said. 'His ticker finally gave out. It was a helluva thing, Christian. He called me to the hospital, told me I put spice in his last few years. Only time I ever saw the old boy with tears in his eyes.'

'How about that half-mill he owed you for the Rhodes trick?' Hatcher asked with a smile.

'That was the best part of it, Christian, the old boy was a class act to the end. There was this beat-up old strongbox in the corner of the office, didn't even look like an antique. When I went to the hospital the night before he passed on, he gave me the keys to his office and then he gave me the key to that chest, said it was full of personal things, and when he died I could go through it and throw away what I didn't want. So I did. Lo and behold, there was half a million dollars in gold coins in it' – he held up a finger – 'and a piece of silicon the size of your fingernail.'

'Silicon?'

'A computer chip. So I took it to a friend and mounted it on a computer board, and when I activated the program, it was like a diary. Phone numbers, names, background on most of the rich taipans on the island and a lot of Orientals – all the secrets of Tsu Fi were there. Christian, next to that little piece of sand the half a million looked like a bucket of sand. I didn't think the old Tsu Fi recognized the existence of computers.'

'Which reminds me, how're things upriver?' Hatcher asked.

'Changed,' Cohen said. 'I don't go upriver anymore.'

'Oh? Why?'

'Most of the old gang is gone.'

'Hiekaya?'

'Dead. And Ty San. Joe Cockroach. Jimmy Chow. All of them.'

210

'What happened?'

'They started scrambling, killing each other off. The only one who got out whole was Sam-Sam. Now he's got this gunslinger working for him, an Iranian name of Batal. I hear he was with the SAVAK before the Shah split. A real mean one, Batal. There's another killer up there who ran out of Haiti with Baby Doc. Used to be with the Tontons. Calls himself Billy Death.'

'What the hell are Iranians and Tontons doing up there?' Hatcher asked.

'Dollars, I guess. They're Sam-Sam's newest guns,' said China. 'Sam-Sam lives mostly off tribute, knocks off the Chinese coming down from Shanghai or from out in the provinces, steals their goods, cuts off their feet and hangs them off the mast as a warning to others.'

'Were you worried maybe they'd dust you?' Hatcher whispered.

'Not really. They need me,' said Cohen. 'I still finance a lot of the action up there. Besides, I have a lot of friends, loyal friends. This isn't Chicago, the triads tend to get along with each other – even the Chiu Chaos stay pretty much in their own backyard. One of the things I learned from the old Tsu Fi: Never eat the whole pie, always give a piece to the other guy.' Cohen paused pensively for a moment, and added, 'Now, you, on the other hand, you left footprints all over the place.'

'It was part of the job.'

'Whatever it was, you made a lot of enemies, Christian. And I don't flatter myself that this is a social visit, much as I love you.'

It was not a criticism. Hatcher knew what Cohen meant. In the past there was always *something* one of them needed from the other.

Their conversation was cut short by the appearance of Sing, Cohen's enormous Chinese bodyguard, who suddenly appeared quietly in the living room behind them. He cleared his throat to summon Cohen. Cohen went in the other room, talked in low tones for a minute or two, and came back. Sung Lo remained in the room. Cohen's mood seemed darker.

'A problem?' Hatcher asked.

'I'm not sure,' Cohen said seriously. 'Are you in trouble, Christian?'

'Why?'

'Just curious.'

211

'I may need a favor,' Hatcher said finally.

'Must be something going on for you to come back to Hong Kong,' Cohen said. 'You know Tollie Fong is the new *san wong* of the White Palms?'

Hatcher nodded.

'They all think you're dead. The minute Fong knows you're here, he'll try to kill you. If he misses, Joe Lung'll have the whole damn White Palm Triad on your ass. They'll follow you to the North Pole if they have to. We're talking about family honor, blood oaths, saving face, the whole ticket. It would be better if you were left dead.'

'I know the score.'

'Well, you act like you forgot,' Cohen said. 'This is their turf, Christian. As long as you're in this house, you're safe, but I wouldn't give a Confederate dollar for your chances out in the colony. I love you, pal, and I hate to see you leave, but you can't stay in Hong Kong. Somebody's already got a tail on you, old pal.'

'Yeah. I think it's the Hong Kong police. A sergeant named Varney with the Triad Squad paid me a visit this morning. He claims my name popped up in their computer when I went through customs.'

'You don't believe him?'

'I believe the computer part of it, that could happen. But this Varney seems a little *too* interested in me. They followed me from the hotel.'

'Humph,' Cohen said pensively. 'This Varney just showed up at your room?'

'Yes.'

'I don't trust anybody, particularly where you're concerned,' said Cohen. 'I'd forget whatever brought you here. Go home, Hatch.'

'I can't do that.'

'Why? What's so special about this trick?'

Hatcher told Cohen the whole Murph Cody story, ending with the death of Windy Porter and the disappearance of Wol Pot.

'Right now, I don't have a lead except this ghost camp in Laos. If it existed, somebody upriver knows about it. Maybe I can get a name, some lead before I go to Bangkok.'

'Bangkok! Shit, it's worse in Bangkok,' China said, his voice going up an octave. 'Fong spends half his time wasting dissidents up in the Golden Triangle and the other half getting laid at the Royal Orchid Hotel. Why don't you just go over to Macao and hatch an egg in his front yard.'

'There's five million people in Bangkok. I can keep away from Fong and his bunch.'

'Hell, a damn cop already knows you're here. You think you can just slip in and out of Bangkok without stirring up something? And you have no other leads?'

'A picture of Cody and his hoochgirl. Does the phrase "Thai Horse" mean anything to you?'

Cohen looked at him and smiled for the first time since Sing discovered the house was being watched.

'Thai Horse? Why?'

'It popped up somewhere.'

'Come here,' Cohen said, leading Hatcher back into the bedroom. He pointed to the ivory statue of the horse by the bed. 'That is a Thai Horse,' he said.

'The statue?' Hatcher said with surprise.

'That's right. It's a real treasure. Authentic Thai Horse, about third century B.C. Been kicking around for a *long* time.'

'What is a Thai Horse?' Hatcher asked. My God, could the reference to the Thai Horse at the Wall have meant a statue, a simple gift? he wondered.

'The mythical ghost horse,' Cohen said. 'Supposedly stolen from the King of Siam. According to legend, it carried Thai heroes to heaven after the great wars. Legend has it that a Chinese brigand stole the horse and brought it here to the first emperor of China in exchange for a pardon. They renamed it the Celestial Horse, the *Tian Ma*. It was the *Tian Ma* that delivered the first seven emperors of China to the mountaintops around the colony when they died, then the gods turned them into dragons. When the rule of the Han Dynasty ended, the horse disappeared and was never seen again.'

Hatcher whispered, 'Where'd you get it?'

'From an artifacts museum in Peking,' he said with a wink. 'Don't ask me how much I paid to get this little darling lifted.'

Hatcher stroked the smooth sides of the handsome ivory horse. Could there be any significance to the reference other than as a statue? he wondered. Finally he said, 'Well, that doesn't add anything to what I know, which is damn little.'

'Have you got *any*thing else on the fire?' Cohen asked.

'I've got a man doing some checking for me in Washington,' Hatcher said. He looked at his watch. 'I can call him now. If he comes up with anything, I'm going to play out the hand.'

'Or –'

'I'll trash the job and go home.'

213

'Then I hope the son of a bitch doesn't even turn up *your* name,' Cohen said. 'I'd sure as hell rather have you gone than dead.'

FLITCRAFT

Sergeant Flitcraft was waiting in the reception room of computer operations in the Pentagon when Sergeant Betz arrived at work. Betz was a tall, paunchy man in his late forties, a short-sticker with a cushy job and less than two years to go before retirement. The broken blood vessels in his nose attested to his penchant for scotch, particularly Dewar's. He and Flitcraft went back a long way. Bragg. Korea. Nam. Betz scowled at Flitcraft, the smiling, tough black sergeant, who had somehow managed to stay in the service although he walked with a limp, supported by a cane. Flitcraft, too, was close to retirement. Betz knew Flitcraft wasn't there on a social visit.

'Got some confidential entries for you this morning, Sergeant,' Flitcraft said, standing as Betz entered.

'Yeah, right,' Betz said. 'C'mon down.' He turned to the receptionist. 'Give Sergeant Flitcraft a class-three permit,' he said.

She reached in a drawer and pulled out a blue name tag, filed its number on a registry and handed it to Flitcraft. She knew him and assumed he was there to give Betz classified information for the general computer. The blue pass permitted him to go only as far as the general offices, a bank of small windowless boxes, through a door to the left of reception. The door to the right opened into the general computer system and was guarded by a marine.

Flitcraft followed Betz into his office, a small cheerless cubicle with just enough space for a desk, a file cabinet, a computer terminal and one other chair.

'You got some entries for me there, Sergeant?' Betz asked, easing open a desk drawer.

He knew Flitcraft, knew he worked for a special unit known only as Shadow Section, and that he was trustworthy. Since Flitcraft did not have a C-1 classification, he did not have access to secret computer files. Flitcraft took a quart of Dewar's White Label from his briefcase and slipped it in the drawer, which

214

Betz eased shut with his knee. Because the office was under constant surveillance by a roving video camera, they played this game of charades.

'We've got some low-grade classified reports here for general entry,' said Flitcraft, sliding a sheaf of immaterial reports across the desk to Betz. Betz looked at them, casually lifted the cover sheet and read on a slip of paper on page two: 'Classified POW files.' Betz looked at Flitcraft as if to say, 'Who cares?'

Flitcraft raised his eyebrows and shrugged as if to answer, 'Who knows? You know how the brass are.' Silent looks exchanged between noncoms who had been in the system a long time and knew that a lot of information was classified simply to prevent the news media from gaining access to it through the Freedom of Information Act.

Betz slid open the tray on his desk and checked a list of code names and numbers. He wrote several down on a slip of paper and attached the slip to the top of the file. He set it aside in plain view of Flitcraft while he filled out a receipt, which he signed.

Flitcraft memorized the list immediately:

52-767-52116
Sidewinder
9696
Cherry
Monte
Cristo
Zenda

Betz handed the phony receipt to Flitcraft, who put it in his briefcase.

'See ya,' Flitcraft said. They shook hands and he left the office.

So far, so good. Flitcraft went straight to the men's rest room on the same floor, entered a stall, and wrote the list down before he forgot it. Then he left the Pentagon and hailed a cab.

The office of Shadow Section was in a private office building near the White House. To the casual observer, it was a small personal communications company in the private sector. Very few people knew that it was a branch of military intelligence.

Inside the office, which was identified only by the name Interplex on the door, was a bank of computers and interconnected communication systems that gave the three men, who dressed in civilian clothes, access to satellite and computer information all over the world.

Flitcraft ran the operation with the help of two other noncoms. All three had served Sloan in the past, and all three had suffered

215

wounds that should have resulted in medical discharges from the service. But Colonel Harry Sloan protected his men, and they, in turn, were thoroughly devoted to him. They would have given up their tongues rather than discuss the work they did.

Flitcraft got a cup of coffee and sat down in front of one of the computers.

Flitcraft was accustomed to the complex entry and silent codes needed to gain access to the government's general computer and then into specific classified files. These were a series of numbers and names that had to be entered upon prompting from the terminal. The system also had a double-entry silent code series that had to be entered without prompting. If these were not entered, the main computer immediately triggered a hack tracer. Within seconds the base computer registered the phone number and identity of the interrogating computer and then denied further access to the system.

It was a clever double-entry system designed to prevent hacking into these confidential files. In addition, each specific file category had its own set of bypass codes that were changed weekly, adding still another deterrent to hacking.

Flitcraft entered the modem program, permitting him access to other computers over regular phone lines. He typed in the general number for computer records and then a prompt requested his access number. He checked the list Betz had given him. The access number was 52-767-52116. A second prompt appeared immediately, requesting the code name for general files. Flitcraft entered 'Sidewinder,' the code name for entry into all classified files.

Now came the touchy part, for the computer did not ask for the ID number of the bypass code; it simply prompted a response to the question 'Specific File Number.' Without knowledge of the anti-hacking system, a hacker would have entered the code name requested and immediately sent an alarm to the tracer.

Flitcraft entered the ID number Betz had provided, 9696, followed by the code word 'Cherry' and bypassed the hack tracer. The computer repeated the question 'Specific File Code,' to which he entered 'Monte,' which was followed by a second prompt. He entered 'Cristo.'

Bang, he was in the general POW file. On the next prompt he typed in 'Zenda,' and the menu of all subdirectories appeared, followed by two questions: 'Subdirect or subject,' permitting him either to enter directly into a specific file or to search for one under general subject matter.

216

The sergeant smiled. Now the detective work began.

For the next three hours, Flitcraft typed in questions, seeking the answers Sloan had requested at 3 A.M. that morning. He checked under North Vietnam, POW camps, temporary camps, unverified reports, individual air sightings, reports from POW debriefings. Flitcraft was an expert at digging out obscure information.

When he was finished, Flitcraft had a list of temporary holding camps, none of which seemed to fit the description Sloan had provided, and several cross-referenced POWs. He had narrowed the list several times through cross-referencing.

But four returning prisoners had reported they had been held in what appeared to be the same temporary camp at different times between 1969 and 1972. The camp's commandant was identified as 'Thysung,' 'Taisung' and 'T'sung,' all close enough to be the same man.

The locations, which Flitcraft pinpointed on a map, were all close to the Laotian border and generally within fifty miles of one another, although the exact location was hardly accurate. None of the four POWs had stayed in the camp for more than a few weeks. There was also a report from a B-52 crew that had sighted what it believed to be a POW camp in the same area. And another report of a recon flight over the location two weeks later that reported the camp no longer existed.

Significantly, however, all four of the POWs had reported that there were half a dozen men who were prisoners in the camp when they arrived, and were still there when they left. One stated he 'had heard there was a VIP being held in the camp,' and another had reported a rumor that at least one of the permanent prisoners was 'collaborating with Charlie.'

Flitcraft ran a check on the four POWs. One was deceased, one was in a mental institution, the other two had been discharged. He traced them down and got current addresses and phone numbers.

For various reasons, none of the information was considered credible or significant by the Army. That was understandable, since the reports were isolated and not verifiable, and since the locations seemed to be those of temporary holding camps. But the four locations and the B-52 sighting were all on the Laotian side of the mountain range called the Chaîne Annimitique, and all mentioned the village of Muang, which was six hundred miles north of Saigon.

217

Flitcraft also checked out Murphy Cody. As far as the computer was concerned, Cody was dead.

Flitcraft answered on the first ring.

'This is Hatcher, N3146021,' he said. 'Do you need a voice print?'

'You're clear, sir,' Flitcraft answered.

'Did you turn up anything?'

Flitcraft rather proudly told Hatcher that his information indicated that the ghost camp did exist on the Laotian side of the Chaîne Annimitique near the village of Muang. Four debriefed prisoners had stayed in it for various periods between 1971 and 1973, the longest for five weeks. And the four had reported the name of the commandant or warden, variously, as 'Thysung,' 'Taisung' and 'T'sung,' all close enough to imply that it was the same man. The locations, too, indicated it was the moving camp Schwartz had called Huie-kui.

Flitcraft had also phoned an ex-Hanoi POW who had known a man who was in the camp at one time. 'He had the impression there were several prisoners being held there on some kind of permanent basis,' Flitcraft said.

'Any mention of Murphy Cody?' asked Hatcher.

'No, sir,' said Flitcraft. 'The name never came up.'

'Did any of the reports mention that a VIP was being held in the camp?'

'Yes, sir. But the closest to anything specific was that there were several prisoners who were segregated from the rest of the group. Like maybe they were permanent party, something like that.'

'Any reason why?'

'I could only reach this one subject,' said Flitcraft. 'He said they might have been collaborators, but he was guessing. Besides, what would the percentage in that be? One prison camp is as bad as the next.'

Flitcraft had a point, although the possibility of collaboration certainly was not out of the question.

'I wonder why the MIA commission never followed through on these reports?' Hatcher wondered out loud.

'I pieced this together from a bunch of scattered reports,' said Flitcraft. 'There were a lot of these transient camps, and nothing to pin them down. After the war, they just vanished.'

Maybe not, thought Hatcher.

'Thanks,' he told Flitcraft. 'You tumble on anything else,

feed it to the colonel in Bangkok. I may be hard to reach for a couple of days.'

'Yes, sir.'

'Nice job, Sergeant.'

'Thank you, sir. Good luck.'

Hatcher cradled the phone. It wasn't much, he thought. But it was enough to make the upriver trip a necessity. Someone up there would have dealt with the Huie-kui or at least have heard about it. And now he had a name – or three names.

He told Cohen the news.

'Someone upriver had dealings with this camp,' said Hatcher, 'and I'm going to find them.'

'Well, *I* never heard of it,' Cohen said.

'Hell, China, the Ts'e K'am Men Ti knew your sympathies were with America. They did business with the Chinese, the Vietcong, the GIs in Saigon, the Khmer Rouge, but they wouldn't talk about it with a *mei gwok yahn*.'

'You're also on Sam-Sam's list, too. Something about a gun deal that went sour.'

Hatcher took a sip of his drink and didn't answer.

'Well, you just answered *that* question,' said Cohen.

'He was dealing with the Khmer Rouge. The whole mission was to bust up that little party.'

'He's sworn to cut out your tongue and have it for lunch.'

'The old Hatcher *gwai* will pull me through.'

'Sure,' said China, 'I'll tell you something – when the old Hatcher luck runs out, they'll feel the earthquake in New York City.'

'It'll work,' Hatcher said. 'Trust me.'

'Humph,' Cohen mumbled again. Hatcher was heading for deep trouble and he was going it alone, stubborn as usual. He hadn't changed a bit. Sing ended his consternation by appearing suddenly at the doorway.

'The car belongs to the Island Catering Service,' Sing said.

Cohen turned to Hatcher. 'That company belongs to the White Palms. There it is. Fong's bunch is on to you.'

'Then I better get out of here,' Hatcher said.

'Like hell,' said Cohen. 'You're safe here. Fong wouldn't dare attack my home.'

And then after a moment's thought, he added, 'We'll beef up security and everything'll be fine. Don't worry about it. Excuse me a minute.'

Hatcher got up and looked over the side of the balcony. It

219

was thirty feet to the ground, which sloped sharply downward and was covered with vines and ferns. The top of the banyan tree, which was thirty or forty yards from the foot of the balcony, was ten feet below the balcony level. There were four heavy posts supporting the balcony. Heavy spotlights were mounted on the corners of the balcony. The high wall continued down both sides of Cohen's property until foliage blocked his view.

'The back looks fairly secure,' Hatcher whispered. The phone interrupted any further discussion of security.

Sing answered the call and looked up with surprise. He held his hand over the mouthpiece. 'It is for the Occhi di Sassi,' he said. 'A Sergeant Varney.'

Cohen's face clouded up. 'Son of a bitch, what now?' He looked at Hatcher. 'You want to take it?' he asked.

'Let's find out what he's up to,' whispered Hatcher.

Sing handed him the phone.

'Hatcher,' he whispered.

'Sergeant Varney from the Hong Kong police,' he heard the clipped tones reply. 'You remember me, sir?'

'Of course.'

'You did a nice job slipping my men this morning,' Varney said pleasantly. 'But I think I should warn you. Joe Lung went to your hotel room. Now he's on the island and has several men with him.'

'How did you find me?' Hatcher demanded.

'Guessed, sir,' answered Varney. 'I decided to take a chance that you were visiting your friend the Tsu Fi. Point is, we have a safe house near the airport. We'd like to take you out of there.'

'I'll be fine,' Hatcher answered.

'We thought perhaps you would prefer to avoid a confrontation at your friend's home. This man, Lung, is serious, Mr Hatcher.'

'I'm sure he is,' Hatcher replied. 'What do you have in mind?'

'We'll slip in there in an hour and bring you out. I'll have a backup unit with me. We have Lung under observation. I think everything will move smoothly.'

'Call when you get to the gate,' Hatcher said and hung up.

'How about the man on the hill?' Cohen asked Sing.

'Still there.'

'Does he suspect we're on to him?'

'I think not,' said Sing.

'How many men do you have?' asked Hatcher.

'Three in the front, one in the back, the three of us inside,' Cohen answered.

'If Varney's in on it, they'll set up the hit here, China. Lung and his men will probably come in behind Varney. They figure they'll catch us by surprise.'

Hatcher had never seen Cohen this angry before. 'They wouldn't dare attack this house,' Cohen said coldly, but his tone was less than convincing. Then he added, 'If they do, there's going to be hell to pay.'

WHITE PALMS

In a warehouse below the mountain, Joe Lung sat back from a window, watching the house on the peak through powerful infrared binoculars. It was getting dark, but he had a clear view of the balcony in the back of Cohen's home. Suddenly he saw Hatcher appear at the railing of the balcony for a moment, then disappear from view.

'There he is,' he hissed with a combination of satisfaction and hatred.

There were six other men in the room besides Lung, all dressed in black sateen pants and black shirts. All but one of them stood quietly against the wall of the small office with their hands folded in front of them. The one who stood aside, whose name was Wan How, had helped case the house, and was obviously uncomfortable. Lung looked across the room at him.

'You have a problem with this, Wan?' Lung asked.

'It is a fortress,' Wan answered. 'It is thirty feet from the ground to the balcony in the back –'

'I can see that,' Lung snapped impatiently.

'The front wall is eight feet high with electricity across the top. There are scanners in many places in the gardens. And the steel gates are –'

'I will worry about getting us inside,' Lung said. 'You have anything else to cry about?'

Stung by the insult, Wan hesitated a moment. He was a tall man in his early twenties, with long, slender fingers and light skin, an athlete in excellent condition, and he was far from being a coward. 'He is Tollie Fong's mark,' he said softly, staring at Lung.

221

Lung's lips curled back in anger. 'Hatcher is *my* mark. I have been waiting eight years for today. He killed four of our brothers in the triad, *my* brothers. He stole our merchandise. Do not tell me Hatcher is only the *san wong's* mark.'

'He killed Tollie Fong's *father*,' Wan replied. 'I think we should wait for him to return before —'

'You do not have the insides for this, is that it?' Lung said viciously. 'You see this?' He jerked up his black shirt. A long jagged scar stitched across his belly from side to side. 'The bastard *gwai-lo* spilled my guts, but I have enough left to take him. I have a right to this kill, Wan. I am the *san wong's* Number One here. When Tollie is gone, I say what we will do and what we will not do. You understand that?'

Wan did not reply. Embarrassed, he looked at the floor.

'I tell you we are going to hit the house and kill them all.'

Wan looked up, startled. 'You mean to kill the Tsu Fi.'

'Fuck the Tsu Fi!' Lung said, his voice rising. 'He is *mei gwok*, a *gwai-lo* just like Hatcher. He protects our blood enemy. I say get rid of this American Jew.'

The other men showed no emotion at all. They stood silently, inscrutably, while Lung and Wan How argued the wisdom of attacking Cohen's home.

'I disagree,' said Wan. 'We have no fight with the Tsu Fi. If we kill him, we will make many enemies.'

'Enemies make us stronger,' said Lung. 'You are getting weak, man. Too much easy life. The hydrofoil back to Macao leaves every thirty minutes.' He waved him away.

'I have taken the oath,' said Wan How. 'If it is your decision to do this, I will do my part.'

Lung glared at him for several seconds, then nodded slowly. 'Good,' he said.

Lung turned back to the window and stared back up at the house. 'Khan has been watching the house all day. The women are gone. There are five men besides Cohen and Hatcher. Three on the grounds in front, the *gwai-lo* and Sing inside. One man patrolling the back.'

There was a knock on the door.

'Keye?' he said to one of the other men.

'*Hai,*' the man answered and opened the door. Sergeant Varney entered the small office. Lung turned to him with a smile that was almost a sneer.

'Well?' he asked the British cop.

'I made the call.'

222

'And?'

'I'm not sure Hatcher will come out with me,' Varney said. 'He is a very cautious man.'

'Then we cannot take the risk. We will follow you inside the gates. It is the only way through the front. Four men in the front – I will take Keye and three others and go up the balcony at the rear.'

'I can't be in on the killing,' Varney said hurriedly.

'Of course not,' Lung said with a shrug, still smiling.

'And I'm going to have to put on a bit of a show. The man with me isn't part of this. I have to make it look good,' Varney went on.

'I hope you do not shoot too well,' Lung said slowly, his eyes mere slits.

'I don't want my man hurt.'

'Then keep him out of our way,' Lung said sharply, his voice hissing like a snake's, his eyes glittering. 'If he gets out of control, he is a dead man, you understand that, English?'

'Look, I'll be useless to you in the future if you force me to tip my hand,' Varney pleaded.

'Just stay clear when it starts!' Lung repeated sharply, and Varney knew the discussion was over.

He cleared his voice and said, 'Right.'

'We will be ready when you get there. Just do exactly as we discussed.'

Varney nodded, and after hesitating a moment, he left.

'You trust the Englishman?' Wan asked.

'He has been on our payroll for more than a year. He cannot afford to refuse us about this. Besides, he is the one who spotted Hatcher in the beginning.' He turned back to his binoculars and, without looking at his soldiers, added, 'He will be a big risk after this. He has outlived his usefulness to us anyway.'

He turned back to the tall Chinese. 'The Englishman is yours, Wan.' He pointed to two of the henchmen who stood silently against the wall. 'You will take these two and pick up Khan at the Gardens, follow the Englishman through the gates and hit the front of the house. Kill Varney and his partner and everyone on the grounds. My team will take out everyone inside the house. Just remember, Hatcher is a dangerous man – but he is mine. If you must take him on, wound him only, so I may finish the job.'

ASSAULT

Cohen had sent Tiana to Fat Lady's for the night. He sat on the bed and watched Hatcher open the Halliburton case, snap open the video camera and remove the plastic trigger housing. He unscrewed the lens from the telephoto lens and took out the gunsight. He removed the short barrel from the other lens and the two magazines from the batteries.

'That's beautiful,' Cohen said. 'What is it?'

'Austrian Aug,' said Hatcher as he assembled the weapon. 'I need some ammo.'

'No problem,' Cohen said. He gave the order to Sing, and the big Chinese slipped out of the room and returned a minute or two later with four boxes. 'Enough?' Cohen asked.

Hatcher smiled. 'Two hundred rounds oughta do it,' he whispered.

Cohen gathered his small band in the living room, a sturdy-enough-looking bunch dressed in black pants and turtlenecks and each wearing a black cotton mask so they would be well concealed in the dark. All were armed with Mac 10 submachine guns. He spoke to them in Chinese.

'They will probably hit us front and back,' he told them. 'Hatcher, Sing and I will stay in the house. We'll keep the lights out in the house. We'll draw and make them come to us. Louie, you take the roof. George, Joey Chen and Lee – in the garden. Sammy, you'll be on the ground in the back. Anything to add, Christian?'

Hatcher shook his head.

Hatcher had one final thought, but it was one he hesitated to discuss with these men. Joe Lung was the last of the five members of Dragon's Breath, the men who had run dope for White Powder Mama from Thailand to Saigon, and there was a good chance he knew about the Huie-kui camp. He needed to keep Lung alive, at least long enough to try to question him. But that seemed too much to ask of Cohen's small brigade, all of whom were putting their lives on the line for the Tsu Fi – and for him.

Finally he said, 'If there's a chance to keep Lung alive, I'd like to question him.' Cohen looked at him with raised eyebrows. 'But not at the risk of anyone's life,' Hatcher quickly added.

It had started to rain, a light drizzle with a portent of a heavier downpour to come. This was good news for Lung. It would cover sounds of the movement of the gangsters, all of whom wore black shirts and pants.

His driver parked the car on a curved street below Cohen's house. Joe Lung and the other two assassins got out and moved quickly and silently up through the foliage to the foot of the wall that surrounded Cohen's property. The ground here leveled off after sloping sharply away from the house for several hundred yards.

Lung guessed there would be at least one man on the ground at the rear of the house, possibly more, so he made his assault plan accordingly. He tossed a grappling hook up twice before it caught on the wall, then went up the line to the top of the wall and attached a twenty-foot-long insulated jumper to the electric wire on top of the fence, letting it dangle down. Lying flat on the wall, he slid one end of the jumper down the wire until it was taut. Then he crawled back. With the insulated jumper firmly attached, he cut the electric wire. He punched the button on his flashlight twice, then dropped over to the inside of the fence, landing in a crouch in knee-deep vines and straw grass.

Above him, through the trees, he could see the spotlights on Cohen's balcony several hundred yards away, throwing arcs of light on the foliage below. He stayed in the crouch, his ears alert for sounds in the darkness. The other two men dropped quietly beside him.

The drizzle turned into a steady rain.

They spread out quickly until the three mobsters formed a line from the east to the west wall of Cohen's estate. They still had not spotted the guard on the back slope. They moved forward as silently as possible through the tangled vines and grass toward the house, keeping low, looking for a silhouette against the spotlights, each with an earphone in one ear attached to a battery-driven beeper.

It was Lung who spotted Cohen's guard, Sammy, squatting in the cleared area at the foot of the balcony, his eyes searching the area beyond the arc of spotlights. Lung pressed his beeper button twice. The other two assassins heard the beeps and froze. It was up to Lung to take out the guard when their man signaled that the assault on the front of the house had begun. Lung was lying in the high grass perhaps thirty yards from the crouching Sammy, a black shadow with a mask over his face.

Lung raised his rifle, a Mannlicher loaded with a tranquilizing dart that would immediately knock the man unconscious. Better

225

than a bullet, which might only wound the guard and give him a chance to sound an alarm.

He sighted in on Sammy through the infrared scope, then raised it up to the balcony. The lights in the house were out. He lowered the rifle back down, aiming at Sammy's throat, and waited for the signal from the street.

On the roof of the house, Cohen's man watched through binoculars as a car picked up the man near the Botanical Gardens. He whispered into his walkie-talkie, 'They have picked up the man on the hill. There appear to be three others in the car.'

In the darkened house, Hatcher swore vehemently. 'That's it. That son of a bitch, Varney, turned me up to Joe Lung. He's in on it.'

Varney and his assistant, a young Oriental corporal named Henry Dow, reached the top of the mountain. Corporal Dow knew few details about the job. They were taking a man into protective custody, that was all he needed to know. The beefy young corporal had been a cop for four years and never asked questions.

Varney approached the gates of Cohen's estate slowly through the rain. He saw the triad mobster's car turn in behind him, its lights out. The corporal, distracted by the rain, was peering intently through the windshield and did not notice the car. As they neared the gate Varney flicked his lights, then picked up the radio phone, got the police operator and asked for a patch through to Cohen's phone number.

'Their play will be to follow Varney's car through the gates while they're open,' Hatcher whispered.

Cohen relayed the message to the other men. He had a Smith & Wesson .357 and an old Army Colt .45 stuck in a web belt he had strapped on for the occasion. Hatcher laughed at him. 'China,' he said, 'you look ridiculous.'

Cohen smiled grimly. 'Don't underestimate me, Occhi di Sassi,' he said. 'I know how to handle these things.'

'That's a relief to know,' growled Hatcher. He opened the glass door to the balcony. 'I'll check the back.'

He eased out the back door in a crouch and crept to the railing of the balcony. Rain was coming down steadily now and the visibility was poor. Below him, he saw the guard, Sammy, crouched near one of the support posts, his Mac 10 protected by a poncho. Hatcher went back inside to get out of the rain.

Down below, crouching in the wet grass, Lung checked his

watch. Varney would be making his move anytime now. Once the action started in front of the house there would be enough distraction for his men to go up the support posts, over the balcony and hit the house from the rear.

'Here they come,' Cohen's man on the roof said into his walkie-talkie.

In the car behind Varney, one of the assassins saw Varney's lights flick. 'Go!' he said into his walkie-talkie.

Behind the house, Lung heard the order and squeezed off the tranquilizer, watching through the night scope as the dart smacked Sammy in the throat. He saw the Cohen guard fall back against the support post. His eyes rolled up and he dropped against the post in a sitting position. His shoulders drooped and his weapon fell to the ground.

Lung pressed the beeper twice, and the two mobsters in the rear charged rapidly through the grass and rain to the balcony support posts. Lung drew a stiletto from his sleeve, then, grabbing Sammy's hair, pulled back his head and slit his throat.

'This is Sergeant Varney,' the British sergeant said into his phone when he heard Cohen answer his call. 'Open the gates, will you?' He slowed to a stop.

'Here we go,' said Cohen, pressing the gate switch.

As the two big iron grille gates swung slowly open, Varney slammed down the gas pedal. His car lurched forward and roared into Cohen's driveway. His headlights caught one of Cohen's men before the Cohen gunman leaped into the protection of the rose garden.

Behind him, the assassins' car, its tires screaming, roared through the closing gates behind Varney. Varney's car skidded to a stop near the front of the house, jumped a small curb and crashed into the garden. He and Corporal Dow tumbled out opposite doors of the car. Behind them, Lung's killers rolled out of their car into the flower gardens, and as Dow stood up, the driverless car slammed into Varney's machine. It hit the rear fender, glanced off and screeched down the side of the police car. The sturdy policeman shrieked as he was crushed to death between the two cars. Varney, dazed, tumbled from his car only to be cut down immediately by the assassins.

Inside, Sing and Cohen ducked behind a sofa as the door was shattered by a dozen bullets. Glass and lamps exploded in the room. Hatcher, watching from the door of the bedroom, whispered, 'Everybody okay?'

'So far, so good,' was Cohen's quick reply.

227

They could hear the rattle of the Uzis used by Lung's men quickly answered by the deeper roar of the Mac 10's. The night was ripped by gunfire and an occasional scream. Flashes of gunfire reflected through the windows like distant lightning. Cohen and Sing concentrated on the front door, in case Lung's men broke through.

In the rear of the house, Lung and his two men quickly attached leather straps with spikes on the inside to their ankles. They slung belts – like those used by telephone linemen – around the posts, jammed the spikes into them and started up.

Inside, Hatcher saw the first of Lung's killers reach the top of the balcony, leap over the railing and charge toward the bedroom. Hatcher dived behind the bed. In the dark and the rain, the killer saw only movement in the room and fired a blast from his Uzi. The bullets ripped into the mirrored wall, and Hatcher's reflection erupted in shattering glass. Hatcher dropped both hands on the bed and fired a short burst from his Aug. Half a dozen shots stitched the gunman from chin to belly. The shocked gangster was thrown backward as the bullets tore into him. He flipped over the balcony railing and dropped from view.

From the other room Hatcher heard another burst of Uzi gunfire. He ran in a crouch to the doorway of the living room in time to see a second triad gangster zigzag into the darkened room, firing from the hip. Bookcases, vases, flowers and paintings exploded a moment before Cohen stood up from behind the sofa and fired his .357 once. It hit the gunman in the chest, spinning him around, his gun still chattering. Blossoms of down feathers erupted from the sofa. Cohen felt a tug at his side, a sharp pain like a beesting. He looked down. My God, he thought, I'm shot!

The assassin felt the hot bullet burn deep into his chest and rupture his heart while his lungs flooded with blood. His body jackknifed and he fell forward on his face, like a man praying before Buddha.

As Hatcher rolled back into the bedroom he saw Lung vault the balcony. The mobster was silhouetted in the doorway, his face drenched with rain, his eyes glazed with hatred. An instant later he saw Hatcher but not before Hatcher fired a burst at him. Lung jumped to one side but a round clipped his ear, which vanished in a spray of blood and flesh. Hatcher leaped across the bed and dived through the doorway, swinging the Aug as he did.

He punched Lung across the jaw, shattering it, and knocked him back against the railing. But the Oriental was tougher than Hatcher thought. He lashed out with his knife and nicked Hatcher's

228

sleeve. Hatcher grabbed Lung's wrist, shoved it up, twisting it away from him, and the knife dropped from his hand. As Lung flipped backward he grabbed Hatcher, and they both landed on top of the railing. Hatcher hooked his elbow over the wooden crossbar and caught himself. He still had Lung by the wrist, but the falling gangster snapped loose and dropped, twisting as he fell, trying to get his feet under him. He landed sideways, the heavy fall slamming the air out of him and smashing two ribs. Lung bounced down the slope to the edge of the grass.

He rolled painfully over on his face, his broken ribs searing with pain, the side of his face ripped by Hatcher's gunshots. He pulled his knees up under him and staggered in a crouch, down the hill toward darkness.

Behind him, Hatcher wrapped his legs around the post and slid to the ground. He snatched up Lung's knife, which was lying in the mud, and charged down the slope.

Lung leaped into the tall grass, but his broken ribs were more painful than he could bear. He fell with a cry and began crawling the last few feet toward the dark. He was almost out of the spotlight's arc when he felt Hatcher's iron grasp on the back of his collar, felt himself hauled to his feet, heard Hatcher's rasping voice in his ear. 'You son of a bitch,' Hatcher hissed, 'you should have died a long time ago.' He placed the point of Lung's own stiletto against the back of the gangster's neck, pressed on it hard enough to break the skin. 'You've got some questions to answer,' he rasped.

Lung, humiliated and defeated, got his legs under him and lunged upward, ramming the knife deep into his own throat. His cry was like an animal's. Hatcher pulled his hand back, but the knife was buried so deep the soggy hilt slipped out of his hand. He heard Lung's gargling scream, the unmistakable death rattle, felt him shudder and fall limp.

Hatcher stood over him, still grasping his collar. Lung's head lolled forward. Hatcher dropped the killer facedown in the mud at his feet.

'Welcome to hell,' his shattered voice said as he stood over the dead killer's body with rain pouring down his face.

HARD BALL

By daylight Cohen's mansion had become a scene of frenzied activity. Six officers had finished photographing, interrogating and trying to piece together what had happened the night before. Photographers had taken pictures of bodies and cars and the remains of both had been hauled away. Now gardeners were at work repairing the damage in the front of the house.

An official car pulled in the driveway. Colonel Jeffrey Holloway got out and slowly turned on one heel, a 360-degree turn, surveying the battered grounds of Cohen's home.

Holloway was not a pleasant person. The man who headed the Central District of the Hong Kong police was six feet tall, his white hair cropped almost Nazi-short, his face a thin, stern triangle dominated by almost blind-gray eyes. Even in the heat of the morning sun, his starched khaki uniform was unwrinkled.

He strode toward Cohen's front door like a palace guard, so straight he almost leaned backward. He slapped one thigh with a riding crop, his symbol of rank.

Holloway sniffed about the house appraising the damage, then walked down to the open doorway to the guest room. Cohen, whose side had been nicked by a bullet, lay on the bed. Ping, the acupuncturist, leaned over him, placing needles here and there to kill the pain in the wounds, which a medical doctor had already repaired.

When Ping had finished his work, Holloway entered the bedroom. He ordered the man repairing the shattered wall mirrors to leave. Hatcher leaned against the wall and said nothing.

'A gangland fight, two police officers dead, eight others dead. One hell of a mess, I'd say,' he snorted.

'You're a little confused, aren't you, Colonel?' Cohen answered, still not looking at him. 'My home was attacked by triad mobsters. How dare you come in here and imply that I instigated this mess.'

'You've been asking for trouble for years,' he snapped back.

Cohen lay quietly with the long needles protruding from his neck, stomach and knees. He lay there forming his strategy, deciding how best to handle the situation diplomatically. The old Tsu Fi had once advised Cohen, 'Never force a man into a corner. He has no choice but to fight. Always leave a door open for him.'

Cohen sighed and folded his hands across his chest. 'You're walking a very thin wire,' he said to Holloway.

'Is that a fact?' the priggish officer said, raising his eyebrows.

'Your man Varney was on the take,' Cohen said flatly.

230

'Ridiculous!' Holloway snapped, his voice beginning to boil. 'One of the finest officers on the squad.'

Cohen laughed at him. 'First, Varney tipped off Lung that Hatcher was in Hong Kong. Then he led the killers through my gates. And finally Lung's own men killed him to shut him up.'

'Absolute trash,' the colonel bellowed.

'Colonel, Varney visited Hatcher yesterday morning at the Peninsula. Within two hours, Lung broke into the room to kill Hatcher. He missed because Hatcher was out here. Then Varney called Hatcher here and told him the Triad Squad wanted to take him into protective custody. Are you aware of all that?'

Holloway silently glared at Cohen through narrowing eyes.

Cohen went on: 'When he arrived at my gates he patched through a call to this number from his police car. Then he led Lung's men in here. I'm sure all this can be verified by your own records. But I'll bet Varney didn't report Hatcher's arrival in Hong Kong, because he reported it to Lung, not to the police. Or that he planned to provide protection for Hatcher, because he had no such intention. Check your radio operators. You'll find he made a call from his car to my unlisted number seconds before they attacked us.'

Holloway's anger began to slowly change to doubt. 'Very convenient conjecture,' he said uncertainly.

'Not on your life,' said Cohen. 'Hatcher thought the cops were tailing him, but they were actually Lung's White Palm mobsters, who were tipped off by Varney. Or worse, men on your own squad who were on the take, too.'

'You're making irresponsible accusations,' Holloway said menacingly.

'The killers were waiting out there for us to open the gates for Varney,' Cohen said with a sigh. 'He led them in here.'

'Circumstantial. It will be interesting to see what happens when you take *that* story to court,' said Holloway.

'Nobody's going to court,' Cohen said flatly.

'Oh?'

'Colonel, don't give me that stiff-upper-lip shit. Are you interested in the truth?'

'Truth? Hah!' Holloway snorted.

'Listen to me,' Cohen snapped. 'Hatcher threw off his tails on Cat Street. But when he got here, Lung's people were observing the house. That's how Varney located Hatcher – *Lung* told him.'

'And how would we handle that story?' Holloway asked cautiously.

231

'Simple. Report that Varney showed up in response to a help call,' said Cohen. 'He and his man died heroically trying to defend innocent citizens from being attacked by thieves. You give Varney a hero's funeral and I forget the whole matter. Or – you can create the big stink. And we can back up our complaint with your own records. Which way do you like it?'

'How dare you threaten me!' Holloway snapped indignantly.

'Threat, hell,' replied Cohen. 'It's a solution to a very nasty situation.'

'I'll see you in hell first,' Holloway said sternly.

'Colonel, you're bluffing,' Cohen said with a bored air. 'You have the perfect out, take it while you can.'

Holloway sucked his upper lip between his teeth. He didn't say anything for several seconds.

'Call your man in,' Cohen said quietly. 'I'll give him the proper version of what happened.'

The mirrors had been replaced in the guest room and Ping had removed the needles and left when Tiana returned home and rushed to Cohen's side. He put on a good act, wincing with pain, speaking in a trembling voice.

'*Ngo jungyi nei,*' she whispered, putting her arms gently around his neck and caressing his face.

'I love you too, darlin',' he said, winking across her shoulder at Hatcher, who sat on the edge of the bed.

'Why are you not in the hospital?' she asked.

'Too tough,' he said and then started to laugh.

She sat up sharply. 'You are making a joke at me!' she said angrily.

'No, just kidding around.'

'This is not for kidding around!' she said sternly.

'Tell her, Christian. Was I tough? Did I show some stuff here last night or didn't I.'

'He is your friend, he would say anything for you,' she said, staring impudently at Hatcher.

'The Occhi di Sassi does not lie,' said Cohen. 'Didn't think I had it in me, did you, Christian?' he asked proudly.

'I thought the way you handled the colonel was more impressive.'

'Routine!' cried Cohen with a wave of his hand. He pulled up his shirt, displaying his bandaged side. 'And look at that. The Purple Heart, my dear. I've been wounded in action. Another inch, and Buddha would have been sitting on the bed instead of you two.'

'I must see to the rest of the house,' Tiana said, excusing herself.

232

After she left the room, Cohen scowled at Hatcher. 'What's the problem?' he asked.

'Five of your people died here last night,' Hatcher said. 'Just to protect me. I didn't come on this job to get people killed. History's beginning to repeat itself. I should never have come here.'

Cohen leaned toward his friend and laid his hand on Hatcher's. 'Listen to me, Christian,' he said seriously. 'You made a few enemies in your time. You can't evade them. But before you get a bleeding heart, let me tell you, every man here last night had reason to hate the Chiu Chao triads. They all had old scores to settle. Every one of them was here voluntarily and grateful for the chance. And their families will be well taken care of for life. It really had nothing to do with you.'

'Sure. Now you'll be on Fong's list, too,' Hatcher said.

'No,' Cohen answered. 'To attack a man's home is an act of cowardice. Even the triads will be dishonored. Lung hit me without Fong's approval, I'm sure of it. And now Fong owes me an apology. Lung dishonored him – and botched the job in the bargain. Forget it, the old Tsu Fi can take care of himself. You're the only one who still has to worry about Tollie Fong. Are you still determined to go up to Chin Chin land?'

'More than ever. For the first time I've got something positive. A name, China, I've got a name. Wol Pot. It's a starting place. Without Wol Pot, I didn't have anything.'

'Supposing Cody doesn't want to be found. Supposing you turn over a rock and something nasty crawls out.'

'I'll deal with that if it happens.'

'Okay, then there's only one person you can trust who can take you up there.'

'Who?' Hatcher asked.

'Daphne Chien,' Cohen answered.

ch'u-tiao

The house was surrounded by flowers and sat on a quiet street in one of the finer residential sections of Macao, forty miles from Hong Kong by hydroplane. Despite its look of tranquillity, Macao had dark secrets hidden along its cobblestone streets and behind its terraced red and ocher Mediterranean villas. There

233

was still about it a sense of mystery and decadence; it was still a center for the smuggling of illegal Chinese aliens, carried in the dead of night by snakeboat into Hong Kong; a center for gold smuggling; a protectorate for Chinese triad gangsters who freely practiced white slavery, arranged major dope-smuggling deals between Thailand's Golden Triangle and Amsterdam and other Western ports, and ordered the execution of their enemies from behind the façades of peaceful rococo villas. The banyan trees lining the Praia Grande concealed corruption of every kind.

Wang, the retired *san wong* of the White Palms, who was in his eighties and had been for more than fifty years the leader of the outlaw triad, was feeding his tropical fish.

He had handpicked Tollie Fong as his Red Pole when Fong was still in his early twenties and had never doubted the wisdom of his choice. But he had warned Fong that Joe Lung was a dangerous Number One, a reckless and irascible killer, who, as the old man had put it, 'thinks with his gonads.' Now Wang had to deal with the aftermath of Lung's attack on Cohen.

Fong arrived at the house at precisely ten o'clock, having flown in from Bangkok on the early morning flight. The house was a stunning tangerine-colored Mediterranean villa on Avenue Conselheiro, which wound around Guia Hill, and had perhaps the finest view of Macao on the tiny peninsula. It was rumored to have been the hideout of Sun Yat-sen while he plotted the overthrow of the Manchu Dynasty, an apocryphal yarn, but possible. Above it, on the pinnacle of the hill, stood what was left of St Paul's Church, a magnificent ruin destroyed by a typhoon in 1835, while from the rear sun porch of the house, the old man could see far below the oldest lighthouse on the China coast and, beyond it, the South China Sea.

Fong stood at the front door, checking out his reflection in the glass door before ringing the bell. He was an athletic, light-skinned man, a bodybuilder, tall for a Chinese, with gold-flecked black eyes and modishly trimmed black hair that flowed back over his ears, outlining a thin, hawkish face. He preferred Western dress and was wearing a dark blue cotton suit and a scarlet silk tie. Fong was a handsome man whose good looks were marred only by an unnerving inscrutability, for he seemed to be a man without any expression, his face a mask with a mouth that moved. He was ushered through the house by a bodyguard the size of a sumo wrestler.

The old man was in his favorite room at the rear of the house, feeding the saltwater fish in three one-hundred-gallon aquariums.

234

The fish were his proudest possession. He knew each by name and by habit and was chatting with them as he sprinkled brine shrimp into one of the tanks when Fong was ushered into the atrium. Fong stood near the old man and bowed respectfully. Wang nodded his head.

'Welcome back, Tollie,' the old man said without looking up. 'How was your trip to Bangkok?'

'Shorter than I planned,' Fong answered. 'I had to leave before I finished my business, but I can go back tomorrow.'

'What happened at the house of Tsu Fi?' the former *san wong* asked.

'Lung went crazy,' Fong said.

'That is all you have to say about it?'

'What else is there to say?' said Fong. 'I never talked to Lung. He found out Hatcher was in Hong Kong from a police informant named Varney. And he attacked the house. Now they are all dead, including the cop. We'll never really know what happened.'

'I warned you that one day Lung would compromise you,' said the retired *san wong*.

Fong nodded. He was embarrassed that the old *san wong* was forced to deal with an awkward situation that was basically Fong's fault.

'He was fulfilling a *ch'u-tiao* of many years against the American,' Fong said somewhat defensively.

Ch'u-tiao was a blood oath, an oath of honor, and one that by tradition could only be resolved in death.

'So it is ended. And would you have approved of this action?' the old man asked, still playing with his fish.

'Of course not,' said Fong.

'We do not want war with Tsu Fi,' the old man said.

Fong decided to face the subject head-on. 'Maybe it's time to get rid of this *mei gwok* Jew,' he said slowly.

The old man looked up, his eyes mere slits. He stared at Fong for several seconds and the younger man became uneasy, realizing he had said the wrong thing. 'Let me show you something,' he said. He reached in one of the other tanks, opened his palm, and a large yellow tang swam leisurely around his hand.

'Come, Shang, come to your father,' the old man whispered.

The fish finally swam into his hand, pecking at it, looking for food. Wang grabbed the fish and quickly dropped it in one of the other tanks. Almost immediately it was attacked by three of the fish in the new tank, two of them less than half its size. The tang floundered, darted out of the way only to be hit behind the gills by a small black-and-white domino. The tang flipped to its side, wiggling its tail frantically, but it was already moribund. The two men watched while half a dozen fish pecked the tang to death.

'Next to human beings, fish are the most territorial creatures on earth,' the old man said. 'If you inject a stranger into their home, they will kill it. Even the small fish attack it. So the big fish is overwhelmed. Then they break his ballast and he is helpless.' He looked up at Fong. 'Do you understand what I am saying?'

Fong nodded.

'Good. You were the finest Red Pole in the Chiu Chaos,' Wang said, 'but to declare war on the house of Tsu Fi and attack him in his own environment was suicidal, as Lung discovered.'

'I would not make the same mistakes,' Fong said.

The old man stared at him for several more moments and nodded again. 'We do a lot of business in Hong Kong,' he said. 'Cohen is respected and feared among all the Sun Lee On. He is powerful in the business community. Doing business in Hong Kong means doing business with him. You must swallow your pride. Joe Lung compromised you. The rules of the Society require that you make an apology and a gesture to satisfy the insult.'

'That's why I flew back from Bangkok this morning.'

'*Hai*. Then call him now. Arrange a meeting for later today. Get this over with. It is an annoyance I do not care to put up with any longer than necessary.'

'I will do it now,' said Fong.

'*Mm goi,*' said the old man. 'I am also aware that you, too, have a *ch'u-tiao* against the American. If necessary, you must be prepared to put it aside.'

Fong looked surprised.

'I cannot do that!' the new *san wong* said, but his predecessor and mentor cut him off before he could go on. 'You can and will, if it is necessary,' he said with finality and turned back to his fish.

Fong knew the discussion was over. He bowed to his master.

'*Jo sahn,*' he said.

'*Jo sahn,*' the old man answered.

DAFFY

The smell of cordite still hung in the air of the house as they waited for Daphne to arrive. According to Cohen, Daphne was the only person they could trust who still traveled upriver into that dangerous land and dealt with the brigands, mainly in materials, Thai silk and madras cotton, which she smuggled into the colony duty-free. She had two things going for her: nothing intimidated her, which earned her the respect of the pirates, and she dealt in gold. Even the Ts'e K'am Men Ti did not bite that strong a hand.

But Hatcher also suspected Cohen's motives. Could he possibly be playing Cupid? Hatcher's first encounter with Daphne had been the result of a rather perverse Cohen joke. The Tsu Fi had been certain that Hatcher would be attracted to her and just as certain that she would ignore the brash Yankee *gwai-lo*.

Cohen, too, was thinking of that night. In a funny way, Daphne Chien brought the friendship between Cohen and Hatcher full circle, for it was Hatcher's first meeting with her that had strengthened what had been until then a tentative friendship between the two men, a time for sparring and contemplation and even testing. From the beginning, Cohen had seen in his new friend a man of curious and sometimes frightening balance – a man of intense loyalties and an outrageous sense of humor balanced by a dark, deviously clever, dangerous and unpredictable streak. He had seen the dark side of Hatcher's persona, the human trigger that could kill with the suddenness and impartiality of a sprung mouse-trap. And then there was Hatcher's charmingly eccentric side. He slept on the floor, preferred to read in Chinese rather than English, sometimes would go two or three days without eating, and had a bizarre memory, which excluded obvious details and retained only what Hatcher considered important. He knew, for instance, that Sam-Sam Sam was left-handed but could not describe a single one of the tattoos that covered the pirate's body.

Hatcher survived by keeping these two disparate sides of his personality in careful balance, never letting one overpower the other, like a coin perched on its edge.

To Cohen, all of these traits made Hatcher a fascinating, often endearing, and potentially trustworthy friend, but it was at Hatcher's first meeting with Daphne that Cohen had seen a gentle, almost boyish side of Hatcher's personality, although the balance was still there. On the one hand, he was surprisingly naïve; on the other, outrageously audacious.

They had just arrived at the Governor's Ball, the annual mob scene at the Chinese Palace, to which Cohen, as a joke, had conned Hatcher into going, knowing the mysterious riverman hated

237

crowds, cocktail parties, dances and snobs – all the reasons why everyone else went. Hatcher spotted Daphne the moment they arrived at the party. She was standing on the other side of the main ballroom, a stunning, unattainable statue, observing the shoulder-to-shoulder cocktail crowd with an air of icy indifference. Cohen sensed Hatcher's immediate infatuation.

'Forget it,' said China. 'Your eyes are the wrong shape.'

'Who is she?'

'Daphne Chien. Her mother's Malaysian, her father's half Chinese, half French.'

'Amazing collaboration,' Hatcher said half aloud, staring through the crowd at her.

'Every gwai-lo in the colony has tried,' Cohen whispered. 'She won't have anything to do with Westerners.'

'Neither would the Tsu Fi and that didn't stop you,' Hatcher answered. 'You know her?'

'Yeah, I know her,' Cohen answered with an air of apprehension. Social confrontations, particularly in an event of this importance, made him uncomfortable, so he added, 'And I'm telling you, she particularly hates Americans.'

'How come?'

'Her father was a very successful tailor here, built up a very nice business with a few quality stores in the States. Along comes a big American combine, decides his little company has big potential, makes him a lot of promises, then screws him to the wall, edges him out, and starts mass-producing blue jeans using his name and reputation. They got big, big, big, but the old man never saw a dime of it.'

'What was the company?'

'Blue Max, you've probably heard of them.'

'Everybody's heard of it.'

'The old man was so humiliated he tried to kill himself. She saved his life. . . .'

Hatcher was already off and running. Cohen rushed after him.

'Introduce me,' said Hatcher as he threaded his way through the black-tie crowd toward her. Cohen followed, trying to talk as he made his way through the jabbering guests.

'You haven't heard the rest of it,' Cohen said, shouting above the cocktail din.

'So what's the rest of it?'

'She started a new business. Knockoffs.'

Hatcher stopped and looked back at him with a wide grin. 'She counterfeits American blue jeans?' he said.

Cohen nodded. 'She counterfeits Blue Max American-brand blue jeans – at about half their price.'

'Fantastic.'

Cohen nodded. 'Ripped them off for enough to start her own label, became their biggest competitor, then merged with them. And ended up in control. And ended up firing the whole greedy bunch.'

'Beautiful,' said Hatcher.

'It sure was, but it left her with a very bad taste in her mouth for mei gwok.'

'So how come you know her?'

Cohen smiled. 'I set up the merger deal that put her in the driver's seat. I'm one Yankee she likes,' he said.

Hatcher was more determined than ever to meet her. He started back across the room with Cohen at his side.

'Give me some names,' he said.

'Names of who?'

'The guys who ripped her off,' Hatcher said impatiently as they approached her. 'One or two names, c'mon, hurry.'

'Uh . . . Howard Sylvester . . . Allen Mitchell . . . uh . . .'

'That's good enough. Introduce me as – Chris London.'

She got even more beautiful as they got closer, her tall, lithe body encased in a dark green silk sheath that etched each perfect line of her body and seemed to add luster to her almond, almost cocoa-colored, skin, and glitter to deeply hooded eyes that were as green as the dress. Her jet-black hair was tied in a long ponytail that curled over one broad shoulder and fell between her breasts. She wore no rings, her only jewelry being a pair of pear-shaped diamond earrings and a diamond necklace with an emerald and ruby pendant that lay in the hollow of a throat as delicate as a swan's. She smiled brightly when she saw Cohen.

'China!' she cried, 'at last, someone to talk to.'

Cohen kissed her on the cheek, then turned to Hatcher. 'Miss Chien, Daphne, I'd like to introduce a friend of mine, Chris, uh . . .' he faltered, forgetting the second name.

'London,' Hatcher said quickly.

The smile vanished. She nodded curtly. 'Monsieur,' she said in a French accent and a low voice that made one strain to hear her and turned away. Hatcher pressed on.

'I'm a lawyer,' Hatcher went on. 'In fact, I represent some old associates of yours.'

She turned back toward him, her chin pulled down, staring coldly at him from under ebony eyebrows.

239

'Oh?'

'Yes. Howard Sylvester and Allen Mitchell.'

Nothing changed in her face, but Cohen almost swallowed his tongue. He could see his friendship with Daphne Chien vanishing with every word Hatcher spoke. Hatcher stepped close to her, took her elbow very gently and steered her toward the terrace.

'You see, they've put together quite a dossier on your knock-off business, prior to the merger? They feel that they have a fairly strong case against the new Blue Max. . . .'

Their voices died out in the crowd as Cohen stood watching them. Her eyes were the eyes of a killer, and then suddenly they both stopped and faced each other. Hatcher leaned over to her and spoke very quickly. Her mouth dropped open, she seemed to lose her composure for just a second, then there was an exchange, back and forth, and when it was over, Hatcher bowed, kissed her hand and left. He strolled back to Cohen, smiling.

'Lunch tomorrow,' he said. 'Just the two of us. Wait here, I'll bring you a drink. Scotch, a dash of water, no ice, right?' And he was gone again.

Daphne followed a few seconds later, glaring at him as she drew to within inches of him.

'Why didn't you tell me he was Hatcher?' she said.

'I have no excuse whatsoever,' Cohen stammered.

She stared after Hatcher as he edged through the crowd.

'Are you really having lunch with him?' Cohen asked.

'Yes,' she said.

'What did he say to you out there?' Cohen asked.

She smiled vaguely, stared at him for a second and said, 'Ask him.' And then she too was gone.

'What did you say to her?' Cohen asked when he returned with the drinks.

Hatcher shook his head. 'I'll never tell,' he said.

Now Cohen sensed a different Hatcher. The hair trigger seemed to be on safety. The hard, brash edge seemed softer, more contemplative. It was not that he felt Hatcher was getting soft, but rather that the two sides were slightly out of balance. And while Cohen liked that new side, it also worried him. If Hatcher was going upriver, he could not afford to lose that old edge. In the land of the Ts'e K'am Men Ti, instinct precluded provocation. 'Shoot first' was the law of survival.

The doorbell ended his ruminations.

The woman in the doorway was the color of café au lait and

240

she stared down at Cohen through almond-shaped green eyes. She was tall and elegant, dressed in a pale pink shantung silk jacket over a ruby-red silk sheath, an outfit that was sexy, yet in good taste. As she entered the house she kicked off her shoes with long, cocoa-colored legs.

'Hello, China,' she purred softly and kissed him on the forehead. Then without hesitation, she asked, 'Where is he?'

'Out on the balcony.'

'Has he changed?'

'He's a little older, like all of us. Picked up a few more scars.' But he didn't go on. She was already on her way to the deck.

'I never thought I would see you again,' she said, standing in the doorway. 'You *look* like the same old Hatcher.'

Daphne's *ch'uang tzu-chi* was also stimulated by the sight of him, alive, after all the years. For the year after they met, Hatcher had lived with Daphne whenever he was in Hong Kong. He left without warning and returned the same way, never discussing his business. She had heard of him before they met – Hatcher, the daring Yankee river pirate, the lone wolf feared even by the mighty Sam-Sam Sam himself. It was only after he was gone that new rumors started. That he was a paid assassin. That he worked for the CIA. That he nurtured friendships and then double-crossed those closest to him. That he was a member of a secret section of the Army called *Ying bing*, shadow warriors.

Having known him for a year, they were rumors Daphne dismissed, for she had seen both sides of him – the cold side that went off in the night to do whatever deeds he had to do and the other side, the caring lover, to whom sex was fun, not a conquest, for whom it was open, and slow, sometimes agonizing play that ended in what he called 'the purest feeling,' the small death, the orgasm that was his one positive, total escape from reality, as momentary as it might be.

She knew also in her heart and from her experience with him that any or all of the stories could be true.

But it didn't matter. He was alive and he was here and, like Cohen, she remembered the night she had met Hatcher, a night she would never forget.

She had hardly been able to contain her anger at this impudent mei gwok *lawyer as he led her out of the crowded ballroom of the Chinese Palace and onto the terrace. And she was just as angry that Cohen had introduced them. Then he stopped and smiled at her. 'My name's not London, it's Hatcher,' he said in perfect*

241

French. 'And I think what you did to those Americans was lovely and I can get you Indian cotton, top grade, delivered wherever you want it, for half of what you're paying now, which should be worth as much as – at least a ten percent markup for you.' He paused for a moment, then added, 'Not only that, but I can make you laugh a lot.'

She had stared at him for several seconds, amazed at his audacity, and drawn to his gray eyes. But she quickly recovered.

'How much?' she asked.

'How much what?'

'How much cotton can you deliver, how fast and at what cost?'

'I'll have to figure that up. I don't do that kind of thing in my head.'

'Neither do I,' she heard herself say.

'Lunch tomorrow. Strictly business. I'll have the figures, you bring the check. No managers, no accountants, no lawyers, just you and me.'

'I warn you, I don't compromise.'

'Neither do I,' he said. 'Everybody loses in a compromise. I negotiate. When you negotiate, everybody wins.'

'Oh? How so?'

'You decide up front what you don't really care about. Narrow it down to what's important. That's your line. I'll do the same. Trust me, we'll deal fast and have time to do a lot of laughing before the meal is over.'

'How come laughter is so important to you?' she asked.

He smiled. 'Laughter is the key to heaven,' he said.

And to her surprise, she had agreed to lunch.

There had never been any cotton deal between them.

But he had made her laugh – a lot. And he was right, it was the key to heaven.

'I'm going back to my room,' Cohen said from the living room. 'My side is beginning to act up a little.'

They ignored him. He shrugged and went off toward the rear of the house.

There was an awkward minute or two when neither Daphne nor Hatcher knew exactly what to say. She broke the ice.

'What happened to your throat?' she asked, staring at the scar on his neck.

'I was in a very bad prison. I spoke when I shouldn't have. A guard decided to discourage me from ever speaking again.'

'Is it painful?'

242

'Not anymore.'

'I am glad,' she said, then raised an eyebrow. 'Your voice is very sexy.'

'*Merci*. Wasn't it always?'

'Not like now,' she said. Then after a pause, 'What happened to you? You just vanished. Everyone thought you were dead.'

'I went back to America to do a job and got in trouble. Three years' worth of trouble. In a prison where *every*thing was forbidden.'

'And what of the other three years?'

He shrugged. 'I figured I was history by then, Daffy.'

She threw back her head and laughed, a throaty laugh that set off bells in his memory.

'Daffy,' she said. 'I have not heard Daffy for so many years. No one else would ever call me Daffy.' She let the laugh die and then said quietly, her green eyes flashing, 'No, Hatcher, you were never history. Not for me.'

He let it pass.

'Is Cohen serious?' Hatcher asked her. 'Can you really help me?'

'Straight to business,' she said. 'So it's going to be like that, eh?'

'I'm sorry,' he said. 'I feel a little awkward. I know I owe you –'

She put her fingers against his lips. 'You owe me nothing. We made no promises. I shared my bed with you . . . with anticipation. Sometimes even . . . impatience.'

He remembered, the words conjuring moments of delirious joy, but he pushed the thoughts away again.

'I owed you at least a proper good-bye,' he said.

'Is that why you came back? To say good-bye to the friends who thought you were dead?'

'Perhaps,' he whispered huskily. Then, trying again to avoid the inevitable, he said jokingly, 'Besides, I could use a sauna treatment at the Estoril. And the Thai massage there –'

She turned and walked to the bedroom door. 'You don't have to go to the Estoril Hotel to get a massage, Hatcher,' she said. 'And you must say *jo sahn* properly before you say *joi gin* again.'

He followed her into the room.

'How can you help me, Daffy?' he asked.

She walked to the other side of the bed. 'I told China I would help – but only on my terms.'

Hatcher looked at her suspiciously. 'Uh-huh, and what are they?' his frayed voice asked.

'You must stay out of Macao.'

'I have no reason to go over there now.'

'And we must do this thing exactly as I say.'

Hatcher smiled. 'You haven't changed a bit,' he said.

'Agreed?'

'I'll think about it.'

'What is this about a prison camp, anyway?' she asked.

'I'm trying to find someone,' he said. 'We were comrades in the Navy together. His father is a hero in America. He may have been in a prison camp in Laos. It was called Huie-kui. The commandant's name was Taisung, or something like that. I figure somebody must have done business up there during the war. Maybe they'll remember something.'

She turned her back to him and stared out at the bay, shaking her head. 'You're looking for one man?' she said.

'It's why I came back,' he said. 'All the rest of it – you, China – that's all a bonus.'

'Perhaps we can sneak upriver and avoid Sam-Sam, maybe I can set that up. There is only one man I think who might help you. You remember Samuel Anstadt, the one they call the Dutchman?'

'I never met the Dutchman.'

'That's because he operated in Laos and North Vietnam. I buy material from him now. But ten years ago he sold drugs, guns, clothing, everything, to the Vietcong.'

'Can we get him down here?' Hatcher asked.

She shook her head.

'He is wanted by the Hong Kong police. They would recognize him in a moment. But there is a place called Leatherneck John's in Tsang, forty miles upstream.'

'An American joint?' Hatcher interrupted.

She nodded. 'A lot of dealing and drinking is done there,' she said. 'Drug deals are made and so is the exchange. It is a kind of – free spot. We can meet the Dutchman there, but only if we're sure Sam-Sam Sam is out of the area.'

'You're not going,' Hatcher said.

'Of course I'm going. They will only talk to you because I ask them to. I will have to make the deal.'

A forgotten shard of mirror glittered in the corner, reminding him of the night before. He had put China's life at risk. Now he was about to do the same to her. Once again, he was taking, not giving, like the old times.

'Maybe –' he started.

She whirled and glared at him with flashing green eyes.

'No *maybe*. Yes.'

They were almost nose to nose, her eyes demanding agreement. They stared at each other.

'There is one other thing. . . .' He stared down at her, the brash smile she remembered playing at his lips.

'Yeah?'

He reached out cautiously with one hand, stopped an inch from her mouth, then slowly moved his fingers to her mouth, touching her lower lip with his fingertips, exploring it with his forefinger, squeezing it with his thumb and middle finger until it pointed toward him. Her tongue glistened an eighth of an inch from his finger, flirted with it and finally swept across it, and his finger, moistened, slipped more easily across her lips.

'*Hai* . . .' she said.

Her eyes closed and she tilted her head back and he leaned to her, gently squeezing her mouth as his touched hers. Her breath came out in a rush and she bit his lips, explored them with her tongue until finally the tease was no longer a tease but a passion.

She reached up and slipped her jacket off, let it fall to the floor as they kissed.

He reached up with his other hand and untied the slender string on one shoulder, then the other, but she pressed against him, keeping the dress from falling. She slid her hand between them, pressed the flat of it on his stomach. Her fingers nimbly unbuttoned his shirt. She slipped her hand inside, sliding it across the hard muscles, her thumb encircling his navel. She slid her fingers under his belt, turned her hand toward the floor, slid it down until she felt him rising to meet her hand.

Then she leaned back. And the dress slipped slowly down, dangled for a moment on her hard nipples, then slipped over her breasts and down to her hips. They kept kissing, their eyes closed as their hands explored each other, gave each other clues.

With her free hand she undid his belt buckle, unsnapped his pants, slipped her hand around his buttocks until they dropped off, then did the same with his shorts; he reciprocated, loosening her dress until it too fell away. She was naked under the dress.

Their lips were still locked together as she took his hand and moved it slowly to her stomach and then down, until it was between her legs and then she pressed it hard against her and began moving it up and down, then moved her hand, pressed the back of her hand against the back of his until they were stroking each other in perfect rhythm, their lips moving in the same rhythm.

'My God,' he whispered into her mouth, 'slow down.'

He felt her twitch, press more tightly against his hand.

'*Cheng . . . nei*, now, *cheng nei* . . .' she said as her breath became shorter, more urgent. 'Please . . . please . . .' And she began to grind against his hand, began stroking him faster and he began to move with her hand. She was trembling now, she sucked in her breath and rose on her toes and he could feel her getting harder under his fingers and then as she cried out she thrust him into her.

She ground her head into his shoulder, her muscles taut, trembling as he continued to massage her, faster and faster, lowering her slowly onto the bed until her arms fell away and he was over her, his eyes closed, his biceps twitching, and then suddenly he took in a breath and held it as he, too, exploded. She reached up with both arms, wrapped them around his neck and pulled him down on top of her, still grinding against him and he could feel her tightening again.

'*Cheng nei*, Hatcher . . .'

yen dui yen

It did not surprise Cohen when Tollie Fong called him. It was customary – a requirement of honor by anyone who belonged to the triad societies, whether it was the traditional society, the Sun Lee On, or its underworld offshoot, the Chiu Chao. As was the tradition, Fong suggested a meeting that afternoon in an offbeat restaurant deep in Wanchai. They agreed on the basics. The meeting was set for four o'clock. Each would have three representatives of his own triad with him; each would select a judge from the Society in general to monitor the meeting; there would be no weapons. The attack on Cohen's house was not specifically mentioned.

Cohen selected his most conservative *cheongsam* for the meeting. He left in the Rolls at three-forty-five, taking with him Sing, who was already out of the hospital, and two other members of his 'family.' Hatcher and Daphne were still behind closed doors in the bedroom. No need to tell them about the meeting yet.

The Rolls swept quietly down the mountain, past the governor's mansion and the U.S. consulate and down Connaught Street to noisy, rowdy Wanchai and then crept through teeming streets, threading its way between rickshas and pedestrians, to Lan Fung Alley, a dismal and deserted connector. A small sign in hand-painted calligraphy halfway down the narrow alley announced the presence of Lon Song, a tiny, nondescript restaurant favored by locals. The driver parked the Rolls as close to the entrance as he could get, and Cohen entered behind Sing and his two other aides.

Lon Song was a narrow, feebly lit place, barely big enough to accommodate its ten tables. The smell of garlic hung heavily in the air. It was four-ten and it was deserted except for the owner, an elderly but very erect man with a wisp of gray chin whiskers. He stared at Cohen through bifocals, smiled and bowed.

'It is an honor, Tsu Fi,' he said.

'Are the others here yet?'

'*Hai*. Also the judges.'

'*Ho*,' Cohen said. He and his three men followed the old man back through the dingy corridor to a door at the rear. The owner opened it for him. There was a small landing and a staircase that led down to a cellar room, a room that was dusty and poorly lit and obviously rarely used. In the center was a small table with two chairs facing each other on opposite sides. A tea service sat in the middle of the table. There were two cups.

Following tradition, Tollie Fong, who had committed the insult, had arrived first. He sat on the side of the table facing the stairwell. Behind him stood his three aides, their arms crossed over their chests.

There were two other men in the room. One was Sam Chin, an elder in the Chinese community and a respected banker, who was the *san wong* of one of the most honored triads in the Sun Lee On. The other was Lon Tung, *san wong* of the House of Seven Drums, one of the most dangerous of the Chiu Chao triads. They were there to monitor the meeting, to make sure there was no violence and that whatever the problem was it would be resolved satisfactorily, either with accepted apologies, or with a formal declaration of war between the two houses. Among the triads, a sudden and undeclared attack from one on another was considered dishonorable. Members of the offending family were ostracized. Fong's alacrity in asking for the meeting was obligatory.

Fong stood as Cohen came down the stairs. He smiled a barely discernible smile. His reputation as the most ruthless assassin in the Chiu Chaos was undisputed.

He and Cohen sat down facing each other. Fong poured each a

247

cup of tea. Nobody else spoke. Not even a throat was cleared. Fong took a sip of tea before starting. Cohen leaned back, sipped his tea and stared across the table at Fong, *yen dui yen*, eye on eye. The stare could not be broken until the problem was resolved, one way or another – either with forgiveness or with war.

According to tradition, the two men spoke through their judges, a ritual designed to prevent direct confrontations. Thus sarcasm and tonal inflections were removed from the negotiation. Fong held up one hand and Tung leaned over as Fong whispered in his ear.

'I returned from Bangkok as soon as I heard about the unfortunate incident at your home last night,' Tung said, repeating Fong's whispered remarks.

Sam Chin leaned over Cohen, who whispered his response.

'*Mm goi*,' Chin repeated what Cohen had said. 'I am pleased you have acted so promptly.'

'You understand that this attack was not done at my command? I did not order such an insult to your home.'

'I do now, since you say so,' was Cohen's response.

'I have come to offer an apology,' Fong said through Lon Tung.

The conversation continued in this vein – Fong whispering his comments to Tung, who repeated them, and Cohen replying through Chin.

'You have violated my house,' Cohen's judge replied. 'A dishonor to the oath of the triads.'

Fong quickly whispered a lengthy answer, his eyes beginning to glitter in the feeble light.

'It was not me. But it was my Number One, and Lung has paid dearly for his sins. I come to apologize for his stupidity, and to ask that the Tsu Fi forgive me.' He paused while Tung repeated his comments, then before Cohen could answer, whispered something further. Tung said, 'And to offer compensation for this insult.'

Cohen leaned forward, playing the game to the hilt and whispering hurriedly to Chin. 'I am sorry, I did not hear the last,' he said.

Tung said, 'Tollie Fong has offered to make compensation for the insult to the Tsu Fi.'

Cohen finally nodded. He took another sip of tea before whispering his retort to Chin.

'Then I accept your apology,' Chin repeated.

'*Mm goi*,' Tung said with a nod of his head. 'And what compensation does the Tsu Fi feel is proper?'

Cohen took a sip of tea, his eyes still locked with Fong's. Then he whispered slowly to Chin. Chin looked surprised, but only for a moment. He stood up and said, 'As tribute, you must set aside this feud with the *mei gwok* Hatcher.'

The men on both sides of the room were startled by the demand. The judges, Chin and Tung, stared at each other. The demand, they knew, would cause trouble. Anger boiled up in Fong. Hate dilated the pupils in his eyes. By the *san wong's* orders, he must grant the demand, but he had to protest to save face.

He shook his head but still remained *yen dui yen* with Cohen. 'I cannot do that,' he whispered to Tung in a voice thick with hatred and loud enough for Cohen to hear. 'The *mei gwok yahn* murdered my father.'

'It is my understanding that the *mei gwok* killed in self-defense,' Cohen whispered in a voice just as loud, not waiting for Tung's translation.

'He dishonored the House of Fong, just as Lung dishonored your house,' Fong answered crisply, still *yen dui yen*, but now speaking directly to Cohen.

'Then it is an even trade,' Cohen quickly answered.

The response disarmed Fong for a moment. Fong was a killer, not a negotiator. 'No! Not until Hatcher joins Lung in hell is it an even trade. What you ask is unreasonable.'

Cohen held his hands out in a gesture of futility. 'Nevertheless it is the price you must pay for Lung's dishonor.'

Fong slowly shook his head, his eyes still locked with Cohen's, growing more angry with each word.

'I made a blood promise, the oath of *ch'u-tiao*,' Fong said slowly.

'Honor is honor,' said Cohen. 'I say the feud is over.'

'And I say this thing between Hatcher and me is not your business,' Fong said, leaning toward Cohen.

'Then I cannot accept your apology,' Cohen said with brittle authority.

Sam Chin stepped forward and cleared his throat. '*Deui mju*,' he said, bowing, 'it occurs to me that perhaps the Tsu Fi might offer a tribute more acceptable to the Tsu Fong so that this dispute may be resolved peacefully.'

Cohen was adamant. By tradition, Fong was virtually obligated to accept any demand within reason.

249

'No,' he said. 'My home has been compromised. I have a right to this request. It is particularly fitting because Lung made this attack for the purpose of killing the *mei gwok*, who was my guest.'

'And I, too, say no,' Fong quickly answered.

'Then I'll let it be known everywhere that Tollie Fong has violated his oath to the Sun Lee On.'

'I am not of the Sun Lee On, I am Chiu Chao,' he said.

'We are all cousins in the oath,' said Cohen. 'If you betray the house of Tsu Fi, you betray the Chiu Chaos and all triads.'

'So it shall be,' Fong said, with a sneer in his voice, forcing the issue. He picked up his teacup and smashed it on the table. Cohen leaned back, startled by his outburst. Fong slashed the knife edge of his hand into the broken bits of china.

'You are declaring *zhanzheng* on the Tsu Fi,' Tung said, obviously surprised that Fong was taking this confrontation to the limit. 'The Tsu Fi is right. You will face the wrath of both the Chiu Chaos and the Sun Lee On.'

'Then I, too, must declare war – on the Tsu Fong,' said Cohen. He stood up and, with disdain, swept the broken cup on the floor.

'You have one hour to get out of Hong Kong,' China said.

Fong stared up at him and his lips curled slightly.

'You may still reconsider,' Chin said slowly.

'You have guts, Cohen, to threaten the new *san wong* of the White Palms.'

'This island belongs to me,' Cohen said with finality. 'If you have any doubts about that, you're dumber than I think you are.'

Fong stood up slowly. 'You are a fool, Yankee,' he said, 'to make blood over this *mei gwok* spy. He is a liar. He cheats his friends. He kills those who trust him.'

'My kind of guy,' Cohen answered. 'Your hour is running out.'

Fong stared at him for a few moments more.

'All right,' he said finally. 'I will not dishonor the *san wong* of the White Palms. But you humiliate me, *mei gwok*,' he said to Cohen.

'It'll pass,' Cohen said, and Fong bristled again. He turned to each of the judges, bowing to them in turn, and stormed up the stairway followed by his men. Lon Tung followed quickly behind him. Cohen's shoulders slumped. He had won. His heart was rapping against his ribs, but he had succeeded and avoided a blood feud between himself and the White Palms.

Sam Chin touched Cohen's shoulder. 'I have never known you to be so difficult in such a negotiation,' he said.

Cohen looked over at the elderly man.

250

'I agree,' he said wearily. 'Unfortunately, San Wong, nothing else was appropriate.'

Tollie Fong stood outside the restaurant waiting for the car to be brought to him. There would be no war between the Tsu Fi and the Tsu Fong. The compromise with Cohen still stung, but it had been necessary. For now he would have to put aside his *ch'u-tiao* to kill Hatcher, but that was acceptable, in fact, it fit perfectly with his plans. He had waited eight years to get Hatcher, he could wait a few more weeks. But in Tollie Fong's mind, Hatcher was a dead man. It was just a matter of time.

The shadows outside were growing longer. Daphne lay beside Hatcher, turned and pressed against him, moving slowly until almost every inch of her touched his side.

'I hope you do not cause all kinds of hell up there,' she said. 'Bad for my business.'

'Good for your business. Maybe we'll get rid of Sam-Sam for you,' Hatcher growled, turning toward her, pressing her tighter.

'I may hold you to that promise of Indian cotton you made – how many years ago?'

'A long time,' he said. 'I'll see what I can do.'

'When are you leaving?'

'As soon as we finish upriver.'

'And you won't be back.'

He started to say something, but she put her hand over his mouth. 'China told me everything. I know it is dangerous for you in Hong Kong. I just want to know this time. I would like to say *joi gin* properly.'

'You have already,' his voice growled.

She put a long leg over his hip and pulled him even closer with it.

'I'm not through yet,' she said huskily.

SMOKE

A pale, dyspeptic, extremely nervous young under-under-under-secretary named Lamar Pellingham, Jr., greeted Sloan at the entrance to the embassy and immediately confided that this was his first experience with death on a foreign shore.

251

'It's impossible, absolutely impossible. Forms, forms, forms,' the pasty-faced man groaned. 'I've never seen such red tape.'

'Yes, I know what a problem these things are,' Sloan agreed solicitously. 'You'd think they'd be glad to get rid of the remains instead of making it so difficult.'

'Yes. Right. Of course,' the diplomat answered, somewhat startled by Sloan's nonchalance. 'Uh, the maids packed up everything – that is, everything but what was in his desk. We sealed that room, left it – the desk, I mean – alone. You know, in the event there was, uh . . . classified material there.'

He spoke every word as though it were a hot coal he was spitting out of his mouth. It was obvious he found the entire matter repellent.

'Excellent decision,' said Sloan. 'I'll check it out.'

'Have you seen the police?'

'Not yet. I came straight here after checking into the hotel. Do you have the police reports?'

'No, the investigator, a major, uh, Ngy, wouldn't give anything up. A real mean one, said he needs it for the investigation,' Pellingham stammered quickly. 'But I have the other things. Come with me, please.'

The nervous junior diplomat led Sloan back through the ornate passages of the Thai embassy to his office, a cheery but small cubicle near the back of the building. He riffled through a stack of folders in his 'Hold' box and handed Sloan an envelope marked, 'Porter. Final Papers. Confidential.'

'Everything's in there,' Pellingham said. 'All the forms, his insurance papers, even his last expense report.'

'Interesting. I'll just take these along,' Sloan said.

'Perhaps I should, uh, make a copy?' Pellingham stammered, rubbing his cheek with the palm of a sweaty hand and turning what started out as a statement into a question.

Sloan smiled his reassuring smile. 'If it would make you more comfortable,' he said, 'a copy will be fine.'

'They say it's, uh, a case of an innocent bystander, killed more or less by accident, if it's possible for someone to be murdered by *accident*.' He hesitated and, when Sloan made no response, added, 'Not exactly a hero's death. But I suppose it's best for our purposes. I mean acceptable under the circumstances.'

'Acceptable,' Sloan said. 'An excellent way of putting it. I can see why you picked the diplomatic service.'

'Well, thank you, sir,' Pellingham responded. 'I meant for the family and all.'

252

'Of course. I know exactly what you mean, and I agree,' Sloan said, trying to put the young man at ease. 'Look here,' he went on, 'no need to worry about this any further. I'm here now. It's in my hands.'

'But . . .'

Smiling, Sloan handed the envelope back to Pellingham. 'Why don't you make your copy while I check out Porter's things.'

'Yes, yes, good idea. You, uh, know where to ship the remains and his effects?'

'It's all arranged.'

'Oh, thank God,' the neophyte diplomat said with relief.

'Just show me Porter's suite while you're copying the report, hmm?'

'Right, right.'

The young man watched as Sloan entered Porter's suite, wondering whether he should accompany him. But Sloan closed the door and he stared at it for a full minute before scurrying off to the copy machine.

An hour's search produced nothing of value to Sloan but a five-by-seven leather-bound, three-ring notebook. Porter's diary, a veritable autobiography of the man beginning in January of that year. Sloan stuffed it in his briefcase. He checked over everything else and found nothing else related to the Cody-Wol Pot case. After getting the copy of the Porter documents, he headed back to his hotel.

He peeled off a soggy shirt, pulled a table under the ceiling fan and spent the rest of the afternoon going through the diary. Porter had certainly been keeping a wary eye on the little Thai. The notebook was complete up to the day Porter died. The expense account meticulously included fifty cents for a Coke at a place called the American Deli in Patpong 'while performing surveillance.' Porter had turned into the ultimate bureaucrat.

Then the need began gnawing at Sloan. He became distracted and finally closed the file folder and the notebook. As the sun began to set he stared out the window at the city of golden spires and domes, shimmering in the dying rays of the sun, watched as they got dimmer and dimmer until finally they winked out like dying candles. The need was in him and the night lured him out of the room, down to the crowded main street.

A two-seater with a wiry, energetic little driver waited near the entrance of the hotel. 'Sir, sir,' the little fellow said, trotting beside Sloan as he walked toward the row of taxis at the door. 'Got good *tuk-tuk*, best price in town. Very fast.'

Why not, thought Sloan. There were hundreds of the noisy machines in the city. It would be impossible to trace his movements.

'All right, lead on,' Sloan said.

'My name is very complicated,' he said. 'You can call me Sy, my American friends call me Sy.'

'Right,' Sloan said, settling back in the somewhat uncomfortable seat, and gave him an address in the waterfront district.

The trip across town took only fifteen minutes, but Sloan's heart was already a thundering drum in his chest by the time they got there.

The place had not changed, would never change. The tart smell of the river gave way to a much sweeter odor. It attacked his brain and intoxicated his spirit as he went down the narrow stairs, which creaked and groaned underfoot. As he descended the odor got stronger, headier.

The master waited as usual at a desk near the door. This one was new, but they all looked alike. Wrinkled, bowed old men with faded eyes and sunken faces, they were the dream masters, the killers of nightmares and assassins of pain, and the guides to the Elysian Fields. As he followed the old man back through a narrow passageway, Sloan began to feel a little light-headed. They entered a long narrow room lined with drab canvas cots. Silk screens stained by age and misuse separated the beds. A gray veil of smoke clung to the ceiling. It was like walking through hell.

Sloan followed the dream master to the third cubicle. He lay on his side on the bed, got comfortable, watched as the old Thai tamped the black cube into the bowl of the long pipe, lit it with a taper, and sucked fire into the cube until it glowed. Then he held the thick stem against Sloan's lips. The colonel took a deep breath, felt the oily smoke as it surged into his lungs, invaded his bloodstream, streaked up to his brain.

As the opium took effect, Sloan felt electrified. His body hummed, then became numb. Old bruises and wounds were healed. Pain vanished, stress evaporated. The doom diminished. The old Thai shrank before his eyes and slowly vanished in a golden mist.

Sloan groaned and rolled over on his back.

He let the haze envelop him, embraced it, walked through to the other side.

To a place of green fields and flowers.

A deep blue sky was overhead and the sun warmed him.

254

Somewhere nearby, the sea crashed on rocks.

He lay down in cool grass.

His anxieties were washed away by the caressing breeze that wafted over him.

Here there was no death. No cries of pain, nor enemies nor dirty jobs to be assigned. No nightmares.

There was only tranquillity.

It was the only place left where Sloan could find peace.

THE TS'E K'AM MEN TI

Hatcher and company left two hours before dawn, sneaking past the harbor patrols and customs boats in the Bujia Ngkou, the bay at the mouth of the Beijiang River that becomes Hong Kong harbor, and then heading west into south China along one of the many tributaries of the jungle-choked Xijiang River. By the gray wash of dawn they were thirty miles upstream.

They came in two boats. The first was a long, narrow snakeboat, heavily powered, with a thatched cabin near the rear. Behind it was a thirty-foot 600 hp Cigarette boat, capable of skimming the water at sixty miles an hour. Hatcher, Daphne, Cohen and Sing, who doubled as helmsman, and another gunman, Joey, were in the first. There were four Chinese gunmen in the second, on 'loan' to Cohen from a friendly Chiu Chao triad known as the Narrow Blade Gang, as backup in the event the Tsu Fi got in trouble. They all felt comfortable, since Daphne's intelligence had reported that Sam-Sam was farther upriver and was not expected back to the Ts'e K'am Men Ti stronghold until the next day.

Early in the trip, before they got to the river, everyone had been tense and wary, on the lookout for harbor patrols and customs boats. Now they relaxed as the long wooden boat cruised quietly along the river, hugging the bank to avoid being too obtrusive and followed by the impressive Cigarette.

Cohen was a strange sight, dressed in a *cheongsam* with a pistol belt around his waist, sitting like a crown prince on his canvas lawn chair, staring ahead into the darkness, muttering a continuing monologue questioning his sanity, Hatcher's, Daphne's – in fact, the whole damn trip. He had insisted upon arranging for the boats and the gunmen.

255

Finally Hatcher growled, 'Listen, China, nobody stuck a gun in your ear and ordered you to come. It was your idea to round up the guns, get your beach chair there and come along for the ride.'

'Well, I couldn't talk you out of it,' Cohen answered.

'What's that got to do with it?'

'You know what I mean,' Cohen said. 'What the hell's so special about this guy Cody anyway?'

'I told you, we went to school together.'

'That doesn't float,' Cohen said with disgust.

'Hell,' Hatcher said, 'maybe I wanted to do one last job that had . . . some sense of . . . humanity . . . honor maybe.'

'"War, he sung, his toil and trouble; honour but an empty bubble,"' Cohen intoned.

'Dryden,' Hatcher replied. 'How about "Mine honour is my life; both grow in one;/Take honour from me, and my life is done."'

'Richard the Second,' Cohen answered, and after a moment's meditation added, 'I hope to hell all this poetry's worth the trip.'

'Don't we all,' answered Hatcher.

'Let me tell you something maybe you don't know about Sam-Sam,' Cohen said, starting a rambling monologue that eventually had a point. 'First time I ever met him was when I saw you, when the Tsu Fi sent me up here to Chin Chin land the first time. Sam-Sam was kind of the new kid on the block, okay? He came down from Peking because he was an ardent capitalist at heart, which didn't go over well in Peking. This was about six months before that time I met him. I don't know what he did in Peking, but whatever it was, he had developed the most blasé attitude about killing I've ever seen. I mean he would just as soon put a bullet in your brain as step on a bug.

'I was dealing mainly with Joe Cockroach, he was like the agent for everything. You made a deal with Joe and he got it all together – one price, one guy to pay. It was a comfortable way to do business. Also I trusted Joe. I knew him before in Hong Kong when he was in the import business. So maybe the third time I go up there, Sam-Sam comes up to me and says from now on it's him and me doing business. He'll make a better offer, he says. And I tell him, "Sam-Sam, I can't do that because I've been dealing with Joe for too many years and, besides, things don't work like that up here at the Ts'e K'am Men Ti."

'So Sam-Sam walks out on the deck – we were in this barge and I was in Joe's office, Joe is outside doing something – and

Sam-Sam walks out the door and next thing I know I hear two shots, *pumf, pumf,* just like that, and I dash to the door and look out in time to see Sam-Sam with the gun still smoking and he grabs a handful of Joe's shirt and lifts him up with one arm and throws him in the river. And he looks over at me and he smiles and he says, and this is a quote, he says, "Now it is not a problem anymore." And he laughs. Six months later he controlled the whole damn river.'

'I know all that stuff, China,' Hatcher said with a sigh.

'Yeah, but here's what you don't know,' Cohen said rather elegantly. 'Joe Cockroach came to Hong Kong from China. He did this and that, nothing very successful, then he went up to Chin Chin land and got in the smuggling business. Then he sent for his brother to come down. His brother was Sam-Sam Sam.'

'Sam-Sam isn't going to be around,' Hatcher said gruffly.

'Yeah, right, that's what we're all hoping,' Cohen intoned. 'That Sam-Sam won't be around.'

They fell silent again and Cohen began to doze, his head bobbing, then woke up suddenly, but drifted off again. In the eerie twilight before dawn he looked like some ancient Chinese philosopher.

Daphne and Hatcher sat beside him on the hardback benches provided in the snakeboat. Hatcher was leaning back, his long legs stretched out in front of him. Daphne reached out and slipped her hand in his. He squeezed it gently and held on to it as they peered straight ahead into the waning darkness.

She leaned over him and said softly in his ear, 'You like this, don't you, Hatch? Living with your heart in your mouth.'

'It can become addictive.'

'Did you ever marry, Hatcher?' Daphne asked.

'Nope.'

'Is that the reason?'

He thought for a moment, and said, 'Maybe.'

'Ever thought about it?' she asked.

'No,' he said immediately, and was surprised at his answer. 'The thought never occurred to me.'

'Why not?'

Hatcher did not answer immediately. He thought of all the stereotyped reasons.

'I live day to day,' he said finally. 'Marriage is also yesterdays and tomorrows.'

He turned and looked back at her. 'Or maybe I've just been

too damn selfish all my life to think about anyone else. Why? Is this a proposal?'

They both laughed softly in the darkness.

She shook her head. 'No,' she said, 'I'm not the marrying kind either.' She paused for a moment and then asked, 'Do you ever worry about dying?'

'Nah,' he said quickly, 'I gave that up a long time ago.'

The river broke up into a dozen twisting streams and creeks that coursed through the thick jungle. This was the northern rim of the Southeast Asian rain forest. A few miles to the north, trees gave way to foothills and then mountains, but here the jungle was still fresh and verdant. Chinese patrol boats, limited in number, ignored the area, which was like pirate Jean Lafitte's stronghold in the early 1800s, a drifting, lush green empire of assassins and privateers who could vanish in an instant up one of its many creeks and rias or disappear into jungle hideouts defended by mines and booby traps. It was a sprawling black market, its barges and boats of contraband protected by nature and by the brigands who called themselves the Ts'e K'am Men Ti, the Secret Gate Keepers, and dominated with vicious authority by the ruthless Sam-Sam Sam, and his henchmen, the SAVAK killer Batal and the Tonton assassin Billy Death.

With the sun, the jungle creatures in this marginal rain forest began to awaken and the underbrush came alive with morning sounds. Adjutant storks squawked, gliding frogs bellowed and leaped from tree to tree, hornbills pushed through the foliage with their powerful beaks vying for food with fruit-eating bats. High above them all, eagles drifted leisurely through the blood-red sky seeking breakfast.

By noon they were near the small villages of Jiangmen and Shunde. They slipped past them. By midafternoon they were deep in the jungle.

'We're coming to the Ts'e K'am Men Ti cutoff,' Daphne said.

Hatcher studied the map she had sketched before they left. It showed a narrow cutoff snaking away from the main river to the south. Four miles up the cutoff was another branch that twisted off to the east through the jungle, then cut sharply west forming a narrow peninsula, an elbow in the stream, like the trap in a sink, and easy to block in the event someone tried a hurried retreat back toward the main river. Leatherneck John's was on the far side of the elbow.

Hatcher pointed to the tight little peninsula and traced his finger straight across its base, away from Leatherneck John's.

258

'This where we are?' he whispered.

'About there.' Daphne nodded.

'So if we got in trouble at the bar, we could forget the boat and come overland, straight back here, right?'

She nodded.

'How far is it?' he asked.

'A mile or less,' she said.

'Okay,' Hatcher's voice rasped, 'that's our fall-back position. We'll have the Cigarette boat wait here and we'll go around the bend in the snakeboat. If we get in trouble, we run overland, like rabbits, back here, forget the small boat.'

Cohen said, 'How many men do we take with us?'

'Sing goes in the bar with us, covers our ass,' said Hatcher. 'Maybe one other shooter to stay with the snakeboat and keep his eyes open in case Sam-Sam should show up. The other three stay with the Cigarette. If we have to run for it they can cover our retreat. If it goes smoothly, they'll just follow us back.'

'Sam-Sam will not be back until tomorrow,' Daphne reiterated.

'Uh-huh. Well, there's always the unexpected,' Hatcher said, half aloud. 'I'll stop worrying about Sam-Sam when we get back to Hong Kong.'

'You are very cautious,' Daphne said with a smile.

'And still alive,' Hatcher answered. 'Let's put it together and get on up there.'

As they entered the domain of the Ts'e K'am Men Ti the jungle sounds merged with other sounds. Human sounds. While the sun began to sink behind the trees a strange chant drifted through the trees from in front of them.

'What's that?' Cohen asked.

Daphne said, 'The women are singing a *hanchi*, some kind of good-luck song.'

'I've never heard that before,' Cohen said.

'It's Cambodian, I think,' Daphne said.

'Are they Khmer Rouge?' Hatcher asked.

She shrugged. 'Khmer Rouge, free Laotian guerrillas, river tramps. Who knows. Remember, the women are just as mean as the men, and maybe a little quicker.'

The stream was no more than a hundred feet wide. As they rounded the elbow they saw the first signs of the Ts'e K'am Men Ti. There were three barges lashed to trees hard on the bank to their right, jutting out into the small river. Sing had to swing out to get around them. On the first, there were two hooches, side by side on the back of the barge, like guard stations.

259

A dozen women, all bare-breasted and wearing red bandannas tied tightly around stringy black hair, chanted as they cleaned the deck. On one corner of the barge two large woks were smoking as another woman stirred vegetables for dinner into them. A man sat on another corner fishing.

'Quite a domestic little scene,' Hatcher growled.

'Sweet,' Cohen said, 'like a Fourth of July picnic.'

There were five or six crates of electronic equipment stacked in the center of the deck of the second barge, sloppily covered by a tarp. Beside it, the third barge held only ten or fifteen cases of ammunition. Hatcher checked the ammo through binoculars: 9 mm., .30 caliber, .38 caliber, a crate of .45s.

'A lot of bullets and very little inventory,' said Hatcher.

'Sam-Sam's probably got his heavy stuff stashed a little farther upriver. He's not expecting customers,' Cohen offered.

'Good,' said Hatcher.

Beyond the barges, another hundred yards up the creek, was Leatherneck John's, a large, ugly square with thatched sides and a corrugated roof. It jutted out over the creek on stilts and was surrounded on both sides by makeshift piers, like a shoddy mud-flat marina. Several boats of various descriptions were tied up at the pier. One of them was a scruffy-looking Chris Craft, at least twenty years old, a tattered German flag dangling from its radio antenna.

Daphne said, 'The old white fishing boat is the Dutchman's.'

'Good,' Cohen whispered. 'Maybe we can get out of here in a hurry.' He swept the binoculars farther upstream. A heavily laden barge, well covered with waterproof tarpaulins, hugged the bank a hundred yards past the bar.

'Jesus,' Cohen breathed.

'What?' Hatcher asked.

'Check the barge farther upstream,' Cohen said and Hatcher lifted his glasses.

'Fat city,' said Cohen. 'That's the store.'

As they watched, a man came out on the front of the barge and stretched, then began to urinate into the river. He was a tall, very thin black man with greasy hair kneaded into pigtails held in place by a red headband. His blue shirt was open to the waist and he had an AK-47 over his shoulder and a H&K 9 mm. pistol in his belt. He was wearing gold-rimmed Porsche sunglasses.

'Uh-oh, that's the Haitian, the one they call Billy Death,' Cohen said. 'He's the one likes to cut off people's feet. Look down at the bow.'

260

Hatcher swung the binoculars down and searched the front of the barge. There, hanging by a cord, appeared to be a pair of shoes. Hatcher flipped the switch on the glasses and increased the focal length, zooming in tightly on the shoes. He could see the rotten gray skin of an ankle sagging over the top of one of the shoes. Flies buzzed furiously around it.

'My God,' Hatcher gasped.

'It should be all right,' Daphne said. 'He doesn't know you. He probably won't pay any attention to us.'

'Yeah,' said Cohen. 'Just business as usual.'

Sam-Sam's barge was a sprawling floating flatbed, stacked with contraband and ammunition. He had a dozen of his best men with him and seven women, some of them concubines, some tougher than the men. Batal was along but Billy Death was not. The Haitian didn't like the river.

'What is the problem with Billy Death?' Sam-Sam asked Batal.

'He cannot swim,' the Iranian answered.

Sam-Sam thought that was funny.

'He is afraid to ride the barge because he cannot swim?' Sam-Sam said with a laugh.

The Iranian nodded.

'Hell, I cannot swim,' Sam-Sam said, smacking his chest with an open hand.

'Neither can I,' Batal said, and he started laughing too.

A racket from the rear of the barge broke up their merriment. The helmsman came running forward.

'What was all that about?' Sam-Sam demanded.

The helmsman pointed toward the rear of the barge.

'Generator blow up,' he stammered.

'Well, change it. Throw that one overboard and hook up another one.'

The helmsman shook his head.

'Do not have,' he said.

'We do not have a spare generator?'

The helmsman shook his head. He stared down at the deck.

'Only one generator?' Sam-Sam stormed. 'We got every fucking other thing on this damn barge. We got TVs, stereos, we got Thai silk and cotton from India. We got cigarettes from America, France, England, Turkey, Egypt. So why do we only have one generator? So? Anybody got an answer to that?'

He raged around the deck kicking at things and cursing to himself, his snake eyes darting from one person to another.

261

Suddenly he drew his pistol. The men and women on deck moved back as a group. Sam-Sam stalked the deck like an insane man, twirling on the balls of his feet, glaring from one face to the next.

'Who takes responsibility?' he screamed.

His clan stared at him, afraid to speak.

'Who wants to eat a bullet?' he yelled. His voice carried into the jungle and echoed back. 'Anybody?'

He waited for a few moments more, enjoying the fear etched on the faces of his band. Then suddenly he wheeled and emptied the gun into the forest. Birds scattered, shrieking their complaints.

Sam-Sam turned back to his crew and laughed. His crew relaxed. There was a wave of nervous laughter.

'So – we go back,' Sam-Sam said with a shrug. 'What is the big rush to go anywhere?'

LEATHERNECK JOHN'S

Sing guided the snakeboat into the dock beside Leatherneck John's and they tied it down.

'Everybody stay loose unless there's trouble, okay?' Hatcher said.

Sing and Joey, the other gunman, nodded. Sing followed them down the makeshift dock to the bar. A large slab of ebony over the door had 'Leatherneck John's Last Chance Saloon' carved into it, and a line below it, 'Founded 1977.'

Hatcher was surprised when they entered the place. He had expected the bar to be a tawdry, ramshackle oasis in the midst of the Ts'e K'am Men Ti's contraband market. But the big room was clean and neat. On one side there were twenty or so tables and a pool table that had seen better days. A black man with thick hair tied in a tight ponytail was sleeping on his side on the pool table. He was wearing olive drab combat pants and a Hawaiian shirt, and was using his bush jacket as a pillow. On the other side was the bar, a long, fancy oak bar with a slate top.

'The last time I saw a bar that fancy was in Paris,' Hatcher said.

'Came from a joint in Mong Kok,' Cohen said. 'The way the story goes, Leatherneck John won the whole place in a crap game

262

and shipped it up by barge. But – up here you can hear anything.'

The place was deserted except for three men, including the one sleeping on the pool table.

One was a big man sitting on a barstool sipping a glass of beer. He had less hair than the billiard balls, and was dressed in khaki, his ample stomach folded over a military web belt. This would be the Dutchman, Hatcher thought. His bald head was sunburned and peeling. Years of hard living on the river had ravaged his face, leaving behind a puffy, ruddy orb laced with broken blood vessels. His nose was swollen and warty, and his eyes were buried under thick lids, giving him a sleepy look.

And then there was Leatherneck John himself. He was an enormous man, towering at least six foot three, and easily weighing 220 pounds, his red hair trimmed close to the scalp, a thick, neatly trimmed beard concealing the bottom half of his face, the sleeves of his camouflage shirt rolled up almost to the shoulders, revealing biceps the size of a truck tire. Leatherneck John looked like an old topkick. Burly was a perfect word to describe his size and bulk. Not fat, but big and solid. Formidable. His hair was shaggy and turning white. His eyes glittered with gaiety, as though he had just heard a joke and had not started laughing yet. A retired topkick, thought Hatcher, has to be. He looked past the big man and saw the six stripes, pinned to the wall with a Marine K-Bar knife.

'No hardware permitted inside the room, cowboys,' Leatherneck John said in a voice that was friendly but left no room for argument. Hatcher and Cohen gave Sing their weapons. The Chinese bodyguard stuck the short-barreled Aug and Cohen's .357 in his belt and stepped just outside the door, where he leaned against the wall. The other Chinese gunman in the snakeboat had moved to the back, near the tiller, where he sat with his Uzi tucked against one leg.

Hatcher strolled over to the bar. The wall behind the bar was a collage of Marine paraphernalia. Medals hung haphazardly: a Purple Heart, a Navy Cross – Hatcher lost interest after those two – along with an M-60, two M-16s, an 870 riot shotgun and a .45 Army-issue automatic, and photographs, belts, a canteen. The counter below was a shambles of ammo belts, boxes of ammo and several loaded clips.

Hatcher made a fist, his thumb above the knuckles lying flat and pointing straight out. This was a *dap*, among 'in-country' vets a sign that they had been in Vietnam. The ritual could be

263

carried further with a series of slaps and knuckle knocks to indicate the unit they served with. John stared down at the first, looked back up at Hatcher and a sort of smile crossed his lips. He made a similar fist, slid open an old-fashioned ice chest and took out two beers. He stared at Hatcher with his twinkling eyes as he popped the tops. He smacked one down on the bar in front of Hatcher.

'I never forget a face,' he said.

'A noble attribute,' Hatcher whispered.

'I saw you once in Nang. This was, uh, let's see – maybe '73, around that time.'

Hatcher smiled but did not say anything.

'You're Hatcher,' Leatherneck John went on. 'I recognized you when you walked in the door. I was with a guy in the Seals, knew who you were.'

'If you say so,' Hatcher whispered.

'A lot of talk about you up here,' John said with a slow nod, his mouth curling into a grin.

'Is that a fact?' Hatcher replied.

John nodded. 'I hear all sorts of things,' he went on. 'I don't know whether you're a good guy or a bad guy. The jury's still out on that.'

The man on the pool table stirred, turned slightly and peered sleepily over his shoulder at Hatcher and Leatherneck John.

'Don't believe everything you hear,' Hatcher said. He held the wet can up in a short salute and took a deep swallow of the cold beer. He decided to take a chance on Leatherneck John.

'I'm looking for a guy,' Hatcher said. 'Navy pilot named Cody, went down in the Delta in '72.'

'Never heard of him,' John said, making work to end the conversation.

'He may have been in a Cong prison camp up around Muang.'

'Never heard of him,' John repeated. He leaned over the bar toward Hatcher. 'See, what you got here is a very volatile situation. I mean, there's no reason whatsoever for any of these creeps up here to even say hello to each other, let alone get along, okay? But in here, this is like the Free State of Danzig, y'know. You don't ask questions. You don't *answer* questions. You get along.' He made a circle in the air, waving it around the room. 'In here, it's my rules. Nobody argues with me. You get outa line, you deal with me. And that's just the way it is.'

'Thanks,' Hatcher said.

The black man on the pool table had turned and was facing the group now, still feigning sleep, although he was watching the action through half-closed eyes.

'Howdy, Miss Chien,' John called from the bar as Hatcher returned to the table, 'welcome back to the Last Chance. What'll it be? Dinner, booze or barter?'

'Got any brandy?' Cohen asked.

'The best. Armagnac '78.'

'Dey are my guests,' the man at the bar said in a heavy Dutch accent as he walked toward them. 'Put it on my bill.'

The man took Daphne's hand in a large, hairy paw and pumped it while appraising Cohen and Hatcher.

'Goot to see yuh,' he said.

'And you, Dutchman,' she answered. 'This is the Tsu Fi.' She nodded towards Hatcher. 'And this is our friend, Tom.'

'Tom, huh,' he said skeptically. 'I hear you come to fish.'

Hatcher grinned a quick, passing grin as he stared the Dutchman down. 'Just looking for an old friend,' he growled.

'I see you met John,' the Dutchman said, making conversation.

'We exchanged amenities.'

'*Ja*, sure. Vell, let's sit and talk, den, I got to move on.'

He motioned to a table and they sat down. Hatcher stared hard at him, sizing up the heavyset trader. His swollen eyes were bloodshot and his mouth curled in what seemed like a perpetual sneer.

The Dutchman leaned over the table and said in a whisper to Hatcher. 'Look, I know who you are, okay? No problem. I ain't interested in your beef vit Sam-Sam.'

'What do you know about my beef with Sam-Sam?' Hatcher croaked casually.

'Vell, you know how talk goes.'

'No,' Hatcher said, still staring at the trader, 'how does it go?'

The Dutchman looked at Daphne with a question: Why was the Yankee being difficult? She looked away. It was Hatcher's game and she decided to stay out of it.

'I ain't looking for trouble,' the Dutchman said. 'I come because Miss Daphne ask me to, okay? I know all about you, *Ying bing*. I just vant to keep it clean, see? Don't do me no goot, they know I'm talkin' to you.'

Ying bing. Shadow warrior. Nobody had ever called him that to his face before. Hatcher let is pass.

'Just curious,' Hatcher said. 'I hear there's a misunderstanding between us.'

265

The Dutchman raised his eyebrows and laughed.

'Misunderstanding? *Ja*, dat's goot. Some misunderstanding. He says you owe him fifty thousand dollars. And proper interest.'

'That's ridiculous,' Hatcher whispered, shaking his head and chuckling, 'A roll of the dice to Sam-Sam.'

'I don't tink it's da money, although it is a consideration, I'm sure,' the Dutchman said. 'He says you disgraced him.'

'What the hell,' said Hatcher, 'hijackers got the guns. Cost me a penny or two, too.'

'Dat's not da vay he says it happened,' said the Dutchman, taking a sip of beer and wiping his lips with the back of his hand.

'You can hear anything you want to hear,' Hatcher whispered, dismissing the comment with a wave of his hand.

The Dutchman looked furtively around the empty bar and said, 'Sam-Sam says you vere Company.'

Hatcher chuckled and leaned back, feigning shock. He shook his head. 'Come on.'

'He says you set him up. Dat you used his money, bought da guns, and sold dem to the Chem guerrillas and da Chems used dem against the people he vas going to sell dem to.'

'I'm not that devious,' Hatcher said casually, at which Daphne, Cohen and the Dutchman all stared at the floor rather than disagree. The Dutchman fit a cigarette into an ivory holder and lit it with a gold lighter. He leaned back, blowing irregular smoke rings toward the ceiling, watching them dissipate.

Leatherneck John brought the drinks to the table.

'Anything else you need, just yell,' he said and drifted back to the bar.

'What else does Sam-Sam say?' Hatcher asked.

'He says you sleep vit da Devil,' the Dutchman said. 'He says you haff an instinct for da throat and are not betrayed by conscience. He says you lie vittout moving a muscle and kill vittout a taste for blood. And he says you could negotiate vit God and get da best share.'

'He knows you well,' Cohen said with a grin.

'Sounds like he's describing himself,' Hatcher said.

The Dutchman laughed too, and raised his beer in a half-hearted salute.

'So – vat is it?' the Dutchman asked.

'I'm trying to find out if the Vietcong had a floating prison camp called Huie-kui in northeast Laos. They may have called it the spirit camp. This would be late 1971, early '72.'

266

The Dutchman looked at Daphne and then back at Hatcher.

Daphne took out an envelope and laid it on the corner of the table. She kept her hand over it. 'Five hundred dollars Hong Kong, as agreed – *if* the information is reliable,' she said.

It was the first time Hatcher had heard about paying the Dutchman, but he did not intercede. He would settle up with Daphne later. This was not the time to discuss it.

'Dey had several camps over dere,' said the Dutchman.

'This would be on the other side of the mountains, near Muang.'

'Muang, *ja*,' the Dutchman said with a nod. 'Across country, utter side of da Annimitique.'

'That would be it,' said Hatcher, his eyes glowing. His pulse picked up a few beats. 'Did they move it around?'

'*Ja*, to keep from choppers.' He pointed toward the ceiling.

'You did business with them?'

The Dutchman shrugged. 'So?'

Hatcher took out the photograph of Cody and Pai that Schwartz had given him. 'Look,' he said, 'I don't give a damn about the camp itself or what the Cong did. The war's over. I'm looking for a friend of mine.'

'All you Yankees tink your friends are still alive over dere,' said the Dutchman.

Hatcher handed him the photograph.

'This guy here,' he said, pointing to Cody.

The Dutchman held the photograph a few inches from his face and squinted at it. He shifted positions a little, turning the photo to catch the light and looked hard at the picture for almost a minute. As he was perusing it Daphne looked at the rear door and stiffened. Hatcher casually followed her gaze.

Billy Death stood in the doorway, his AK-47 cradled in his arm. Leatherneck John stared hard at him.

'Hey, Billy,' he said, 'park the piece. You know the rules.'

The black man stared across the room at Hatcher's table.

Leatherneck John took down the shotgun and, holding it by the slide, jerked his wrist. The carriage slid up and back, charging the weapon.

'You deaf?' Leatherneck said, laying the shotgun on the bar aimed in Billy Death's general direction. 'My house, my rules. The gun stays outside.'

Billy Death sucked a tooth, then stepped back out the door and leaned his machine gun against the wall.

'The peashooter, too,' Leatherneck yelled.

Death took the pistol out of his belt and laid it beside the AK-47. He strode to the bar, walking on the balls of his feet, his hands hanging loose in front of him, like a boxer.

'Japanese beer, cold,' he said, in the singsong accent of Haiti.

Leatherneck John popped the top off a bottle of beer and put it in front of the Haitian.

'Who are the Yankees with the Dutchman?' Billy Death asked.

Leatherneck John stared at him for several seconds, then he said, 'Harry Truman, Winston Churchill and Eleanor Roosevelt.'

The Haitian's brows knit together.

'You know better'n to ask questions in here, Billy,' Leatherneck John said. 'Repeat after me: "It's none of my business."'

At the table the Dutchman paid no attention to Billy Death. He looked up at Hatcher.

'Maybe,' he said finally, in answer to Hatcher's question.

'Maybe?'

'*Ja*. Skinnier. Very tired-looking. Und a beard, so I couldn't bet on dis.'

'Was he sick?'

The Dutchman pursed his lips and then shook his head. '*Nee*, not sick. Maybe . . . drugs.'

'He was on drugs?'

'I vould say dat.'

'What drugs?'

'Well, I vould say a little smoke. Maybe powder.'

'Skag and grass?'

'Is possible.'

'You sold shit to the Vietcong there?'

'Drugs vasn't vat I was selling, but . . .' He let the sentence dangle. At the bar, Billy Death lowered his sunglasses over his nose and stared over the top of them at the table. Hatcher glared back. Their eyes locked for a moment or two, then Death turned away.

'When was this?' Hatcher asked.

'Vas long time ago. I would say, let me see, I vas moving Thai silk to Saigon vit Henrickson, the Finn, and he vas kilt vintertime, '75. Vas dat summer. *Ja*. Last time vas about June, 1974.'

''74,' Hatcher said half aloud. 'And he was a prisoner?'

'*Ja*.'

'You said the last time. How many times did you see him?'

'If it is him, *Bing yahn*, maybe three, four times. But I vill not swear to it. I'm sure it vas da girl but –'

'The girl?' Hatcher interrupted him.

268

'*Ja*. Da girl I'm sure of.'

'You saw this girl with this man?' Hatcher repeated, pointing at Cody and Pai in the photograph.

'I saw da girl. I tink it vas dis guy. Like I said –'

'You mean the Cong let her stay with him?'

'I just saw dem talking.'

'Maybe he was, uh – what we call a trustee. You understand "trustee"?'

'*Ja*, sure. Dey trust him. He does tinks for dem, dey let him outside the vire a little bit each day, watch da utter prisoners. She bought some tinks.'

'Christ,' Hatcher muttered under his breath. 'What did she buy?'

'Quinine pills. Smoke. Penicillin. China Vite, and also to buy some shoes and shirts. Clothing.'

'How did she pay?'

'Like da Arvies.'

'North Vietnamese dollars?'

The Dutchman nodded.

Hatcher looked at Cohen, who whistled low and shook his head.

'Let me get this straight. You think you saw this man in June 1974, about twelve clicks south of Muang on the Laotian side of the Annimitique mountains in a moving Vietcong camp with this girl and she got quinine, China White, clothing and penicillin and paid for it with Arvie money.'

'*Ja*, is correct.'

'How big was this camp?' Hatcher asked.

'Small,' said the Dutchman. 'Maybe twenty, twenty-five prisoners, half a dozen guards and da varden.'

'What was the warden called?'

The Dutchman thought for a moment and said, 'Taisung.'

'And this prisoner was outside the compound, right?'

'*Ja*. Dere vere six, seven outside.'

'Cleaning up?'

The Dutchman nodded.

'You recognized all these guys?'

'From da clothes. Dey vere vearing clothes bought from me.'

'What were the other prisoners wearing?'

'Vork clothes. Mostly gray. Dey kept the Yankees away from the Vietnams.'

'Vietnams? What do you mean, Vietnams?'

'Dese udder prisoners, dey vas all Vietnamese. Political prisoners, Yankee sympathizers, like dat.'

269

'You mean this was a prison mostly for Vietnamese political prisoners?' Hatcher said with surprise.

'*Ja*, till dey could move 'em north to Hanoi.'

'I'll be a son of a bitch,' Hatcher said.

'Vhy don't you ask John. Dere's a rumor he vas once in prison camp.'

'Where?'

The Dutchman shrugged. 'Ask him,' he answered. He raised a hand, and Leatherneck John popped open another beer and brought it to the table. Hatcher handed him the photograph.

'Know any of these people?' he asked.

John took the photograph and looked at it. 'Why, should I?' he asked.

'I don't know,' Hatcher said. 'He was a POW. I heard you were too. I thought maybe –'

'The slope ain't born could catch me and hold me,' John said without animosity.

'I'm just asking.'

'I'll tell you the same thing I told Billy, cowboy. Around here there ain't no yesterday. When I get outa bed in the morning, life starts over. I forgot more'n I remember.'

'He's a friend of mine,' Hatcher said. 'I'm trying to help him.'

'No shit. Supposin' he doesn't want help.'

'That's possible. If I find him and that's the way it is, I'm long gone.'

'Good for you.' John looked at the photo again and laid it back on the table. 'Nice-lookin' woman,' he said and started back to the bar.

'Semper Fi, pal,' Hatcher growled.

John stopped and turned back toward him.

'How's that?'

'Semper Fi. You were a marine, you know what that's all about. This guy and I were mates. Maybe he's in trouble. Maybe he needs something. I want to make the offer, that's all.'

'So find him and make it.'

'Yeah, right.'

Leatherneck John smiled pleasantly and returned to the bar, but Hatcher decided to try once more. He followed Leatherneck John back to the bar. Billy Death stared down the length of oak at him and said, 'You here to buy or sell?'

'Neither one. I'm a tourist,' Hatcher whispered. Billy Death sneered at him, threw a handful of coins on the bar and left. Hatcher turned back to Leatherneck John and leaned toward him.

270

'How about the girl?' Hatcher asked. 'Have you ever seen the girl?'

'I told you, I got amnesia, cowboy,' Leatherneck John said. 'Hell, I don't even remember my last name.'

Hatcher laid an American hundred-dollar bill on the bar.

'That's nice,' Leatherneck John said. 'I ain't seen a yard in a long time. Mostly Hong Kong dollars hereabouts.' He stared at the bill for a moment, picked it up and rang up the sale on the cash register. Turning back to Hatcher, he said, 'I sell booze, food and silence. You want a little jolt, a little toot, a smoke, I can maybe help you out.' He counted out ninety-five dollars, H.K., and laid it on the bar. 'And that's *all* I got to sell, cowboy.'

'*Mm goi*,' Hatcher said.

'You're welcome,' John said, still smiling.

Hatcher gathered up the change and returned to the table.

'I don't like the way this is shaping up,' Cohen said quietly. 'You got your information. If there's nothing else —'

'I guess you're right,' said Hatcher. He held the chair for Daphne and they all stood up. The Dutchman laid his fat hand on the envelope and looked at Daphne with raised eyebrows.

'It's yours,' Hatcher said.

'*Bedankt*,' the Dutchman said, stuffing the envelope in his inside jacket pocket. 'Haff a safe trip back.' He walked across the room to the man on the pool table and shook him.

'Let's go, Jawnee,' he said.

'Yeah, yeah,' the black man with the ponytail answered sleepily. 'Pick me up around back.'

'You come now,' the Dutchman said gruffly and left.

'That Tonton's got me worried,' said Cohen. 'He was a little too interested in us.'

'Curiosity,' said Hatcher. 'Hell, it isn't —'

He stopped and looked out the window at the Dutchman, who had reached the Chris Craft and was getting ready to leave.

'I just thought of something else,' he said. 'You all go to the snakeboat. I've got to ask the Dutchman one more question.'

'Hurry it up. The sooner we're out of here, the better,' Cohen answered nervously.

The man with the ponytail sat up on the edge of the pool table, his legs dangling above the floor and watched Hatcher leave. He jumped to the floor and walked casually toward the door.

Outside, heat seeped down over the jungle like warm syrup. The Dutchman was checking his fuel supply. He looked up as Hatcher approached the boat.

'*Ja*?' he asked.

'One more thing. This Taisung, the warden of the camp, you know what happened to him?'

'He ran for it,' the Dutchman answered without stopping his work.

'Ran for it?'

'*Ja*. I don't tink he vas too vell thought of in Hanoi.'

'Why?'

'Drugs, booze. Dey vere all corrupt, y'know.'

'How about the prisoners?'

'I don't know 'bout dem,' the Dutchman said with a shrug.

'Where did Taisung run to?'

The Dutchman capped the fuel tanks and purged the fuel lines as he thought about the question. He stepped over the gunwale and stood close to Hatcher. As they spoke Hatcher became aware of movement downriver, at the bend in the elbow. It was a barge, moving slowly around the sharp curve in the narrow river.

'Bangkok,' he said.

'Bangkok?'

'*Ja*, Bangkok.'

'One more thing,' said Hatcher. 'Does Thai Horse mean anything to you?'

Cohen was surprised at the mention of his statue. The Dutchman too looked surprised.

'Vere did you hear about Thai Horse?'

Hatcher's heart jumped. Cohen seemed even more bemused.

'Around. Does it mean anything?' Hatcher urged.

'Rumors.'

'What are they?' Hatcher asked eagerly.

'Only dat dere is a heroin-smuggling outfit in Bangkok called Thai Horse. Very dangerous bunch, not to mess vit dem. Dat's all. Booze talk, I tink.'

Cohen tried to hide his obvious surprise. Hatcher hesitated. The more he dug, the worse it looked for Cody. How much did the Dutchman know?

'You don't believe it, then?' he asked, trying to keep his voice from showing any emotion.

'I believe only vat I can see and touch,' said the Dutchman.

'But it's possible?' Hatcher pressed on.

'Vell, as you know, in Bangkok everyting is possible,' the Dutchman said with a wave of his hand.

The Dutchman was looking downriver, toward the barge. Hatcher ignored it. He needed one more answer. But before he could ask it, the Dutchman's face drained of color. His eyes bulged.

'*Mijn God!*' the Dutchman said.

Hatcher turned and looked. The barge was halfway around the bend. Standing on the front of the boat was Sam-Sam Sam. Hatcher felt a momentary jolt, a combination of fear and surprise – he had expected them to come the other way. Now Sam-Sam was between them and the Cigarette boat. They were cut off, and there were at least twenty men and women on the barge.

In the bar, Leatherneck John said, 'Jesus, the shit just hit the fan.'

'It's Sam-Sam,' the Dutchman whispered to Hatcher with awe. 'Get out uf here, man! I don't even know you.'

Hatcher grabbed his jacket in a tight fist. His tormented voice left little room for argument.

'Have you seen him there? The warden?'

'He has been seen,' the Dutchman quickly stammered. 'He does some business over dere now. He is passing himself off as a Thai.'

'A Thai? You know what he calls himself?'

'Vol Pot,' cried the Dutchman, squirming out of Hatcher's grasp. 'He calls himself Vol Pot.'

THE BEST DEFENSE

With the information that Wol Pot had once been the warden of the Huie-kui camp, Hatcher's heart was racing as he rushed down the pier to the snakeboat. Cohen was watching Sam-Sam's barge through binoculars.

'I don't think he knows we're here yet,' Cohen said. He lowered the glasses and looked at Hatcher. 'Maybe we ought to run for it, back to the Cigarette boat.'

Hatcher took the glasses and studied the barge. 'He'll cut us off once he recognizes me. Why don't you people take the snakeboat and I'll go overland, back to the cutoff and meet you there.'

'No!' said Daphne. 'We came together, we'll leave together.'

'This is no time for heroics,' Hatcher whispered, still watching the barge.

'She's right,' Cohen said.

'Look, I'm the only one he wants. The *ch'u-tiao* is between us, not you people.'

As they watched through their binoculars, Sam-Sam Sam strolled the deck and stretched. One of the women came out of the cabin. She was still getting dressed and was as ugly as Sam-Sam.

'See him?' Cohen asked, without lowering his binoculars.

'Uh-huh.'

'Had himself a little matinée,' said Cohen. 'Phew, look at that woman, she'd gag a maggot.'

'This isn't the Miss Universe contest,' said Hatcher.

'More like Miss Mud Fence of 1912,' Cohen said, swinging his glasses around and checking out the rest of the barge.

As Hatcher watched, another man joined Sam-Sam, a swarthy olive-hued man wearing a white cotton shirt open to the waist. Two gunbelts crisscrossed his chest from shoulder to waist and an M-16 rested casually across his shoulders. There was a pistol in his belt and a machete. The three men stood on the foredeck of the barge, looking at the water and chatting.

'You're right, they look like they expect an invasion,' Cohen said.

'That must be the Iranian,' said Hatcher.

'Yeah. Batal.' Cohen lowered his glasses. 'So, now what do we do?'

'I'll hit the woods, go overland back to the Cigarette boat,' Hatcher said.

'I don't think so,' said Daphne, pointing behind them. Far out at the end of the pier, Billy Death was talking into a walkie-talkie.

'Think he made me?' Hatcher asked. He focused his glasses on the Haitian, who was pointing toward them as he spoke. 'Yeah, he made me,' he added.

He swung his glasses back to the barge and was staring straight into Sam-Sam Sam's binoculars. The pirate lowered his glasses. His mouth curved into a grin, then a leer, then formed the word 'Hatcher.' He raised his AK-47 and charged it.

'Love at first sight,' said Cohen.

'Behind us,' Daphne said.

Billy Death and another brigand were coming down the pier toward them.

'Sing, you and Joey take care of those two,' Hatcher snapped.

The Chinese gangster nodded curtly and he and Joey took

274

their Uzis, climbed up on the pier and walked slowly toward Billy Death.

Watching from the doorway of the saloon, Leatherneck John said, 'Christ, it's beginning to look like *High Noon*.'

At the snakeboat, Hatcher made an instant decision. They were outnumbered twenty or thirty to one. Hatcher grabbed Cohen by the elbow and shoved him into the snakeboat. 'Daphne,' he yelled as loud as he could, 'get inside the saloon, out of range.'

He turned the key and cranked the snakeboat's engine to life.

'Take the tiller,' Hatcher ordered Cohen, and grabbing his briefcase, he ran to the front of the long, narrow boat and lay down flat on the bottom. He opened the case and took out a small square of gray C-4 plastique. He molded it quickly into a thick rope about two feet long and two inches thick.

'Where the hell are we going?' Cohen demanded.

'Head for the barge,' Hatcher yelled back.

'What?'

'Trust me!'

'You're nuts, Hatcher, you're just plain fucking nuts,' Cohen yelled as he steered the skinny boat toward Sam-Sam's barge.

Daphne backed slowly toward Leatherneck John's saloon, watching the snakeboat and the face-off between Cohen's men, Sing and Joey, and Billy Death and his man. Leatherneck John reached out and, grabbing Daphne by the arm, pulled her inside the door of the saloon.

'You're gonna get yourself killed out there,' he snapped.

'Can't you help, please?' Daphne pleaded.

'Not my fight, ma'am,' Leatherneck John said emphatically. 'I gotta live up here.'

'Then give *me* a gun!' she hissed at him, her eyes afire with anger and fear.

The black man with the ponytail stared out the door.

The snakeboat was zigzagging its way toward the barge. Half a dozen gunmen were firing at it. Bullets tore through the thatched hooch at the rear of the boat and erupted in the water around it. Cohen was guiding the boat's dodging course toward the barge while Hatcher lay in the front firing intermittent bursts at it while he wrapped the coil of C-4 around the prow of the boat.

'Keep dodging them,' he growled.

Onshore, Sing and Joey reached the pier. They were half the length of a football field from Billy Death and his man. The two Chinese stopped.

275

'No farther,' Sing ordered. As he held up his hand another of Sam-Sam's river rats jumped from behind the corner of the saloon and jammed a knife into Joey's back, just above the waist. Joey turned with a roar of anger and grabbed his attacker, but the wound was lethal. His arms went limp and he fell off the pier into the river.

Sing grabbed the man around the neck and snapped it with one hard twist. The man dropped. Sing turned toward Billy Death and his sidekick and fired a burst down the pier. It hit the sidekick shin-high, and he toppled to the dock with a scream. As Sing fired a second burst into the fallen thief, Billy Death got off a double burst. The bullets ripped into Sing. He fell to his knees but tried to get up, still firing. Death shot him again. Sing fell facedown, dead.

'Pretty tough Chink,' Leatherneck John said.

'I make that about twenty to two now, not exactly what I'd call fair odds,' said the man with the ponytail.

'Odds don't mean shit up here,' Leatherneck John said.

The man with the ponytail walked resolutely to the bar and took down the M-60 hanging behind it. Curled below it on a shelf was a fully loaded ammo belt. He threw the ammo belt over one shoulder and headed for the door.

'Hold it!' Leatherneck John demanded.

'Don't worry,' said the ponytailed man, 'I'm going outside.'

'Not with my piece.'

The man swung the muzzle of the M-60 toward Leatherneck John.

'I'm borrowing it,' he said flatly as he walked out the door.

Leatherneck John said nothing. He stood watching with his mouth hanging open and his hands on his hips.

Billy Death ran past the door of the saloon and started down the riverbank, running with his back to the ponytailed man.

On the boat, Hatcher had the C-4 plastique wrapped around the prow. He armed a small black contact fuse and, reaching over the front of the boat with his head down, twisted it into the soft plastic explosive. Bullets stitched a line down the rail of the snakeboat, inches from Hatcher's ear. The barge was coming up fast.

Hatcher turned and crawled back to the thatched cabin.

'Let's go!' he said to Cohen.

'Go where?'

'We got to get out of here. This thing's going to blow sky-high any second!'

'Why didn't you tell me you were going to do something like this?' Cohen yelled. Bullets tore into the rail near him. Cohen went berserk. He stood up, let go of the tiller, and holding his gun hand straight out in front of him, started firing his .357 at Sam-Sam.

'We've got to go now!' Hatcher yelled and dived into Cohen's stomach, driving the little man backward into the side of the thatched shed. The side collapsed. Hatcher and Cohen plunged through the flimsy cabin, out of the speeding boat and into the river. The snakeboat, driverless, etched its crazy course toward the barge.

Hatcher and Cohen hit the water with such force that it momentarily knocked Hatcher's wind out of him. He felt Cohen's body wrench and then slip away from him. Hatcher tumbled once in the water, spread-eagled and stopped his motion. He lunged to the surface, took a deep breath and dived hard, his arms and hands sweeping the water around him.

Nothing.

He surfaced, took another deep gulp of air and dived again, taking powerful strokes and searching the dark water with his hands. Still nothing. Then as he surfaced he saw Cohen's head bob up a few yards away. Cohen was half conscious, disoriented.

Hatcher took three hard strokes, reached out and grabbed Cohen's arm by the sleeve. 'I gotcha, pal, relax.'

Behind them, the snakeboat drove straight toward the barge. Batal looked at it and saw the gray cord of plastique around the bow. He screamed and dived overboard as the boat charged into the barge. Sam-Sam leaped to one side as the snakeboat hit and rose up out of the water, its prow several inches above the side of the barge. The hull of the snakeboat shattered and the prow tore into a stack of TV sets, smashing through tubes, scattering them like blocks. Tubes burst like firecrackers. The contact fuse smacked against the casing of one of the TV sets and the plastique exploded.

Sam-Sam was ten feet away when the barge erupted. He felt the sudden burst of hot air just before the concussion tossed him into the air like a broken twig. The force of the explosion ruptured his vitals and ripped his body apart. A moment later the explosion set off the gas tanks; the rear of the barge burst like a balloon. Fire and debris showered the air. Men and women on the barge were scattered like confetti.

The explosion lifted Batal out of the water, and blood spurted from ears, nose and mouth. He plopped back down into the river

277

unconscious and sank slowly to the bottom as bits and pieces of the barge splashed into the water and sank with him.

'Beautiful,' said the ponytailed man with a smile.

'Holy shit!' was all Leatherneck John could muster.

A hundred yards away, the concussion of the explosion knocked both Hatcher and Cohen underwater. Hatcher lost his grip on the stunned Tsu Fi again. Cohen came up gasping, heard the chatter of submachine gun fire. Geysers of water sprouted from the river around him, shocked him into full consciousness. He splashed around like a hooked marlin, gulping air. The river erupted a few inches from Hatcher's face as another burst ripped into the water. This time Hatcher saw where it was coming from. Billy Death stood near the river's edge, fifty yards away, firing his AK-47.

Hatcher turned and zigzagged away from shore, yelling to Cohen to follow him. Another burst showered past him, *bip, bip, bip, bip, bip*.

A half-mile downstream, behind the barge, the Cigarette boat hugged the shore. The men in the boat had seen Sam-Sam return and had followed the barge upstream, hugging the shore to keep out of sight. Now all hell was breaking loose in front of them.

'We go see,' the leader of the three Chinese backup men said, pointing toward the barge.

The barge was tilting rapidly and the Ts'e K'ams aboard were too busy scrambling for safety and hauling their wounded to the shore to worry about Hatcher. Another explosion rent the barge, a gorge of flame roared out of the stacks of ammo boxes, followed by a wrenching explosion as the boxes exploded.

The explosion distracted Billy Death, who lowered his gun and walked uncertainly toward the barge.

Then the *pop-pop* of 9 mm. shells began as the heat cooked them off and they began ricocheting off the barge, ripping into the trees, and plopping harmlessly in the water. The barge was now fully ablaze.

Billy Death hesitated, then turned his attention back to Hatcher and Cohen. He raised the AK-47 to his shoulder and aimed at the two figures struggling in the river.

Behind him, seventy-five yards away, the ponytailed man stepped outside, and standing under the porch, he swung the heavy M-60 up, smacked the cartridge belt into the receiver and charged the first round into the chamber. He threw the rest of the belt over his shoulder and walked toward Billy Death.

'Hey!' he yelled. 'You, the one they call Billy Death.'

The Haitian turned toward him. The man stood with legs spread out at the edge of the river with the M-60 aimed squarely at the ex-Tonton assassin.

'Drop the gun,' the man ordered.

Billy Death stared uncertainly at him, then back out at Hatcher. He hesitated a moment too long before he swung the AK-47 around at the man with the M-60.

The heavy machine gun roared, kicked, rippled the muscles of the ponytailed man. Half a dozen shots ripped into Billy Death's chest. His own gun went off harmlessly into the air as he was spun around by the burst. His knees buckled. He floundered, staggered to the edge of the river and fell to his knees in the water. His arms went limp, the AK-47 fell into the water and his chin dropped to his chest. Billy Death fell sideways and rolled over on his face in the water.

The man walked back into Leatherneck John's, unloading the heavy machine gun as he strolled across to the bar. He put the M-60 back on the rack and dropped the ammo belt on the shelf below it.

'You better be long gone when they get this mess under control,' Leatherneck John said.

'I was thinking the same thing,' the ponytailed man said.

'Why the hell'd you do such a crazy thing?' the barman said.

'I told you, I didn't like the odds.'

'That's it, you didn't like the odds?'

'You know what a HALO drop is?' the ponytailed man asked.

'Sure, high altitude, low open parachute jump,' Leatherneck answered.

'I did a HALO drop in the Delta back in '74. It was dark and the wind changed and I missed my zone by half a mile and came down in a bamboo thicket behind Gook lines. A bamboo shoot went right through my foot and came out my shin, right here.'

He pulled up his pants leg and pointed to an ugly scar near the middle of his shinbone.

'I was pinned to the ground by this ten-foot shoot of bamboo and Charlie was all over the place. Then all of a sudden this guy appears from out of nowhere, breaks the shoot off and piggybacks me a half a mile back to the drop zone. Then he's gone again, just like that. Never said a do-mommy word to me the whole time. Later on, somebody told me it was this guy Hatcher everybody calls Occhi di Sassi – Stone Eyes. Now, do you understand?' He turned to Daphne. 'Tell Hatcher Jonee Ansa says thanks – we're even now. You might also tell him to check out a section called Tombstone in Patpong. Place called the Longhorn. A lot of the ex-GIs in Bangkok hang out there.'

The ponytailed man turned and vanished out the rear exit of the saloon.

On the river, the Cigarette boat suddenly burst through the smoke pouring off the barge. The pilot saw Hatcher and Cohen in the river. He steered the sleek speedboat toward them and slowed as he pulled beside them. One of the gunmen reached over the side and grabbed Hatcher's wrist. They locked hand to wrist and he pulled him up. Another of the henchmen reached over the side and pulled the still-groggy Cohen aboard.

The slender boat cut an arc in the river, swung into the dock and picked up Daphne and then roared back through the broiling smoke of the ruined barge, which tilted crazily as if struggling to stay afloat and then slid hissing and groaning to the bottom of the river.

'Well, I'll say one thing for you, Christian,' Daphne said, 'you sure know how to burn your bridges.'

jo sahn

As they headed back downriver, darkness settled over the boat like a shroud. Cohen and Hatcher had stripped off their wet clothes. Now they were huddled in the cabin of the big boat to keep warm. Daphne had remained on deck.

'I can't believe you do this kind of thing for a living,' Cohen said.

'Did,' Hatcher corrected.

'As far as I'm concerned, you're still doing it,' Cohen said. 'In the last twenty-four hours I've had all the excitement I'll ever need.'

'If it's any consolation, so have I,' Hatcher said with a smile. 'Got any brandy on this tub?'

'All I've got is some Amaretto.'

'Not on an empty stomach.'

Cohen huddled deeper into the blanket. He stared at Hatcher for a moment and then said, 'Give it up, Hatch.'

'Give what up?'

'Don't be thick.'

280

'I told you, before, China, I can't do that.'

'Yeah, I know. Honor, integrity, old school tie. Isn't it a little late for that?'

'It's not a little late for Murph if he's in trouble.'

'You heard what the Dutchman said. He was a junkie!'

'He said he thought he was doing a little pot, for God's sake.'

'And collaborating.'

'All guesswork.'

'God, you really are giving him the benefit of the doubt. You know enough already to –'

'Look, here's all I *know*,' Hatcher said, cutting him off. 'I *know* that Cody could have gotten out that plane fifteen years ago. I have reason to *believe* that he was in the Huie-kui camp and that Taisung was his warden and the girl was with him there. I *know* a man named Wol Pot claims to have seen Cody in Bangkok and now Taisung is in Bangkok calling himself Wol Pot. I also *know* that Windy Porter was tailing him and got killed for his trouble, probably by a Chiu Chao killer. And I have reason to *believe* that Wol Pot may have worked for Tollie Fong and got in trouble and that's why he came to us. You put that all together, China, and that's good enough reason for me to go to Bangkok.'

'You also *know* that Tollie Fong'll kill you on sight.'

'He made a promise, *yen dui yen*, to lay off both of us.'

'And you trust his word? His *ch'uang tzu-chi* ends only when one of you dies. A blood oath, Christian. If necessary he'll create an excuse to break the *yen dui yen*. C'mon, don't act naive.'

'China, when I set out on this job, I didn't believe for a minute that Murphy was alive. Then I had doubts. Now the equation is swinging the other way. Now I think he is alive. And if he is, I'll find him. And fuck Tollie Fong.'

'Be sure to kill him first.'

Hatcher reached over and ruffled Cohen's hair. 'I love you too, buddy,' he said. 'I always seem to be taking something away from my friends, never giving anything back.'

'It's always worked both ways.'

'That's a kind thing to say.'

'Kind my ass, don't get maudlin,' Cohen said. 'We lost you once. Then we found you. Now we're going to lose you again, this time for good. I know that, so does Daffy.' He waved his hand toward the deck. 'Why don't you go say good-bye to her.'

He lowered his head, staring at the floor, and shrugged the blanket up around his ears.

'Thanks, China.'

'Yep.'

Hatcher started out the door. Cohen did not look up. He said, 'I'd like to know you're safe and sound on that island of yours. How about a call when it's over, if you can still whisper.'

These were people who loved him enough to risk dying for him, and there was no proper way to say good-bye. Each clue took him closer to the past and then led him further away from it. But Hatcher had no choice. His mission was to find Murph Cody, and there were no more answers in Hong Kong, the answer had to be in Bangkok. And the closer Hatcher got to solution, the more he feared what it would be.

She was sitting in the bow, watching the wake boiling behind the boat in the moonlight. He sat down beside her and, holding the blanket, wrapped it around her shoulder and pulled her to him.

'Was it worth it, Hatcher?' she asked.

'I think so,' he said. 'It confirmed a lot of questions.'

'Such a price!'

'Yes, isn't that always the way it is.'

They sat quietly for a while and then she asked, 'Do you have a woman?'

Hatcher hesitated for a moment. Was Ginia *his* woman? She certainly would object to the term. But in his heart, Hatcher now realized he had made an unspoken commitment to her. He had never expressed it, but she *was* his woman. He felt for her, wanted to care for her, to make her happy. He wanted some semblance of permanence in his life. Ginia meant all these things and more.

'Yes,' he said finally.

'You had to think a long time.'

'I've never really thought about it before,' he said. 'I've assumed a lot.'

'What is her name?'

'Ginia.'

'Ginia,' she repeated, as if testing the name. 'And what is she like?'

'Very independent. Very smart.'

'Beautiful?'

'Yes. But not in the same way you are.'

'I do not understand that.'

Hatcher tried to think of a way to describe the difference between the exotically alluring Daphne and the naturally

282

beautiful Ginia. Finally he said, 'She does not take a man's breath away as you do.' Not exactly true, but a permissible white lie.

'You are diplomatic with time,' she said with a smile. 'Does she understand you as I did?'

'She doesn't know anything about my past.'

'Or your friends?'

'Or my friends.'

'And will you ever tell her?'

'I suppose someday, if it seems proper.'

'Do you love her, Hatcher?'

That stopped him. These were questions he had never asked himself; now Daphne was forcing him to deal with them.

'That would be something new for me, eh, Daffy?' he answered, avoiding a specific response. 'The kind of love you're talking about has been missing from my life for a very long time, if it was ever there at all.'

'It was there, Hatcher. You never let anyone see that side of the coin, but I got a peek a few times. And China says you are two people. The man we all see and the man nobody sees. Does Ginia see that other man?'

'I think that's the only one she does see.'

'Then she is very lucky.'

'I still seem to be doing the same old things.'

'There is a difference. There was a time when you seemed to . . .' She hesitated, trying to find the right word.

'Enjoy it?' He finished the sentence for her.

'Yes,' she agreed. 'Enjoy it.'

'Perhaps. But nothing is accomplished by looking back. What's done is done.'

He took her cheek in the palm of one hand and turned her to him.

'I love you, Daphne. You have never escaped my thoughts. But I never thought of us in any settled-down kind of way. That kind of sharing? Hell, neither one of us ever seemed to want that.'

She looked away. *Speak for yourself*, she thought, but she said nothing, and Hatcher realized that in trying to be honest he had hurt her. To him, the relationship with Daphne had been like a long one-night stand for both of them, a wartime romance with no future and no permanent commitment. Now it was too late. He had made another world for himself, a world so different from hers that there could be no place in it for her, no hope of a permanent relationship between them. Life on his island would bore her to death. Besides, he had once cut his ties with this dark and dangerous world, the world of Daphne, China Cohen, Harry Sloan and the Ts'e K'am Men Ti, a world that was her whole existence. Now he had to cut those same ties again.

'You are right, we were never interested in that kind of sharing,' she said, and saved him the pain of hurting her even more.

As they cruised silently through the mouth of the Macao Runs the lights of Hong Kong twinkled to their left. He stared at them as they grew closer and the skyscrapers took shape in the darkness.

'I will get off first,' she said. 'They know where to stop.'

'Daphne . . .'

She put her fingers to his lips.

'We have said and done it all, Hatcher,' she whispered. 'You will not be back this time. But I know in my heart that it is as painful for you as it is for us. *Choi qui see yong qup haipon.*'

The Chinese said it well: 'Killing the past scars the soul.'

BOOK
THREE

S*et honour in one eye and death i' the other, And I will look on both indifferently.*

Shakespeare, Julius Caesar
Act I, Scene 2

THE JUDAS FLOWER

In April the winds sweep down the mountainsides of northern Thailand, chasing away the last of the monsoon clouds and wafting across the fields of red, white and purple flowers. The flowers sway like rows of ballet dancers as the sun burns down on them and they burst into bloom and the mountainsides and fields become a tapestry of color.

But like some species of butterflies that live only for a single day, the flowers die quickly, each leaving behind a pale green seed pod that looks like an onion on a stick. In the months before April the plants toil day and night to produce alkaloids, which are stored in these seed pods. When the pod is cut, the milky alkaloid oozes out and quickly dries and darkens.

When the petals fall, the hill people in their flat straw hats appear on the steep slopes where the flowers grow and move through the rows, slicing the sides of the pods and gathering the thick sap with iron spoons before it hardens.

General Dao, the *phu yai ban* of the Hsong hill tribe had watched the previous spring as his villagers tapped the pods. As village headman it was his custom to sit like a god on his black horse on the crest of the hill with the strap of his M–14 draped around his shoulders like a sling, his arms resting on the butt and barrel of his weapon, observing the harvest while his two shotgun guards sat nearby. The guards took turns scanning the sky and valley with powerful binoculars, watching for signs of federal troops or helicopters, while below, on the sides of the hill known as Powder Mountain, the field workers tapped the pods.

As *phu yai ban*, Dao was elected by his fellow villagers. Like his father, he settled disputes of every kind, listened to the problems of his villagers, and negotiated for the Hsong with the outside world. The Hsong were part of a tribal sect called the Phui Thong Luang, the Spirits of the Yellow Leaves, a small, elusive group whose isolation had enabled them to maintain customs and traditions that were centuries old.

Dao was a compact man, hardened, as were all the Hsong people, by the harsh life of the mountains. He was thirty-seven and looked fifty-five, although he was still handsome, with a face that was a bronze square, a wide mouth and a broad, flat nose.

He preferred dark green military clothing to traditional garb, as did his men. His black hair was wrapped with a red bandanna. Occasionally he would take the binoculars and watch the women workers, who wore brightly colored blouses with striped yokes, colorful pants fitted tightly around the hips and draped at mid-calf – called *pasin* and resembling old-fashioned pedal pushers – and large, flamboyant turbans of gaily colored material woven with silver beads.

The sap they were gathering was opium gum.

The natural alkaloid was morphine.

And the pretty little purple, white and red flowers were *Papaver somniferum*, which proliferate like weeds in Southeast Asia. No innocent garden flowers, the somniferum poppy is a metaphor for the best and worst in man, a symbol of good and evil. It is both heaven and hell contained in a white pod that is not much bigger than a man's thumb. Like the mythical song of the Sirens, the promise is alluring but the reality is deadly, for while opium begets painkilling morphine, it also begets heroin.

Dao did not know any of the statistics or demographics of drug use. He did not know where his packages were going, who would buy them, or who would eventually use the product of his crop. He had never heard of a spike or a jolt or a rush or a high or uppers, downers, hash, pot, boo, toot, coke, smack, crack, H, horse, lid, hit, popping, chipping, mainlining, tripping, acid or poppers. He did not know that his crop might kill some pitiful junkie half of a world away or that teenage gangsters might die in the street fighting over an ounce of the white powder that would eventually be refined from the sap of the little flowers. He had never seen a hypodermic needle. It was the cash crop of the village and had been for years, and to Dao and the rest of the Hsong tribe there was nothing wrong with selling it.

But the government had said it was wrong and had begun a program to coerce farmers into growing coffee, mushrooms and maize instead of poppies. There had been trouble in the hills. The Leums and the Lius and many other hill tribes had been attacked by the army and had their crop confiscated and burned, but the government had never approached Dao. His tribe was large and controlled a difficult, rugged section of the mountains. He was a fiery and independent leader as well as a dangerous adversary. Dao controlled only 250 hectares of poppy fields – about a hundred acres – hardly enough to start a war over. Besides that, the young general, as *phu yai ban*, was supposed to report to the government's district director, but two years earlier he had expelled the *nai amphoe* from Hsong and the government had never replaced the man.

But the young general still followed the same precautions. When the sky had turned red and the river sparkled like gold, Dao rode down to a small hooch located at the center of the fields and went inside. The place smelled sweet like new-mown grass. The opium gum had been brought there and wrapped in one-and-a-half-kilogram packages called *joi*. There it would retain its potency indefinitely unless refined.

The packages of gum, which looked like dark brown cake icing, were stacked in saddlebags. A ten-kilo package of gum and another containing one kilo of the same substance lay on the wrapping table. Dao took out a knife and twisted the point into one of the packages, drawing back a small, sticky dab, which he rolled between his fingers until it was a small ball called a *goli*. He put it under his tongue, closed his eyes and sucked on it, rolling it around in his mouth. Then he smiled. Excellent.

That night the packages were loaded on mules, and before dawn, Dao and four of his most trusted men led the mules off through the forest toward the House of the Golden Lady. They rode for two hours through dense brush, staunch spears of bamboo as tall as pine trees, enormous teak trees choked with crawling vines. They rode along paths only the best-trained eyes could spot, paths that were acrawl with deadly krites and patrolled by black panthers and tigers.

They stopped when they heard the familiar deep rumble through the towering overgrowth ahead, tethered their horses and walked the last mile as though mesmerized by the rumble, which finally crescendoed into a roar. When at last they broke out of the jungle, they were at the mouth of a deep, rocky gorge, veiled by sprays of mist that billowed out around them from the thundering waterfall called the Golden Lady at the far end of the vale. Struggling over slippery rocks at the edge of the river until the earth was trembling underfoot, they finally found the entrance to the cave known as the House of the Golden Lady.

Hsong leaders had been hiding their opium gum here for centuries. Now the place was better than ever, for it was not only suicidal to reach on foot but inaccessible to government choppers. They stacked the *joi* of opium gum deep in the cave, covered them with straw paper, and there they remained until the time to deal.

Now it was fall and the previous day the Chiu Chao boss had

sent his messenger to the Hsong village to request a meeting. Dao had sent the Straw Sandal back to his boss with the kilo of gum as a gesture of goodwill, so they could check the quality.

Most of the hill tribes still sold opium gum in its raw stage, but the Hsong tribe had its own refinery, a crude but effective little factory in a room no larger than a bedroom. The Chiu Chaos preferred to refine their own heroin, but the Hsong had always produced the powder themselves. It was a matter of pride to Dao as well as of economics. It takes two thousand poppies to make a kilo of opium gum. A kilo of gum sold in the hills for seventy dollars, a kilo of China White sold for nine hundred dollars. To Dao the difference was worth the effort. It meant more rifles for the men, more pigs and buffalo, and perhaps even a new truck for the village, bolts of Thai silk for the women, and for himself, a new radio with shortwave. He had no idea that the same pound of heroin was worth half a million dollars in New York, or that it would be stepped up six or seven times after that, making the street value close to four million dollars.

That night the Hsong cranked up the little furnace. They mixed ten kilos of gum with water and cooked it in an enormous brass wok until it was a dark, thick mass that looked like heavy molasses. Then they poured it into an ancient wooden press and squeezed the water out. What was left was a kilo of morphine base granules. Mixed with water and acetic anhydride in a small still and dried under grow lamps and pressed again, it produced a brick of pure white powder, which they branded with a stamp: 999. The mark of Hsong and a guarantee that the one-kilo brick of China White was 99.9 percent pure heroin.

Just after sunrise, the chopper took off from Chang Mai and headed for the village of the Hsong, seventy miles away. The day before, Tollie Fong had sent his Straw Sandal to General Dao to arrange the meeting. The ritual of dealing was a formality, but one they had performed at villages like this all over northern Thailand during the past few months. The emerald-green mountains slipped below them and grew more rugged and less penetrable. Mountain roads twisted up the sides of the lush peaks and ended suddenly at landslides or were simply devoured by the foliage. From the air it was easy to see why the army was frustrated in its attempts to discourage or destroy the poppy crop here.

Fong sat in the copilot's seat of the chopper with his three aides in the seats behind him – the White Fan, who was in charge of rituals and for this trip would also serve as Fong's secretary and financial adviser, and two gunmen, Billy Kot and Soon. The messenger had completed his duties and returned to Bangkok.

The White Fan, an ancient seer pushing eighty with wispy white hair and the remnants of a white goatee, wore the traditional silk *cheongsam* of the Chinese and had devoted his life to tradition and ritual. He hated to fly, particularly in this mixing bowl of an airplane, but his inscrutable face gave no hint of his discomfort. He sat with his eyes closed and his small black bag of tricks between his feet. Soon, a reliable executioner, dozed beside him, unconcerned by the flying.

Economics, as well as killing, was Tollie Fong's business. Getting the smack from the hills to the marketplace, whether it was Singapore or Marseilles, New York or Grand Rapids, was also his business. Fong had first been introduced to the trade while he was still in his early teens by his father, who had gone to college in the United States and understood Americans. Fong remembered that night well.

1962. The eve of the Chinese New Year, the Year of the Tiger.

Outside their window, there were dancers and dragons in the street. Firecrackers rattled in the gutters and the stars over Hong Kong were concealed behind a glittering wall of skyrockets.

Young Fong, not yet fourteen, wanted to be out there with the rest of his friends, but his father was insistent. He had called his *bing yahn*, his soldiers, to a meeting and the White Palm executioner leaned toward his five officers and placed his hand on his son's knee. 'I have spent several hours with the *san wong* and it is important that you understand our new plans.

'First, you must understand about Americans. They are very self-indulgent. They are eager to try new things. They are very sociable and they go to great lengths to impress their friends. They tend to do things in great masses. They live on borrowed money and their goals in life are security – and pleasure.

'Now they are becoming involved in a great turmoil over the fighting in Vietnam. There is revolutionary protest by the young people. And' – his eyes lit up – 'they have discovered drugs. Marijuana, peyote, the chemical called acid. It is just beginning. The *san wong* believes these young people are ripe for other drugs.

'Until now, the customers for powder have been mostly beggars, people of the streets, thieves and thugs. There is some trade with the very wealthy, but very few users in between. The Sicilians control the trade.

'So we have three plans. First, it is time to move on the Sicilians. This will not be done easily, but we may be able to supply them and use their people for our own distribution.'

'Can we trust them?' one of the *bing yahn* asked.

'Never! Always be wary of them. When it is convenient, we will make our war and destroy them, but that is a long time away. For now, we must help create the demand and make the deals, so we need the Sicilians. Second, the American soldiers in Vietnam and Thailand are at our very door and the war is growing. There will be many more soldiers coming. This war will last a long time, as it did with the French. We will sell them powder at cost plus ten percent.'

'At cost?' one of the *bing yahn* said with surprise.

'Plus ten percent, to create the need,' Fong corrected. 'And they will take this need back to the States with them and pass the need on to their friends and they will all grow old with the demon. These will be *our* customers. They will be accustomed to pure China White and will not be satisfied with the Turkish and Mexican brown shit the Sicilians sell. Finally, we must encourage the hill people to grow more poppies, for the demand will be greater than any of us realize. All other business in which the White Palms are involved must come second to this.'

That was the night he had assigned his five captains, who called themselves the Dragon's Breath, to open the markets in Saigon and keep them supplied.

'We must plan this move most carefully and then wait,' he said, 'for it will be two or three years before we make our move, but it is a good plan and it will work.'

When his captains had left, the older Fong turned to his son. 'You must understand the economics of this business,' he said softly but firmly. 'There are millions, perhaps billions, of dollars at stake. Right now your destiny is to follow me as Red Pole of the White Palm Chiu Chao. But this business will open things up for you. The more you know, the more important you will become. Who knows how far you can go. . . .'

The Red Pole had prepared his son well. Tollie Fong's mentor was Joe Lung, who would later be the only member of the Dragon's Breath to survive Hatcher's brutal massacre on the Mekong. Lung guided a vigorous training program. A year with the Ninja in Tokyo, six months with the SAVAK in Iran, another six months with thuggee Sikhs in Bombay. And another year spent with a master of tai chi and karate on Okinawa.

But always there was the business of the trade to learn, and Fong learned it from the experts by interning in the business offices of the Chiu Chaos in Hong Kong, Bangkok, Singapore and Seattle. Before he was twenty he was in New York learning the business of the street and had already killed three times, for his main role in the hierarchy of the White Palms was still to take his father's place as the Red Pole executioner.

As the new *san wong* of the White Palms, Fong would have made his father proud, for he had become an expert at the economics of the trade. Now the profits were so enormous that police could be bought and whole nations could be corrupted. Dope smuggling had become the most profitable business in the world, and a fifth of all the heroin sold in the United States came from the Golden Triangle in northern Thailand. And despite his *ch'u-tiao*, his blood oath to kill Hatcher – the man who had executed his father and now Joe Lung – the business of powder had to come first, for he had stretched his authority by setting up deals with the most productive hill tribes in the Golden Triangle.

Each year he had spread his empire farther, moving more deeply into the Triangle, taking dangerous risks with the suspicious and volatile mountain bandits. Every time the government burned out a field or coerced a hill tribe into planting coffee or mushrooms, Fong went deeper and found new tribes willing to cultivate the lucrative poppy.

His gamble had paid off handsomely. Fong now controlled the flow of Thai heroin for all the Chiu Chao families, and that was almost 5 percent of all the heroin that came out of Thailand. And in secret conclave, the Chiu Chaos were at that very moment, confirming him as *san wong*, master of all the families.

Fong needed someone to take his place as enforcer, someone he could trust. He decided that someone would be Billy Kot.

Handpicked from among the many assassins who served the White Palms, Kot was bright, clever, awesomely ruthless and, in Fong's eyes, the most efficient killer in the world, next to Tollie Fong himself. Kot was only twenty-six, but he was a college graduate, and now it was time to move him up.

Leaning over the back of the seat, Fong began a dialogue with Billy Kot, who leaned forward with his ear close to Fong's mouth.

'You must learn this part of the business because you are going to be the next Red Pole.'

Kot reared back in surprise, for the news was totally unexpected.

'It is more than just the business of the Red Pole,' said Fong.

'You must not only enforce the rules of the Society, you must also control negotiations up here as well.'

'I understand,' Billy Kot said, trying to control his excitement at the news. 'I promise to be worthy of your trust.'

'You must learn the ways of each of the hill leaders. To us they are like arteries to the heart. They must learn to trust you. And they are all different.'

'What of General Dao?'

'General Dao has been head of the Hsong tribe for fourteen years, since he was twenty-two,' Fong began. 'For three hundred miles in every direction, the tribes fear the Hsong.'

'Is he a warlord?'

'He does not start things, but he does not bow down either. They have not waged war on anyone for at least ten years.'

'So he is a tough guy,' Billy Kot said.

'Very. The army is afraid of him. Two years ago he threw out the *nai amphoe*, and Bangkok never even replaced the man. He is not like some of the others, always crying about the federals burning their fields, trying to gouge a few extra dollars for every *joi*.'

'Is he friendly?' Kot asked.

'He smiles,' Fong answered with a shrug, 'but he is cautious. The secret is to treat him with respect, never threaten him. An insult or threat, even an unwitting one, could be mistaken as an act of war. His *bing yahn* would drop us all on the spot. At the very least he would end our arrangement. So be careful.'

'I will just listen this time.'

'No, do what your spirit says. If you make a slip, the White Fan will warn you. He will stand or sit between us and Dao and to the side, partly facing us. If he shakes his head, stop talking, and he will handle the problem.'

'How much gum does the Hsong produce?'

'He is not a big producer, but the powder is as pure as it gets and he does it all, including the refining. Each year he has increased his production. I don't know what the yield will be this year.'

Below them they saw a village, not large, perhaps a hundred hooches, forming neat patterns on a high, lush mesa. Beyond it was Powder Mountain, its poppy fields denuded by the harvest. The pilot jockeyed the chopper around and put it down beside a dirt road at the foot of the mountain.

'This is the main village,' Fong said as they crawled out of the plane. 'There are three or four smaller ones around. And the

294

Hsong *bing yahn* live in the jungle. They are everywhere, do not underestimate them.'

'How many soldiers?' asked Billy Kot.

'I have no idea,' Fong answered. 'Three hundred maybe.'

'Weapons?'

'Everything. Subguns, M–14s, grenade launchers, a lot of small stuff. Very well armed.'

A battered antique of an army truck was waiting for them. They crawled in the back and sat facing each other as it rattled and rocked up the barely passable road to the village, thirty-five hundred feet above the valley floor.

'He can use a new truck or two,' said Fong, nodding to the White Fan. The old man made a mental note of it. He never wrote anything down.

Kot watched as the truck climbed the dusty road. He spotted a momentary flash of sun on steel in a tree, saw movement in another.

'His *bing yahn* are everywhere,' he said.

'*Hai*. Real monkeys,' Fong answered with a nod.

When they reached the crest of the hill, the truck stopped in front of a small hooch, a box of a house with one door and one window, which sat apart from the rest of the village. An armed guard stood at the side of the door.

'Just watch how it is done,' Fong said.

The formalities dated back to the time of the Opium Wars in China, almost a hundred and fifty years ago. Fong posted Soon on the opposite side of the door and entered the hooch with the Fan and Billy Kot.

It was a small room with four mats on the floor in the center, two facing each other, two stretched between them, forming a square in the middle of the room. Dao stood in front of one of the mats with two of his troopers posted in each corner of the room behind him. Beside Dao stood the *fai thaan*, a man whose face was etched with the crevices of time and whose teeth were stained dark brown from chewing betel nuts. The *fai thaan* was the cook and chief refiner of the Hsong tribe. At his feet was a small package wrapped in flat green leaves.

Fong walked casually to the center of the room and, facing Dao, pressed the palms of his hands together and bowed in a *wai* to show his respect for the Hsong leader and the brewer of magic powder. Dao answered the *wai* and then the Fan took his place facing the old cook and put his black bag at his feet. Kot stood behind Fong.

'I would like to introduce my *bing yahn*, Billy Kot, to the general,' Fong said. 'He will soon take my place as White Palm Red Pole.'

A look of concern crossed Dao's face. 'Is something wrong?' he asked.

'No, no,' Fong answered hurriedly. 'I am to become *san wong* of the Chiu Chaos. From this day on, Billy Kot will be my eyes and ears and voice. He will speak for me and he will negotiate fairly with all the tribes that supply us with powder.'

Dao looked at Kot for several seconds, studying the young man's smooth features. He had eyes like his boss's, hard and glazed with abstract menace.

'So he is learning?' said Dao.

'*Hai*,' Fong answered.

The general appraised Kot once more and nodded curtly with a smile.

'Ho,' Dao answered, slapping his right fist into the palm of his left hand, a sign of acceptance. They did not shake hands, because to touch another in Thailand is considered an insult. He sat cross-legged on the mat in front of him. Fong did the same, followed by the Fan, the new Red Pole, and the *fai thaan*. It was only after they were seated that Dao acknowledged the Fan.

'Are you well, Phat Lom?' he asked. The old man nodded and smiled faintly as he opened his bag and took out an abacus. He placed it in front of him.

'*Hai, hai*,' Dao said, nodding briskly. Then he slapped his hands together and smiled broadly. 'So, now it is time to deal,' he said, and nodded to the *fai thaan*, who carefully unfolded the leaves from the package. The white brick branded '999' gleamed on the mat before them. He picked up the snow-white square with both hands and offered it to the White Fan, who took it, held it in one hand, and weighed it by feel, first holding it on its side in the palm of his hand, then turning it on end. He nodded once, curtly, indicating the weight was proper. He stood and walked to the window and held the brick in the sunlight and studied it for several minutes, blowing gently on the surface. He scraped up a fingernailful and, holding it to a nostril, slowly inhaled it. He waited for another minute or two for it to take effect, then he scraped up another fingernailful and put it in his mouth and tasted it. Finally he returned and placed the brick in front of General Dao.

He held up three fingers to Fong.

Khuna-phaap di thi soot. First quality.

296

'Excellent as always,' said Fong. 'How much did you get this year?'

'Ninety hundred and thirty-five *joi*,' Dao answered, obviously proud of the yield. Fong, too, was delighted. Almost fifteen hundred kilos of gum, a hundred fifty kilos of heroin.

'That is fifty kilos more than last year,' he said.

'A very good year,' answered the general.

On the previous buy, Fong had paid nine hundred dollars per kilo. He looked over at the Fan, whose fingers were shooting the small colored balls of the abacus back and forth. The Fan held up two fingers, then three, then one, then a fist. It was a simple code, which only Fong and the Fan understood.

Although Kot did not understand the code, he made some quick calculations in his head. Not bad, he thought. A mere $135,000 for 150 keys of pure smack.

Fong turned to him and asked him what he thought the price should be. It was an unexpected test. Actually the price was immaterial. Considering the Chiu Chao profit margin, they could easily afford to pay Dao four or five times the normal price and hardly feel it. But this was business, and a dollar was a dollar.

Kot tried to think like the Red Pole. He had to weigh two things: first, whether to raise the price at all and, second, if so, how much to raise it without spoiling the general. Upping the price fifty dollars a *joi* would not hurt them that much. It would be significant enough to impress the hill chief and still not appear overly generous.

'Fifty more a *joi*,' Kot answered.

Kot knew from the slight twinkle in Fong's eye it was a good answer. Fong turned back to the general. 'My bid would have been twenty-five,' he said with a smile. 'The new Red Pole is more generous than I.'

General Dao was obviously pleased. The Fan showed no expression. His fingers were busy working the colored marbles on the abacus. He held up another combination of fingers.

The entire package would cost $142,500, or 2,850,000 bahts.

'How does two million eight sound?' Fong asked.

'I am most pleased,' Dao said, slapping his fist into his palm. The deal was concluded. Fong reached into the black bag and took out several packets of purple baht notes and stacked them neatly in front of Dao. When he had stacked the entire two million plus, he did a *wai*.

'The entire amount as agreed. When can Mr Kot expect delivery?'

297

'Will three days be satisfactory, starting in the morning?' Dao asked.

'Excellent.' And he, too, smacked his fist in his palm. 'And if it will not offend the general, I would like to make the Hsong a gift of two new trucks, to celebrate the new Red Pole.'

Dao was both surprised and pleased. Two new trucks in the bargain! 'You are very generous, my friend,' he said. 'The Hsong will be most happy to work with Mr Kot.'

'*Mai*,' Fong said with a nod and rose. They left the hooch and Soon joined them as they walked back to the truck.

Fong was pleased with his choice of Billy Kot and he slapped his new Red Pole on the arm.

'You did very well in there,' he said reassuringly. 'I do not think you will have any problems.'

'*Mm goi*,' Billy Kot said with a *wai*.

'One hundred and fifty kilos of pure for a hundred forty thousand dollars and two trucks,' Fong said. 'What does that come to, White Fan?'

The Fan had already figured up the profit, based on the morning street price in Manhattan. He flashed his fingers in the code. 'Three million, seven hundred thousand dollars,' Fong said, beaming. 'Fair work for one day.'

Wherever there were human beings, there were dope traders ready to prey on them. In the Hotel Vitosha in Sofia or L'Hotel Pique in Marseilles or the Garden Hotel in Amsterdam, Syrians, Turks and Lebanese met with Chinese, Sicilian and American gangsters to trade in heroin, cocaine and marijuana. They were the power bosses of the dope trade. They had developed the shipping routes from the Orient to Amsterdam, London and Rome, and from there to major ports in North America, where one thousand kilos – 2,200 pounds – of heroin went for a billion dollars and change before it was even cut for the street.

Their partners were the Sicilians, for in the years since the end of the Vietnamese war they had made their agreements with the American mobsters and spread their deadly powder to most of the major cities in the United States.

The drug lords had turned smuggling into a bizarre art, a deadly game of hide-and-seek between 'mules,' the couriers who did the actual heroin smuggling, and drug and customs agents. The lethal powder was smuggled in hollow gemstones, icons and statues. In Tampax and condoms. In dolls, books, diplomatic pouches, and major shipments of coffee, soybeans and bamboo.

298

It was dissolved in water and then suitcases, paintings, rugs and clothing were soaked in it and carried or shipped into the United States. Smugglers buried it in the desert until they made their deals, then sent it across borders by feeding it to their camels, addicting them, and training them to follow specific routes in order to get more.

For every drug bust there was a new scheme. For every pound that was confiscated, ten pounds got through.

In Bangkok and Hong Kong, Tollie Fong and his White Palms had developed the most obscene and terrifying smuggling techniques of all. Now it was time to make a major drug move on the United States. They had almost three tons of 99.9 percent pure China White secreted in Bangkok ready for a mass shipment to America.

The prediction made by Tollie Fong's father twenty-three years earlier was finally coming true. The years had been good to them. And Fong had the perfect plan. It had been approved by the old *san wong*.

Tollie Fong was positioned to make war on the sworn enemy of the Chiu Chaos, La Cosa Nostra – the Mafia.

A SUGGESTION

Earp came out of Sweets Wilkie's office and went up the steps and through the glass beads into the Longhorn Saloon's 'Hole in the Wall.' The Honorable was seated in his stuffed chair, his imposing presence making it seem like a throne. He was reading as usual. The fringed lamp was the only light on in the large alcove. There was no one else in the room, and the lights over both the poker and pool tables had been turned off. Earp pulled up a chair and sat down beside him.

'Little late for you, isn't it?' he said.

'I'm engrossed,' the Honorable said, without looking up.

'My man in Hong Kong just called.'

'Um-hum,' the Honorable said, still reading his book.

'A man named Hatcher is coming in on the morning plane. Hatcher is an assassin. He works for Sloan.'

'Perhaps a coincidence?'

'Not a chance. Sloan comes in. Now Hatcher follows him. No, he isn't coming for the fucking waters.'

299

'And this Hatcher is dangerous?'

'He's wasted half of Hong Kong in the last forty-eight hours. The guy's a walking plague.'

'Would you like a suggestion?'

'Don't I always?'

The Honorable dipped his finger in wine, turned the page of his book and licked his finger. 'Arrange for him to come here,' he said. 'Check him out up close and on friendly territory.'

'That's a little dangerous, isn't it?' Earp said. 'Bringing him right into the living room?'

'If he's as dangerous as you say and he's here to assassinate Thai Horse, he's also very smart. He'll wind up here sooner or later anyway.'

The Honorable looked up and what might have passed for a smile crossed his lips.

'As the Thais say, "It is easier to kill a friendly tiger than a mad dog."'

KRUNG THEP

Hatcher stirred as the 747 banked sharply and swept over Bangkok on its approach to the city and the flight attendant announced their approach to Don Muang airport. Still half asleep, Hatcher remembered Bangkok as a city of gold and silver temples, of spires and domes, and delicate, beautiful women, as fragile as china, swathed in radiant silk.

He pulled back the curtain and it was like looking down on a painting. Even in the gray predawn light with the sun a shimmering promise on the horizon, Bangkok was like a gleaming jewel in the palm of Buddha's hand, and the Chao Phraya River was an endless life line stretching from little finger to thumb. Hundreds of golden domes and spires reached through the morning mist like flowers seeking the sun. It was these holy places and the canals which coursed through the city that defined Bangkok's character and personality. Centuries ago there were no roads in Bangkok; its streets were dozens of canals called klongs that wound through it, their banks draped with flowers and trees. Progress had changed that. A few major water arteries still served the city; the rest had been filled in to become boulevards and lanes. But the flowers remained and the streets were demarcated as much by orchids, bougainvillea and palm trees as they were by gutters and sidewalks. Through the mists of morning, Hatcher occasionally caught a glimpse of the canals jammed with slender, long-tailed *hang yao* laden with fresh fruit, flowers and wares as the river people made their way to the floating markets on the banks of the main river.

As the plane began its descent the sun rose over the horizon, and the morning mist, set ablaze by the fires of dawn, turned to steam, vanished, and revealed in stunning glory a sparkling city of gold.

This was a land so alien to Westerners that it was like flying into another planet. The tourists 'oohed' and 'aahed' at the sight. Everything below them seemed clean and fertile and seductive. And yet he knew that beneath the beauty there was also the agony of great poverty, that children bathed in their own refuse and were sold on the streets, that heroin was part of the rate of exchange, that there were sixty or seventy homicides a month, that the cold steel and mirrored glass towers of the Westerners were slowly corrupting Bangkok's ancient and exquisite beauty, and that automobiles were polluting the city's air. Perhaps, he thought, the Thais would tire of the foreigners and throw them out, as their ancestors had done two hundred years before when the *farang* had tried to replace the gentle compassion of Buddha with the rigid, intractable arrogance of Christianity.

To survive as a *farang* in Bangkok, Westerners had to accept its philosophy even if they did not understand it. Here Buddha was the benevolent saint. Rich Thais bought buttons of gold leaf and pressed them on temples and icons. The poor covered statues with broken teacups. Everyone paid tribute and came to pray, to ask for favors from Buddha, for the Thais thought nothing of asking for a big fish on their line or a winning lottery ticket or a beautiful woman for the night or a handsome man to curl up with when the sun vanished. The subtleties were lost to those from the West whose God, modeled by pompous, arrogant, self-appointed intermediaries, was an angry God, less compassionate, less forgiving, and devoid of any sense of humor. To the Thais, who believed the smile was born in their country, Buddha was a kind and generous God, capable of impish tricks, laughter and infinite joy, a God who asked nothing, demanded nothing, and smiled on those who laid tribute at his feet.

Perhaps that is why, to the Thai, arguing was a sin, raising one's voice was an insult, and anger was intolerable. One had to love a people whose philosophy of life was summed up by their

301

reaction to almost everything: *Mai pen rai*– 'Never mind.' While Hatcher did not begin to understand the intricacies of Hinayana Buddhism, one thing he did understand was that Buddhists believed that our temporary existence on earth was uncertain at best; that concern was folly and anger was futile; that confrontation was an embarrassment, anxiety was a sin, and life was a process of forgiving. It was a philosophy he had tried to embrace, but there were psychological responses so ingrained in Westerners that it was difficult for a *farang* to ignore them.

And while Hatcher had understood and tried to practice the Thai philosophy in the past, this time it was not working for him. He was overwhelmed with anxiety, and what he feared most was what he would learn about Cody in Bangkok. The closer the plane got to the airport, the more his anxiety grew. Even identifying his former friend would be a major problem. Would he still recognize Cody? It had been almost twenty years since he had last seen his friend. And he had probably changed his name.

But Hatcher's greatest fear concerned Cody himself. What was he doing here, and why had he kept his identity a secret all these years? Was he a collaborator? A junkie? A drug smuggler? If he was smuggling drugs, was he tied in with Tollie Fong and the Chiu Chao triads? Or was there some even darker secret that Hatcher could not imagine?

Was Cody actually dead? Even if he had escaped the plane crash fifteen years ago, Cody could have died in the prison camp or in any of a dozen other ways. Fifteen years was a long time.

Hatcher also remembered that there was no such thing as a fact in Thailand. Truth was a crucible for what was real and what was imagined, what was veritable and what was spiritual. At best, a fact in Bangkok was an abstraction of reality, a perception of the individual. Truth was often an illusion and things were never what they appeared to be.

Yet try as he might, Hatcher could not come up with a single positive reason for Cody to remain in hiding.

Finally there was the most gnawing question of all: if Cody was involved in some dark scheme, what would he, Hatcher, do about it? Ignore it and go home? Try to set up the meet with his father anyway? Perhaps Cohen's advice was the best advice of all – turn his back on the whole thing and go home.

That was not a viable option for Hatcher.

He had an obligation to Buffalo Bill Cody. He had made a promise and he meant to keep it.

302

Anyway, he was hooked, he had to play the hand out, no matter what the outcome.

He cleared customs without incident and found a taxi. The trip to town was a surreal fantasy, a wondrous journey through a dazzling array of cultures, sounds and sights that might have hypnotized Sinbad. The city's beauty had always fascinated Hatcher, and now, coming back after five years, he was stunned again by its veiled mysteries and hidden promises.

The twenty-mile trip to town passed quickly, and the lush green fields of the countryside surrendered abruptly to the city as they passed the spectacular Chitralada Palace, the residence of King Bhumibol, the benevolent and well-loved ruler, whose great-great-grandfather, Rama IV, better known as King Mongkut, brought the English schoolteacher Anna Leonowens to Siam in the 1860s to enlighten his children. Although her autobiography, *The King and I*, and the play and movie based on it, had brought fame to Thailand, they were banned as inaccurate.

The taxi passed the Royal Turf Club racetrack, past fields where daily kite fights were a prelude to dusk and over Phadung Klong, the main canal of the city. In two hours the boulevard would be gutter-to-gutter cars, sputtering motorized pedicabs called *samlors*, and *tuk-tuks*, the strange three-wheel two-seaters that weave in and out of the traffic and drive everyone mad and whose name describes the sound of their small motors.

But in the early light of day, the city was as it might have been a century before. They drove down an almost deserted Bamrung Muang Road, where orchids, jasmine and roses cascaded over fences, past estates where young women in embroidered costumes practiced ceremonial dances and flirted with the long shadows of daylight on lawns of emerald velvet. The cool morning breeze sifted through the open windows of the taxi, carrying with it the constant tinkle of temple bells from the wats, the Buddhist temples that were everywhere, their rooftops a delicate mosaic of colored spirals and gold-tiled domes, their eaves adorned with curling yellow finials called *chofas*.

A Thai businesswoman in Western dress, her Mercedes parked by the curb, placed a wreath of jasmine on a miniature but elaborate spirit house and clasped her hands in a *wai*, possibly asking the spirits for a successful day. The tiny temples were everywhere, looking like cluttered, gloriously painted dollhouses mounted on posts. They were always decked with offerings: hand-painted vases filled with roses, smoking joss

303

sticks, necklaces of orchids, notes to the spirits, brightly dyed strips of silk, even food. Seeing the little temples, Hatcher remembered a mercenary named Nickle Knowles, who always offered a bullet to the spirits before a job.

A half-dozen monks in saffron robes rushed out of a nearby wat with their brass alms bowls, seeking their first meal of the day. Two blocks away a country woman, her head wrapped in a brightly jeweled turban and her lips permanently stained brown by the betel nuts she chewed, sat in the middle of the sidewalk stringing jasmine blossoms. And a block farther, a greengrocer was busy arranging his stall with a dazzling array of pineapples, bananas, mangoes and durians, the large, spiky fruit most foreigners hated.

They passed the towering swing of Phatpu, where athletes once swung in giant arcs for the pleasure of the King until the practice was banned as too dangerous, and there the flower-lined streets gave way to the crowded old town. The incongruities continued: a noble but derelict Victorian palace with ginger-bread turrets stood behind a cinema; an enormous three-story-high Buddha rested between two glass and concrete office buildings; a group of street urchins dashed along the curb with the grace of ballet dancers, playing soccer with a rattan ball, rousting a flock of migratory swallows that seemed to flutter constantly in search of roosting places among the statues and temples. And there were touches of Thai whimsy: a barbershop called the Darling, a restaurant called the Puberty, a hotel that rented rooms by the hour called Bungalow Home Fun.

The street ended abruptly at Yawaraj Road, which marked the beginning of Yawaraj, or Chinese Town. As the traffic increased khaki-clad traffic cops in gleaming white pith helmets began to appear, and the driver relied more on his horn than on his driving skills to make his way through the choked alleys. Streets funneled, became narrow and claustrophobic, wound uncertainly past ancient and ramshackle wooden buildings wedged against one another. Occasionally an elegant Chinese pagoda roof topped the otherwise undistinctive rows of shops that offered rare foods, aphrodisiacs, Cantonese vitamins and magic herbs. The streets became more constricted, curving through the Nakorn Kasem, the Chinese market known as Thieves' Market, a misnomer, since most of the shops sold such unromantic articles as toilets, water pumps and light fixtures. The real lure of Yawaraj was the dusty, dimly lit antique shops. Shopkeepers were already busy hauling their clutter of treasures outside,

304

where they spilled over the sidewalks: porcelains, teak furniture inlaid with mother-of-pearl, rosewood screens, brass and copper lamps.

The driver turned into New Road and headed down the last few blocks to the river at the far edge of Yawaraj and pulled up in front of the Muang House, a middle-class hotel, which Hatcher preferred over the luxury hotels of Bangkok. It was air-conditioned, so mosquitoes would not be a problem. The taxi then went down past the produce market to the Oriental.

The restaurant was outside at the back of the hotel on a flower-filled terrace above the broad, sweeping Chao Phraya River. Below it, long boats puttered through the morning mist on the way to the floating market while on the far side the spires of a dozen wats pierced the low-lying veil. It was not yet 7 A.M. The restaurant was deserted except for Sloan, who stood at the railing sipping coffee and staring down at the river. The early morning breeze flapped the jacket of his white raw-silk suit. With his pale blue shirt, he might easily have been mistaken for a salesman or a business executive. He finally took a table near the railing, and with his Ben Franklin glasses perched halfway down his nose, he opened the *Bangkok Post*, one of the country's three English language newspapers, folding it lengthwise the way subway riders do in New York.

There was another reason for Hatcher's gnawing anxiety in coming to Bangkok. Harry Sloan. Expediency was Harry's middle name.

Before the mission ended, Hatcher feared, he might have to stand between Murphy Cody and Harry Sloan.

How much should I tell him? Hatcher wondered. Does he need to know anything?

'*Sawat-dii*,' the head waiter said with a bow. 'Breakfast, please?'

Hatcher pointed toward Sloan and followed the ornately dressed young man to the table. Sloan looked up over his glasses and then down at his watch.

'Right on time,' he said. 'Punctuality, the mark of a dependable man.'

Hatcher ordered fresh orange juice, coffee and an English muffin. When the waiter left the table, he took off his glasses and laid them carefully on a corner of the table.

There was no smile on Sloan's face, although his voice was as soft as usual. 'You've been having yourself quite a time over in the colony,' he said.

305

'What do you mean?'

Sloan smiled condescendingly. 'Just so you understand, I've got a fire under my ass in Madrango. I don't need a shoot-out on Victoria Peak, cops getting blown up, a Goddamn tong war between Cohen and Tollie Fong, a shoot-out upriver with half the Ts'e K'am Men Ti getting knocked off. What I'm saying, all of a sudden the priorities have shifted. Madrango is what's important right now.'

'You're a little confused, Harry,' Hatcher's wrecked voice answered just as softly. 'I didn't draw a line in the ground and dare them to step over it. They were trying to kill *me*. What was I supposed to do, play sitting duck?'

'Nobody expects that.'

'Then let me do my job.'

'You know how important it is to keep the brigade quiet, particularly now. There's too much at stake. Here, in Central America, in the Middle East. Hell, I've got cards all over the table.'

Hatcher stared across the table at Sloan. He shook out his napkin and dropped it on his lap as the waiter brought his coffee.

'You knew the risk when you brought me into this,' Hatcher said, doctoring his coffee with generous amounts of cream and sugar. 'And we both knew I was in trouble the minute that son of a bitch Varney showed up at your door. As you always say, if one person knows, everybody knows. Of course, it didn't help that the bastard was on Fong's payroll.'

'The late bastard, I hear.' The smile returned, the slick tone of voice was back. 'Just remember, in the future these things can be negotiated.'

'There wasn't time for that. They didn't ring Cohen's doorbell and suggest a little pow-wow first –' Sloan's words suddenly sank in and Hatcher stopped for a moment, staring at him. 'What do you mean, they can be negotiated. You can't negotiate anything with the Chiu Chaos.'

Sloan leaned across the table. 'I can handle it,' he said nonchalantly.

'How?'

'We do business with these countries. When we need to put the squeeze on assholes like Fong, there are ways of doing it.'

'Harry, *no*body puts the squeeze on assholes like Fong.'

The waiter came with their breakfast. Sloan had ordered eggs, bacon, toast, fruit. Other guests began drifting into the restaurant.

306

'What the hell happened upriver?' Sloan asked as he salt-and-peppered his eggs.

'I was looking for information,' Hatcher said.

'I hope what you got was worth the body count.'

'When did you start worrying about body counts?' Hatcher said sarcastically.

Sloan leaned across the table. 'Did you find out anything or not?' he said.

'I got some leads.'

'That's it? All I get out of this breakfast is that you got some leads.'

'We'll talk about it if they pan out.'

Sloan leaned back and sighed. He looked back over the river, arranging his thoughts.

Hatcher said very matter-of-factly, 'Harry, I came over here to find Murphy Cody and that's what I'm going to do. And I'm going to do it my way, which doesn't include giving you progress reports every thirty seconds. I said I'd be alive for breakfast today, and here I am. What the hell do you care whether I get into it with the Ts'e K'am or Fong or anybody else? That's my problem. I don't even work for the brigade anymore, I'm just a private citizen looking for an old pal.'

'I admire your talent at oversimplification,' Sloan said and then chuckled. 'Well, I've got some bad news for you, and some worse news for you after that. Which would you like first?'

Hatcher sighed. 'Why do you smile when you say that?' he asked.

'I can be just as perverse as you,' he said. 'The worse news is that they found Cody's dog tags on the site of the crash.'

Hatcher scowled at him, letting the information sink in.

'When did you hear that?'

'Last night. They turned up when the site was checked back in '76. It wasn't in the report because he was already declared dead and the government file was closed when they were found.'

'How did you find out?'

'You know Flitcraft, he doesn't miss a base. He sent a routine inquiry to the POW commission and the insurance company after we got Windy's report. The information on the dog tags was buried in an insurance wrap-up but was never added to the government file. They couldn't have cared less by then.'

Hatcher thought a moment. Actually it was good news to him. It resolved a problem he had in dealing with Cody's identity in the prison camp. 'That could explain why the Vietcong didn't exploit him.'

'I don't get you,' Sloan said.

'Up until now it really bugged me,' Hatcher said. 'It didn't make sense. If Charlie had the son of the commanding general, they were in a good position to do some hard trading, but they never did. Now we know why. He dumped them, Harry, so they wouldn't know who he was.'

Sloan's eyebrows rose. It was obvious that had not occurred to him. 'You have a real knack for making things work for you,' he said.

'I also pinpointed that floating camp called the Huie-kui. It was located on the Laotian side of the Annimitique Mountains around a town called Muang. It was a transition camp for Vietnamese quislings—'

'Well, shit,' Sloan snorted in disgust.

'Let me finish!' Hatcher whispered. 'There were also eight or ten American POWs in this camp, a kind of permanent slave labor. I've got an eyewitness who thinks he saw Cody up there.'

'Thinks?'

'We're talking ten, eleven years ago.'

Sloan scratched his chin with the back of one hand.

'What happened to this camp after the war?' he asked.

Hatcher shook his head. 'I don't know. But I do know the commandant was so corrupt he couldn't go back to Hanoi. He turned rabbit and ran.'

'So it's conceivable that if Cody was in the camp, he could have run, too,' Sloan said.

Hatcher nodded. 'You got it.'

'Where did you hear this?'

'Chin Chin land, from a trader they call the Dutchman. That's why I went up there. It didn't have anything to do with Ts'e K'am.'

Sloan's ego could be stroked. He stared across the table at Hatcher for a long time before he said, 'It's still all maybe and could be.'

'Yes.'

'So we still don't have anything positive but Wol Pot.'

'Right again,' Hatcher said.

'This is MIA shit, Hatch,' Sloan said. 'I'll tell you what I don't think — I don't think there're twenty-four hundred missing Americans doing time in Hanoi, or up there teaching the Vietnamese how to play Monopoly or any other damn thing.

Maybe a handful wandering around Laos or North Vietnam. Maybe a few turncoats. The rest of them were probably tortured to death or shot or died of malnutrition or disease. Those are the ones who weren't killed on the spot. Hell, a lot of good people got wasted in Nam, Hatch. Why torture the ones back home with hope. Besides, back in the real world you can get poisoned by a pill from the drugstore, get run down by some drunk on the highway. There're worse ways to die than serving your country.'

'Why didn't you mention that back in Georgia when you were conning me into this trip?'

'I never said he was alive.'

'You implied it enough to get me over here.'

'Well, I'll say one thing, your attitude is a hell of a lot more positive than it was in Georgia – or even Hong Kong.'

'Let's just say we've elevated a wild-goose story to a premise.'

'That's bullshit. I know you. I can tell when that nose of yours starts working. You're on to something.'

'That's accurate,' Hatcher said with a nod.

'You think Cody's alive?'

'Let's just say I think it more than I did in Hong Kong.'

'Why?'

'Little things. Intuition.'

'But nothing you could take to court.'

'Nope.'

'Uh-huh. Okay.'

Hatcher had left out several important pieces of the puzzle. That the commandant who had escaped to Bangkok was Wol Pot. That the Dutchman thought the man who could be Cody was on drugs. He didn't tell Sloan about the hoochgirl, Pai, and he still had not mentioned Thai Horse. *Why?* he asked himself. *Because he didn't trust Sloan* was the answer.

'The issue is, Is Murphy Cody alive, and if so, what's he into?' Sloan said. 'That's the issue.'

'Back in Georgia, you told me if I found Cody there would be no questions asked,' Hatcher said. 'The old man just wanted to say good-bye, you said. That was the *only* issue.'

Sloan lit a cigar, tapped ash off it and watched the wind break it up and twirl it away. He stared out over the river.

Both men were thinking about other times, times when they trusted and relied on each other, when there was an unwritten, unspoken bond between them that went beyond duty and orders and was an almost psychic link between thought and action. Los Boxes had struck that bond and shattered it.

Now they were skirting the issue, neither of them willing to lay it out to deal head-on with the problem. Sloan didn't want to make a verbal commitment, he never did. In the past, he had always left the dirty words unsaid.

'What this is really about is protecting the general's reputation, keeping the old man from being embarrassed,' Hatcher repeated.

Sloan's eyebrows made little half-circles. 'There could be more to it than that.'

'Like what's Cody been up to for the past fifteen years?' said Hatcher.

'That enters into it.'

'That wasn't part of the deal.'

'Christ, Hatch, you've been doing this kind of thing for almost twenty years. Do I have to draw pictures for you?'

'Yeah, draw me some pictures,' Hatcher whispered.

'Seems pretty simple to me,' Sloan said.

'You're asking me to make a very heavy judgment call here,' Hatcher said.

'You've made them before. What's the problem? Seems to me you're leaning over backwards to give your old school chum the benefit of the doubt.'

'We're not just talking about an old school chum, we're talking about Buffalo Bill's son.'

'That's the whole point,' said Sloan.

'Why don't you just come right on out with it,' Hatcher's tortured voice asked. 'You want me to dust Cody, don't you?'

He's done it again, thought Hatcher, that slick-talking bastard has done it again.

'I want you to find out if he's alive, and if he is, why he hasn't turned up,' Sloan said slowly and distinctly. 'And if he's mixed up in something – unsavory . . .'

He let the sentence fade out.

'Unsavory? Unsavory? Aren't we getting a little cute here,' Hatcher snapped.

'We never had to talk about this kind of thing before,' said Sloan, his eyes narrowing.

The tickling sensation in Sloan's gut turned sour. What had happened to Hatcher? he wondered.

'Why don't you just lay it out for me,' Hatcher said.

Sloan still wouldn't commit. He stared into space, puffing on his cigar.

'You're telling me you want Cody hit,' Hatcher said, and there was genuine surprise in his voice.

310

'I'm telling you you have options, like you always did.'

'Well,' growled Hatcher, 'I don't want the option. I didn't come over here to kill anybody. I came to find out whether Murphy Cody is dead or alive, period. Now you're throwing a lot of new rules at me.'

'No rules –' Sloan said.

'I'm not going to make that kind of decision,' Hatcher whispered.

'Then call me,' Sloan said flatly. 'I'll make it for you.'

'This guy was a war hero, Harry.'

'So was Benedict Arnold.'

'What do you know that I don't?' Hatcher demanded.

'Not one fucking thing,' Sloan snapped back.

'Then it seems to me you're drawing some pretty harsh conclusions.'

'Well, what the hell conclusion would you draw?' Sloan appealed. 'You sized it up yourself a minute ago. The guy is missing for fifteen years. Then he apparently turns up alive in Bangkok and doesn't want anybody to know it, and now Windy Porter's dead and this Wol Pot is on the run. Supposing the two Chins who wasted Porter were running interference for Wol Pot. Suppose he and Cody are in something together.'

'Suppose, suppose, suppose,' Hatcher said angrily. 'Hell, we're not even sure Cody's alive. This Wol Pot could be pulling some kind of a scam on all of us.'

'Hey, I buy that, okay,' Sloan agreed. Then he said, almost offhandedly, 'If that's the way it is, dust the little bastard off, too.'

'Is it really that easy for you, Harry?' Hatcher asked. 'Dust off Cody, dust off the Thai.'

Sloan sighed. His shoulders drooped and he suddenly seemed ten years older.

'We've been fighting these shadow wars for too many years to change now,' Sloan said wearily.

'And if Murph's clean?'

'Then set up the meeting with Buffalo Bill. Look,' he sighed, 'you do what you have to do, I do what I have to do. You start looking for answers to a lot of questions, you're gonna be dead, Hatch. That's basic and you know it. You don't have time for that. All we got is clicks and reflexes. You got two choices on any given day – do it or don't do it. If you don't know the options going in, if you haven't made the decision, they'll get you. Have I ever told you any different? Has there ever been any question in your mind about that?'

311

'Not before now,' Hatcher said without looking at Sloan.

'Then maybe I've got the wrong man.'

'Maybe so.'

'You want out?'

Hatcher thought about it. He had mixed emotions about Murph Cody. One man thought he was a hero, another thought he was a maniac. Now the mission had taken on new complexities. It was no longer a question of is he alive or isn't he, but whether he should stay alive or not. Hatcher knew if he bowed out, Sloan would bring in someone else, someone who would do the job without thinking, some expedient butcher.

And what are you, Hatcher, he thought to himself, *an inexpedient butcher?*

In Hatcher's mind he was the only one in a position to make that judgment call. Much as he hated it, Sloan had done it again. He had put Hatcher in the middle. To Hatcher there was only one alternative.

He nodded slowly. 'I'm still in,' he said. 'If he's alive, I'll find him.'

'Then what?'

'Then I play it by ear.'

Sloan stared across the table at him for several moments, then said, 'Fair enough.' He slid a manila envelope across the table to Hatcher.

'What's this?' Hatcher asked.

'It's everything the embassy had on Windy Porter, for what it's worth. His diary has a few locations that might help you.'

'How about police reports?'

Sloan chuckled again, as if he were enjoying heaping bad news on Hatcher. He finished his coffee and dabbed his lips with his napkin.

'Well, uh, that's the other bit of bad news. We've had a little trouble with the local cops.'

'What kind of trouble?'

'They're playing hard to get. They stiffed a runny-nosed embassy errand boy, told him they're holding all of Windy's stuff until they complete their investigation and they won't talk about it.'

'They probably don't have much anyway.'

'You'll be dealing with a major named Ngy. I'll be tied up making the arrangements to get Windy back to the States. If you need me, call Flitcraft, he can always get in touch.'

'Is this Ngy going to give me a bad time?' Hatcher asked.

312

'They don't call him the Mongoose for nothing,' Sloan
answered.

THE MONGOOSE

When Hatcher left the Oriental, he checked out the taxis and
limos in front of the hotel. It was his custom to hire a car for a
week at a time so it would always be available at a good price.
And he also looked for a driver who was street-smart, somebody
clever who knew where to get answers.

The Mercedes and Rolls-Royce limousines were lined up first,
followed by more conventional cars, Plymouths and Toyotas.
The drivers, all smiling, held open the doors and motioned him
inside. They were all too clean, too civilized and uniformed. He
looked past the row of limos and cabs to a small, wiry Thai
standing beside a three-wheel *tuk-tuk* near the end of the line.
The little man appeared to be exercising. He stepped back
suddenly and thrashed his arms in a series of hard jabs, sparring
with an imaginary opponent, then jogged forward, threw a hard
kick that was shoulder-high and turned back, jogging in place.
He saw Hatcher watching him and smiled.

The little man jogged past the big expensive cars to Hatcher
and bowed. He was wearing cutoff jeans and a white t-shirt with
'Harvard Drinking Team' on the front in dark blue letters.

'*Sawat-dii,*' he said, a general greeting in Thai that could
mean anything from 'Hi' to 'Good-bye' and bowed again to
Hatcher.

'*Sawat-dii, khrap,*' Hatcher answered. '*Phom maa jaak
Muang Saharat.*'

He was about five five and in his mid-twenties, with a flat nose
and a wide face. A mixture of Thai and Chinese, Hatcher
thought. Like many Thai men, he wore a tattoo on his shoulder.
Hatcher recognized the tattoo as Kinnari, the half-woman,
half-bird goddess, a harbinger of good luck.

'I know you are American, I speak English,' the lad said
proudly.

'*Sabai-dii.* What's your name?'

'Tsi Tei Nyk. Everybody call me Sy.' He exhibited two ragged
rows of ruined teeth. 'You name?'

'Hatch.'

313

Sy pointed back and forth between them. 'Sy, Hatch.'

'You got it right.'

'Good stuff.'

'Yeah, good stuff,' Hatcher agreed. 'You exercise like that a lot, do you?' He threw a couple of playful punches to make his point.

'I am a boxer,' Sy said proudly, sticking out his chest in an exaggerated show of pride. 'I drive *tuk-tuk* until I get money to quit.'

He jumped back and thrashed his arms in another series of jabs, threw another hard kick, and jogged in place. 'I practice every morning at dawn for two hours. And thirty minutes each afternoon I practice my moves.'

'You want to work for me for about a week?'

'A week? Do what?'

'Translate for me.'

'Everybody here speak English. And you speak Thai,' Sy said.

Hatcher nodded. 'Yeah but not *Sabai-dii*. You get me around, tell me about people. Help me get things done. No problems.'

'Ahh. No problems,' Sy said, and suddenly he understood what he was being hired for. '*Mai pen rai*.'

'That's right, *mai pen rai*,' Hatcher agreed. 'So how much?'

'Every day. All the time?'

'I sleep late,' Hatcher said with a smile.

Sy chuckled and nodded slowly. 'I gotcha. Sleep late, stay up late.'

'That's about it.'

Sy, his hands folded behind his back, paced back and forth in front of Hatcher, his forehead wrinkled in a frown. 'I will have a fight tomorrow night, so I cannot work then.'

'Okay.'

'And I must do my moves each afternoon.'

'I understand,' said Hatcher. 'Where do you fight?'

'Everywhere. Tomorrow at the Royal Park near Wat Phat,' he said proudly. 'If I get good enough, someday I will become a member of the King's guard.'

'That's what you want, huh, to be a King's guard?'

'Yes. I have asked Buddha for that gift every day for twelve years. I wear the *hai-huang* and tattoo to guide me to that job.'

He reached inside his shirt and took out a circular brass ornament on the end of a silver chain. A reclining Buddha was engraved in its center. The Thais were big on amulets, which

314

they called *hai-huang*, meaning 'worries away,' and some had amulets for every occasion. There were stalls and shops that specialized in amulets near all of the four hundred wats in Bangkok.

'That's a handsome *hai-huang*,' said Hatcher. 'Okay, I'm sure we can find thirty minutes for you to practice every day. Maybe I'll even go to the fights with you.'

'I will get you ticket,' the driver said excitedly, thrusting his leg out to the side in two hard kicks.

'Okay, so how much?' Hatcher asked again.

Sy stopped and held out his hand, the fingers splayed out. 'Fi' dollars, American bucks.'

'An hour?' Hatcher said.

'All day.'

'Five dollars a day?' Hatcher said with surprise.

'And I eat.'

'Right. Five dollars a day and meals.'

'*Chai*,' the little Thai said.

'You're worth more.'

'More?'

'Twenty bucks a day.'

'A day!' Sy said, his eyes growing twice their size.

Hatcher nodded.

'I am rich man,' said the delighted Sy. 'I will rent a car.'

'Can you drive a car?'

'Sure, okay.'

'Okay, I'll throw in the car,' said Hatcher.

'Throw in?'

'I'll rent the car.'

'A jeep?' Sy said excitedly.

'No, something better.'

'Jeep is good. Take bumps good.'

'Too hard on the ass,' Hatcher whispered. 'And too hot.'

'Merkedes?' Sy said, coming down hard on the c.

'How about a chevy?'

'Chevy? Ah, Chevrolet?'

'*Chai*,' Hatcher answered.

'Okay,' Sy answered with a shrug.

'Okay, here's what we do. We're going to the police station. Then we're going back to my hotel, rent a car and then I'm going to study some reports for an hour or two. You can practice.

315

There's a small park across from the hotel. Then you and me, we'll check out Bangkok.'

Major Tan Ngy stood behind the desk, his hands clasped behind his back, his face a mask, staring at the memorandum that lay in front of him. He was annoyed, annoyed that the chief had ordered him to cooperate with the Americans, annoyed that the Americans had even asked to interfere with the business of the Bangkok police. And that's what the American was coming for, to interfere.

Why was it that the Americans always felt they could step in and take over? No matter where they were in the world, they expected reports – and *authority* – to be handed over to them, just like that. The death of the American intelligence officer, Porter, was a local police matter, a homicide on the streets of Bangkok. It was not the business of the United States Army or military intelligence or this Hatcher. It was *his* business. Ngy was head of the homicide division of the Bangkok police and he had nothing against Americans in general, but he did not like their interfering in his business.

Ngy was an excellent police officer, tough, resilient, uncompromising and honest, all of which had earned him the nickname the Mongoose. The Mongoose did not need Americans snooping around, implying that his investigative abilities were inferior or inadequate.

That was the worst part about it – he had nothing to report. His investigation was stymied. The trail was growing colder by the day, and Ngy knew that with each passing hour the killers moved a little farther out of reach. Now the Yankee would come in and offer to solve the matter, just like that. He had dealt with Americans before. Arrogant. Presumptuous. Conceited. Superior. And yet he would have to be almost obsequious. The chief's memo was quite clear about that. Be friendly, it said. Not just courteous, *friendly*!

It was not going to be a good day.

He looked at his watch. Fifteen minutes. In fifteen minutes the American would arrive. Oh, he would be prompt. My God, were these people *never* late? He would make the usual salutatory comments. He would be patronizing. He would smile a lot. Then he would offer to assist the local police. It was always *assist*.

At two minutes before the hour, Ngy's assistant tapped on his door and almost reverently announced the arrival of Hatcher.

316

Ngy walked over very close to the police sergeant. 'He is an American Army officer, not the president of the United States,' he hissed under his breath.

'Y-y-yes, sir,' the sergeant stammered, surprised at the major's subdued but vehement outburst.

'Show him in,' Ngy said, marching back to his desk.

Hatcher approached the meeting with the same anxieties as Ngy. He didn't want to stir up anything. He wanted the Americans to stay off the case, but he wanted copies of the police reports and a sense of their progress. He wasn't sure just how to pull that off without raising Ngy's suspicions. But he was sure that he would not mention Wol Pot, Cody, Thai Horse or any other aspect of the case.

Hatcher was surprised at how big the office was. This was, after all, the office of a homicide cop, not the prime minister. It was a high room, hollow-sounding, with spotless tiled floors, its sparse furniture polished and free of dust and blemishes. Papers fluttered listlessly on desks, stirred by the ceiling fan. The sounds of traffic and bells ringing and people moving were a murmur from behind closed shutters.

The major was short and trim, neatly dressed in a khaki business suit, a pale blue shirt and a yellow tie. His mustache and hair were trimmed with infinite care, his nails were manicured, his black boots buffed to a blinding shine. His face was a mask, revealing neither pleasure nor pain, surprise nor ennui, friendliness nor antagonism.

Murder at a poker table, thought Hatcher.

Hatcher knew all about him. He had worked his way up through the ranks, attended the American FBI training academy, spent six months working with police in New York City, had once been part of a team that had tracked heroin movements from the Golden Triangle into Malaysia, a team comprised mostly of U.S. Drug Enforcement agents. His arrest record was the envy of most department heads.

Ngy was a precise man, it wasn't hard to tell. Everything about him was precise. The way he was dressed. His office. His desk! Everything on it was arranged in perfect geometric patterns, letters, pens, blotters, phone, all in tight little squares.

Precise, precise, precise. A man with a big ego and one easily bruised. Hatcher would have to be very careful dealing with this cop whose underlings, behind his back, called him the Mongoose.

'Major,' Hatcher said in his most sincere tone, 'I'm Hatcher. Can't tell you how much I appreciate your time.'

317

Ngy's smile struggled not to be a sneer. 'It is my pleasure, Colonel,' he said earnestly. 'I am embarrassed that such a thing could happen here. I had hoped Bangkok was more civilized.'

Uh-oh, thought Hatcher, he's having trouble with it.

'These things happen,' Hatcher said. 'Do you think robbery was the motive?'

Aha, fishing, thought Ngy. He's being subtle. Well, it won't hurt to give him a little bit.

'No,' Ngy answered. 'Nothing was taken. It appears he stepped into a fight and was killed for his trouble. There are witnesses who saw the whole thing.'

This is a smart cop, thought Hatcher. If there are witnesses he's picked them clean, no need for me to appear interested. That'll throw him off a little. Hatcher decided to give him a little something in return.

'That sounds just like Windy – that was his nickname, Windy – anyway, he was that kind, always ready to help someone in trouble.'

Ngy nodded, still smiling. 'I see,' he said. He seems to be leading me down this dead end, thought the Thai policeman, a chance killing. Didn't he know that Ngy knew that Porter was an intelligence officer? Intelligence officers were not likely to be killed by chance.

'Ironic, isn't it,' Hatcher went on, 'an intelligence officer getting killed like that. He . . . deserved . . . I don't know, a more . . . exotic death.'

Clever! thought Ngy. That clears the air about Porter's job. He poses the problem and then answers it. *What is the game here?*

'Well, we haven't ruled out other considerations yet,' Ngy said. 'It's just that from all the surface evidence it appears he was just an unfortunate good Samaritan.'

Is he here because he knows something we don't know? thought Ngy. Perhaps Porter was on some questionable intelligence job and Hatcher is here to find out how much we know. Ngy decided to drop his hook a little deeper. 'Was he . . . uh, involved in anything that might have a bearing on the case?' Ngy asked.

Hatcher shook his head. Good, thought Hatcher, he doesn't know a thing. He's really fishing now.

'No, actually his job was pretty much confined to embassy security. He wasn't a working field agent. Windy was close to retirement. This was considered a kind of easy job to go out on.'

318

Ngy thought, *Do I trust him*? If what he says is true, then the Porter case could very *likely* be a chance encounter that ended in death. It would make the lack of arrests somewhat more palatable to his superiors.

'Well, rest assured we are doing everything in our power to find the killers. We have adequate descriptions of both of them, and the man in the other boat.'

'Other boat?'

Well, obviously he hasn't spent a lot of time on this matter, thought Ngy. Even the papers had reported that there was a man in the other boat. I'll give him some more free information. See how he reacts.

'The one who seemed to be the intended victim,' Ngy said. 'He jumped in the river when this all started. It could very well be some kind of grudge fight between street gangs and your Major Porter stumbled on to it. There was also a prostitute involved – but there was no implication that the major even knew her. I assure you we don't suspect any connection between them.'

'Thank God for that. This has been rough enough on his wife.'

Ngy thought, perhaps he can help with the note. He reached into the folder and took out a five-by-seven sheet of lined three-ring notebook paper. It was stiff and faded and the blue ink was smeared.

'We found this,' Ngy offered. 'But even our handwriting experts cannot decipher what was written on it.'

Hatcher looked closely at the paper, turned it over and looked at the back. It was the page from Porter's diary on the day he died. He dropped it back on Ngy's desk, not wanting to seem too eager.

'Probably his grocery list,' Hatcher said with a chuckle.

'Probably,' Ngy said with an equally forced smile.

'Perhaps I could show this to some of his associates. I may be able to turn something up that will help you.'

Ngy was immediately suspicious again. But he decided his fears were unfounded. This Hatcher appeared to have no interest in the case other than to officially report he had looked into it. Thus far he had made no attempt to interfere. Ngy decided a concession or two would be all right.

'I see no problem there,' Ngy said with a smile.

Okay, thought Hatcher, now comes the breakthrough. 'Good,' he said. 'Well, I know you're busy. I'm here really to see that the remains get back safely. Let the family know that the police are working on it. You know how it is, they're on the other side of the world. . . .'

Ngy nodded vigorously. Why not put him at ease, he thought, get rid of him once and for all.

'Perhaps,' said Ngy, 'it might help if you took a copy of the investigation report back to the family. Let them know that we're doing everything possible.'

Hatcher could hardly contain his joy. Point, game, match, set.

'Excellent idea, Major. I'm sure it will help.'

Harmless, thought Ngy after Hatcher had left. Apparently the Americans trusted Ngy's handling of the case.

Sy and Hatcher returned to the hotel, where Hatcher rented a dark blue two door Chevy sedan. Then he went up to his room, ordered a bottle of Jack Daniel's and a pot of Thai tea. He turned up the air conditioning, turned on the ceiling fan, peeled off his shirt, poured himself a cup of tea and laced it with whiskey, and sat down on the rattan sofa with all the files spread out on a coffee table.

The report was short and simple and told him very little. Witnesses reported that a man had made an arrangement with a prostitute named Sukhaii who worked on the Phadung Klong near New Road market. While they were in the cabin of her boat, a *hang-yao* approached and two men got out and started to board the boat adjoining Sukhaii's. The American, Windy Porter, apparently went to the aid of the prostitute and was stabbed by one of these men. He fell overboard and his body was retrieved quickly by several boat people. The man with Sukhaii jumped overboard and escaped the scene. The killers escaped in the *hang yao*, which was later recovered with its owner, who also had been stabbed to death. The autopsy showed two stab wounds, one in the lower right chest, the other straight down into his neck, by a thin blade knife that had coursed down seven inches and pierced the heart.

It could be coincidence, thought Hatcher, that the killers had used a killing thrust that had become a trademark of the Chiu Chaos.

The officers making the report assumed that the two intruders were attempting to rob the prostitute and her mark and Porter unfortunately had interceded. Descriptions were vague. One of the killers was described as 'a Chinese man with a streak down the side of his face and a bad eye.'

Police had been unsuccessful in locating the mark who had

320

jumped overboard and swum for his life. Sukhaii had given them an insignificant description of him – five six, 150 pounds, brown eyes, black hair, narrow face. No name. According to the report, the killers had said nothing to her.

Was it Wol Pot? If so, why did Porter mix it up with the two men who were obviously after the ex-Vietnam prison commander? Perhaps it was simply chivalry. More likely, Porter knew that if they lost Wol Pot they would also lose Cody. So he'd tried to help out.

Hatcher pored over every slip of paper, writing down anything that seemed significant. There were more than a dozen locations mentioned in the daily diaries, although it appeared that Porter practiced a very simple surveillance and did not ask any questions about Wol Pot or Taisung or whatever the hell his name was.

He added to his list every location that was mentioned more than once, including the American Deli. Porter had been there three times, once with a notation: 'Ate lunch while observing subject from across the street.' He also had attended several sporting events, including the horse races and boxing matches.

Hatcher also added to the list 'Tombstone' and 'The Longhorn,' the two locations mentioned to Daphne by the ex-GI at the Ts'e K'am Men Ti battle. When he was finished he had a list of fifteen or twenty locations. Then he started checking them more carefully, trying to form some kind of profile of this Wol Pot in his mind.

As soon as Hatcher was gone, Sloan left the hotel and took an air-conditioned limo to the embassy. He signed the necessary papers and made the necessary arrangements to ship Major Porter's earthly remains to San Francisco on an Army transport leaving the next day. In all, the Porter business took a couple of hours. He lunched with Harvey Kendall, a diplomat familiar with DEA and NSA operations in the area, and made small talk for an hour.

Then he took a *tuk-tuk* to Yawaraj. Driving into Chinese Town was like entering the wide end of a funnel. They went down one twisting, tortuous street to another and then to an alley suffocated by row shops and then another alley, even more claustrophobic, and from there to its dead end at the river.

The old man who ushered Sloan through the innocuous-looking door was as old and wasted as the doorman the previous night. His eyes were unfocused burned-out coals, his face was caved in and as wrinkled as a pitted prune, and he was skeletal.

321

The timbers and slats were webbed by spiders. The old place creaked and groaned with age. Below him, Sloan could see the desk and, behind it, cubicle after cubicle. Faintly, he could hear an occasional cough, and softly, far back in the room, a vague tenor voice was crooning an Irish lullaby. The old man led Sloan down the rickety wooden stairwell into the den, into smoke that swirled in wispy whirlpools under a broad ceiling fan that hung on the end of a long, slender pole, which vanished up into darkness. The sweet mown-grass odor of opium drifted up the stairway, and Sloan's mouth went dry with anticipation.

He paid for his pipe and followed the old prune-faced man to a cubicle with two narrow cots. He lay down. It was hot in the room, and he peeled off his tie and opened his shirt to the waist. He was already dizzy from the fog of opium smoke that settled like morning mist on the floor of the large room. His eyes kindled with excitement as he watched the old man roll a *goli* of thick, brown-black opium between his fingers and stuff it in the bowl of the pipe and stoke it up.

While Sloan waited, his mind drifted to Hatcher and his growing rejection of the brigade. *Damn you Hatcher, damn your soul*, Sloan thought to himself. You can't reject all the good guys we had in the brigade. God, look what's happened to them. Eddie Conlan dead in Libya. Ike Greenbaum burned to a crisp in a crack-up in Chile. Dick Mazzetti running some half-assed security outfit in Florida and drinking himself to death in a wheelchair. Jack Burbank blinded by terrorists in the Lebanon embassy explosion. Molly McGuire, one leg short, serving out his time in the Immigration Service. The *Immigration* Service, for God's sake. How many times had he saved Hatcher's ass? And mine? They had all put their asses on the line, Hatcher as well. Were any of them less heroic because they didn't wear a uniform? Who could say they weren't heroes?

The old man took a deep draw and passed the pipe to Sloan, who drew deeply on the pipe, felt the hot smoke burn down his throat and fill his lungs. He quickly forgot Hatcher and the brigade. He turned away from thoughts of the past and almost immediately he was euphoric, his mind in another time and place, his cares and worries dismissed from his mind. He closed his eyes and saw green fields drifting with the wind. He did not hear the person enter the cubicle or the squeaking of the other cot.

'Did you see Hatcher?' a voice asked.

Sloan answered without opening his eyes. 'Yes.'

322

'And?'

'He's getting closer. I told you he could find him. It's just a matter of time.'

'Has he spotted Wol Pot?'

'No.'

'Does he know who Wol Pot really is?'

'He didn't say.'

'And Thai Horse?'

Sloan was tired of talking, tired of thinking about questions and framing answers. He was at the doorway of the Land of Nod and then as he entered he said dreamily, 'Didn't mention Thai Horse. Didn't mention Wol Pot. Didn't mention bangles, baubles or beads or moonlight and roses. Nightingales in Berkeley Square. Pigeons on statues and bright yellow ribbons. Didn't mention any of it. Look, Hatcher will find Cody. He's onto something, I can tell. I know him as well as I know myself. He's the best there is.'

AN APPOINTMENT IN PARIS

Ismala Hadif, who had been code-named the Hyena by Interpol and the CIA, was possibly the most wanted terrorist in the world. CIA had positively identified him as the instigator of the bombing of airport terminals in Vienna and Rome in which a total of sixty-seven people, mostly women and children, had died, eighteen of them American kids on a summer tour, all under sixteen. He was also the prime suspect in a Berlin nightclub bombing in which thirteen had died, nine of them women, and was believed to have killed an American ambassador's wife in Tunisia during a failed attempt to assassinate the ambassador himself. His acts of terrorism and assassination had been documented for four years, and yet he moved through the free world as freely as a breath of air, a master of disguise and audacity.

Among experts in terrorism, Hyena was the most hated man on a long list. An ingenious and dedicated fanatic, Hyena was trained in Libya and lived in Tehran. He had left his home a week earlier, and intelligence sources had spotted him and followed him to Cairo, where they had lost him.

Another pursuer had not.

Hyena had been quietly tracked on a circuitous route that had ended in Paris, where he was now travelling with a forged Turkish passport, credit cards and papers identifying him as a salesman for a cigarette company in Ankara. Hyena, who was fluent in several languages, including Turkish, and shaved his beard and dyed his hair gray, adding twenty years to his appearance. Contacts had changed his eyes from dark brown to blue. Lifts in his boots added two inches to his normal height of five eight. He was staying in a large and costly chain hotel near the center of the city, a departure from his usual procedure.

His target was General Karl Shustig, the American military genius who was also an expert in security. Shustig had been chiefly responsible for some recent masterly security measures, measures that had foiled Hyena's plans on two previous occasions. But Shustig was guilty of violating his own safety rules. A man addicted to habit, he followed the same routine every day; he was picked up at the same hour, driven down the same streets to his office and returned in the same way. A car went ahead of and behind his vehicle, but this was hardly adequate security. Shustig had become complacent after four months in Paris. He had dismissed the possibility of a terrorist attack on himself.

To Hyena he was a perfect target. A personal friend of the American president and a man rumored to be the next member of the Joint Chiefs of Staff, he was also an easy hit. A bomb capable of destroying an entire city block would be planted in a sewer main on the route to Shustig's office. Hyena would activate it from two blocks away by radio control as Shustig's car went over the man-hole. The explosion would destroy most of the block and certainly atomize the general's car.

Two days before, Hyena had scouted out the sewer line, picked the location, and found among the loose bricks and slime on the sides of the narrow tunnel a perfect place to hide the bomb. Even a last-minute inspection of the sewer lines would not reveal the presence of the explosive.

Hyena was content with his preparations. He would plant the bomb tonight and do the job the following morning. A tape claiming responsibility for the assassination had already been prepared and would be delivered to radio stations ten minutes after the deed was done. He walked back through the wide tunnel with the sounds of the Paris sewer roaring in his ears. Hate motivated Hyena, murder satisfied him. If he died, his two sons would follow soon after him. The way to heaven was a river of Western blood.

324

He did not see the bearded man in the shadowy tunnels behind him. As clever and cautious as Hyena was, his tail was better than he.

Earlier in the day this same bearded man had entered the West German embassy wearing overalls, carrying an electrician's tool chest and using false credentials identifying him as an electrician. The guard had asked him to open the case and he had lifted the drawer straight up, high enough for the guard to see under it. He waved the bearded man on. Once inside, the bearded man knew every inch of the building. He had been studying its floor plans for days. He had gone straight to the utility closet on the lower floor, found a folding aluminum ladder stored there, and carried it to the storage closet adjacent to the reception room on the first floor. He stepped into the reception room and looked it over. It was a towering room with a thirty-foot ceiling. An enormous glass chandelier with hundreds of small teardrop ornaments dangling from its mirrored sockets cast a bright orb over the entire room. The room was filled with people preparing a reception that night. In the confusion the bearded man went unnoticed. He studied the room for several minutes, paying particular attention to the chandelier, then left.

Now the bearded man was watching from the restaurant on the mezzanine of the hotel when Hyena returned. He got up and walked quickly to the elevator, got off on the fourth floor, walked up one floor and waited until he heard the elevator doors open. He cracked open the door slightly, watched as Hyena went by, waited until he got out his key, then slipped through the door and walked toward Hyena.

The terrorist turned with a start, then relaxed. The man was stooped and looked about sixty. He had a gray beard and white hair. The bearded man smiled and Hyena nodded curtly before opening the door. The bearded man took three steps and chopped him viciously at the base of the skull. Hyena dropped straight to his knees. He was unconscious before they hit the floor. The bearded man grabbed the back of his collar to keep him from falling, shoved him into the room and closed the door. He threw Hyena on the bed, put on a pair of thin plastic gloves, stripped Hyena, gagged him, and tied him naked to a chair. He put a DO NOT DISTURB sign on the door, turned on the TV loud, pulled over another chair and sat down facing Hyena. There was a leather band tied around Hyena's wrist with a key attached to it. The bearded man reached into his sleeve and drew out a stiletto. He sliced the leather band and took the key.

325

He slapped Hyena's face several times. The Arab's eyes fluttered open, and when they managed to focus, Hyena looked at the bearded man with terror. He tried to talk, but the gag was so tight it was cutting the corners of his mouth. The bearded man held a finger to his lips. 'Shh,' he hissed very softly.

Then he reached out suddenly and grabbed Hyena's face in one hand. His grip was like a vise. Hyena could not move his head; the bearded man's fingers stretched almost from one ear to the other. His other hand appeared before Hyena's face holding the narrow dirk, honed to a gleaming edge. The blade was seven or eight inches long. He held the point of it just under Hyena's left eye, its point drawing a pearl of blood. Hyena's eyes fluttered. The bearded man could smell his fear.

'Where is the bomb?' the bearded man whispered in perfect Arabic. He let go of Hyena's face and held the key in front of his eyes. 'Where is the case that goes with this?'

Hyena shook his head furiously. The bearded man grabbed his face again, held it tightly.

'I ask one more time, then you will lose this eye. In the end I will find it anyway. Save yourself pain and me time.'

Hyena shook his head again.

The bearded man jammed the knife point in, twisted it, and very deftly popped out Hyena's left eye.

Hyena's scream was stifled by the gag. The bearded man held a mirror before Hyena's pain-glazed right eye and the Arab killer stared in horror at the bleeding hole in his face.

Hyena's head was throbbing. He felt sick to his stomach and the room was rocking in and out of focus. The bearded man screwed off the top of the hilt of the knife and removed a small round honing dowel. He began to sharpen the knife. The blade rang in the air like a bell as he swept it back and forth across the stone.

Is he going to cut my throat? Hyena wondered. Good God, who is he? Will I die without knowing who killed me?

The bearded man stared at him, still half smiling, and said softly, 'You will never sire another child killer.'

He shoved his knees between Hyena's knees and spread Hyena's legs with his own. He placed the knife flat against Hyena's crotch. The razor edge rested against Hyena's penis.

'The bomb?' the bearded man whispered in Hyena's ear. He twisted the knife slightly so it bit the flesh. Hyena's good eye closed with pain.

'Quickly,' the bearded man whispered. 'I am running out of

time and patience. Tell me, and I will cut your throat and you will hardly feel it and you will be dead very quickly. Otherwise, you die with humiliation. The Hyena will go to heaven as a eunuch.'

Hyena swallowed. Sweat poured down his face and chest in rivers. His eye throbbed with pain. He could feel the blade of the knife slicing into the side of his manhood. He opened his remaining eye and looked toward the bed.

The bearded man pulled back the mattress. A small black briefcase lay between mattress and springs. He took the key that had been fastened to Hyena's wrist and unlocked the case.

The bomb was impressive and formidable. Plastique and a lot of it, enough to take out the Eiffel Tower. The case contained both a radio control unit and a timer. The bearded man turned back to Hyena and smiled.

'I am a man of my word,' he said quietly. He grabbed a handful of Hyena's hair and pulled his head back. Hyena's Adam's apple bobbed like a fishing cork in his throat. The bearded man slit Hyena's throat to the jugular.

He closed the case, threw the mattress back in place, untied Hyena and let him fall in a pile on the floor. He removed the bomb carefully from the case and left the radio device in it. Then he laid the floor plans of the West German embassy on the bed, crossed to the door and looked cautiously into the hall. Empty.

He left the DO NOT DISTURB sign on the door and walked down two flights of stairs to his own room and entered it. He was already packed, and the room had been charged in advance to a blind account with a Geneva address. He had one small suitcase and the black tool chest when he left the hotel. He went straight to the airport and checked his bag, went to the men's room, opened the tool chest and took out a pair of overalls and put them on. Then he took another cab to the West German embassy.

He showed the security guard the false credentials identifying him as an electrician, opened his case and lifted the drawer out so the guard could see the tools in the compartment under it. The guard waved him on. He entered by the side door, went straight to the storage room, took the tall ladder and went quickly to the crowded reception room and set it up. A rigid-looking German approached the bearded man as he started to climb up to the towering chandelier. The bearded man held up a light bulb and pointed to the chandelier, and the German shrugged and went away.

He removed the drawer of his tool chest, reached under it, and pulled free the bomb that was attached to the underside of the drawer by small suction cups and carefully attached it to the pipe that supported the giant glass dome. He set the timer for 6:30 P.M.

Five minutes later he had replaced the ladder and was gone. He walked four blocks, hailed a cab and returned to the airport, where he retrieved his suitcase and left the tool chest in the same pay locker. He went into a stall in the men's room and opened the suitcase. There was a small battery-operated makeup mirror and a makeup kit inside, and he removed his wig and makeup, pulled off the overalls and stuffed them in a brown bag with the makeup. He put on a white shirt, blue tie and a sports jacket and closed the suitcase. When he left the stall, he dropped the bag with the makeup in it in a trash can.

The American ambassador was a tall, deeply tanned man, who, although in his sixties, was in excellent physical condition and looked forty-five. And he could be persuasive. Tonight was an extremely important reception, for his mission was to convince the representatives of several European countries that terrorism had reached epidemic proportions. In effect, it was time to declare war on terrorists, although he knew that several of the countries had been spared any terrorist attacks and were reluctant to incur the wrath of the Arab killers by making any overt moves on them.

At six-five, as he was getting ready to leave for the reception, he received an urgent phone call on his red phone. There was reason to believe that an extremely dangerous Libyan terrorist known as Hyena was in Paris, he was told. This was confidential information, but security would be critical, and extra precautions were being taken at that very moment. The phone call went on for ten minutes as a state department under secretary explained in boring detail what was going to be done.

'Listen here,' the ambassador said impatiently, 'I'm going to be late for a very important reception. Can't we discuss this first thing in the morning?'

The flustered secretary apologized and rang off.

'God, these officious little pipsqueaks in State drive me mad,' he complained to his wife. 'Now we're going to be late.'

'Let's twist its tail tonight, Geoffrey,' he told his driver as they got in the limousine. 'We're running late.'

A block later an accident delayed them another ten minutes. The ambassador glared at his watch.

'Damn,' he said to his wife, 'we're going to be almost a half hour late. Damn, damn, damn!'

Ambassadors from Finland, France and Holland were in the receiving line when the bomb exploded. There was a moment of deafening sound, of fire and light, as the crowded room was illuminated and assaulted simultaneously. The boom of the bomb was followed almost immediately by shrieks of pain and terror. The chandelier had shimmered and burst, its hundreds of glass ornaments reduced to thousands of gleaming shards. The deadly glass darts projected by the force of the explosion streaked down into the crowd below. Like chunks of diamond shrapnel they ripped into the dignitaries. Pale women in expensive gowns, their faces suddenly shredded by bits of glass and metal, staggered into one another. Ambassadors in cutaway coats were driven to their knees and assassinated by glittering arrows of death. And in the momentary silence that follows any shock and before chaos breaks out, the chandelier, weakened by the explosion, swung feebly and then its support snapped and it plunged down on top of the dead and wounded in a great splash as the rest of the glass shattered on impact.

'M-my God,' the American ambassador cried out as they turned off the main street into the drive of the embassy. Ahead of them in the garish beam of their headlights, people in their evening finery, bleeding and blind, were staggering out of the shattered reception hall into the street.

KLONG GIRL

Sy was in a small park across the street, practicing his moves. He looked good, a quick jabber with good legs. Hatcher reached in the car window, tooted the horn and the driver came immediately.

'I am looking for a girl named Sukhaii who works on the Phadung Klong near New Road,' Hatcher said.

'Is she a whore?'

'Yes,' Hatcher replied, repeating the girl's description from the police report. 'Five two, sixteen years old, ninety pounds. A real princess, they say.'

'Of course she is a real princess,' Sy said with a shrug. 'Who would go with an ugly whore?'

329

'That's very philosophical,' Hatcher said.

'It may take a little time to find her,' Sy said, 'the water babies do not stay in the same place on the klong.'

'While we're at it,' said Hatcher, 'I'm also looking for these two people.' He showed Sy the photograph of Cody and Pai taken in Vietnam fifteen years ago.

'Is this old picture?' Sy asked.

Hatcher nodded. 'Fifteen years,' he growled.

'They change a lot,' Sy said.

Hatcher nodded again. 'I'm sure of it,' he said.

'This is American and Thai girl?' Sy asked.

'No. The man was an American flier, but the girl was Vietnamese.'

'Ah,' Sy said. He stared at the picture for at least a minute and then nodded and passed it back to Hatcher.

As they drove through the crowded streets, Hatcher reflected on his plan. First, try to find the girl, since she was the only person who had actually seen both Wol Pot and Windy Porter's killers. Then he would start checking out Porter's surveillance locations to see if that produced anything. Near the top of the list was the section called Tombstone and the Longhorn Bar. The subject of Thai Horse was touchy, since it involved street gossip. Was there really a Thai Horse, and if so, was it a gang? A man? Wol Pot or Cody? Or someone new? Because Hatcher could not tie it directly to Cody, he would play that by ear.

The trip to Phadung Klong took only a few minutes; the intersection was a few blocks away, just past the sprawling produce market now almost deserted for the day and across a short arched bridge at the klong. It took Sy three stops and the better part of an hour talking to river people to get a lead on the girl.

'They say she works closer to Rama Four Road,' he said returning to the car. 'We find her, *mai pen rai.*'

They drove parallel to the klong, separated from it by thick banyan trees, flowering orchids and shacks built on stilts over the banks of the river. At Rama Four, Sy parked the car and disappeared down the bank of the klong. He was gone for another fifteen minutes.

'She has moved to Klong Mahachai,' he said when he got back. 'But it will be difficult to locate her until tonight. We should find her near the Maharaj Road crossing close to the Thieves' Market in Chinese Town.'

At dusk they drove to Maharaj Road, and Sy once again

scouted the banks of the klong. He was gone only a few minutes this time.

'We have luck,' he said proudly. 'Come.'

He led Hatcher along the edge of the klong, past several boats.

'You be careful, okay, *pheuan*?' Sy said. 'Sometime the girl boss he looks to steal your money, watch, you know? But I be behind you,' he said, pointing down the row of snakeboats and houseboats that were tied to the bank and to one another. There were many young women sitting in the bows of the boats, smiling, appraising, inviting a bid from the crowds along the canal. Hatcher followed Sy as they threaded through the crowd of gaping tourists that was already beginning to gather on the bank and past several boats until the little Thai stopped a man who was heading upstream with a fishing pole.

'Sukhaii?' Sy asked 'You know which is her boat?'

The old man smiled gleefully, nodding vigorously, and pointed over Sy's shoulder to a long boat practically at their feet.

'My trip,' Hatcher said and walked uncertainly across the first *hang yao* and past a muscular Thai, who stared at his chest as he passed but did not look at his face. He scrambled aboard the second boat as a young girl, no more than sixteen, came from under the thatched hooch at the rear. Lowering her head slightly, she stared at him over her nose. Her eyes got dusky brown. She had it down to a science.

'Sukhaii?' Hatcher asked.

'You know my name?' she said, surprised.

Hatcher nodded. '*Chai*,' he said.

'You want do some *sanuk*?' she asked in shattered English. She pulled him close and rubbed against him, still smiling. She was warm and soft to the touch and had a sprig of jasmine behind one ear. For a moment Hatcher thought about having a little *sanuk* with her. He gently took her by the arm so she wouldn't bolt and held up an American fifty-dollar bill.

'I am not here for fun,' he said in Thai.

The girl look startled and tried to pull away from him.

'Look,' he said, 'fifty dollars American. That's one thousand bahts, two purples. You want this?'

The girl stared at the fifty and Hatcher dropped her arm.

The muscular Thai in the other boat stared casually across the deck at them but said nothing.

'What for?' she asked cautiously.

'There was a man here the other night when the killing occurred in the next boat. He jumped overboard.'

331

'*Chai* . . .'

'What did he look like?'

The girl thought for a moment and held her hand up about five and half feet above the deck.

'This tall. Very brown eyes. Black hair. Thin face. About like you heavy.'

'Built like me but shorter?'

'*Chai.*'

'Any scars – uh, marks on his face or body?'

Sukhaii's eyebrows rose. 'Ah, *chai, chai* . . . *he* has dragon. Here.'

She laid her hand on her chest.

'A tattoo of a dragon?'

She nodded.

'Now, this guy, he was in a big hurry, yes?'

She nodded her head vigorously. 'He was afraid.'

'I'm sure. Now, the way I see it, he didn't have time to get dressed before he went swimming,' Hatcher whispered.

She looked at him suspiciously but did not answer.

'He probably didn't take his clothes with him –'

'*Chai, chai,* took clothes –'

'*Mai,*' Hatcher said, shaking his head. 'No time.'

'I told police –'

'I am not the police. I don't care what you told the police. And I do not tell the police anything.'

'I tell police *everything*,' she said defiantly.

'I think perhaps he may have left his pants behind –'

She shook her head frantically. '*Mai, mai*. No wallet.'

'I didn't say anything about a wallet,' Hatcher said softly.

The young girl was beginning to panic. She looked past Hatcher at the Thai on the other boat.

'Look here, I'm not from the police, I am *Amehricaan*,' Hatcher said. 'All I want are the ID papers that were in the wallet. I don't care about anything else, you can keep the money or anything else of value. I just want the papers, understand?'

Her eyes shifted behind him again. He turned. The Thai stood near the port side of the boat but did not come aboard. He was dressed in a purple *pakoma*, a kind of man's sarong-pants and a white cotton tank shirt. There was a large tattoo of an orchid with a snake entwined around it on his right forearm. He smiled briefly at Hatcher and then looked at the girl.

'What does he want?' the man asked Sukhaii in Thai.

Hatcher interjected. 'I was offering the young woman fifty

American dollars for the identification papers in a wallet left here the other night. No questions asked. I'll forget I was ever here, okay? No police. It is personal. All I want are the papers.'

The Thai came aboard and walked close to Hatcher. He was two or three inches shorter, but his body was hard and veins etched his biceps. He studied Hatcher's face for a full minute through eyes the color of mud. Behind him, Sy stepped on the other boat, waving away the water babies and vendors who squawked at him.

The tattooed man lowered his eyes and said, 'You wallet?'

Hatcher shook his head. '*Mai*.'

'You friend's wallet?'

Hatcher did not lie. He shook his head again. '*Chai*.'

'Huh,' the Thai said. He stepped past Hatcher and whispered to the young prostitute. She stared up at him for several moments and nodded. 'How much?' he asked and she whispered, 'Ten thousand bahts.'

Five hundred dollars, thought Hatcher, *and the girl was probably holding back another hundred or two. Wol Pot did okay.*

'Why did you keep it from the police?' the Thai whispered.

'I thought he might come back,' she lied, and he said, 'Then get it and I will deal with the *farang*.'

He did not say the word for foreigner with any contempt and he was perfectly at ease and relaxed, as if he and Hatcher were old friends. If his whore's swiping the wallet upset him, it didn't show. He motioned Hatcher inside the hooch, so the other river people could not see them. Nervously Sy moved closer.

Sukhaii went to a chest, took out a snakeskin wallet and gave it to the Thai, who opened it, took out a handful of purple bahts, and stuffed them in his pocket.

'I am sorry,' she said repentantly. He shrugged and said casually, '*Mai pen rai*,' motioned her to leave and then leafed through the wallet and found a small gold amulet in one of the compartments. It joined the money. He looked back at Hatcher.

'Sixty dollars American,' he said. His smile grew a little larger. Hatcher had forgotten that in Thailand the first price was never the final one.

'*Khit waa phaeng pai*,' Hatcher answered, as was expected of him. 'Fifty-five,' he countered.

The Thai's smile grew larger still and he shrugged. 'Fifty-seven, if it is what you want,' he said with a broad, broken-toothed grin and handed the wallet to Hatcher to check, and Hatcher leafed quickly through the contents.

333

'Good,' he said, handing the Thai the fifty-seven dollars. '*Khopkun. Sawat-dii.*'

'Now, one more thing,' Hatcher said to the girl, taking out a twenty-dollar bill, 'another twenty American if you will tell me what the man with the knife said to you.'

'He said nothing!' she cried out quickly.

But the Thai was eyeing the twenty. He looked at the bill and then looked out of the hooch at the river for several seconds. 'Tell him.'

'But they said –'

'*Tell him!*'

The girl was almost out of breath with fear. 'They said they would cut my face until I looked like a grandmother,' she said weakly, staring at the floor.

'Why would they do that?'

'If I told the police anything about them.'

'What else?'

'They asked if I knew an address.'

'Whose address?'

'It did not make sense. It was the horse in the myth.'

'Thai Horse?' Hatcher asked eagerly. The girl nodded. The Thai reached out slowly and plucked the twenty from Hatcher's fingers. The seventy-seven dollars joined the rest of the booty. Then the Thai reached to the back of his belt and brought out a teak billy club a foot long. He stood four or five feet in front of Hatcher and smacked the club in the palm of his hand.

'Maybe you give me rest of money or maybe you gold Rolex, hey?' the Thai said, still smiling.

Hatcher backed up a foot or so. His body began to tense up and his eyes narrowed. 'Not another *salehng*,' Hatcher whispered hoarsely.

The smile stayed, but the Thai's eyes got a little crazy. He spread his feet and stood with the club held out at his side.

'I hurt you,' the Thai pimp said.

The words were hardly out of his mouth when Sy jumped on the boat behind him. The Thai spun around and took a hard backhand swipe at Sy but it was wide, and before he could swing again, Sy kicked him twice, hard kicks, one in the chest, one on the point of his jaw. The Thai fell back against Hatcher but jabbed the stick underhand into Hatcher's stomach. Though the blow glanced off Hatcher's side, it caught him off guard, and the Thai broke loose and charged Sy. The little man hit him with three hard jabs straight from the shoulder. The Thai's head

334

bobbed, but the punches did not stop him. He kept coming. He grabbed Sy in a bear hug and lifted him off the deck. Before he could throw him overboard, Hatcher reached out and dug iron fingers into the Thai's shoulder. He dug deep, found the nerve he was seeking and ground it against the Thai's shoulder blade.

The Thai was temporarily paralyzed. His arms dropped, the club clattered on the deck and Sy twisted loose, stepped back a step and hit him in the face with a double combination: *whip, whip, whip, whip.*

The Thai staggered backward clutching a bleeding nose and fell against the side of the hooch. The small shack collapsed, and he toppled to the deck covered with bamboo strips and lay dazed for a moment. Hatcher stooped over him, picked up the billy and tossed it into the river. The Thai wiped the blood off his surprised face.

'I am boxer,' Sy said and motioned to Hatcher to follow him off the *hang yao.*

Hatcher looked down at the stricken Thai and smiled. *'Sawatdii,'* he said with a half-assed salute.

They went back up the bank of the klong with Sy strutting ahead of him, brushing aside the roving vendors and prostitutes. When they got to the car, he held the door open for Hatcher.

'You looked real good in there, *pheuan,'* Hatcher said and crawled into the sedan. He went through the papers and found the passport. According to the information on it, Wol Pot was five six, weighed 154 pounds and lived on Raiwong Road, which was in Chinese Town. But Hatcher had something even better than a description.

He was staring down at the passport photograph of Wol Pot, the Vietnamese whose real name was Taisung, the commandant of the Huie-kui prison camp.

ROGUE TIGER

He would come to be known as Old Scar. He lay in the tall grass at the edge of the pond watching the chital stag rutting in the mud fifty feet away. He had been stalking the herd for three hours, sometimes lying motionless for thirty or forty minutes at a time as they moved down through the sandy nullah and out of the ravine into the flat plain and from there through the ten-foot-high bamboo grove to the water hole.

In his day, Old Scar had been a magnificent tiger, over five hundred pounds, faster than any male within a hundred miles, indomitable, and so powerful he had once brought down a seven-hundred-pound buffalo and hauled it with his iron jaws almost a quarter of a mile to his family and then hid the carcass twenty feet above the ground in a tree. This had been some tiger.

Now he was old and crippled by rheumatism. Old battle wounds ached when he crawled. His teeth were yellow and one of his cuspids was broken off. And a huge, ragged scar etched his face from between his eyes down the side of his muzzle to his jaw, the signature of a younger, more aggressive male who would have killed any other tiger of that age and infirmity. But Old Scar had still been a little too tough for the young buck, and he had shown enough stuff to take a draw and walk away from the fight with only his wound.

Old Scar carefully placed one enormous paw in front of the other, creeping by inches toward the unsuspecting deer so as not to rustle the dry leaves under him. For all his twenty-two years he had hunted the same way, with the stealth and patience and speed he had learned watching his mother. He was moving by pure instinct now. Except that all his tricks were failing him.

The stag raised his head suddenly and sniffed the air. There was no wind, so he had not yet picked up the tiger's scent, but he was wary. The herd was spread out and knee-deep in the water. They knew better than to go any deeper, for the pond was also the home of several crocodiles. But they were vulnerable and the big five-hundred-pound buck was responsible.

Old Scar was rigid in his crouch. His once powerful legs were hugged up against his belly, ready to spring, his ears forward, his tail erect. But he had lost his touch and a leaf crackled suddenly under him; the chital spooked and ran, and the herd scattered with it. Old Scar charged after the stag as it darted this way and that, turning suddenly back toward the water. Old Scar dodged with the chital, got inside its turn and was within striking distance. But as he made his big move the stag kicked out both its rear legs. One hoof caught Old Scar in the right eye and the pupil burst like a marble exploding. The tiger roared with pain, took one futile, prideful swipe of his mighty paw and missed by a mile.

The stag and the herd were gone.

Old Scar collapsed in the water, roaring with the pain in his

336

legs and shoulders and from the eye he had just lost to a deer. He rested, panting, in the warm water for an hour and then dragged himself to the muddy banks and rolled in the soft, wet earth to heal his aching body.

The situation was getting desperate. It was his twentieth try in two days, and his twentieth miss. The day before, a careless lemur had moved within striking distance and then had outrun him, dashing up a tree to safety. There had been a time when Old Scar could have taken the tree in three bounds. But he had wearily turned in defeat and skulked away from the monkey's shrieked insults. Old Scar was very hungry.

The herd did not return, and finally he decided to move to another watering hole. He was going back into the territory of another young male, but Old Scar had no choice. He was too tired to go any farther. As he stalked carefully through the brush, a sharp scent stung his nostrils. It was an odor that stirred old longings in the tiger. The smell of a tigress in estrus. And then he heard her growling, a strange, demanding and instantly seductive call, and he heard the male answer her from nearby. Old Scar hunched down and crept forward, peering through the tall grass and saw the female approach the male, begin to nuzzle him, arouse him, and then she lay down and he straddled her. Old Scar watched, remembering his younger days when the females wanted him and flirted with him.

Old Scar moved on, picking up another scent. Chital. He could smell its fresh blood and he knew the male had been lured away from his dinner by the female. He crept forward, following the scent of the freshly killed deer until he found it, hidden deep in a bamboo thicket where even the vultures could not see it.

Old Scar lay on his empty belly and as hungry as he was he fastidiously dressed the dead animal as all tigers do. He started at the rear, licking away the blood, then ripping into the rump with his shearing teeth, pulling out the intestines with his incisors, and cleaning the bones with a tongue like sandpaper.

Old Scar could put away forty pounds of food a day. He had not eaten in three days, and he consciously kept from purring as he ate so as not to attract the male. He could hear the other two cats screaming in ecstasy and he knew it was safe to keep eating. But then he heard the other male rolling over and snorting. Still hungry, the old giant crept off through the tall grass. He knew he could not survive another fight with a young tiger. It was getting dark, so he found a hollow tree and slept the night.

Now he had been wandering aimlessly for two more days,

337

unsuccessfully seeking food, and his hunger was turning to anger. Then Old Scar found himself in a place that was vaguely familiar. He began to recognize landmarks and remembered things from his youth. This was where he had begun life, where his mother had taught him all the tricks before sending him out to find his own territory.

He patrolled the plot of land, looking for traces of other tigers, but there were none. Old Scar realized there was very little grass here. And there were houses built around one side of the lake. And where there once had been a large bamboo-fringed bay there were vegetables growing. The forest was now a hundred yards from the lake with only reeds to provide cover for him.

The tigers' two biggest enemies, progress and man, had stolen more of their domain. But Old Scar was too tired to go any farther. On the far side of the lake he could see people moving about. He crawled on his belly, sneaked into the lake and crouched there quietly, cooling himself, bathing his wounds and drinking the cool water.

It was near dusk when he saw the child: a girl, no more than three years old, a naked toddler who had wandered away from her mother's eye. She strolled along the water's edge, kicking at it, making splashes.

Old Scar watched her with his one good eye. She looked like a monkey, perhaps more meat. She didn't appear as fast and she had no tail. He pulled his legs up under him, got ready. His ears leaned forward, his lips crept back away from his teeth.

The little girl danced straight to him. When she was perhaps five feet away, she saw the giant, hunched in water up to his shoulders, his yellow eyes afire, his broken teeth twinkling. Before she could scream, the tiger lunged. One giant leap and Old Scar had her in his jaws. As he would have done with any animal, he bent her head back like a deer's, bit hard into the throat and suffocated her. Then he turned and sneaked back to the safety of the jungle with his kill. He settled down and started to lick off the blood.

He had tasted better meat and his eye had festered and he was feverish and agitated, but the kill was easy and the food was nourishing. The next day he sneaked back down to the lake. This time he crept closer to the village, close enough to see another child playing in the dirt at the edge of the village.

In the next week Old Scar killed two more children, a crippled old monk and a full-grown woman who was doing her wash in the lake.

338

That was when Max Early was called in. That was when the party started. And that was when Hatcher finally began to unravel the riddle of Murphy Cody.

DOGS

At first, Wol Pot's wallet seemed to yield very little besides his passport. There was a driver's license with an address on Rajwang Road in Chinese Town, two bet tickets from the racetrack, obviously losers, and a ticket to a boxing match, now past. According to Wol Pot's papers he was a 'produce salesman.'

There was nothing else of interest in the wallet.

Over breakfast, Hatcher spread the two photos, of Wol Pot and Pai and Cody, in front of Sy.

'I'm also looking for this guy,' Hatcher confided, tapping the picture of Wol Pot.

Sy studied the photographs for a few moments.

'I think on this girl since yesterday,' he said. 'She is most beautiful. I maybe see her but . . . I think that about all beautiful women.'

'Do you remember where?' Hatcher asked.

Sy shook his head. 'He is with this girl?' he asked, pointing to the photo of Cody.

'Maybe, maybe not. I don't know. The GI is the one I'm looking for.'

'Okay,' Sy said. 'Where do we go first?'

Hatcher took out his list of locations from Porter's day book. Unfortunately Porter's diary contained notations on locations and times but no addresses and no comments. He also had the address from Wol Pot's passport, an address in Yawaraj. He took out the sheet the Mongoose had given him, the water-streaked page from Porter's diary dated the last day of Porter's life, and spread it out on the table. That was all he had to go on, that and a note to check out a bar called the Longhorn in a place called Tombstone and another note: 'Thai Horse?' He smoothed the water-ruined sheet carefully on the table and perused it once more, but the only thing legible was part of one entry: ' . . . try, 4:15 P . . .'

'Address from passport is in Chinese Town,' Sy said. 'Rajwang Road. We start there maybe?'

'Good idea,' Hatcher said. But it wasn't. The address turned out to be phony – a non-number along the river on the edge of Chinese Town. The closest number to it was an ancient building that in disrepair seemed ominous. Its wooden walls were faded and peeling from the sun and rain, the windows were boarded over, and it seemed to sag in the middle, as though the very floors were tired. A deserted old relic squeezed between two other deserted old relics. Hatcher tried the doors of the three warehouses but they were nailed shut. Deserted buildings. Obviously nobody lived in them. Wol Pot's address was an empty pier.

What was Wol Pot doing there? Obviously Porter had been following Wol Pot and made notations of every place the man went. The first two locations on the list were restaurants in Chinese Town, but they yielded nothing. Hatcher assumed that Wol Pot had eaten there. The managers of both studied Wol Pot's photo for a long time, then shrugged. 'Maybe' was the consensus.

'What's next?' Sy asked.

'You know a place called the Stagecoach Deli.'

'Okay,' Sy said. 'Very near here.'

'We'll try it next.'

They drove through noisy, tacky Patpong with its blaring loudspeakers outside gaudy bars and dazzling neon signs, fully ablaze in midafternoon, and turned at a place called Jack's American Star and the San Francisco Bar, which advertised topless go-go dancers who performed 'special shows.'

Then suddenly they were on a street out of the past, away from the neon glare, the bellowing loudspeakers and the hawkers. It could have been a street in any Western American town and even in the daylight there was about it an unreal atmosphere. Sunbeams, like spotlights, sliced through the late afternoon mist from the nearby river, and it was eerily quiet, like a ghost town.

'Stop here!' Hatcher ordered as they turned into the street. He got out of the car, surveying the strange, winding road. A wooden marker had been tacked over the regular street sign. CLEMENTINE WAY, it read.

'This has to be the section they call Tombstone, right?' Hatcher said to Sy.

'That's good guess. I saw in the movie over at Palace one time. *The O.K. Gunfight.*'

'*Gunfight at the O.K. Corral,*' Hatcher corrected.

'That's it, Burt Reynolds.'

'Lancaster.'

'*Chai*,' Sy said, smiling his row of battered teeth.

Hatcher walked down through the mist, past the Hitching Post, which had elegant Western boots and tall cowboy hats displayed in the window. He checked the menu pasted to the window of Yosemite Sam's, and it reminded him of home: Brunswick stew, chili, spareribs and pork barbecue. The Stagecoach Deli was a few doors farther down the street. It had swinging doors and an imitation Tiffany window but offered lower East Side New York fare. A little farther on was Langtry's Music Hall. The photographs in its two-pane windows were of naked Thai and Chinese dancers, but it too conformed to the Western motif that dominated the street. The windows also featured old posters of entertainers from the gay nineties. Lillian Russell, Houdini, Lillie Langtry and Eddie Foy. It did not open until 6 P.M.

He walked down one side of the street, crossed over and came back up the other side, passing other quaint spots. An ice cream parlor called Pike's Peak, a ham-and-egg joint called the Roundup, which advertised American doughnuts in its window. A movie theater, the Palace, which according to its marquee played American double features.

And there was the Longhorn, its flat roof dwarfed by a soaring onion-domed wat directly behind it. The Longhorn's sign was shaped like a giant scroll, rolling over the entrance from one side to the other. There was an old-fashioned wooden Indian propped by the swinging doors and long wooden bus-stop benches on both sides of the door, and a balcony over the sidewalk supported by unfinished four-by-fours.

Someone had gone to a lot of trouble to make this small, isolated section authentic.

A large black man was sitting on one of the benches in front of the bar's beveled glass window, drinking a can of Japanese beer. He was leaning back against the window of the saloon with his eyes closed, letting the afternoon sun burn a hole in him. Every so often he would take a swig from the can.

Hatcher crossed back to the Stagecoach Deli and checked out the short street. There was a hint of music and conversation from behind the closed doors of Tombstone but none of the hawking and loudspeakers of Patpong, a block away.

The notations in Porter's notes said, 'Stagecoach Deli, taxi, 10 A.M., 1 hr'; the following day, 'Stagecoach Deli, noon, 45 mins'; and the day after that, 'Palace Theater, 2:30 P.M., 35 mins.' Did

341

that mean Wol Pot had come to these places in a taxi or had he been watching them *from* a taxi? He could have eaten at the Stagecoach Deli in forty-five minutes but he had spent only thirty-five minutes at the Palace Theater, hardly time to see a film.

The two places formed a perfect triangle with the Longhorn as the apex. He took out the water-scarred sheet the Mongoose had given him, and studied the partially legible entry.

' . . . try, 4:15 P . . . ' was still all he could decipher.

The entry could have referred to Langtry's Music Hall: 'Langtry, 4:15 P.M.' It fit. Was it possible that Wol Pot had been observing the Longhorn four days in a row, each day a little later than the day before? He remembered what the ex-soldier upriver had told Daphne. 'Go to the Longhorn in Tombstone, a lot of Americans living in Bangkok hang out there.'

An ironic scenario popped into Hatcher's mind. Perhaps Wol Pot had lost track of Cody. Wol Pot was looking for Cody, and Porter was following Wol Pot.

'I'm going to take a look at the Longhorn,' Hatcher told Sy.

Before Hatcher could cross the street, another man came down the sidewalk toward the bar. He was wearing tan safari shorts, a faded red tank top, and red, white and blue sneakers. A red bandanna held scruffy blond hair out of his eyes.

He had a dog on the end of a long leather leash. It was a big, ugly, dumb-looking animal, which looked like a cross between a Great Dane and a spaniel with some hound dog thrown in. He had sleepy yellow eyes, a long, slobbery muzzle and a long, skinny tail that drooped until it rose at the end. His coat was shiny deep brown except for a large white spot that looked as if someone had thrown paint on his shoulder. There was nothing symmetrical about the spot; it covered half his face and then dribbled down his chest, where it was speckled with brown spots. The dog didn't walk, it loped, and it didn't look bright enough to scratch an itch.

The black man opened one eye, saw the dog, and started to chuckle to himself. The chuckle started at his big, burly shoulders and rippled down to his portly waist. He kept his mouth shut but eventually the chuckle burst out in the form of a loud snort, followed by a stream of beer.

'Lord laughing out loud, would you look at that big, lazy, ugly, dumb-ass, sissified, silly-tailed dog over there.'

'Excuse me, you talkin' about my dog, Otis?' the man in the red, white and blue sneakers said with a scowl.

342

'I'm talking about that big, lazy, ugly, dumb-ass, sissified, silly-tailed dog right there. Would his name be Otis?'

'What do you mean, "would be"? His name *is* Otis'

'Well then, that's who I'm talkin' about.'

'You're really pissing me off, brother, I told you, that's *my* dog.'

'If you don't say anything, nobody'll know.'

'I'm proud of that fuckin' dog, man.'

'Then you're dumber than he is.'

'Maybe you'd like to gum your dinner tonight. Maybe you'd like to pick your teeth up off the floor and carry them home in your pocket.'

'Yeah, and maybe you'd like me to pull your tongue down and tie it to your dick.'

'Lord God a'mighty, you must be having a lucky day. You must think this is the luckiest fuckin' day in your lousy, worthless, fuckin' *life*.'

'I don't need luck to grind you into the street and make a big ugly spot out of you.'

'I hope you've made your peace with God. I hope you've kissed that wart-faced, fat, smelly old whore of a mother of yours Ah-dee-fuckin'-*ose*, because you're about to be nothin' but patty sausage.'

'Shit, I don't know how you lived this long, somebody hasn't parked a sixteen-wheel goddamn Mack truck in that ugly fuckin' mouth of yours, it's big enough, that's for damn sure.'

'I'll kick your ass all the way back to King Tut's court. I'll kick you right outa this *cen*tury.'

'Well then, why don't just get to it, motor mouth.'

'Kiss this sweet earth farewell, motherfucker.'

'That'll be the day, you stand-short, rubber-muscled dipshit.'

'Why don't you stop talkin' and start fightin'.'

'Well, what are you waiting for, you little dork, a goddamn band or somethin'. Goddamn *fire*works. Goddamn invitation from the fuckin'*pres*ident.'

'Listen, they friends most time,' Sy confided to Hatcher. 'I bring Amehrikaan tourist here alla time, they buddies usually.'

'*Buddies*!' Hatcher answered with surprise.

'Most time.'

The white man tied the big dog to one of the posts in front of the Longhorn and struck a classic boxing pose, holding one fist close to his face, snapping his nose with his thumb and shooting his other arm out tauntingly.

'Get serious, Potter,' the black man said with a smile. 'I'll whack you into the sidewalk, won't be nuthin showin' but the top of your miserable head.'

'Well, get at it, Corkscrew, get at it,' the man called Potter said, dancing about.

A large man with shoulders like a bison's stepped out of the Longhorn and stood with his hands on a waist the size of a ballet dancer's. He had snow-white hair and a white handlebar mustache, and he wore cowboy boots and jeans and a holster with a .357 Python jammed in it.

Hatcher watched the display with open-mouthed awe. What we got here is a time warp, he thought to himself.

The white-haired man stepped between Potter and Corkscrew and laid a gentle hand on their shoulders. 'What the hell's going on?' he asked.

'He's making fun of my dog,' Potter snapped.

The white-haired man looked at the dog and smothered a laugh of his own.

'You know what that dog's name is?' asked the black man, still struggling to keep from laughing. 'Otis. Otis, for God's sake. His name's enough to make a grown man cry.'

Potter struggled to get at him and the big man pushed him gently back.

'Just take it easy, Benny,' the white-haired man said. 'Come in, I'll buy you both a drink. You can leave Otis tied up there on the post.'

Benny looked stricken.

'Somebody'll steal him,' he said, panic in his voice.

Corkscrew broke out in gales of laughter, but the white-haired man tried to be diplomatic. 'I don't think so,' he said quietly. 'I don't think anybody'll steal your dog.'

'Not unless they're real, real hungry,' said Corkscrew through laughter that was approaching tears.

'Damn it, Corkscrew, I've had enough!' Benny roared.

'Aw hell, c'mon,' Corkscrew said, '*I'll* buy the damn drinks.'

The white-haired man herded them both into the saloon. Otis watched them go, then flopped down on the sidewalk, snorted, and fell sound asleep.

'Who's the big guy with the–' Hatcher said, twirling his fingers at the corners of his mouth.

'Mr Mustache? That is Earp,' Sy answered.

'Earp?'

Sy nodded once emphatically.

344

'Not *Wyatt* Earp?' Hatcher asked, almost sarcastically.

Sy reacted with surprise.

'You know him?' he asked.

'No, I just guessed.' Hatcher sighed.

'That very good,' Sy replied, obviously impressed.

'I think I'll just check that place out,' Hatcher said, heading across the street toward the door of the Longhorn.

'I wait here,' Sy said. He started practicing a few moves on the sidewalk.

'Suit yourself,' Hatcher said.

When he stepped inside, the time warp was complete. He waited for a few seconds, letting his eyes grow accustomed to the dark interior. Then he fixed the details of the place in his head so he wouldn't forget them. It seemed remarkably authentic, a big room with green shades over the tables and sawdust on the floor; ceiling fans lazily circulating the air, which smelled of bar drinks and hamburgers; an antique bar that stretched the width of the room, and obviously had come from America, with a beveled mirror behind it, which made the saloon seem wider; large letters engraved in the glass that spelled 'Tom Skoohanie' and under the name, 'The Galway Roost, 1877'; a beat-up old buffalo head with one eye and a black patch over the other; faded daguerreotypes and drawings of famous outlaws, lawmen and Indians on one wall, a vintage Wurlitzer jukebox in a corner, turned very low, playing an old record – Tony Bennett's 'Younger Than Springtime'; in another corner, a bulletin board covered with notes, business cards and patches from Army, Navy and Marine units; on one side of the room, raised a couple of steps above the floor, a smaller room behind a beaded curtain.

The man called Wyatt Earp sat at one end of the bar chatting with Corkscrew and Benny, who seemed to have forgotten their differences.

The bartender was a tall, elegant black man in a black T-shirt covered by a suede vest, blue jeans and cowboy boots. He wore a cowboy hat big enough to take a bath in with a red, yellow and green parrot feather stuck in its band. The only other person in the main room had long blond hair and sat hunched over the bar.

Nobody gave Hatcher a first look as he walked toward the bar, yet he felt a sudden chill, like a cold wind blowing across the back of his neck, and the hair on the back of his arms stood up. He felt uncomfortable, as if, uninvited, he was entering a

345

private club. Why had Wol Pot come to Tombstone day after day for short periods of time? Was he indeed watching the Longhorn? Was he following Cody? Thai Horse?

Was the answer to the riddle of Murph Cody somewhere in that room?

TOMBSTONE

Hatcher knew he would have to proceed with caution. If Cody was alive and in Bangkok, he obviously did not want to be recognized, so it was reasonable to assume that anyone who knew him was protecting his identity. Did someone here know about Huie-Kui, the ghost camp? Or Wol Pot, Cody, Thai Horse? He knew caution was called for – about what he said and to whom.

'What's your poison?' the bartender asked in a deep cultured voice that was almost operatic.

'*Singha*,' Hatcher answered.

'Draft, bottle or can?'

'Draft.'

The bartender filled a frosted mug with Thai beer, all the while keeping his eyes on Hatcher. 'First drink's on the house,' he said, sliding it down the bar. Hatcher held out his hand and felt the cool, wet glass slap his palm.

'*Khawp khun*,' he said.

'You're welcome.'

The black man's face was friendly but his sparkling eyes were suspicious.

'You don't look like the average tourist we get in here,' he said, casually running a rag over the highly polished bar. 'You have the look of a man who did some time in-country.'

'Military intelligence out of Cam Ranh,' Hatcher answered.

'Special Forces,' said the bartender. 'I was never sure where the hell I was. Where you from?'

The man who was slouched over the bar sat up and leaned on his arms, staring at Hatcher through faraway gray eyes; eyes that were bloodshot and drowsy. Clean-shaven with his long, blond surfer's hair tied back in a ponytail, he had on an unbuttoned khaki safari jacket with sweat stains half-mooning the armpits, no shirt, a pair of white tennis shorts and old-fashioned high-top Keds. Hatcher could not guess his age, which could have been

346

thirty-five or fifty. The man said nothing. He just stared at Hatcher for a while, then turned back to his half-empty drink and stared into it.

'I like to keep moving, never nest anywhere for too long,' was Hatcher's whispered answer.

'What brings you to Bangkok?'

'Vacation. My driver said this was the place to come. Who knows, I might bump into an old pal.'

'Who knows?' the bartender answered, noncommittally.

Hatcher patted the bar, trying to keep the conversation alive, and said, 'I'm guessing this bar didn't come from anywhere near Thailand.'

'You do know your bars,' said the bartender. He stroked the worn top affectionately. 'This one and the mirror and old John Ford up there,' he said, wiggling a thumb over his shoulder toward the one-eyed bison's head, 'came here from one of the finest saloons in the U.S.'

'Is that a fact,' said Hatcher.

'Old Skoohanie was a Texas cowboy – and one lucky Irishman. One night he wandered into a gambler's tent in Abilene – when Abilene wasn't much more than a passing thought – and runs forty bucks to six thousand. Ends up owning the tent, the tables, the bank, the whole megillah. That was the beginning of the Galway Roost.' He stopped long enough to draw himself half a glass of beer.

'Which doesn't explain how it got here,' said Hatcher.

'There was this mealymouthed little sapenpaw name of Edgar Skoohanie in my outfit in Nam who was always bragging about this bar of his,' the bartender went on. 'So I told him if he ever wanted to sell out, let me know. Sure enough, one day I get a call and the voice on the other end of the hook says, "This is Edgar Skoohanie, remember me?" Like anybody with an IQ of more than ten would forget a name like Edgar Skoohanie, right, and I says sure and he says things aren't going well for the old Roost and he's gonna change it into a disco! A fucking *disco*, for God's sake. We kicked it back and forth and I end up with the bar and the mirror and Edgar throws in old one-eyed John Ford there and next thing you know, I'm in business. Twelve thousand purple for the lot and four thousand more to get it shipped over.'

The bartender never spoke in terms of American money, he talked of bahts, one baht being about five cents American; of purples, which were five-hundred-baht notes, or browns, which were ten bahts, or greens, which were twenty, or reds, which

347

were a hundred. He paused again, this time to draw Hatcher another beer, then said, 'What else was there to do but open up the Longhorn?'

'Bet a good story goes with the bullet hole in that mirror,' said Hatcher.

'Not as interesting as the one that goes with that voice of yours,' the bartender answered.

'Talked when I should have listened,' Hatcher growled.

The barkeep responded with a barracks-room laugh. Two gold teeth gleamed from the side of his mouth. A full carat's worth of diamond twinkled from the center of one of them.

'I do like a man who can joke about his mistakes,' he said, sticking out a hand big enough to crush a basketball. 'Name's Sweets Wilkie, I own the place.'

'Hatch,' Hatcher answered.

As Wilkie and Hatcher talked, two Thai girls entered from a door at the rear. They were beautiful young girls with long black hair that cascaded down their backs almost to their waists. They were dressed in cowgirl miniskirts, cobra-skin cowboy boots and fake pinto-pony vests, their budlike breasts holding the vests at bay. Neither of them could have been more than fifteen. They hit Sweets Wilkie from both sides, giggling and wrapping their arms around him and kissing him on both cheeks.

'This is Jasmine, we call her Jazz, and this is Orchid,' Wilkie said, obviously enjoying the attention. 'We been married about a year now.'

'You and Orchid?' Hatcher asked. Wilkie looked surprised and said, 'Hell, both of 'em.'

'Both of them!'

'Been married and divorced six times since I been here and I'm yet to lay out one baht for alimony. I figure this time I'll double up – maybe I'll get a little luckier.'

His glittering grin lit up the darkened bar. He swatted the girls on their ample derrières and they moved on down the bar.

'Welcome to Tombstone,' the blond man suddenly mumbled, nodding as though he were about to fall asleep, and continuing to stare into his drink.

'Meet Johnny Prophett, the official poet laureate of Tombstone,' Wilkie said.

'My pleasure,' said Hatcher.

Prophett looked over his nose at Hatcher, smiled wanly, and held out in Hatcher's general direction a hand that was cold and lifeless.

348

'How many Americans live in Bangkok?' Hatcher asked.

Prophett stood up unsteadily, hopping two or three steps on his right foot. His eyes were beginning to water and he shrugged his shoulders and scratched his arms, and Hatcher realized, seeing him on his feet, that Prophett was rail-thin, almost emaciated. Prophett held his arms out at his sides like an evangelist on a roll. 'Four, maybe five hundred,' he said. 'In all shapes and sizes. Engineers, salesmen, tennis bums, stock racketeers, gamblers, walking wounded, cynics, miscreants, displaced persons, antisocials. You name it, we are it.'

Well, thought Hatcher, *that narrows the odds on finding Cody from five million to one to four hundred to one.*

Wilkie said casually, 'Just a bunch of relocated Yanks.'

'God's fucked up, man,' Prophett meandered. 'Supposed to be dead on the far side of the river. Bloody boatman hasn't figured out what happened. Even a poet has a hard time making any sense outa that one.'

'Right,' Wilkie agreed and Hatcher nodded, although neither of them knew what Prophett was talking about. 'Johnny's doing a book,' he said by way of explanation and winked.

'Bombay and tonic,' Hatcher said to Wilkie.

Wilkie took the glass, put in a handful of ice cubes, and filled it with soda water.

As Prophett rambled on, a man came from behind the beads, shaking his hands as though they were cramped. He was a bizarre sight, a husky man pushing six feet, walking with a little strut, his shoulders rocking back and forth. He wore jeans and a white sleeveless T-shirt. The skull imprinted on the front had a rose in its bony teeth and *Grateful Dead* printed across the back. His arms were thick and muscular and his hands, although large, had slender, almost delicate fingers. Thick black hair curled around his shoulders and tumbled down over his forehead. What was bizarre was a thin, red line that ran from his forehead down across the bridge of his nose to the point of his chin. His face was painted black on one side of the line and white on the other.

'That's Wonderboy, our resident minstrel,' Prophett said.

Wonderboy walked to the bar and held his hand out toward Sweets Wilkie.

'My luck's on vacation,' he said. 'The box, Maestro.' Wilkie handed him a four-string guitar, polished and well worn, an instrument obviously cared for with great affection. The strange-looking man walked over to the Wurlitzer, pulled the plug with a booted foot, and sat down next to it.

He closed his eyes and laid his head back against the wall and started singing: '"Hey Jude, don't let her go. . . ."'

It was a beautiful voice. Clear, deep, a touch of whiskey in its high tones, and he gave the song such a plaintive plea that one wanted to grab Jude and shake some sense into his head.

Prophett leaned over and whispered, 'Five feet from a flame-thrower when it took a mortar. Nobody really wants to see what's under that paint.'

As the afternoon wore on, the bar began to fill up. Wilkie commandeered Benny Potter to help as the bar began to stack up two deep. His eyes watering, Prophett began hunching his shoulders and absently scratching his arms. A man entered the Longhorn walking with a funny little jump step, as if he had just fallen off a two-story building and landed flat on his feet. He had the trunk and arms of a weight lifter but skinny spindles for legs. He skipped straight to Earp and whispered something to him. Earp got up and went behind the bar and through a door into the rear of the building somewhere. The man with the funny walk went up the steps and through the beads into the small alcove.

'That's Gallagher,' said Prophett. 'Gerald Gallagher from Hobart, Indiana, owns a club called Langtry's across the street. Naked girls. Not ladies, girls. Gallagher doesn't hire them if they're over twelve. In Gallagher's book, any woman over twelve is menopausal. In the United States, he'd be stoned to death in the public square.'

'How come he walks so funny?' Hatcher asked.

'His jeep hit a land mine. The floorboard almost put him in orbit,' said Prophett. 'His feet never woke up.'

'I assume you were in Nam,' Hatcher said to Prophett.

Prophett stared back into his glass. 'Hell, I was with Gallagher the day he blew up. I left a leg in that jeep.'

He held out his right leg and tapped on it with a knuckle. It made a metallic sound, *ping,* like hitting an empty water pipe.

Prophett, Hatcher said to himself, *that name is vaguely familiar.*

Earp came back into the bar and went up through the beads into the Hole in the Wall. He sat down beside the Honorable, who was watching two men play eight ball.

'That's Hatcher down there talking to Johnny,' he said.

'Ah, you followed my advice, then.'

'Sy didn't steer him here, he turned up on his own.'

'As I predicted.'

350

'Don't get smug on me. I'm not so sure it's a good idea, playing along with this guy.'

'I knew he would end up here sooner or later,' the Honorable said, proud that his intuition had paid off. Earp took a long cheroot from his vest pocket and lit it, twisting it slowly between his fingers so it would burn evenly.

'He's flashing around a picture of Wol Pot. Also Cody. And he works for Sloan.'

The Honorable made a temple of his fingers and rested his mouth against its peak.

'He told Sweets he was here on vacation, but Sy connected with him after he had breakfast with Sloan,' Earp went on. 'He's not here by accident.'

'Chance perhaps. They both are here, they both –'

'Let's be serious. He's tracking, and I say if he's here this quickly, he's too close.'

'Don't let your paranoia cloud good judgment.'

'I say he's on to something.'

'A fair call. Maybe you can find out what.'

'I say Thai Horse takes him out.'

'*Kill* him?'

'Don't you understand, this is a very dangerous man. I know him by reputation. He was a sanctioned assassin in Nam. They sent him out with a list. When he scratched off the last name, he came in and got another list. He's not some dumb gumshoe from San Francisco.'

'All the more reason to be cautious. I gave you my suggestion. Get next to him. Befriend him. Find out what he's doing here. You can't go around just recklessly knocking people off, Mr Earp. Regardless of what we call it, this is not the O.K. Corral.'

Earp glanced down at the bar. Hatcher and Prophett were chatting. The whispering man seemed to show no interest in what was going on behind the beads.

'I will also remind you that Porter was killed here.'

'So?'

'So even if you decide to do something rash, don't do it in Bangkok. Lure him out in the countryside somewhere. Two in a row would attract a lot of attention from the Americans.'

'Great idea,' Earp said flatly. 'I'll just invite him on a picnic.'

'You must be resourceful. You sound like you're panicking. You still have the advantage, Wyatt. We know more about him than he knows about us. Now you must find out why he's here.'

'I don't think you could torture that out of him.'

'You know what they say about getting more with candy than sour cream.'

'This man moves very fast. This is his kind of game.'

'If he is connected to Sloan and you kill him, they'll send somebody else.'

'Not if it's done right.'

The Honorable leaned back and smiled. 'That's all I'm suggesting, dear friend,' he said with a wave of his hand. 'Whatever you do, do it properly. As you pointed out, it is a dangerous game and he's very good at it.'

'Very good doesn't cut it. He's an expert.'

As Earp spoke a boxy man in tennis shorts and a white T-shirt got up from the poker table and approached a portly gentleman in white. He drew up a chair and sat down facing the white-haired gentleman, who put aside his book and took a sip from the wineglass as the dark-haired man leaned forward and spoke to him in whispered tones. The older man nodded sagely as the other spoke and pointed to the card game behind the glass-beaded curtain.

Earp turned on his barstool, facing the main room, took out his .357 with the special barrel and laid it casually on the corner of the bar. Hatcher watched the ritual with more than mild interest.

'That's Eddie Riker, the ice cream parlor, remember? talking to the Honorable,' Prophett rambled on to Hatcher, nodding toward the older man. 'The Honorable is the official banker of Tombstone.' His nose began to run and he sniffed, then began scratching his side. 'Kind of sets his interest on what the loan's for, a little less for eating money until payday than, say, to cover a turn of the cards at the poker game up there in the Hole in the Wall.'

'And the guy with the cannon is the Brink's man?'

Prophett laughed. '"Brink's man," that's slick. The Brink's man is Wyatt T. Earp, known to us as W.T. He kind of covers the money box, case somebody should take a notion to heist it. Him and that piece he calls his Buntline Special.'

'Looks like he can handle the job.'

'The Thai police leave us alone, they let old W.T. keep things quiet.'

'That's a helluva weapon,' said Hatcher, nodding toward the Magnum. 'You could walk to Milwaukee on the barrel.'

Prophett started to laugh again. Up above, the Honorable opened the strongbox and took out what appeared to be a loan note. He scribbled on it and slid it to Riker, who scribbled on it, and then the Honorable counted out five purples and slid them across the table. Riker nodded his thanks and went back to the game.

'Riker is have a bad day,' said Prophett.

Wilkie ambled back up the bar.

'How we doing here?' he asked.

'I'll have a beer,' Hatcher said. 'Wouldn't mind turning a few cards, either.'

Wilkie stared at him for a moment and then said, 'They're kind of funny about who plays in the game. But if you hang around long enough and they get to know you, they'll invite you.'

'Kind of a closed corporation,' Hatcher suggested.

'Kind of.' Wilkie went back down the bar and started talking to a customer.

'Was Sweets who started Tombstone,' Prophett said, and his words began to run together. 'Sweets and Wyatt. Sweets was an English professor at Tuskegee Institute, got his master's with honors from Atlanta University, what'd they do? They drafted him. A teacher, a *teacher*, man, and they dumped him in Nam and the teacher became Sergeant Wilkie and he looked around at what was happening and he never went home. Opened the Longhorn, then Eddie Riker started up Pike's Peak –'

Wilkie's eyes cut toward Prophett. He was smiling at his bar trade, but Hatcher could tell he was listening to Prophett ramble on about Tombstone and the Longhorn. Suddenly he turned and went to the end of the bar and said something to Corkscrew. The black man got up without looking down the bar and went behind the beads.

'– and Corkscrew and Potter opened Yosemite Sam's. Wonderboy opened the Stagecoach,' Prophett mumbled on, staring down at the bar. 'Max, he couldn't stand anyplace dark, closed up, he went down south to do some farming. And Kilhanney, poor fuckin' Kil – that goddamn Taisung . . .'

Hatcher, lulled by the low, rambling conversation, was suddenly jerked awake. He tried not to show his surprise when Prophett said the name. *Taisung*! Wol Pot's real name.

Before he could continue, Prophett was cut off. 'Hey!' Wilkie called from down the bar and Prophett looked up, startled. Wilkie moved quickly back up to them. 'Easy, kid,' he said, rather sternly. 'Save it for the book.'

Hatcher looked around at the Hole in the Wall. Vaguely,

behind the veil of beads, he could make out a woman among the seven players at the table.

The woman playing poker got up and left the game, standing just behind the curtains for a moment while she counted a handful of bahts, then proceeding into the main room. She was a handsome woman, big-boned and broad-shouldered, with hardly any waist at all. Her blond hair was turning white, belying her features, which placed her under forty. She was wearing a loose-fitting white cotton blouse and a skirt of turquoise Thai silk and thong sandals.

Hatcher remembered her from pictures as being smaller, more delicate, a woman dwarfed by the camera equipment and canvas bag slung over her shoulder. Saigon, toward the end. Melinda Prewett had won a Pulitzer Prize for her pictures of destruction, fear, hatred and pain. When the war ended, she had left a lucrative job with *Life* magazine and vanished. 'My camera has nothing else to say,' was her swan song.

She walked directly toward him, stuffing the fistful of bahts in her skirt pocket and stopped when she got to Johnny Prophett. She put her arm around his shoulder and whispered, 'Hi,' in his ear. His face lit up and he laid his cheek against the back of her hand.

'Howdja do?' he asked.

'Made midgets of 'em all,' she said softly in his ear. 'Time for your medicine.'

'Right,' he said, his speech beginning to get worse. 'Meet Hatch. He's on vacation from the world.'

'That's nice,' she said. She stared hard at Hatcher for several moments, then smiled and said, 'Welcome to Tombstone, Mr Hatch. Enjoy your stay.'

LEG WORK

Taisung!

The mention of the prison camp commandant by Prophett was definitely a break, but how did it fit in? Obviously Prophett had known the commandant of the Huie-kui prison camp before he had changed his name to Wol Pot. That could mean only one thing to Hatcher – Prophett had been in the camp or knew people who were.

354

Several questions troubled Hatcher. Did Prophett know where Taisung/Wol Pot was now? Did any of the other regulars know him? Did any of them know Cody? And who or what was Thai Horse and did he – or it – fit into this picture anywhere?

Hatcher took an ice-cold shower to kill the effects of the afternoon of beer drinking. He thought about Ron Pelletier. They had worked in the brigade together many times. Sloan had told him Pelletier was working immigration out of Chuang Mai, which was in the hill country 430 miles to the north of Bangkok. Pelletier had been in Thailand for two years. Perhaps he knew something, *any*thing, that would help unravel the riddle of Murphy Cody. Pelletier was an old friend and a man he could trust. He made a call to the night number of the Immigration Service and left a message for Pelletier, knowing it was a long shot.

He stretched out on the floor, naked under the ceiling fan, watching the shadows whirling above him as images galloped through his brain: the painted face of Wonderboy as he sat in the corner singing; one-legged Johnny Prophett, reeling around the bar; Gallagher hot-footing it across the room; the Honorable sitting in the corner dipping his finger in wine and turning the pages of his book while Earp with his cannon watched over everyone.

His thoughts kept going back to Prophett and he opened his *ch'uang tzu-chi*, picturing the emaciated writer as he tried to remember where he had heard that name. All he really knew about him was that he was a writer and had lost a leg in a jeep accident.

Then suddenly he sat up.

Paget!

It wasn't the *name* that was familiar, it was the *face*. But it didn't fit the name Johnny Prophett. His name was James Paget. He had seen Paget's byline and picture many times during the war.

Why had he changed his name to Prophett? And if he had changed his name, had others among the regulars changed theirs? And why? Hatcher decided to take another long shot. It was 9 P.M., 9 A.M. in Washington. Flitcraft would be in the office by now. He put in the call and went through the security drill.

'I've got some names I'd like you to check on,' he told his Washington contact. 'I don't have much else, but let's see just how good you really are. One of them is a civilian. James Paget. A journalist . . .'

355

He dictated the other names of the regulars he had committed to memory: Max Early, who had been attacked in a tunnel by bats and now lived on a farm because he couldn't stand closed-in places; Potter, who, with Corkscrew, had held off a whole company of Vietnamese but lost Corkscrew's brother while they were at it; Eddie Riker, who was the best damn slick pilot in Nam; Gerald Gallagher, who walked like a man on hot coals; and Wyatt Earp, a great-grandson of the real Wyatt Earp, who had been a full colonel in CRIP and had done four tours back to back. Bits and pieces.

'I've also got two nicknames – real long shots,' Hatcher said, giving Flitcraft Wonderboy and Corkscrew.

'I'll get back to you,' said Flitcraft, unfazed by the skimpy information Hatcher provided on these men.

Hatcher ordered a salad and coffee to the room. As he was eating, the phone rang. He snatched it up, thinking perhaps it was Flitcraft.

'Hello?'

'Hatch?'

'Yeah?'

'Pelletier . . .'

The big man sat hunched over the corner of the bar. He was well over six five, with the beefy shoulders and chest of a professional football player. His right sleeve was tucked in the pocket of his field jacket. His remaining hand was enormous and his wrist was the size of a hawser. Time and duty had ravaged and scarred his face. His gray-flecked mustache was trimmed below the corners of his mouth, and his black hair was balding at the temples and turning white around the edges. Dark brown eyes glared unflinchingly from behind slightly tinted, gold-rimmed glasses. A mean-and dangerous-looking man, he did not smile easily, nor was he prone to casual conversation. When he did have something to say, he said it in a deep, flat, clipped monotone.

Hatcher had worked with Pelletier many times and in many places through the years and knew him to be a staunch and loyal ally and a relentless enemy. Before joining the brigade, Pelletier had been a career marine and had once carried two wounded men at the same time for a mile through the South Asian jungle. Big men.

Pelletier looked up as Hatcher entered the bar, and what might have passed for a smile crossed his lips. He offered the enormous hand.

356

'Original bad penny,' he said. 'Good t'see you, mate.'

'And you,' Hatcher's ruined voice answered sincerely.

'Glad you're alive. Heard all kinds of rumors,' Pelletier said, his eyes boring in from behind the glasses.

'Like what?'

'You were dead,' said Pelletier. 'Knew that was shit.'

'What else?'

'Sloan dumped on you. Did a bad stretch in Los Boxes. He sprang you. You did a Judge Crater.'

'That's pretty accurate.' Hatcher nodded.

'That son of a bitch. 'N'you're still in bed with him?'

'Not really, I'm doing a little free lance involving an old friend.'

'Anybody I know?'

'I don't think so,' Hatcher answered, and the big man dropped the subject immediately. Years in the brigade had taught both men not to ask too much about any mission unless they were personally involved. 'You look pretty rough yourself, Ron. What happened to the arm?' Hatcher asked.

'Gangrene. Crunched it in the field, couldn't find a saw-bones.'

'Where?'

'Afgo . . . 'Bout you?' he nodded toward Hatcher's throat.

'They don't permit talking in the Boxes. I cleared my throat at the wrong time.'

'Jesus.'

'Whatever you've heard about that place, it wasn't bad enough.'

Pelletier drained his glass and held the empty up to the waitress.

'Lotta good guys went across, Hatch,' he said.

'Yeah.'

They sat silent for a few moments while the girl brought their drinks.

'Keeping busy here?' Pelletier asked, making conversation.

Hatcher shrugged. 'Been hanging out in a place called the Longhorn.'

'Sure, down in Tombstone,' Pelletier said.

'What do you think of the place?'

Pelletier shrugged. 'Good American food down there. Bunch of expatriate Americans turning a buck.'

'Know any of them?'

Pelletier shook his head. 'Ain't been down there in a couple months. Place called Yosemite Sam's has good ribs.'

'What've they got you doing?' Hatcher asked.

'Sloan got me a berth with immigration. Got six months t'go on my thirty years. Finish my time, keep my retirement.'

357

'I suppose he has his moments.'

'Suppose. Chicken-shit job, checking locals looking to emigrate.'

'What else?' Hatcher asked casually.

Pelletier hesitated long enough to swallow half his drink and wipe his mouth with the back of his hand. He stared at Hatcher for several seconds, thinking the question over, then he chuckled. 'Been keeping an eye on the hill tribes, see who's big in 999.'

'What's the word?'

'Your old pal Tollie Fong's real busy. Still on your case?'

Hatcher nodded. 'Remember Joe Lung?'

'That pig sticker.'

'He tried to dust me in Hong Kong a couple of nights ago. He won't be sticking any more pigs.'

Pelletier smiled. 'Good riddance.'

'I'm sure Fong intends to honor his *ch'u-tiao* against me.'

'Maybe too busy right now. Chiu Chaos cornered a lot of this year's crop.'

'How much?'

Pelletier shrugged. 'The DEA thinks Fong's got two, three tons of pure, stashed.'

'In Bangkok?'

Pelletier nodded, finished his drink and ordered another, then said, 'Having trouble moving it. Feds're looking for a big shipment. A *big* shipment.'

'When?'

'Any day. Concern you?'

'I'm not sure,' Hatcher answered. 'Have you heard any talk about an outfit called Thai Horse?'

Pelletier's eyebrows rose. 'Heard that one too, huh? You don't miss a trick.'

'What do you mean?'

'Street rumors. Jerry Cramer in the DEA says the word is around that a bunch called Thai Horse has been clipping Fong's couriers. That's all it is, rumors.'

'Know anything about them, any details?' Hatcher asked.

Pelletier shook his head. 'A mean bunch, what I hear. Knocked off three of Fong's couriers. As I get it, a couple months ago they were buying babies off the street here, killing 'em, stuffing 'em with skag.'

'My God!'

'They got dumped down on the Malay border. Driver got away.'

358

'They're worse than the Chiu-Chaos.'

'Suppose. Fong's done worse.' He shrugged. 'So far they only took Fong for maybe a hundred keys. Drop in the bucket.'

Hatcher's mind did some fast arithmetic.

'That's four million dollars' worth of White *before* it hits the street,' he said.

'What's two hundred twenty pounds against three tons?'

'Bad face for Fong, makes him look bad. Others might try.'

This time Pelletier's smile broadened. 'Be a shame, huh? You take that fucker out, Hatch, they'll give you downtown Chicago.'

'I'm just looking for a guy, not looking for trouble.'

'You've changed,' Pelletier said.

'Time'll do it to us all.'

'If you need any help . . . ' Pelletier said, letting the offer hang in mid-sentence.

'Thanks,' Hatcher said. 'If I get in trouble there's nobody I'd rather have back me up than you.'

'Yeah,' Pelletier said without a hint of emotion, 'same with me.'

When Hatcher left the bar an hour later, he was unaware of movement in the dark shadows of a closed shop across the street. Glittering eyes watched him hail a taxi. As it pulled away a tall Chinese man stepped from the shadows, entered a car that was waiting nearby. It followed Hatcher all the way back to the hotel.

INVITATION

The next morning, the *Bangkok Nation* told Hatcher that aside from the daily races at the Phat racetrack, Sy's boxing tournament was the only other sports event of the day.

The big story on the front page was the bombing of the West German embassy in Paris. Seven people, including the Finnish and Swedish ambassadors and their wives, had been killed. The American ambassador had arrived late and missed the explosion.

In a related story, French officials stated that the infamous terrorist known as Hyena, whose body was discovered later in the day in a hotel room, was believed to be responsible for the attack. Their conjecture was that Hyena had later been murdered in an internal dispute with one of his own people.

Hatcher threw the paper aside and studied the photograph of

359

Wol Pot for several minutes, memorizing his eyes, the shape of his face, his ears, the configuration of his nose and lips, committing them to his *ch'uang tzu-chi*, the window to his mind. He tried to imagine what Wol Pot would look like if he shaved his head or grew a beard or mustache. The keys were Wol Pot's eyes, savage and merciless, his ears, which were large and stood away from his head, and his nose, which was long and narrow, unlike that of most Indo-Chinese, whose features tended to be more blunt and heavy.

In his *ch'uang tzu-chi*, Hatcher isolated a strip from Wol Pot's forehead to the tip of his chin, concentrating on that area of Wol Pot's face.

Hatcher spent most of the morning checking out the crowded and noisy Sanam Luang produce market, showing Wol Pot's photograph to stallkeepers and boat people, hoping perhaps someone would recognize the man who had listed himself as a produce salesman on his passport. Nothing. He visited the passport office in the hope that Wol Pot would be remembered there. Certainly he must have applied for a new passport. But once again he ran into a wall of shaking heads and silence. It was highly likely that the elusive Wol Pot had purchased a fake passport, which was not that difficult to do in Bangkok.

A check of the rest of the locations in Porter's book proved uneventful. Hatcher's best lead to Wol Pot seemed to be his penchant for sports, although spotting the little Vietnamese in the crowds that attended the horse races and boxing matches seemed unlikely. The trip to the horse races yielded nothing but crowds of frenzied bettors, since the only thing Thais seemed to like better than sports was gambling.

He returned to the Longhorn in the late afternoon and gave Sy the rest of the day off to prepare for his boxing match that night, promising he would use the ringside ticket Sy had given him. The crowd would be smaller than at the track, and since the tickets in Wol Pot's wallet were for a previous boxing match it was obvious he liked the sport.

Wilkie seemed delighted to see him. Up in the Hole in the Wall, there was a great deal of activity among the regulars. The poker game had been suspended, and several of them were sitting around the table, talking excitedly. W. T. was leaning back in his chair, sighting down the barrel of a .30 caliber rifle with a gold inlaid barrel and a stock of hand-carved teak. A formidable weapon and a beautiful one.

'You're a betting man, Hatch,' Wilkie yelled as he entered the Longhorn. 'Better hop up there and get in on the fun.'

'What's going on?' Hatcher asked, entering the Tombstone inner sanctum.

'Tigers!' Prophett said with a touch of awe in his voice.

'*Tigers?*' Hatcher said with surprise.

'A tiger, to be precise,' Earp said, polishing his rifle with a chamois cloth. 'A rogue tiger running crazy down the peninsula. Killed a couple of kids and an old man. Max Early has put together a hunt.' He seemed in a more friendly mood than he had been the day before and obviously was excited by the thought of the excursion.

'Kind of sudden, isn't it?' Hatcher responded.

'This is a man-eater,' said Potter. 'He's not going to sit around waiting for us to rent tuxedos for the affair.'

'It goes down tomorrow morning whether we're there or not,' said Earp. 'And we're gonna be there. This is one bad animal.'

'Everybody kicks in two purples, killer take all,' Wonderboy said. They were like kids planning a holiday.

'Sweets will hold the wagers. He has to stay here and mind his store,' said Corkscrew.

'How about the rest of you?' Hatcher asked.

'We're declaring a holiday,' Gallagher said brightly.

'We're taking the dawn plane to Surat Thani,' said Earp. 'Leaves at five A.M. Takes an hour. Max'll pick us up, takes another hour to drive to his place. We'll be tracking the bastard by eight. With any luck we'll be back on the seven o'clock flight tomorrow night. It'll sure perk up your vacation. Interested?'

'This an official invitation?' Hatcher asked.

'Why not?' said Riker. 'The bigger the pot the better.'

'How about a weapon?' Hatcher asked.

'Max'll fix you up,' Corkscrew said with a wave of his hand.

Max Early was the only one of the regulars Hatcher had not yet met. The tiger hunt was a perfect opportunity to get closer to these men and particularly Prophett. Thus far, his only glimmer of a lead was Prophett's mention of Taisung.

'*Pai-tio*, soldier, great *sanuk*,' Corkscrew said with a grin. The Thais tended to divide everything in life into two categories: *mai-tio*, which was serious stuff, like work, and *pai-tio*, which was *sanuk* – fun.

'You'll love it, Hatch,' said Potter. 'Give you something to talk about when you get back to the World.'

'Why not, maybe I'll get lucky and pay for part of the trip,' Hatcher said.

'Great! How many've we got now?' Wonderboy asked.

'There's you, Melinda, Johnny, W.T., Corkscrew and Potter, Gallagher, Ed Riker, Hatch here, and Max, of course – that's nine,' said the Honorable, who was keeping a list.

'Are you the official referee of this operation?' Hatcher asked with a smile.

'I'm treasurer and chief logistician of this little club,' the Honorable said to Hatcher. 'I'll take one purple for the plane ticket and put your change in the ledger.'

'Fair enough,' Hatcher said, handing him the purple note.

Riker rubbed his hands together eagerly and said, 'Not a bad little pot. Five thousand bahts.'

'Give Sweets two more for the bet and you're officially in,' Earp said. 'And be at the airport by four-forty-five or you may not get a seat. This is one game you don't want to miss.'

And a strange game it was, thought Earp. We're watching him while he watches us. Grudgingly, he admitted to himself that the Honorable was right – they had to isolate Hatcher and find out what his game really was. And now Max had provided the perfect solution to the problem. For if Hatcher was as dangerous as Earp suspected, what better way for him to die than chasing a killer tiger.

A TOUGH GAME

Hatcher arrived at the small boxing arena a little after seven. It was mid-city at the rear of one of the stunning Wat Suthat. Although the main event did not start until ten, Sy was a preliminary fighter and was scheduled to fight at about eight o'clock.

This was not a big-time *Muay Thai* match but was like a tank-town fight in the United States, a testing place for young Thai fighters looking for a place on the big-time cards held four times a week at the Lumpini or Rajadamnern stadiums.

Noise, heat and confusion greeted Hatcher as he entered the small arena, which was surrounded by betting windows and Thai bookmakers. The betting was frantic. It was still daylight and it was hot, and the Thais, who gambled with great passion, were a noisy and frenetic mob, sweating and screaming and waving their bahts overhead looking for a bet.

Added to the general confusion was the music that accompanied

362

the fights, a traditional but cacophonous blend of woodwinds, banjolike stringed instruments, a semicircle of tuned gongs, and several different kinds of drums. The overall effect made a cat fight sound melodious by comparison.

Since two Thais had won the flyweight championship of the world a few years earlier, both traditional *Muay Thai* and Western boxing were featured on the card. The fans stood around a large garden at the rear of the arena, like the paddock at a racetrack, watching the boxers warm up and making their choices. The *Muay Thais* worked almost in slow motion, like ballet dancers, while the American-style fighters jogged about the grass paddock like American fighters warming up. But if the *Muays* practicing their ballet-like moves seemed somewhat dainty, nothing could have been further from the truth; they were by far the more ferocious battlers. There had been a time in the past when these Thai fighters had bound their hands with hemp on which ground glass had been sprinkled and fought until one of them collapsed. Now they wore lighweight gloves – no glass permitted – and there were five three-minute rounds. The referee could also stop the fight in the event of an injury.

It was well known in martial-arts circles that a good Thai fighter was a vicious opponent and almost unstoppable.

Sy was wearing a dark blue jacket with a green and red cobra coiled on its back, its white mouth open and threatening. He took it off and handed it to his trainer, a hard-looking box of a man with a crushed nose and thick eyelids. Beneath the jacket, Sy wore red silk boxing shorts with his name printed across the leg in blue Sanskrit. He was also wearing a cord around his head and his left bicep, traditional trappings for Thai boxers. The band around his head was tan and white with a stiff ponytail that stuck straight out in back with a strip of blue silk dangling from it. The thong tied tightly around his left bicep had his good luck amulet strung to it. His feet were bare.

Sy moved with incredible grace, his eyes almost hypnotically fixed, standing on one foot, then on the other, spinning slowly as the music played at twice the normal tempo in the background. Then suddenly as he spun around he lashed out with several ferocious kicks, slashing his arms in a series of one-two punches, then spinning around again and ending in a slow-motion pirouette.

Hatcher was impressed. He went back to the betting area, weaving his way through the yelling, gesturing crowd, keeping an eye out for Wol Pot, although he realized the odds of spotting

363

him in such a crowd were far greater than the odds against Sy winning his match. Hatcher bet a purple on his driver, the underdog in his fight, taking the long end of a five-to-two bet. If the little Thai won, Hatcher stood to gain 750 bahts, about thirty-seven dollars, which he planned to give to Sy as a bonus.

For the first few bouts, Hatcher cruised the crowd around the betting windows and bookies and checked out the screaming gallery during the fights, paying little attention to the action in the ring.

No Wol Pot.

At six-thirty, Sy was ushered into the outdoor ring. On the edge of the city, lightning streaked across the sunset sky accompanied by the distant rumble of thunder, but nobody paid any attention to the threatening storm.

The referee, as in Western boxing, introduced Sy and his opponent, a larger and huskier fighter named Ta Tan.

No biting, wrestling, judo, spitting, butting or kicking the opponent when he is down, the referee warned in Thai, explaining that there would be five three-minute rounds and the match would be stopped in the event one of the fighters was injured. There was a loud chorus of boos and catcalls at the latter announcement.

The ritual of the fight began. The music stopped and the crowd became silent. Sy lowered his head and folded his hands in the traditional *wan*, thanking his trainer and praying to Buddha, telling his God that he believed he had the 'right' spirit to win his battle. Gautama Buddha spoke of four noble truths: first, existence is suffering; second, suffering is caused by desire; third, eliminate desire and you eliminate suffering; and finally, the eight 'right' rules by which one eliminates suffering – right understanding, right thought, right speech, right bodily conduct, right livelihood, right effort, right attentiveness and right concentration. Sy repeated these to Buddha, promising to abide by the rules and live the 'right' life.

After the prayers the music began slowly, providing background for the two fighters, who circled each other in the ring, showing their moves. Sy seemed a more classic fighter than Tan, whose style was less poetic. He seemed more of a brawler, less quick than his smaller opponent.

The first round passed without incident, a dizzying exchange of kicks and punches, most of which missed their mark as the two fighters parried and studied each other's style.

In the second round, Tan moved from his corner fast and

364

struck first, jogging forward on one leg while with the other thrusting at Sy with short, stabbing kicks. Sy easily avoided the first moves, dancing away from him, spinning around and parrying Tan's kicks with his own feet. Then Tan did a change-up, switching legs quickly, parrying and leaning sideways and throwing a hard kick at Sy's groin. It connected but it was high. The little Thai grunted, doubled up and backed away, but Tan pursued him, punching now with lefts and rights, which Sy dodged by moving his head away from the blows until Tan landed a hard punch on the temple.

Sy spun around and lashed out with his right foot, slashing it into Tan's side. The larger fighter took the blow with ease, charged Sy and threw a series of lefts and rights, his gloves smacking loudly as they caught Sy on the cheeks and jaws. The crowd, sensing a kill, was on its feet, screaming for a knockout.

Tan, the brawler, although slower and more clumsy than Sy, had the advantage of size and weight. He bulled in, kicking and punching while the little Thai dodged and danced, trying to avoid the blows. He could not avoid all of them. They rained down on his head, and the kicks found their mark on stomach and thigh. Sy twisted one way and then the other while Tan seemed to have complete control of the match. The bell saved Sy from further damage.

He sat in his corner, casting an occasional glance at Hatcher and smiling. There was a trickle of blood at the corner of his nose. Sweat poured in rivers down his hard, lean body.

Sy was tougher than the crowd thought. The third round began much the same way as the second with Tan charging out, kicking and punching and then going for the change-up, switching feet and lashing out much as a Western fighter might change his lead from right to left. But Sy had psyched out his opponent's style, and he, too, did a fast change-up. Now he suddenly started showing his stuff. He ducked inside Tan's combinations and lashed out with a brutal uppercut that grazed Tan's jaw, throwing him off-balance. Sy jumped back and landed two quick kicks to the stomach, switched feet and caught Tan with two more vicious kicks. Tan staggered back, stunned by the sudden ferocity of the little fighter. Sy took immediate advantage. He came in fast on one foot, then quickly changed feet and landed a sizzling kick on the bridge of Tan's nose. Blood spurted like juice from a ripe orange. Tan backed away, shaking his head and fell into a protective pose.

Now it was Sy who became the pursuer. He feinted with two

kicks. Suddenly he switched feet again, turning the upper part of his body almost parallel to the ground, and lashed out with a brutal kick to the groin. The larger fighter roared with pain, spun around and dropped to one knee. He took a six count, then, bellowing like a bull, charged Sy from his knee.

Sy was expecting the charge. He spun around, landed a brutal kick on the side of Tan's neck, snapped three right-left combinations straight into Tan's face. The bloody nose got bloodier. Then he kicked again, this time with deadly accuracy. The blow snapped Tan's head back. He stumbled backward, obviously in trouble. One eye was beginning to swell shut. In desperation he charged the smaller fighter, wrapping his arms around him, pinning them to Sy's sides and snapping his head against Sy's forehead.

The crowd reacted with boos, their affections quickly switching to the underdog. The referee moved in quickly and separated the fighters, admonishing Tan, who jogged back away from Sy. The little man's nose was bleeding from the head blow. He shook it off, waved off the referee, and began to stalk the big man. The bell ended the round.

Sy's trainer was babbling in Sy's ear, and the small fighter was listening and nodding. Hatcher continued to scan the spectators between rounds, hoping he might get a break, although it was an odds-on bet that Wol Pot was not there. This was not, after all, a major bout.

The fourth round, Tan changed his tactics. He moved more precisely, more like a Western fighter, feeling Sy out, looking for an opening. Sy moved gracefully, dancing around his heavy-footed opponent.

Suddenly, ferociously, Tan slashed his foot out and landed a direct hit in Sy's groin. The little Thai doubled up in pain and fell against the ropes.

The crowd wasn't sure whom to scream for.

Tan stepped in like a tiger and landed three grueling punches to the face. Sy was down on one knee, shaking his head, blood spattering down his chest and mixing with the sweat. He glared up at Tan, and Hatcher saw hate in his eyes. This was the look of a killer. Sy wiped the blood from his face with a glove and shook his head when the referee leaned over and said something to him.

Now he was back on his feet, bolstered by the cheers of the crowd.

Tan charged again, using his flat-footed jogging step to get inside Sy's defense. But then the little Thai did something

366

amazing. He cartwheeled away, landed on his feet behind Tan, and as the bigger man whirled to face him, took three short jump steps, leaped in the air and snapped two kicks straight into Tan's face and landed back on both feet.

While Tan was still staggering under the blows, Sy jogged in again, feinted with a kick, and landed two right-left combinations straight to the point of Tan's jaw.

All four punches found their mark. Tan staggered backward and Sy did his change-up step again, jogging in, switching feet, leaping up and lashing out with a double kick before he landed back on both feet again.

Hatcher was on his feet, screaming with the rest of the crowd.

Bemused, hurt, dizzied by the ferocity of the attack, Tan threw a desperation roundhouse killer punch. It whistled a quarter-inch from Sy's jaw.

Sy smacked him with two fast lefts and slammed a right into the corner of Tan's jaw just under the ear. *Whap!*

Tan spun around, fell face forward into the ropes, bounced off and sat down hard, flat on his ass. He looked around the ring through glassy eyes.

The referee started counting. On six Tan was on his side. On eight he had both feet under him. On nine he shoved himself to his feet.

The referee stepped back.

Sy moved like a shot. He zigzagged across the ring while Tan tried to get him in focus. He never saw the last two blows.

The first was a kick to the top of the stomach, which doubled Tan over.

The second was a blistering right hand that had all of Sy's 120-plus pounds behind it. Tan's head snapped like a punching bag. He fell straight to the canvas, bounced on his knees and fell face forward to the never-never land of the deck.

Angels couldn't have awakened him.

Sy was leaping around the ring, holding his hands over his head, a picture of pure joy. His trainer charged into the ring, lifted him up in a bear hug and danced around the square with him.

The crowd was going crazy, throwing programs, hats, amulets and bottles into the ring.

Hatcher started to laugh as he applauded. That, he said to himself, was one helluva fight.

Hatcher waved his winning tickets over his head, yelling, as best he could, to Sy as his trainer hopped around the ring with him. 'Seven hundred and fifty bahts, pal, *seven hundred and fifty* bahts!' At that moment, Sy could not have cared less. Buddha had believed him. He had taken down the big man. And the crowd was cheering for *him*.

In his excitement, Hatcher did not notice the old Chinese watching him. The man was tall, but stooped. He had gray wispy hair and a white beard, and was wearing a silk *cheongsam*. As Hatcher left the arena the old man followed him.

Hatcher made his way back across the arena floor and went outside to one of the five pay-out windows. He felt the first cool splats of rain. Thunder and lightning were bare seconds apart. Hatcher stood in the line checking out the crowd.

He noticed the ears first. They were big and stood away from his head. Then the nose. In profile, the man's nose was long and slender, almost a hawk nose.

The man, who was two rows away and slightly behind him, was the right size. Five six, 150 pounds. His head was shaven clean, but hell, anybody can shave his head, thought Hatcher. Besides, Hatcher was really only interested in the area from the man's forehead to his upper lip. He called up his *ch'uang tzu-chi*, remembering all the details in the photograph of Wol Pot. The nose and ears matched the picture.

Now for the eyes. That would tell Hatcher for sure, those eyes would do the trick. But the chunky man was wearing sunglasses and in profile Hatcher couldn't see his eyes that well.

It began to rain a little harder. More lightning with the thunder right on top of it. The man caught him staring. Hatcher turned away, monitoring him through his peripheral vision. The man stared hard at Hatcher but did not take off the glasses.

The stooped old Chinese lingered under the rim of the arena, out of the rain, watching Hatcher.

Hatcher reached the window, and the cashier counted out his winnings. He walked back through the crowds around the window and stood near the back of the arena, watching the man with the big ears as he collected his winnings.

Hatcher stared straight at him until he was sure the man saw him, then slowly moved back into the shadows of the arena. It began to rain harder. The man was wearing black pants and a white shirt, and he huddled his shoulders against the rain and leaned forward, peering toward Hatcher.

He took off the glasses and squinted toward the shadows.

Hatcher got a clean view of the eyes. Cold, lifeless, ruthless eyes. Big ears. The aquiline nose.

368

It was Wol Pot.

A crack of lightning coursed through the sky and struck somewhere nearby, accompanied by a deluge.

Hatcher stepped back out of the shadows and started through the crowd toward Wol Pot, who wheeled and headed for the exit. Hatcher bolted, threading his way through the crowd that was lining up to bet on the next fight.

He raced after the Vietnamese traitor, so surprised at actually finding the POW commandant that he failed to notice the stooped old man who was watching him.

The rain was coming down in driving sheets that acted like a veil. In the rush of the crowd to escape the rain, the old Chinese lost sight of Hatcher; he ran into the rain, frantically searching the crowd. He rushed to the main entrance and stepped out into Thi Phatt Road. Crowds of people rushed by seeking shelter from the rain. Neon signs glowed in the early darkness. Desperately the old Chinese turned and hurried toward the alley that ran beside the arena.

Hatcher had kept Wol Pot in view, muscling through the scattering crowd as he raced after him. The chunky Vietnamese turned abruptly and darted through the side entrance of the stone wall surrounding the practice grounds and into an alley off Thi Phatt Road. He huddled against the stone wall as the storm gained in intensity and lightning streaked the darkening sky.

He heard the door open behind him and he started to run.

Hatcher was two dozen feet behind him as Wol Pot ran toward Thi Phatt Road. He decided to try a bluff.

'Hold it right there, Wol Pot,' he yelled hoarsely so he could be heard above the din of the rain. 'I don't want to have to shoot you.'

The ruse worked. Wol Pot slowed down, then stopped, moving back against the wall again, seeking the shelter of the jasmine and orchid blossoms that spilled down the wall. He slowly raised his hands shoulder-high, afraid of what might be behind him. Who was this *farang*? he wondered, but did not turn around. Wol Pot was a devout coward. If he was to be killed, he did not want to see it coming.

Hatcher walked up behind him and stuck his middle finger in Wol Pot's back.

'Bang,' he whispered in Wol Pot's ear.

The stubby man whirled, realized he had been duped and started to bolt, but Hatcher grabbed him by the throat and slammed him back against the stone wall, back among the wet

369

jasmine blossoms. Water poured down Hatcher's face, and he could feel it seeping into his shoes. Then as suddenly as it had started, the rain stopped. Heat broiled up from the hot pavement and turned to steam around them.

'I came halfway around the world to talk to you,' he whispered. 'Now you're going to answer some questions for me.' Hatcher quickly frisked him.

'I don't speak English,' Wol Pot stammered in Thai.

'We'll speak Thai,' Hatcher snapped back in Thai.

'W-w-what do you want?'

'I want Murph Cody.'

The old Chinese turned down the alley adjacent to the arena and walked through the swirling steam caused by the brief, intense rainstorm. In the red glow of the nearby neon signs the steam looked like the fires of hell. The old Chinese peered through the steam. Somewhere in front of him he heard voices. He reached under his robe and drew out a silenced .38.

'Cody!' Wol Pot stuttered in English. 'Who are you?'

'A friend of Windy Porter's, the man who was killed trying to save your hide on the klong.'

'I don't know —' Wol Pot began, but Hatcher took the passport out of his pocket and held it in front of Wol Pot's eyes.

'Don't lie to me, you miserable do-mommy, you were there, with the girl.'

Wol Pot's snake eyes squinted with fear. He began to cringe, shrinking deeper among the damp flowers. Neon lights from the nearby street cast a red glow across his face.

'Why do you want Cody?' he whined.

'You wanted to trade him to Porter for a visa, isn't that right?'

Wol Pot's eyes lit up. 'Are you from the embassy?' he asked hopefully.

'Just let me ask the questions.'

'I didn't know about Porter until I saw it in the paper. I didn't know it was him,' Wol Pot whimpered.

'I've got a deal for you,' Hatcher's shattered voice hissed. 'You give up Cody and I won't turn you over to the American military for your war crimes.'

The POW commandant shook his head, and water dribbled down his bald pate into his eyes.

'Where is Cody?' Hatcher demanded.

'I do not know.'

'Don't lie to me, you little squid, I'll—'

'I do not know, I swear to you. He has vanished. Why would you want him anyway?'

'Maybe he's a friend of mine, too.'

'He is scum!'

'You're a hell of a one to talk.'

'Cody is a heroin smuggler. He is a thief and a murderer. And worse, he is a child killer.'

'What the hell are you talking about?'

'He murders children and stuffs their bodies with China White. That is why he calls himself Thai Horse.'

'Cody is Thai Horse?'

'Yes, that is what he calls himself.'

The information shook Hatcher. He stepped back a moment, staring at the ex-prison warden.

It was the last thing Wol Pot/Taisung ever said.

Hatcher did not hear the silenced shot until it hit Wol Pot in the chest. It went *thunt* and the chunky man grunted and rose up, as if standing on his toes, then fell back against the wall. Two more shots followed in quick order. *Thunt, thunt.*

Hatcher wheeled around and fell to one knee in time to see the ancient Chinese, aswirl in the steam, aim the gun at him. He stared at Hatcher, the gun held in front of him in both hands. Hatcher jogged to the left, then shifted back sharply to the right. But the stooped old man didn't follow his moves. He raised the gun abruptly and backed slowly toward Thi Phatt Road, the neon-stained red mist swirling around his stooped figure until he vanished into the crowded road.

Wol Pot sighed pitifully and slid down the wall into a sitting position. His mouth was open and gasping for air. A red stain began to spread around the three holes in his shirt front. His eyes rolled back and his head fell to one side, and he slumped on his side.

Hatcher jammed fingertips into his throat, feeling for a pulse, looking up and down the alley at the same time. The man was dead. Steam rose around him from the hot, wet sidewalk. Thunder rumbled on the other side of town as the storm went on its way down the coast.

Hatcher decided to get out of there. He turned and followed the old man into Thi Phatt Road. Hatcher flagged a cab and went back to the hotel. *Tuk-tuks* whipped in and out of the sidewalk-to-sidewalk traffic as the taxi crept across town toward the waterfront. That was all right with Hatcher. He needed the time to sort out the last fifteen minutes.

371

Obviously the old Chinese had been following Wol Pot.

Or following him.

He thought about the old Chinese in the swirling steam of the alley, aiming the gun at him, ready to kill until something changed his mind. What happened? Who was the old man and why did he murder Wol Pot? Not that the bastard didn't deserve to be killed, or that there weren't plenty of people around eager to do the job.

But what concerned him most was Wol Pot's contention that Murph Cody and Thai Horse were one and the same, and that he was a heroin smuggler. Did he work for Tollie Fong and the Chiu Chaos? Did the Longhorn regulars know Murph Cody? The questions were still buzzing in his head when he got to the hotel.

'I've got some information for you, sir,' Flitcraft's crisp voice said.

'Let's hear it, Sergeant,' said Hatcher.

'The bad news is that I struck out on the nicknames, Wonderboy and Corkscrew. Wilkie was First Cav, a line sergeant. Got a chestful of medals. No current address since his discharge. Earp was a full colonel in CRIP. Did four tours in Nam, retired in 1976. No current address.'

'Uh-huh. How about the others?'

'That's when it gets interesting.'

'What do you mean, "interesting"?' asked Hatcher.

'Riker, Gallagher, Potter and Early are all listed as missing in action and presumed dead.'

'All *four* of them?'

'Yes, sir. They all went missing in 1972. Here's something else: the journalist, Paget? He disappeared the same day and in roughly the same place as Gallagher.'

'Anything else?'

'One more thing. Both Gallagher and Riker were in trouble when they disappeared.'

'What kind of trouble?'

'Riker for striking a fellow officer and Gallagher for grand theft. He ran a service club in S-town and was skimming off booze and cigarettes, then selling them on the black market.'

'Flitcraft, you ought to get a medal.'

'Thank you, sir. I'm still checking on Wonderboy and Corkscrew.'

'Forget it. This is all I need.'

372

'I might still turn up something on them.'

'Don't need it,' whispered Hatcher.

'Thank you, sir.'

Hatcher lay back down on the floor with his hands folded over his chest. His heart was racing. Suddenly the pieces of the jigsaw were beginning to fall in place. A picture was beginning to form in Hatcher's head, but two major questions still plagued him.

How exactly did Murph Cody and Thai Horse fit into the puzzle?

And he still wasn't sure whether Cody was dead or alive.

Perhaps the answer to those two questions lay at the end of the plane ride to Surat Thani.

FONG

Daphne Chien lived in one of the high-rise apartments at the foot of Victoria Peak, its split-level, two-story living room looking across the harbor toward Kowloon. Its balcony was a jungle, dripping with plants and ferns.

She usually worked late in her office two blocks away on the top floor of one of the glass banking towers, leaving for home at about 7 P.M. On this day she was even later. The sun had already dropped behind the western mountains and the streetlights were burning when she took the elevator to the street, where her limousine was waiting. She was dressed as she usually dressed for work, in a man's gray silk double-breasted suit, a dark blue shirt open at the collar with a red scarf tied around her throat.

As she got in the limo she was watched from a Ford car half a block away. It was equipped with a cellular phone. Before the limo left the curb, the man watching Daphne dialed her home phone number.

The phone in her apartment rang twice and stopped, one ring before the answering machine intercepted it. A moment later it rang again, this time only once.

Tollie Fong stood in the shadows of the apartment. He smiled. She was on her way. He went back up to the bedroom and checked it out. There were four long strips of silk tied to each corner of the bed. He drew a stiletto from his sleeve and placed it on the dresser next to a pair of pantyhose. He put the tape recorder on the nightstand beside the bed.

373

Then Tollie Fong went back down and stood behind the front door of the apartment and waited.

When Daphne came in, Fong moved so fast she was still reaching for the light switch when his powerful hands wrapped around her neck and his fingers pressed deep, felt the nerve, felt her stiffen and then go limp. He caught her before she hit the floor, lifted her, and carried her up the stairs to the bedroom. He laid her on the bed spread-eagled and tied her feet and hands with the silk cords. He turned on the tape recorder and picked up the stiletto and waited for her to regain consciousness.

THE HUNTERS

Old Scar was napping in a bog at the foot of a tall banyan tree when he heard the trucks coming. Earlier he heard the elephants, grunting and snorting and blowing dirt on themselves, but he ignored them. But then when the vans came and there was the sound of many voices, he sat up suddenly, grimacing and opening the ducts in his cheeks, lifting his nose and smelling the wind, but it came from behind him and he couldn't get a whiff of the group that was perhaps two hundred yards away.

Old Scar knew he was up against dangerous enemies. No young buck tiger, this. This was a whole army. His yellow-green eyes flashed ferociously and his lips pulled back from his teeth in a fanged snarl as he strolled slowly and arrogantly through the trees, away from the vans and people and toward the stand of bamboo and tall grass west of the lake, a mile or so away, where his fiery orange and black stripes would blend in with the tall, dry grass.

He wasn't in a hurry. His shoulders and legs hurt. The arthritis was worse than usual this morning and he was hungry. And he was too old and tough to be scared of anything.

Fresh pugs led toward the lake. The Thai guide, Quat, had found them an hour or so earlier. He laid his hand in one of the paw marks. The perimeters of the print were a good inch or two greater than the hand.

'Cat's on the prowl,' Early told the hunters. 'I sent a man on down to the village. The townsfolk will stay inside until this is over.'

'What do you think?' Earp asked.

'Wind's shifting,' Early said, sniffing at the air like an animal. 'If he gets downwind of us he could make a real chase out of this.'

Max Early stared from under the sagging brim of a khaki safari hat. He was a little under six feet tall with thick brown hair and a full beard. His khaki tank top clung tightly to a hard, muscular body, and he had thick, hard legs that strained his tennis shorts. His body was tanned and his beard bleached out by the relentless tropical sun.

He squatted down and, with a stick, sketched out a crude map in the dirt. The group gathered around, drinking beer and smoking and staring over his shoulder at the scribblings in the sand. He explained the area to the hunters.

At the top of the map was their encampment, and at the bottom left, south and east of the camp, was the lake and the village. Between the camp and the lake were two miles of jungle, which stretched east and west for about a mile. Toward the bottom of the map and west of the lake was a broad plain perhaps half a mile square. It was the danger spot, Early explained. At its edge was a bamboo thicket about fifty to seventy-five yards wide that twisted from the lake to the fields. The bamboo was fifteen to twenty feet high and very dense. Between it and the jungle there was a stretch of short buffalo grass followed by two hundred yards of tall elephant grass, which Early said was eight to ten feet high. The short buffalo grass and the elephant grass and bamboo were all handy hiding places for the big cat. Beyond the village and west of the thickets were cultivated fields.

'We're looking at roughly four square miles of brush and tree bays,' Early said. 'Just remember, he can climb a tree, burrow into a stump, lie absolutely motionless for hours in the tall grass –'

'Is he likely to attack a man?' interrupted a nervous Wonderboy.

'He's already eaten three – size isn't going to stop him.'

'How big we talking about here?' Gallagher asked.

'Upwards of five hundred pounds from the look of him and his pug size,' Early answered. 'Also he's blind in his right eye and maybe a little arthritic, which means he's got a nasty temper in addition to being pissed off and on the run.'

'Great,' groaned Riker, peeling off his shirt. He was powerfully built, a hairy man with several scars streaking his belly and lower ribs. He slipped on a pair of Ray-Ban sunglasses.

'Just what the hell does all that add up to?' he asked.

'Five hundred pounds of bad cat,' said Earp with a big grin. 'He gets a leg up on you, Riker, this picnic could turn into a funeral.'

As Early had explained the plan of attack, two of the hunters would ride each of the three elephants. They would be spaced about a hundred yards apart. What Early called his 'noise boys' would walk between the *chaangs*, yelling, beating on pans, shaking up the old cat and keeping him on the run. Hopefully Old Scar would run toward the hunters on the ground who were to shoot only if they had a clear target with nobody in the field of fire. The elephant riders would shoot only in an emergency.

'When you get to the south perimeter, spread out about three hundred yards apart but close enough to keep each other in sight,' Early had advised them. 'When we start the drive south toward the village, move toward us. Get on the inside of the bamboo but stay in the short buffalo grass. Don't get in that *chaang* grass, you get lost in those thickets, you're lunch for the cat. Or one of us could accidentally pop you off. When you get a shot, go for his body. He'll be moving, so go for the mass.'

'Won't the elephants run the cat off?' Riker had asked.

'Elephants don't scare tigers,' said Early. 'In the wild, they tolerate each other. But I saw a cat jump a twelve-foot bull elephant once and tear off half his ear.'

'Does anything scare a tiger?' asked Corkscrew.

Early thought for a moment, then said, quite seriously, 'Not that I can think of. This guy's old. He appears to be blind in one eye and he's hungry and he's slowed down some, that's why he's turned man-eater. But he's smart, don't kid yourself, and spookier than a pregnant cobra.'

'In other words, unpredictable.'

'Totally.'

They had drawn cards to see who would ride elephants and who would be the shooters on the ground. Melinda and Johnny Prophett were on one beast with a driver, W. T. and Early shared a second, and Gallagher and Riker rode the third. Potter, Wonderboy, Corkscrew and Hatch would be on foot.

As they piled in the van, Earp tossed Hatcher a half-smile.

'Good luck, soldier,' he said.

'Same to you.'

The old van rattled across the lush and fertile South Thailand landscape. Breathtaking green fields bloomed on both sides of the road and fruit trees speckled the uneven countryside. There was a sense of endeavor and hard work about the area, probably because of the powerful beasts that worked the land. Domestic elephants were almost as prevalent as water buffalo. There was also a lot of places for the tiger to hide.

Hatcher checked the 375 H&H Early had loaned him, saying, 'Kicks like a mule, but it'll drop an elephant straight on his ass from two hundred yards.'

They drove the two miles across non-roads. In the midmorning sun, the village lay deserted. The doors of the hooches and thatched huts were closed. Wonderboy huddled up against the side of the van, clutching his rifle as though he were afraid it was going to fly away. Sweat streaked the strange black and white paint on his face. Hatcher could see the twisted burn-scarred skin beneath the makeup. He could almost smell Wonderboy's fear.

'Don't worry, kid,' Hatcher said. 'I'll keep an eye on you.'

'I'm okay,' the musician mumbled.

The four men spread out along the back end of the broad grassy area west of the lake but close enough to keep one another in view. Corkscrew and Potter were at one end of the stretch, Wonderboy and Hatcher at the other. They were in the open and the sun blazed down on them. Hatcher broke out in a sweat when he got out of the van.

Ahead of Hatcher was the thick wide stand of fifteen-foot-high bamboo. Through the cramped stalks, Hatcher could barely make out the short grass that stood waist-high on the other side of the bamboo stand.

The only sound was the buzzing of flies and insects. Not a bird twittered and the wind was barely more than a sigh, occasionally stirring the grass. Hatcher put on his sunglasses and walked cautiously along the edge of the bamboo, stopping every few feet to listen and look.

He was not far into the field when he heard the noise boys start their serenade. It was far away. Occasionally one of the elephants would add its voice to the chorus.

Hatcher looked to his left at Wonderboy, a small figure moving cautiously parallel to the bamboo thicket. The noise got louder as he approached the bamboo stand. He looked back at Wonderboy. The kid was standing in front of the towering stalks of bamboo, looking up at them in obvious wonderment.

Not paying attention, thought Hatcher, and subconsciously he began to walk toward Wonderboy.

Old Scar was hungry, but he followed his usual course, ambling down through the trees to the elephant grass. He was at the far end of the stand when he caught the scent of the men. They were between him and the lake. He lurked in the tall, reedlike grass. Then the clamor behind him got louder. Through the earth he could feel the heavy-footed elephants getting closer.

If he left the grass he would be in the open, which meant running through the rice fields.

Old Scar's tail switched angrily. He hissed, turned and skulked through the grass toward the lake, keeping his belly close to the ground so he wouldn't give away his position. He found a dead tree and crawled behind it, peering out with his good eye through the naked branches, waiting. This was his territory. He had walked it out and sprayed it. He had nowhere else to go.

Wonderboy stood at the edge of the tall bamboo, marveling at how high and straight they grew. His heart was pounding so hard he could hear it thumping in his ears. He remembered Max telling them to be extra careful in the bamboo thickets and the tall grass. The bamboo grew close together, so he could barely see between the stalks. Fearfully he entered the thicket, shouldering his way through it. He started singing to himself. Then he began singing aloud, but very low, scat-singing the chorus from 'Suite: Judy Blue Eyes': *'Da da da da do . . . dat dat de da da do . . .'*

The singing calmed his nerves. He decided to go through the bamboo to the edge of the short grass and wait. He could see only a few feet in front of him. Wonderboy had thought he was finished with taking risks, yet here he was, testing himself, stalking an angry, half-blind, man-eating five-hundred-pound cat that could jump out of nowhere at any moment. The sporting aspect of the hunt suddenly seemed stupid to him. It would be so much easier, he thought, to spot the tiger from the elephants and kill it.

Hatcher, too, moved cautiously through the bamboo. The noise boys and elephants were much closer now. It was pure cacophony. If the old cat was in there, he would soon make his move.

Hatcher was thinking about Wonderboy, wondering whether the kid was thinking smart. Scared as he was, he might just

378

stumble in the grass. Grass could be deceiving. The kid could walk right up and step on the cat's tail before he saw him. Hatcher broke through the bamboo stand to the short buffalo grass. Fifty yards on the other side was the tall grass, moving slightly with the light breeze.

Hatcher walked along the edge of the bamboo thicket toward Wonderboy with the waist-high grass swishing past him and insects swarming in his wake. He walked, stopped and listened, then went on.

He began to tense up. The noise boys and elephants were nearing the far side of the tall grass.

Through the twigs of the dead tree, Old Scar could see one of the elephants looming above the tall reeds and hear the thrashers beating on the pots and yelling although he could not see them. The old tiger was thirsty. He was hungry. He had lost his patience.

One of the big elephants started into the tall grass. Old Scar's keen ears heard sounds other than the beating of pots and yelling. He moved away from the tree stump, crawling on his belly, soundlessly moving through the grass toward the lake.

From atop his elephant, Max Early scanned the sea of tall elephant grass, a wide strip three hundred yards deep that stretched almost half a mile from the lake to the cassava fields. Beyond it was the strip of short grass and the tall bamboo. Below him on the ground, Quat was checking the ground, looking for the pugs of the rogue cat. He found the tracks leading into the grass and pointed toward the lake.

'*Anta rai*,' Quat said softy. '*Seua, thaleh saap.*'

'He says it's heading toward the lake and that's dangerous,' said Early. 'I was hoping he'd break out of this grass into the open and run for it.'

Early blew a single sharp blast on a chrome whistle. It pierced the air, a sound higher than the clatter the noise boys were making. Everything stopped.

The elephants, spaced about a hundred yards apart, stopped and began pulling up tufts of grass with their trunks and eating them. Nobody moved. There wasn't a sound. Then Early thought he heard something. He leaned forward, his sharp ears listening.

'What the hell's that?' he said, half aloud.

'You see something?' Earp asked.

379

'I *hear* something. Listen.'

They listened. Earp cocked his head to one side.

'Is that somebody *singing*?' Early asked.

'Singing?'

'I swear to God I hear somebody singing. Sounds like it's coming from over there in the bamboo.'

'Got to be Wonderboy,' said Earp.

'Is he nuts?'

'He's scared. Yell over there and tell him to shut up.'

'Uh-uh. If the kid answers, he'll pinpoint himself.'

'The tiger isn't after him.'

'We don't know what that tiger's thinking.'

'Something wrong?' Riker called out.

Early held his hand up and put his fingers to his lips. He pointed to Riker and then swept his hand across the elephant grass and the low reeds toward the wide strip of bamboo. He urged his own beast straight ahead, peering through his glasses in the general direction of the sound he had heard.

'Get ready,' he said softly to Earp.'We may have a situation on our hands.'

Hatcher was moving quickly down the edge of the bamboo strip toward Wonderboy when he heard the whistle. The noise men stopped beating their pans. He stopped and waited for a moment. It got deathly still.

Then he, too, heard the singing. Wonderboy was closer than he thought. And he was somewhere in the bamboo thicket, a dangerous place to be. Hatcher doubled his pace, moving down the outer edge of the bamboo thicket until he could hear Wonderboy's soft song somewhere nearby. He entered the thicket, moving as quietly as he could toward the voice. The tall stalks of stiff bamboo clattered as he made his way through them toward Wonderboy.

Old Scar, too, was startled by the whistle. Then the noice stopped and the silence confused him. He stopped and listened, heard the elephants pulling up grass.

He heard the sound in front of him: '*Do do do do da . . . dat dat do da da do . . .*'

And he heard someone coming through the grass behind him. He waited, his muscles tightening. The elephants started moving again; he increased his pace.

Old Scar was spooked. He decided to go through the bamboo

to the open field beyond and make a dash for it. His instincts told him to move as quietly as possible until he was in the open. There was activity all around now. Enemies were closing in on him.

He crept forward again, out of the tall elephant grass into the short stuff. Now he really hugged the ground, moving one paw in front of the other, stealthily, cautiously, slowly crawling toward the bamboo, moving away from whoever was coming up in the rear, moving away from the elephants, his good eye jumping nervously, checking the route as he crept toward the strange sound.

Early stopped his elephant again and scanned the grass with his binoculars. He stopped, freezing the glasses on one spot.

'Something?' Earp whispered.

'Not sure . . .'

Early watched the tall grass swaying in the wind. Then he saw one short stretch moving against the wind, almost imperceptibly, like a ripple in the ocean. The movement stopped. Then it moved again. Another four or five feet and stopped again.

'Jesus,' Early breathed, 'there it is.'

'Where?' Earp asked.

'There, moving toward the bamboo in the short grass. Once it gets near the bamboo, if it sees anything it'll probably charge.'

Early handed the binoculars to Earp and directed the elephant toward the movement. The big animal lumbered forward as Earp peered nervously through the glasses.

'I don't see it,' Earp said.

'Right in front of us, about a hundred yards. Watch the buffalo grass,' Earp said.

Then Earp saw the ripple, the slight movement through the short reedlike grass, then it stopped again.

'Jesus, you're right,' Earp said.

'Where the *hell* is Wonderboy?' Early asked.

The elephant moved quickly toward the thicket.

'Can't we start the racket again, scare it off?' asked Earp.

'No, none of that,' Early snapped. 'That cat's crazy. That cat's a Mexican jumping bean. We shake him up now, he might just charge out of pure cussedness.'

Early's voice was clear and clean: 'Wonderboy, stop singing. Back out of that bamboo strip real slow. Don't answer me, just do it. Now!'

'Shit,' Hatcher said, hearing Early's caution. But he didn't stop. He didn't have time to stop. He kept moving ahead.

381

Old Scar, too, heard the man yell and stopped. Then he saw movement a few yards away. His lips peeled back from his fangs and his nostrils sniffed the air. The noise stopped. He kept moving forward.

Through his good eye he saw movement in the bamboo. It was moving away from him and he followed it. Behind him the elephants were picking up their pace. The ground trembled as they stomped through the tall grass. Old Scar moved faster, creeping toward the tall, hard shafts and the open fields on the other side.

Then he saw the two-legged creature, a strange-looking animal with a face that was half black and half white. It was frightened. Old Scar could smell his fear. The creature was backing into the bamboo that stood between Old Scar and freedom. He was carying a stick. The tiger's claws extended, the muscles in his shoulders rippled as he got ready to charge.

He crept out of the grass and into the bamboo.

'Christ, the cat's in the bamboo,' Early said, still watching the movement through the binoculars.

'Where the *hell* is Wonderboy?' Earp said.

'He's in there, too, I can see the stuff moving. The cat's on to him.'

'Oh, Jesus,' Earp said.

'What the fuck,' Early said, refocusing the glasses. 'Is Hatch in there too?'

'Who the hells knows?'

Riker and Gallagher were veering toward them, and so was the elephant Melinda and Prophett were riding closing in on the bamboo thicket.

Hatcher started to run toward Wonderboy, who had stopped singing. He plunged through the bamboo, which clattered after him as he charged through it, breaking off stalks, stumbling, keeping his rifle pointed up so he wouldn't accidentally get off a shot and hit Wonderboy.

Old Scar, too, was moving faster, creeping through the stalks of bamboo, trying to move without revealing his position. He could see the strange creature ahead of him, backing up, looking around wildly. The creature with the black-and-white face was twenty yards away. Old Scar was accustomed to hunting in the bamboo thickets. He could see the creature, but it could not see Scar.

The strange creature stumbled, lost his balance, turned away from him, thrashing about, trying to stay on his feet.

The big cat charged.

Hatcher saw Wonderboy falter and fall. He heard the bamboo stalks cracking off before he saw the cat. He ran toward Wonderboy, who was floundering around, trying to get in a sitting position.

'Stay down,' Hatcher barked in his shattered voice. 'He's charging.'

'Oh God no!' Wonderboy screamed.

Hatcher was ten feet away from the kid when the tiger broke loose of the bamboo stalks. He threw the 375 H&H up to his shoulder, aimed for the chest of the powerful beast as it charged closer and squeezed off a shot.

Ping!

The rifle misfired.

Hatcher didn't lose a beat. He threw the rifle at the rogue and dived on top of Wonderboy, grabbing his gun and rolling on his side. Nearby he heard an elephant trumpet, felt the ground shake as the big creature charged toward them. But he did not let that distract him. He was on his side and the big tiger leaped from ten feet away, its open mouth showing dripping fangs, its one eye gleaming ferociously.

He had time for one shot. He swung the rifle up and fired from the waist straight into the tiger's face.

Old Scar felt the heat of the explosion, was blinded by the white light, and a millisecond later felt the bullet explode just above his good eye, cracking the skull, burning into his head, searing his brain and snapping his head back.

His forelegs collapsed and he went down, rolling over, snapping off a path of bamboo one after another. They came showering down on top of Hatcher and Wonderboy. The tiger lay five feet away, its enormous mouth still open. A pitiful cry-growl escaped from its throat and it shuddered and began to stiffen.

Beneath him, Hatcher could feel Wonderboy trembling. He got to his knees and looked down at the musician, who seemed to be trying to dig a hole in the ground.

'It's over, kid,' Hatcher whispered. 'It's okay.'

'No, no,' Wonderboy cried, all legs and hands in a tight little pile.

Another shower of bamboo stalks fell around Hatcher, and he heard one of the elephants trumpet almost on top of him. He turned, and stared straight into the muzzles of two guns – Early's and Earp's. Nobody moved. Nobody breathed. Almost as if he

383

could perceive in slow motion, Hatcher saw Early's finger tightening on his trigger.

My God, he's going to shoot me! Hatcher thought as he spun away and ducked and heard the rifle boom.

Behind him he heard the tiger scream again and, spinning around, saw it, half on its feet, take the shot high in the shoulder. It screamed once more and fell dead.

'Told you not to go for the head shot,' Early said.

THAI HORSE

Early's small house was at the end of a narrow, hard-packed dirt road. The road wound through dark, verdant foliage, which choked its shoulders, casting it in deep shadow. Rainbow-streaked macaws and parrots, startled by the van, had insulted the men with angry squawks and shrieks as they returned from the hunt. The thatch-roofed house had a wide porch around three of its sides. The sweet odor of cassava from nearby fields permeated the air.

The big cat had been strung upside down by its legs from a small tree. Several women from the village the animal had terrorized had gathered at Early's house to celebrate Hatcher's kill with dancing and a feast. An elderly Oriental man was stooped over a large pot of Thai stew cooking on an open fire.

Hatcher had been coldly quiet since the end of the hunt. He sat alone on the porch watching the locals celebrate the end of the old rogue. The women portrayed the hunters in the impromptu dance while one woman played Old Scar. Lithe, her face painted yellow, she danced on all fours, darting about as the hunters pursued her.

Infuriated in the tense moments after the kill, Hatcher had snatched the bolt out of the 375 H&H and tossed it to Early.

'Next time you loan a gun to someone maybe you ought to make sure it works,' Hatcher had snapped angrily.

Early had turned the bolt over in his hand, carefully examining it before looking back at Hatcher.

'The bloody firing pin's cracked,' he had said with genuine surprise, thinking it was an act.

'Is that a fact,' Hatcher growled sarcastically.

'What's that supposed to mean?' Early said edgily. 'It worked fine this morning, I test-fired the piece myself.'

384

'Wonderboy and I could both be dead right now because of that weapon.'

'I'm sorry, okay? You think I wanted you to *miss* the cat?' Early said. 'Hell, that's ridiculous, how could I have known you would get the kill shot?'

'You're being paranoid, Hatcher,' said Earp.

'Yeah,' said Riker. 'If we wanted to kill you, you'd be dead.'

Having reacted with more passion than was his custom, Hatcher had shut up and now he sat alone deep in thought. He did not see Wonderboy approach him from the side of the house.

'Mr. Hatcher?' he said. 'It *is* Hatcher, isn't it?'

The musician, who had repaired his streaked face with fresh paint, stood against the wall of the house with his hands in his pockets.

'That's right,' the whispering man croaked.

'You saved my life,' Wonderboy said. 'And I, uh . . . don't know how to thank you. But I want you to know nobody was out to get you.'

'You'd have done the same for me,' said Hatcher.

'No, no,' Wonderboy said, shaking his head. 'I choked, man. It wasn't just that I was scared, I couldn't pull the trigger.'

'Did that ever happen before?'

Wonderboy stared off at the dead tiger from behind his mask, and after a few seconds he nodded.

'So forget it,' said Hatcher. 'You can live forever without ever touching another gun.'

'That isn't it.'

'Then, what is it?'

Wonderboy took his hands out of his pockets. He wrapped them around his chest, hugging himself as if he were cold.

'Survival.'

'Survival,' Hatcher repeated flatly.

'Hell, if it ain't one war, it's another.'

'You won't have to go to any more wars, Wonderboy.'

'Anyway,' he said, 'I don't know how you thank someone who's saved your life. The Japanese have a word for it, but I don't remember what it is.'

'*Ongaeshi*,' Hatcher said.

'Yeah, that's it. It means, you know, like a big debt.'

'It means an obligation to repay,' said Hatcher.

'Yeah. Well, *ongaeshi*, Mr. Hatcher.'

Hatcher stepped closer to Wonderboy and leaned against the wall beside him. 'Would you like to try?' his hoarse voice asked.

'I don't understand.'

'Who is Thai Horse, Wonderboy?'

Wonderboy stared off at the other regulars on the other side of the yard. 'What's a Thai Horse?' he asked, still watching the dancers.

'*Ongaeshi*, Wonderboy.'

'Don't say that.'

'Let's try another one. Is Murphy Cody alive?'

'Who?'

'Murph Cody.'

'What do you want with him?' Wonderboy asked. 'What'd you say his name is?'

'Cody,' Hatcher said softly.

'Yeah, Cody.'

'I have a message for him.'

'A message?'

'That's all there is to it.'

Wonderboy nodded slowly and, moving away from Hatcher toward the rest of the group and not looking at him, said, 'Well, if I should run into somebody by that name I'll tell him you're looking for him.'

Wonderboy walked away. The dancers had finished their musical drama and were fawning over the regulars. Earp was chatting with the dancer who had portrayed the tiger, and Wonderboy leaned over and spoke softly into his ear. Earp looked over at Hatcher and then, taking the yellow-faced dancer by the arm, led her across the yard to Hatcher.

'This is Namtaan,' Earp said. 'She wants to meet the great white hunter. Namtaan, this is Hatcher.'

'How do you do,' Hatcher said.

'It is a pleasure,' she said. 'So you are the tiger killer.'

'We all had a hand in it.'

'And did everyone have a hand in saving Wonderboy's life? You are too modest, Mr. Hatcher.' She looked up at him with penetrating eyes.

'It's not modesty,' Hatcher said, looking at Earp. 'Everybody here depends on everybody else. It's something I missed in the war. My job was a very solitary one.'

'That is very sad,' she said.

'Uh-huh,' he growled with a shrug. 'Well, we Westerners have a saying, "You're never too old to learn."'

'There's the other side of that coin,' said Earp. '"You can't teach an old dog new tricks."'

386

Hatcher smiled. 'Yeah,' he said, 'take your pick.'

'He says you asked him about an old Thai legend.'

'Oh? What legend was that?'

'The legend of the Thai Horse.'

'He was only partly right. I wasn't talking about the old Thai Horse legend, I was talking about the new Thai Horse legend.'

'The *new* Thai Horse legend?'

'I'm looking for one who calls himself Thai Horse,' Hatcher replied, staring straight into her dark brown eyes.

'I do not understand,' she said.

'I think Mr. Earp does,' Hatcher said.

'I don't know what you're talking about,' said Earp.

'Why don't we stop kidding each other,' Hatcher said bluntly. 'I was told that a man named Murphy Cody calls himself Thai Horse.'

'Cody was killed in the war,' Earp said, almost too casually.

'Maybe not,' Hatcher answered.

'And why would he do this? Call himself Thai Horse?'

'Because he buys and sells heroin. He kills others and steals it from them. He buys babies and kills them and smuggles dope in their bodies.'

Namtaan looked at Hatcher for a few moments, then turned abruptly and entered the house. Earp followed her, stopping at the door.

'C'mon,' he said to Hatcher. 'She won't bite.'

The interior of the small house was dark and cool. The windows and shutters were closed against the early afternoon sun and an air conditioner purred softly somewhere. Sunlight slanted through the slats in the shutters, casting harsh slivers on the plank flooring. She sat down on an ancient, battered sofa.

'Sit down,' she said.

Earp leaned against a table sipping his drink. Hatcher sat down on the opposite end of the couch.

'Who is this Cody?' she asked.

'Why are you so interested?'

'Please, cooperate with me for a few minutes,' she said almost plaintively.

As Hatcher and Namtaan talked, the other regulars started drifting into the room. Prophett and Melinda sat quietly in a corner, Prophett sprawled loosely in a chair, making aimless little marks on the floor with the toe of his good foot. Riker leaned in the doorway, drinking a beer, and Gallagher sat on the arm of a chair with his arms folded across his chest. Hatcher tried to ignore them.

'Murph Cody is the man I came to Thailand to find,' he said

387

emphatically. 'I'm only interested in Thai Horse as it relates to him.'

'Why do you seek him?'

'It's personal.'

'Do you know him?'

'We were friends a long time ago.'

'Is that why you are looking for him?'

Hatcher thought about the question for a moment, then said, 'That's part of it.'

'Who told you Cody called himself Thai Horse?' Earp asked.

As Hatcher's eyes became more accustomed to the room he became aware that there was another person there. The old Chinese who had been attending the cook pots had also entered the room. He was a dim figure, an old, stooped man sitting in the darkest corner of the room.

'A man named Wol Pot, a North Vienamese POW commandant during the war. His real name was Taisung and he ran a camp called the Huie-kui in Laos.'

'And how did he know Cody?'

'I think Cody was one of his prisoners.'

'I told you,' Earp repeated, 'Cody was killed in a plane crash in 1972.'

'And how would you know that?' Hatcher asked.

'I read it somewhere,' Earp snapped back.

'A common misapprehension,' said Hatcher.

'Misapprehension?' Namtaan said.

'A lie.'

'Why do you think so?' she asked.

'Because it was to Wol Pot's advantage to turn up Cody. He wanted a visa to the United States. Cody was to be his trade.'

'And why would Cody be that important?'

'His father was general of the Army during the war.'

'Perhaps this informant was playing a game.'

'Perhaps.'

'But you don't think so?'

'No.'

'You give such quick answers, Mr. Hatcher, I hope you don't feel like I am interrogating you,' she said with a smile.

'You *are* interrogating me,' he said.

'This is all a lot of bull,' Earp piped in suddenly.

'I don't think so,' said Hatcher. 'I think Murphy Cody is alive.'

'Because of what that greaseball told you?'

'That has something to do with it.'

388

'I don't believe a word of this,' said Earp. 'He's Sloan's man.'

'I'm not Sloan's anything. He hired me to do a job.'

'Christ, he admits it!' said Earp.

Hatcher tried to ignore them. 'What have you got against Sloan?' he asked.

'We think he hired you to turn up Cody and kill him,' said Earp. 'Do you deny that?'

Hatcher was stymied. What Earp said was true.

'No, I don't deny it,' Hatcher said.

The honesty of his answer obviously surprised everyone in the room.

'But,' he went on, 'I didn't accept the job on those terms.'

'What were your terms?' Earp said with a sneer.

'That I would find Cody – if he was alive – and deliver a message to him.'

Earp turned away in disgust and shook his head. 'Jesus!' he said.

'Listen to me, Wyatt. This started out to be a simple job. Find Murphy Cody and deliver a message, that's all. In Bangkok, Sloan changed the signals on me.'

'Earp whirled to face him. 'How?'

'He wanted me to make a judgment call. If Cody was mixed up in something – embarrassing, he implied I should get rid of him. Sloan never says anything directly. He's a master of innuendo. And incidentally, I have as much right as anybody to hate Sloan. He framed me and I spent three years in a Central American scum hole called Los Boxes.'

'And you still took this job?'

'That's right. I figured if anybody could find Cody I could.'

'And you accepted those terms, right?'

'I had to make a choice: stay with the mission and try to find Cody, or take a walk, in which case Sloan would have brought in some cold-blooded bastard to do the job.'

'What makes you different? You once killed for him on a daily basis.'

'Just like you did in CRIP, right?' said Hatcher angrily. 'I was a soldier just like you were. I did what I was ordered to do.'

The remark shut Earp up for a moment. He looked away.

'You know I'm not stupid,' Hatcher said, sweeping his arm around the room. 'If I wanted to kill Cody, I sure as hell wouldn't do it when I'm outnumbered ten to one.'

'You seem pretty convinced that Cody and this baby-killing dope smuggler are one and the same.'

'I'm not sure what I believe about Thai Horse,' Hatcher said. 'What I do believe is that Wol Pot, or Taisung as you call him, knew Cody was alive.'

'Anything else?'

'The rest is all conjecture. What I call the equation.'

'The equation?' said Gallagher.

'Like a mathematical equation, except that you use information instead of numbers.'

He looked around the room at the rest of the regulars.

'For instance, I know Wol Pot was really a Vietnamese prison commandant named Taisung. I know Wol Pot claimed that Murph Cody is alive in Bangkok. And I also know that Wol Pot was probably telling the truth.'

'Why?' asked Early.

'Another part of the equation. Eventually Wol Pot would have had to produce Cody to get his visa. To reveal himself was risky because the U.S. could have found out about his past. But he was on the run, and his only chance was to produce Cody. Without him, he didn't have anything. It would have been like offering to produce – Elvis Presley.'

'Anything else?' Riker asked skeptically.

'Yeah, there is something else. I also know that Johnny Prophett's real name is Paget, and that he and Gallagher, and Benny Potter, Riker, and Max Early were all reported missing in action at about the same time in roughly the same area of Vietnam. I'm not sure, but probably Wonderboy and Corkscrew could be included on that list.

'So, the equation tells me that it's possible all of them were captured by the VC and were in Wol Pot's prison camp. And since Wol Pot knew Cody, I assume he was there, too.'

Riker snorted. 'You got a lot of guts,' he said.

'Any more to that equation?' Corkscrew asked.

'One more thing. Wol Pot also claims that Cody is a killer and a dope smuggler who calls himself Thai Horse. I also heard from a source in the government that there's a rumor on the street this Thai Horse is a drug dealer.'

'And what's the old equation tell you about that one?' Riker asked.

'Perhaps I should take you off the spot, Mr. Hatcher,' said Namtaan, tapping her breast. 'I am the one known as Thai Horse.'

Hatcher's surprise was genuine, so much so that Namtaan broke into a smile for the first time since they had entered the house.

390

'I did not mean to shock you,' she said.

Hatcher quickly recovered his composure. He started to laugh. 'I don't believe a word of that,' he said.

'Nevertheless, it is true,' she said.

'I gave her the name, Hatcher,' Johnny Prophett said.

'Yeah, everybody knows that,' said Gallagher.

'I don't know it,' Hatcher said hoarsely.

'You don't know a helluva lot, soldier, but you sure do a lot of guessing,' Earp said.

Hatcher stared down at Pai. His recognition of her had come gradually. At first he had thought she was someone he had met before, someone from the past. He wanted to see her without the facial makeup – unlike Wonderboy, whose painted face was his reality.

'Okay, I'll try one more,' Hatcher said, staring at Namtaan. 'I'm guessing your name is Pai.'

'My name is Namtaan.'

'Sure. But it was once Pai. Fifteen years ago in Vietnam. You were Cody's lady fair.'

'That is a nice way of saying it.'

'I have a picture of you taken in 1972. It was obvious you were devoted to him, and I'm sure you still are.'

'Why are you looking for him, Mr. Hatcher?' she said, quite earnestly.

'Like I said, I have a message for him.'

'You have come all this way to deliver a message?' she said with disbelief.

'That's right.'

'And Cody was your friend?' said Namtaan.

'That was a long time ago. But old friendships die hard.'

He stopped, and she continued to stare deeply into his face.

'And if Cody was this baby killer, what would you do then?' she asked.

It was a question that had gnawed at Hatcher since his last conversation with Sloan, a decision he had wanted to avoid. Now he had to make it.

'I didn't come here to judge Murphy Cody,' Hatcher said. 'I'll admit the thought I might have to kill Cody has crossed my mind a lot in the last few days. But no matter what he's done, I'm through playing judge, jury and executioner. I've had enough of killing. Somebody else can do the dirty work from now on. I came to deliver a message, period, and that's what I intend to do.'

In the gloom of the dark room, the regulars were all quiet. There was no doubting the sincerity with which Hatcher had spoken.

'And who is this message from?' Namtaan finally asked.

'That's between Cody and me.'

'There are ways we can find out,' said Earp.

'Not from me,' Hatcher growled.

Riker chuckled at the remark. 'Son of a bitch, I'm beginning to believe that,' he said.

'You feel that responsible to this Cody, do you?' Namtaan asked.

'The message is very personal. I'll make it face-to-face or not at all.'

He suddenly turned toward the old figure in the corner, squinting his eyes and peering through the gloom at him. The last time Hatcher had seen the old man, he had been backing away from him in an alley in Bangkok after killing Wol Pot.

'This old gentleman killed Wol Pot. He also had a clean shot at me, started to take it, and changed his mind. I've been asking myself why ever since.'

'And what did you decide?' Johnny Prophett asked.

'Aw, c'mon,' Hatcher whispered, staring across the dark room at him. 'None of you would've let a stranger do your dirty work. Whatever reason you had to kill Wol Pot, and I can think of a lot of them, if it was to be done, one of you would have done the trick. It's not your style to give the job to an old man.'

'That's very astute,' Earp said.

'So the answer is, he's not an old man. He's one of you.'

He turned back to the old man.

'Right, Polo?' he whispered.

The stooped Chinese stared across the room at Hatcher. Then he started to chuckle. He stood up, and then he stood erect, adding another three inches to his height. He limped across the room toward Hatcher.

'Well, I'm sure as hell older. I haven't heard that nickname since the academy, Hatch,' said Murphy Cody.

THE SECRET OF HUIE-KUI

Hatcher felt a sudden rush of excitement. He had not been sure until that moment that Cody was really alive. Now, looking at his old friend, he felt a sense of relief and joy.

Namtaan opened the shutters. Sunlight invaded the room, filling its dark corners.

'Jesus, Polo, I'm glad you're alive,' Hatcher said.

'I don't remember you as being so tough,' Cody said.

'I didn't remember you with white hair,' Hatcher whispered with a smile, trying to break the tension.

'Part of the act,' Cody said. 'My wife is very good at makeup and disguise. My real hair still has a little color to it.'

'What happened to your leg?'

'Tore it up when I fell out of my plane. How about your box?'

'Walked into a gun butt.'

'Funny how simple stories become after a while,' Cody said. 'With time, an hour-long story is reduced to a sentence.'

He seemed taller than Hatcher remembered and thinner. Whatever bad cards had been dealt to Murphy Cody through the years had taken a toll, although the powdered beard and age lines added illusion to reality.

'Look,' said Hatcher, 'if you think you can trust me, I'd like to have a couple of minutes in private.'

Cody thought about that for just a moment, then turned to the regulars.

'Okay,' he said. 'Leave us alone for a minute, please. Namtaan, you stay.'

The regulars scuffled out of the room.

'I've thought a lot about you through the years,' Cody said, leaning against the windowsill, and stared out across the fields, and then he chuckled. 'We saw some good days together, didn't we?'

'That's a fact,' Hatcher said.

'Remember that New Year's Eve? We went to New York, both ended up in bed with that girl, what was her name?'

Hatcher had to think for a minute before he remembered. 'Linda.'

'Yeah, Linda.'

'A very compassionate soul, Linda.'

'Wasn't she, though,' said Cody. He turned to face Hatcher. 'You know, I've owed you an apology for a long time.'

'You don't owe me anything, Polo.'

'I had dinner in Saigon with my dad about a month before I went down. The last time I saw him. He told me you were in Nam working undercover for him and had been for a couple of years. I

393

felt about an inch tall, remembering what I said that night in San Diego. I guess my mouth ran a lot faster than my brains in those days. For what it's worth, I apologize.'

'Thanks. That means a lot to me.'

'You're a persistent son of a bitch, you know.'

'I've been told that.'

'So what's the message, Hatch?' Cody asked seriously.

'It's from your father.'

Cody was surprised. 'My father knows I'm alive?' he said.

'That's what I was sent over here to determine.'

'Forget it,' Cody said. 'Let the dead stay dead.'

'There's no way to put this gently,' said Hatcher. 'Your father's dying of cancer.'

Cody was jarred. He stared into space, then sucked in his lower lip. His eyebrows bunched together. 'Oh Jesus,' he said, and his shoulders suddenly sagged and the middle went out of him and he reached out and leaned against the window shutters. The seams in his face grew deeper. After it sank in for a full minute, he asked, 'How long?'

'Six months, maybe, if he's real lucky.'

'Oh God . . .' The words choked off in his throat. He lowered his head and tears ran down his cheeks. Pai stood beside him and put her arm around his waist.

'Y'know, I never thought I'd see him again, I took that for granted. I just never thought about . . . that someday . . .'

'He doesn't care what you've done or what you're doing,' Hatcher said huskily. 'He just wants to know you're alive, to see you once before he dies.'

'God,' Cody said. He wiped his face, and the age lines painted on it by his wife came off on his hand, leaving behind the true furrows of age and hard times. He stared out the window for a very long time. Neither Pai nor Hatcher said anything.

Finally Cody said, 'Funny, isn't it, how things you thought were important suddenly become – insignificant. All my life I had to toe the mark. Being Buffalo Bill's son wasn't easy. I couldn't fail at anything –' He stopped for a moment, then shook his head. 'No,' he said, 'that's not fair, I didn't allow *myself* to fail at anything. It was in my head. I mean in my head the finger was always pointing at me from the time I was a kid. It wasn't that he said anything to me. He didn't push me, he didn't have to, he was always there like a – like the giant in the woods you're scared of when you're a kid. When I decided to go to Annapolis instead of the Point, it almost killed him. Shit, he went berserk. Here I was just trying to do something on my own, but, Christ, it was the ultimate insult to him. He ordered me to go to the Point, and when I refused he tried to get my appointment to Annapolis withdrawn. But it was too late.'

Hatcher remembered that night when Cody had torn up his room in a drunken rage because he was alone at Christmas.

'Hell,' Hatcher whispered, 'that was twenty-five years ago.'

'Twenty, fifty, no difference, he never forgot it. And he never let me forget it. That decision to go Navy clouded our relationship from then on. Maybe it still clouds it.'

'Doesn't much matter anymore,' Hatcher said.

'It does to me,' Cody said in a faraway voice.

Cody continued to look out the window, shaking his head, clinging to Pai.

'Look, Polo, I can't say anything for Sloan, and I don't know what the hell Porter's motives were,' said Hatcher. 'Your father doesn't give a tinker's damn what happened or what you're doing. He's dying, for God's sake, he wants to say good-bye. My job is to set up a meeting somewhere safe so you can see each other once more.'

'What irony,' said Cody. 'As Prophett would say, two warriors facing each other across the river and no way to say good-bye.'

'His abstract poetry eludes me,' Hatcher snapped with a touch of irritation.

'Don't you get it?' said Cody. 'As far as the world is concerned, we're all dead. In Prophett's metaphor, we all crossed over the river. We can't go home because there's no home to go to. And some of us couldn't go home if we wanted to. You know about Riker and Gallagher?'

'I know they were both in big trouble when they disappeared. I assume Prophett can't go back because he's a hopeless junkie, you can tell by looking at him. Wonderboy – he's learned to live with his face. But you, Corkscrew, Potter, Max Early –'

'It all started back before Nam. Hell, my dad and the admiral arranged my marriage like a couple of feudal kings arranging a wedding for the good of the realm. It was like living in a strait-jacket, my wife and I were barely civil. The old man was over here. So I volunteered for the Black Ponies.'

'In the end it all came down on Cody,' Pai quietly interrupted him. 'He had volunteered for the Black Ponies so nobody could say he was looking for an easy time of it. The losses were like snakes in his head, I could see it every day.'

'It wasn't just me,' Cody said with a touch of bitterness. 'It was

395

the mission. It's always the fucking mission. You set out to do what you have to do regardless of the cost. But then you begin to wonder, Hell, is the mission right or wrong? You probably don't understand that, Hatch.'

'More than you might think,' Hatcher said.

'The final irony is I became one of the losses. That morning I had picked up a letter for John Rossiter, my gunner. But I forgot to give it to him. I never carried any ID – shit, I knew if I went down and they knew who I was, who my father was, then school was out. So all I had was that letter and Rossiter burning to a crisp, the whole jungle afire behind me. I saw that chopper coming in and I thought, God, I'm gonna get out of this. Then suddenly it turned around and just – flew away.

'Then the bullets started hitting around me, the fire was all over – so I threw away my dog tags. Next thing I knew, I had my hands up and they were frisking me and they found that letter and all of a sudden I was Gunner's Mate John Rossiter.

'Riker was the first to recognize me. But he kept mum, they all decided to keep mum. But I figured the least I could do was act like the ranking officer.'

'He tried negotiating with Taisung,' Namteen said. 'To get medicine for Wonderboy and morphine for Johnny and keep Max out of the hole so he would not go crazy.'

'And food, just food,' Cody said. 'I became the camp negotiator, the pimp. The fuckee. If Prophett needed heroin, I sold a piece of myself for heroin. If Wonderboy needed medicine, another piece for medicine. Another piece to keep Max out of the hole so he wouldn't go stark raving mad. I was Taisung's slave.'

'The trouble was, I really didn't have anything to trade for,' Cody said. 'And then . . .'

'And then?' Hatcher repeated.

'And then Pai came to us,' Cody said.

Unsure whether Cody was alive or dead, Pai had set out to find him. She knew only to go northwest and northwest she went. In Vietnam she was Vietnamese. In Cambodia, she was Cambodian. In Laos, she became Laotian. Wherever she was, she smiled and talked and listened. She worked when she had to for food and then moved on. She waded through the rice paddies, dodged the Khmer Rouge, slept in trees to avoid wild animals, almost died twice with fever.

She kept going, crossed the Annimitique, found the remains of one camp – the telltale holes dug in the ground, the remnants of

396

bamboo cell doors – devoured by vines and ground crawlers. The skeletons. She moved on, encouraged and discouraged at the same time.

And then one day she heard the voices – the unmistakable profanity of GIs – and she crept through the jungle grass and saw the camp and that night she crept up to the holes in the ground they called cells and softly called his name as she crept from one to the other and finally she heard Cody's unbelieving voice answer, 'Pai?' and she lay across the crisscrossed bamboo doors, reached down and felt his hand take hers.

'Oh, Cody,' she whispered through her tears, 'at last I have found you.'

It had taken her six months to get to the Huie-kui.

'Oh, Cody, at last I have found you,' Cody repeated her words. 'God, I can't tell you how I felt at that moment.'

He stopped and swallowed hard and then said, 'And finally . . . I had something to offer Taisung.'

He whispered as if he feared the words would turn to ashes in his mouth, and they hung in the air along with all their terrible implications.

'It was my choice,' Pai said in her soft voice. 'I wanted most to keep Cody alive, to keep them all alive. No one asked me to do what I did.'

'And I didn't stop her,' said Cody, turning and staring straight at Hatcher, and the expression on his face said all that needed to be said about what living had cost him and the woman he loved.

'We stayed alive, most of us anyway. Jaimie Solomon was eaten up with cancer. He got back to the States. Joe Binder died in the camp, and Sammy Franklin died of malnutrition before Pai ever found us.'

'Jaimie Solomon?' Hatcher said, remembering the note that had been left on the Wall.

'The main thing is, Pai kept us there,' said Cody. 'Taisung didn't send us to Hanoi. We honestly believed that if we went to Hanoi it was all over.'

'I seduced Taisung,' Pai said, staring at Hatcher's feet. 'I went downriver and brought him liquor, cigarettes, everything he needed to make life easy for him. Then I brought him China White.'

'That was my idea,' said Cody. 'Hook the son of a bitch. Once he was hooked he'd do anything to get a fix. Johnny Prophett had the connection and Pai was free to move around.'

397

'First, a little for the nose,' said Pai. 'Then the needle.'

'Then we had the son of a bitch,' said Cody.

Earp appeared in the doorway drinking a beer.

'Everything okay?' he said.

'Come on in,' Cody answered. Earp entered the small room and leaned against the wall.

'Jaimie left you a note,' said Hatcher.

'A note? Where?'

'At the Wall in Washington, the Vietnam memorial. He thanked you for Thai Horse. Now I know what he meant. He was talking about the Thai Horse that led the fallen warriors to heaven.'

'That's right. It was Pai who led us out of that hellhole into Bangkok,' Cody said. 'That's why Johnny called her Thai Horse.'

'The war had been over almost a year, and Taisung was still holding them,' Earp said. 'That's where I came into it. Hanoi was on to Taisung. He was going to run for it and leave us there with a handful of guards. They probably would have killed us. But Pai offered a trade-out. She'd set up an escape and he could come out with the boys. I was living in Bangkok and helped set up the escape route and the boats.'

'We should have killed Taisung when we had the chance,' said Cody, 'but he was too quick for us. He stole one of the boats and made a break.'

'And you just stayed here in Bangkok?' Hatcher said to Cody.

'That's right,' Cody said. 'During the years I was a prisoner, things happened – things that could never be explained properly.' Cody stopped with a sigh, then went on, 'When we finally escaped into Thailand in late '76, I found out I was officially dead. The insurance was paid, my wife had remarried. My kids had a new father. Me? I had Pai and a chance to start over. What was there to go back to, Hatch? I decided to stay dead. When we first got out I used to fantasize about sneaking back just to get a look at the kids. They were one and two when I left, still one and two in my head – they're in high school now. Well, so much for fantasy. Hell, I don't even have a passport.'

'And the others?' Hatcher asked.

'Well, we had Gallagher, who was looking at five to ten years for grand theft, and Riker, who was facing a court-martial for striking an officer. You know Johnny Prophett's problem. He and Melinda stayed here because dope is inexpensive and accessible. That's when Sweets and Wyatt started the Longhorn. Tombstone just kind of grew out of it.'

'How about the rest of them? Corkscrew, Potter, Max Early?'

Earp said, 'When we got out, Early called home to Utah. The phone was disconnected, the house was sold, his wife and two kids were long gone. What the hell did he have to go home to? Corkscrew? And ex-Detroit pimp. Bangkok was heaven compared to that. Besides, the only family he had was his brother and he was killed on that ridge. And Potter? What was his option – a scratch farm in Arkansas and a wife who serviced everybody in the state while he was gone? The irony is that we were all bonded by those years of imprisonment. Corkscrew and Early couldn't reveal what had happened to them without jeopardizing Cody, Riker and Gallagher, so they all stayed dead.'

'The boys on the far side of the river, as Prophett would say,' Cody remarked.

'So what happened? How did Taisung get back into the act?'

'We had this kid. Kilhanney, Ted Kilhanney . . . That's when all the trouble started.'

'Taisung tried to *buy* us, Hatcher,' said Pai. 'To make mules of us.'

'Blackmail?' Hatcher asked.

'Of the worst kind,' Cody said. 'He threatened to expose me, Gallagher, Riker and Kilhanney unless we turned mule for him. That's what he was doing for Fong, recruiting dope carriers. And Kilhanney was the most vulnerable.'

'Who's Kilhanney?' Hatcher asked.

'A real Greek tragedy,' Cody answered. 'A Catholic priest – how do they put it? – fallen from grace. Somewhere between Saigon and Bangkok, he lost his religion. He was giving some GIs last rites and the position was counterattacked. In the camp he lost what little faith he had left. When we got here, he fell in love with the wife of a Thai politician. You think we're screwed up? He was *really* screwed up. He couldn't face the World, and he was torn up with guilt. Naturally he was the most vulnerable and the first one Taisung went after.'

'What happened to him?'

'All Kil was supposed to do was take a plane down to Hat Yai and drive a truckload of women to the Malaysian border. He didn't know their babies were all dead and stuffed with heroin. When the guards discovered what was going on, Kil panicked and made it up here to Max. Two days later he took the bus over to the Phu Khat beach, swam out, and didn't come back. What was left of him floated up a week or so later.'

'That's when we resurrected Thai Horse,' Earp said.

'We made a deal to run twenty kilos of heroin to Amsterdam,

399

and when the courier delivered it, I killed him and dumped the twenty keys in the Chao Phraya River. Then I sent a message to Tollie Fong and Wol Pot that Thai Horse was taking over. I couldn't do it as Murphy Cody. I couldn't do it as an American. So – I became a Thai, Pai became a Thai. I married a Thai, killed as a Thai; as far as everyone is concerned, I *am* a Thai. Murphy Cody doesn't exist anymore.'

'And we spread the word on the street through Sy that Thai Horse was Taisung's operation,' said Earp.

'Killed two birds with one stone,' said Cody. 'Fong lost face and put the finger on Taisung. The only edge we had was that Taisung never told Fong who we were.'

'The whole deal was done with phone calls,' Earp said. 'The little creep never showed his face.'

'He was watching you, though,' said Hatcher. 'Up until the day Windy Porter was killed. Were you behind that?'

Cody shook his head. 'Tollie Fong.'

A silence fell on the room for a few moments. Cody seemed out of talk. Hatcher picked it up. 'I can guess what happened after that,' he said. 'Fong thought Wol Pot had double-crossed him, so the little bastard had to get out of the country. That's when he blew the whistle on Murph.'

'And Sloan sent you in to find me,' said Cody.

'Look, forget Sloan,' Hatcher said. 'He's out of it. He took Porter's body back to the States.'

'Bad guess, soldier,' said Earp. 'Sloan is in Bangkok right now. In a place called the House of Dreams in Chinese Town.'

'That's bullshit,' Hatcher said.

'He's an opium head,' Cody said. 'The House of Dreams is an opium house. We've been watching him since the Wol Pot contact. He sometimes goes there for days a time.'

'*Sloan!*'

'Want to see the place?' said Earp. 'It's a Chinese junk used for moving produce into the city.'

A Chinese junk, thought Hatcher, remembering the address on Wol Pot's passport that had been an empty pier. And his profession: produce sales.

'I appreciate your loyalty,' said Cody, 'but the man is a junkie, no better or worse off than Johnny Prophett.'

'And guess who owns the junk?' said Earp.

'Tollie Fong,' Hatcher said.

'Correct.'

'So you think Fong is blackmailing Sloan?' Hatcher said.

400

'It makes sense. We'ver seen him go there half a dozen times. And we've seen him leave. We've got a pretty good little intelligence network, Hatcher. You think it was luck, walking into the Longhorn and tumbling on to the regulars. The only thing lucky about it was that you hired Sy. He was supposed to be following you.'

'Don't tell me he's one of the regulars.'

'He makes good tips bringing tourists to the Longhorn,' said Cody. 'He's also one of the best drivers in Bangkok. He was helping out.'

'So you knew where I was every minute,' Hatcher said.

'Tucked you in, got you up,' said Earp. 'Tumbling on to Wol Pot was a real stroke, though.'

'And you were following me?' Hatcher said to Cody.

Cody nodded. 'We didn't know for sure whether you knew where Wol Pot was or not. You could have been meeting him.'

'Why didn't you kill me, too?' asked Hatcher. 'You thought about it.'

Cody nodded again. 'You're right. I just couldn't do it. We decided when Max called about the tiger to get you down here and check you out.'

'And what if you had decided I was here to kill Murph?' Hatcher asked.

'All of us would have put a bullet in you,' Wyatt Earp said emphatically.

Hatcher appeared troubled. 'There's something missing here,' he said. 'Tollie Fong never had trouble recruiting mules before. Why would he suddenly be relying on somebody like Wol Pot?'

'He's moving a lot of junk from the hills to Bangkok and from there to the States,' said Earp. 'He's got at least a thousand keys of ninety-nine pure hidden in Bangkok right now. He needs to move it – a lot of it, and fast.'

'And we know where it is,' Cody said.

Hatcher shook his head slowly. 'If you're thinking what I think you're thinking, forget it. It's not your problem.'

'But Fong is,' said Riker.

'Forget Tollie Fong,' said Hatcher sternly. 'The triads'll hound you until they kill all of you. Stop now. Just let Thai Horse vanish into the woodwork. Fong won't bother you anymore.'

'You don't really believe that,' said Cody.

'Look, you say he's involved in something big. He doesn't have time to look for you or Thai Horse. And if you kill him, it'll never stop. I killed Fong's father in 1976 and he's still after me.'

'I say we hit him, take him out once and for all,' said Earp. 'Solves your problem and ours.'

Hatcher shook his head.

'Listen to me, when I said I was done with killing I meant it. I came on this trip thinking I was performing a simple humane act. Instead I've had to fight practically every day to stay alive. The hell with it, no more killing. The sooner I get out of Bangkok, the better.'

He turned and walked out of the house.

'You think he is right, Cody?' Pai asked. 'You think Tollie Fong will forget?'

'Sure,' said Earp. 'And next season the Pope's gonna play second base with the Mets.'

Melinda was sitting on the porch when Hatcher walked out. She looked up and for the first time she smiled at him.

'Do you understand now?'

'Most of it,' he said. 'I'm a little confused on details.'

'Like what?'

'Like you and Prophett.'

'I'd like you to understand about Johnny and me, maybe it will explain what holds us all together. It's not fear of being discovered.'

'I know it isn't fear. I'm a fast read.'

Hatcher looked at her and thought about all the passion that had been in her pictures. She had been to able to predict the perfect moment on the faces of the victims of war, the soldiers, the enemy, the innocent bystanders who seemed always to get the worst of it; to capture the fear and frustration and the awful confusion of the young and the despair and the awe and the agony of the old when faced with the obscenity of death. And almost as if she were reading his mind, Melinda went on, 'Johnny was something. Not afraid of anything. And dreams – God, did he have dreams. But he wasn't prepared for Nam. It overwhelmed him, and he was like, I don't know, a little boy in a closet who needed somebody to reach out and hold him. He really needed me. He'd cuddle up against me at night, curl into all the right places, tell me how much he loved me. I was drawn to his poetry. And I guess to his weaknesses, too. But Indian country was like a magnet to him. And so was the needle. When he didn't come back that last time, I waited and waited. I knew he wasn't dead.'

'How did you find him?'

'Pai. She called me one day. I didn't know her and she was

very secretive. "Come to Bangkok" is all she said, but I knew why. I was on the next plane out.'

'The spike'll kill him, you know,' Hatcher whispered.

'Of course,' she said. 'I've always known I'll outlive him. Every time he takes a shot I think it'll be his last. He comes to me and he puts his arms around me and I can feel all the futility and defeat in his body. That's when I just pray I'll have him one more day, before the needle takes him away. I can't imagine what it's going to be like. The loneliness of not having him anymore.'

'Fong will kill Murph, Hatcher, like he had to kill Wol Pot. That's why we have to destroy Tollie Fong first.'

'I'm out of it. Do what you want. I've done my job and I'm going home,' he said.

Hatcher thought about the trips Pai had made downriver to score for Taisung – and for Johnny; about the deals she had made for them; about the logistics of getting Jaimie, who was dying of cancer, back into South Vietnam so he could get home.

'Leave Tollie Fong alone,' Hatcher whispered. 'You prod him, he'll be like an angry bull. Leave him alone and it will all pass. Believe me, I know this man well.'

'How about Sloan?'

'I have to see him once more – there's something that needs to be finished between us.'

'And what'll you tell him about Murph Cody?'

Hatcher looked at the tall, sad-eyed man who had once been his brash boxing colleague, looked across the yard at Wonderboy, who was playing his guitar and singing softly for the Thai dancers, and at Pai, who had traded her youth, her nationality, her very soul, for the man she loved.

'I'll tell him the truth,' said Hatcher. 'I'll tell him Murph Cody is dead.'

PLAYBACK

The sun was close to the horizon when he got back to the hotel. Hatcher was tired and dispirited, and at first did not notice the tape recorder sitting on the table beside the bed. He peeled off his dirty clothes, took a shower, came out with a towel wrapped around his waist and lay on the bed, thinking about Murph Cody and the regulars, a disparate group bonded together by love and

403

the need to protect one another. And suddenly he missed the island and Ginia and his friends there, people who asked nothing of one another but trust and friendship. Not unlike the Longhorn regulars. And he admitted to himself that Ginia had brought more happiness and feeling into his life than anything since his days at Annapolis.

He shifted his thoughts back to the regulars. They were going to hit Tollie Fong, he was sure of it, and they would risk everything to do it. And then thinking of Fong, he thought about the assassination of Campon and the bombing in Paris and the death of the Hyena. The police were speculating that he was killed by one of his own people, but Hatcher was familiar with the Hyena – he always worked alone. Pieces began to fall in place in his head.

Then he noticed the small hand-size tape machine. He stared at it, wondering where it had come from, before he reached out and picked it up.

Lying on his back, he flipped on the play switch. The voice froze him: 'Hatcher, do I have to tell you what this is, or do you recognize my voice? Perhaps it will help if I stir your memory. Does Singapore mean anything? It should, Hatcher, that is where you murdered my father. Or the rivers, where you killed my father's most loyal soldiers. Or the house of the American Jew, Cohen, who calls himself Chinese, where you murdered still more of my men. Do I need to tell you my name? No, I think not.

'I am certain that you know I have made a promise to my *san wong* to put aside the *ch'u-tiao* I have sworn against you. And I will honor that oath even though you have dishonored my family and spilled our blood.

'And while my promise also includes Cohen, it does not include *all* your friends, Hatcher.

'Listen for a moment, here is another voice for you to recognize.'

There was silence on the tape for thirty or forty seconds, a hollow sound. Then Hatcher heard someone enter a room farther away, in another part of the house or apartment or whatever it was. A woman's voice was humming as a door opened.

Then she screamed.

It was a scream of surprise and fright, followed almost immediately by the sound of someone being hit – a groan? It was difficult to make out. A moment later there was the sound of heavy breathing, of footsteps on stairs, then Fong's voice again: 'It will be a few moments more, Hatcher. I had to use a little force to subdue your friend.' The machine went dead for a moment, then

404

the hollow sound again followed by a scream and a woman's voice, angry and full of hate: 'You bastard, you bloody bastard, take your hands off me . . .'

Daphne.

He sat straight up on the bed. His heartbeat accelerated. He could not believe what he was hearing, did not want to hear it. He snapped it off and held it in a trembling hand. He knew before the tape spun any further that Daphne was dead. He knew it because Fong would not have left the tape for him to hear if she was still alive. He could not imagine what horror the tape would spew out and yet he hesitated to turn it back on.

The fan whirred overhead in a syncopated rhythm. Outside, the sun slid below the spears and domes of the city's temples. Darkness crept silently into the room and filled its corners and shadows, and still Hatcher sat there with the dreaded tape recorder in his hand. Finally he turned the switch back on and listened to her screams of anger and outrage, listened to the struggle, to things falling and breaking, and finally a sharp crack and a grunt and a sigh.

And Fong's voice, slightly out of breath. 'She is a tigress, Hatcher. Her nails are like scissors. I had to put her away again, but only for a few minutes. She will come around.'

There was a soft, obscene chuckle. 'I think I broke her jaw, Hatcher.'

There was a rustling sound, sounds of activity in the room and Fong's voice again, farther away from the recorder this time. 'I am tying her to her bed, Hatcher. Her hands to the head . . . there. Now her feet. She is tied down on the bed like a star, stretched out for me, Hatcher.'

Daphne groaned. Her voice, pitifully weak and confused at first, then growing stronger, the outrage flowing back into it. Then came the sounds of clothing being torn, viciously, recklessly, and accompanied by Fong's toneless chortling.

'Cut me loose, you pig. You worthless, stinking pig!'

Then she screamed again, this time a scream of great pain, followed by a sobbing deep in her throat.

'This is for Hatcher,' Fong's voice hissed. 'You understand, bitch.'

Her scream tore through the small speaker, distorting it. 'Hatch . . .!'

'I'm going to have to gag her, Hatcher. You'll have to trust me from now on. I'll tell you everything that's happening. I promise you, I won't leave out a single detail . . .'

405

Hatcher flicked it off again. Shimmering marbles of sweat twinkled suddenly on his forehead and coursed slowly down the side of his face as he stared down at the tiny machine. His teeth were clenched so hard his jaws hurt.

He forced himself to switch it back on, to listen as Fong described every disgusting, brutalizing, painful act in detail, to hear Daphne's voice growing weaker, more pitiful, more terrified with each vicious move, and he was numbed by the extent of Fong's sadism, by his total lack of human feeling and compassion, by the horrifying passion with which Fong brutalized, raped and violated her.

Finally he leaned forward until the top of his head was on the bed and beat the mattress with his fists, his rage pouring out in muffled screams and cries.

Fong's voice continued on, its malevolent tones whispered in a deadly mimic of Hatcher's own voice. 'Do you feel it, my dear. Do you feel the point against your throat, hmm?'

Daphne's reply was a painful whimper.

'You know the drill, Hatcher. Place the point of the blade in the hollow place of the throat pointing toward the heart –'

'God, no!' Hatcher cried out through his clenched teeth.

'– then thrust down –'

Her scream was agonizing, even though it was muffled by whatever he had used for a gag.

'– hard and straight –'

Hatcher heard her weak cry.

'– into the heart. Hah!'

Her sharp intake of air. Then the rattle of blood and air in her throat. Then the silence.

'It is over, Hatcher,' Fong's voice whispered into the machine. 'Your friend is dead. And many other friends will die, you *gwai-lo* bastard. It is far from over.'

Hatcher sat for more than an hour, staring into the growing darkness, the tape recorder gripped tightly in his fist, his rage crashing and ebbing in his chest like the waves of the sea, his memories of Daphne Chien surging through his mind. Should he have predicted this would happen? he wondered. Could he have stopped it? He had a moment when he thought it might have been a cruel joke, a perverse play, acted out for his sake.

Finally he called Cohen. It took three tries to get through, and then he heard the familiar Boston accent.

'China?'

'Hi, buddy.'

406

'I'm calling about Daphne –'

'What can I tell you. I feel like a son of a bitch. I should have covered her –'

'It's true, then?'

'How did you find out?'

Hatcher's mouth went dry for a moment. He took a sip of water. 'He left a tape . . . described every . . . every . . . '

'Jesus. Listen to me, Hatch. I've already talked to the *san wong*. I told him Fong was a dishonor and a disgrace to the Chiu Chao, that he's a woman killer and a rapist – shit, you wouldn't believe what I said. I told him if any, *any*, member of the Chiu Chao sets foot in Hong Kong, he's dead. He's disgraced them all, Hatch, the whole damn bloody –'

'China?'

'Yeah?'

'I can't talk any more now, China.'

'Are you okay?'

'Yeah, I'm okay. I just can't talk any more.'

'You watch yourself, Hatch. He's a demon, this one.'

'I know it – see you later.'

'Listen, kiddo, I'll come over there, bring some of my best guys. I can be there by morning and –'

'China?'

'Yeah?'

'Stay home. Later, okay?' He softly cradled the phone.

It had been difficult for Hatcher to accept the reality that for years he had killed with neither hate nor malice, that he had been conditioned and manipulated to the point where inflicting death had come as easily to him as going to the grocery store or voting. If the journey that had started in Los Boxes and ended on a tiger hunt in Thailand had achieved nothing else for Hatcher, it had forced him to deal with the lightless places in his soul, places he had ignored for many years. From 126 he had discovered himself; had learned about camaraderie and trust and love from Melinda and the regulars; about the meaning of friendship from Cirillo and Ginia and Daphne and China Cohen.

And he had learned the true meaning of hate from Tollie Fong.

Hatcher knew he could never shed light in some of the dark places that were part of his nature. He might have been able to set aside the hatred that curled in his gut like an asp, except that he knew Fong's desecration of Daphne had nothing to do with the Chiu Chaos or China Cohen or Harry Sloan or Cody; it was between him and Tollie Fong. Hatcher had started it and Fong

407

was justified in his hatred. Hatcher knew he would continue to wreak his vengeance against everyone close to Hatcher until the *ch'u-tiao* was satisfied.

And Cody and Earp also were right. Eventually the regulars, too, would feel Fong's deadly sting. It had to be ended once and for all. Hatcher knew he could not bury the past without purging it first. Hatcher knew now that he had come to Bangkok because he valued Cody's life. In a savage turn of irony, he had tried to do something decent, and Sloan, who had created the monster within him, had summoned him back to use it again.

There could be no end to the killing yet. Either Hatcher or Fong must die before the blood feud would end.

The little metal cars were replicas of one of the earliest Mercedes racing machines, a single-seater with giant wheels made of real rubber and small plastic windshields. They were made in Germany by the Schuco Company and, when wound up, could reach a speed of thirty miles an hour for about two seconds.

Riker, who had found them in a toy store in the International Bazaar and brought four of them back, was on his knees, blowing dirt from around the axles and dropping single drops of oil into the moving parts. The jukebox was thundering, and Corkscrew and Johnny Prophett were servicing their cars. The regulars were lined up along the wall in the small room behind the glass-beaded curtain, and they had moved the tables back and put several heavy strips of Styrofoam against the back wall and around the legs of the pool table to protect the racing cars when they reached the end of the room. The Honorable, as stern-looking and inscrutable as always, was sitting behind his desk, taking bets, marking the tabs and passing them.

'Okay, c'mon, Corkscrew, get ready. I'm about to make dog meat out of you.'

'That'll be the fuckin' day,' the burly black man answered. He lifted his finger off the back wheels of the small toy car and they wheezed as they spun around. 'Looka there, man. I may be goin' for a record here.'

'Sure,' snapped Riker, winding his car up with a toy key and keeping a thumb on the back wheels.

'Are you ready?' Wonderboy yelled. He was holding a piece of yellow silk that had been checkered with a Magic Marker.

'Drivers ready . . .' he called out, waving the flag over his head. And then he dropped it. Corkscrew and Riker set the cars down and the wheels skittered on the hardwood floors and the two little machines took off toward the end of the room, their springs whining as they unwound and the cars bounding along side by side until Riker's car began to shift to the right and eased against Corkscrew's machine just enough to set it off course. The midget racing car veered, hit the wall and tumbled end over end halfway down the room. One of its wheels flew off and bounced down behind Riker's car as it crossed the finish line and whipped into the Styrofoam barrier. Earp, at the other end of the room, waved the winner's flag.

'Awright!' Riker yelled.

'Foul,' complained Corkscrew bitterly. 'You fouled me, man, drove me right into the wall.'

'Foul, hell, there's no such thing,' Riker snapped back.

The two men stood nose to nose, their fists clenched, bellowing at each other until the Honorable raised his hand and loudly cleared his throat. 'Gentlemen, gentlemen,' he said severely, 'really! This is hardly the way international champions act.'

'What's the decision, Honorable?' Corkscrew asked.

The man in the impeccable white suit cleared his voice and announced, 'Unfortunately, while it would appear that a foul did occur, I must rule that in the absence of any specific regulation concerning the deportment of the vehicles on the course, no foul was committed. The blue car is the winner.'

A general cheer went up and bet money changed hands. Riker counted out his bhats as Corkscrew paid off, snapping the bills into his palm. Then suddenly the room got quiet. Riker turned around. Hatcher was standing at the top of the stairs. His face looked drawn and the color seemed to be drained from it.

'Hey, buddy, what's the matter,' Wonderboy said, 'couldn't stand to leave us?'

Hatcher didn't smile. He walked over and put the tape recorder on the corner of the pool table and snapped it on. The regulars listened, then moved closer as Fong's voice recited his vicious litany.

'Oh my God,' Melinda breathed and, covering her mouth with her hand, turned her back to the table.

When it was over they were all grouped tightly around Hatcher, staring down at the machine. There was no explanation necessary; the tape spoke for itself.

'This lady was special to you, was she?' Prophett asked.

'Does it make any difference?' Hatcher said.

They all slowly shook their heads.

'I made a mistake,' Hatcher whispered. 'This morning when I

409

said Fong was too busy to bother with you? I was wrong. He'll kill and keep killing until he gets to me.'

'So?' said Earp.

'So the only choice is to force his hand. I'll go after him and force him to move on me in self-defense and I'll kill him.'

'Just like that?'

'That's right.'

'You said no more killing this morning,' Melinda said.

'I was wrong.'

'You're going to do this on your own?' said Potter.

'I still have a few good moves.'

'So why the Lone Ranger act?' asked Earp.

'It's my fight.'

'Not true, warrior,' Prophett said. 'It's our fight too. You don't have a monopoly on hate. You got the lady, we got Kilhanney.'

'You can't take the chance, none of you,' said Hatcher. 'You get caught, you blow everything you've put together here. It'll all come out.'

'Well, I've got nothing to hide,' said Earp.

'Me either,' said Corkscrew.

'Or me,' Potter chimed in.

'I say if we're going to do it, we take down the whole works,' said Riker.

'What do you mean?' asked Hatcher.

'I told you before, he's getting ready to make a major move on the U.S.,' said Earp. 'He's got two tons of skag on that junk. I seem to remember hearing you were the one took out the Dragon's Breath back in '72, '73, to try to slow down heroin coming into Saigon. What's the difference between then and now?'

Hatcher, his eyes the color of flint, stared at Earp. What Earp said was true. Wanting things to change didn't change anything.

'You're right,' Hatcher snapped. 'Nothing's changed.'

'We take down the junk, right?' Riker said with a grin.

'You looking for a fight?' said Hatcher.

'Fuckin'-A,' Corkscrew answered for him.

Hatcher walked behind the bar and drew himself half a glass of beer. He sipped it slowly, then wiped off his upper lip with his thumb.

Old instincts were stirring in Hatcher. And old memories. Once, many years before, 126 and 127 had been having one of their long philosophical discussions.

'Sometimes it is necessary for a man to play God,' 126 had

410

said. 'Sometimes God is too busy to take care of things himself and he delegates the authority.'

'How do you know?' 127 had asked. 'How do you know it's not prejudice or hate or envy?'

'Because it will not matter to you,' 126 answered. 'Because it will be a job without satisfaction.'

There would be no satisfaction in killing Tollie Fong. He was simply a volcano waiting to erupt. The time had come, Hatcher couldn't wait any longer. But Fong was no amateur. To do the job right would take everything he had. Just like the old days – as Sloan used to say, 'Do it and do it right.'

'An operation like this, there are only two choices,' Hatcher said. 'Either you go to him or you bring him to you. Either way, we've got to get him right. He doesn't travel alone, and if I count correctly, there're only five of us. We'd have to find the stash, figure out how to get to it – and to him.'

Earp smiled. 'I told you, soldier, we always know where he is. One of us always has the bastard in view. Right now he's on that junk. And you can kill two jackals with one shot.'

'How's that?' Hatcher asked.

'Because Sloan's there too, in the House of Dreams,' came the answer.

A TIME FOR KILLING

Hatcher recognized the area. He had been there once before. Only now at the end of the street beside the two sagging old buildings a large junk was moored, its gangplank stretched to the wharf. Thais moved up and down the plank and argued in loud tones with the men on the deck. On the side of the junk facing the river, several boats – longtails, snakes and klong buggies – huddled around the side of the big boat as the river merchants unloaded their purchases onto their river craft.

'I was here once before with Sy,' Hatcher said. 'That junk is sitting on the spot Wol Pot gave as his address.'

'That was his front,' said Earp. 'He ran the produce haul for Fong, bringing in fresh produce from Chon Buri down the coast. They sell it right off the boat to local dealers.'

'What makes you think his stash is on the junk?'

411

'Because the courier Murph aced picked up the package here,'
Earp continued. 'Sy was following him.'

'The son of a bitch wants to stay as close to his fortune as he
can get,' said Corkscrew.

'And the House of Dreams is in there, too?' Hatcher said.

Earp nodded. 'Fong's junk of plenty.'

'You're sure Sloan and Fong are in there?'

'They were half an hour ago.'

There were five of them in the van: Earp, Corkscrew, Potter,
Riker and Hatcher. Hatcher was wearing his flying belt and a coil
of rope thrown over his shoulder.

There was a clinking of metal on metal as the team prepared
their weapons: Hatcher's Aug, loaded with three extra magazines
in his belt, Corkscrew's 870 riot shotgun and 9 mm. H&K,
Potter's AK-47, which he had borrowed from Sweets Wilkie, and
Earp's trusty .375 'Buntline Special' stuck in one side of his belt,
two pockets full of quick loads and two pipe bombs stuck in the
opposite side of his waistband. Riker had a trusy old M-16.
Plenty of firepower, thought Hatcher. With that kind of firepower, they could hit Fong by surprise and quickly however bad
the odds were. *Hard and fast and no quarter,* he was thinking.
The old wham-bam-thank-you-ma'am approach.

Sy appeared from the shadows and jumped in the side panel
door. When he saw Hatcher, he looked embarrassed and lowered
his head in a sign of shame.

'You don't have to do that,' Hatcher said.

'I am sorry, Hatch,' he said without looking up.

'*Mai pen rai,*' Hatcher answered with a grin. 'I don't know
what you're better at, spying or fighting.'

The little Thai looked relieved. 'I went on board,' he said
excitedly. 'They think I am checking out their stuff to buy. The
Chinese are all down below.'

'How about that bunch?' Potter asked, pointing to several men
in black on the deck of the junk.

'They are Thais,' said Sy. 'They make talk for the food.'

'Salesmen,' Earp said and Sy nodded. 'They'll leave soon. The
junk market closes at nine.'

'Be good and dark by then,' Corkscrew said.

'Let me show you,' Sy said. 'Paper and ball poin', please?'

He was a good spy. Pretending to be a produce dealer, he had
studied the junk well. His map was full of little details, location
of hatchways, stairwells, cabins. The junk was a giant. The main
hold ran the width of the junk and half its length, an enormous

412

yawning cavern that could be filled with lettuce, rice, water-melons and whatever other produce Fong's front men had to sell. On one side of the hold was an open booth, a pleasant, comfortable space with pillows on the floor and a low-slung table where Fong and his men could sit in comfort, sip their scotch and monitor the produce market.

Opposite the booth on the forward end of the main hold was a wooden door leading to the cubicles called the House of Dreams. Nestled in the pro were three small cells.

There was only one stairwell – at the stern end of the hold.

There was an open hatchway near the water level on the river side of the boat through which produce was being off-loaded to waiting boats on the river. On deck, a thin latticework hatch afforded a view of the main hold.

A two-master with a small captain's cabin on the stern end.

'On this side, gas tanks,' said Sy, pointing to the starboard side, above the booth, the side adjoining the wharf.

'How do you know?' Hatcher asked.

'They were putting new fuel in from dock.'

'You don't miss a thing,' said Hatcher.

'Good fighter cannot miss anything,' he answered proudly.

'How many Chinese?' asked Hatcher.

'Fong, Kot, three others. They were sitting in the booth drinking. I do not see Sloan. There are two gunners on each side of hold downstairs, two more on main deck.'

'A mere eleven of them to four of us,' Hatcher sighed. 'You'd think the odds would get better with time.'

'What do you mean, four. I count six of us, if you include Sy,' said Riker.

'Sy stays outside,' said Earp. 'It isn't his fight. But he can provide us with a back-up getaway. You can't go in either, Riker. You can't afford to get caught – you have to keep the van warm.'

'When it starts,' said Hatcher, 'do it fast. Waste Fong and all his boys, burn the junk, and get the hell out. Don't think, just do it. And one more thing – Sloan is mine. We have unfinished business. Sy, find us a snakeboat real fast. And, Riker, keep the engine running. However it goes, this won't take long.'

Earlier in the day, Sloan had sought relief from his nightmares at the House of Dreams. Walking down into its darkened depths, he descended into his own personal hell, following the old man and the smell of opium to one of the cubicles, watching eagerly as the old man rolled the *goli* of thick tar and stuffed it in the pipe,

413

then taking the pipe and sucking its smoke deeply and slipping into his dream world. Lying on the cot, staring up into the darkness, his mind dispelled thoughts of Cody and Hatcher and Tollie Fong as the smoke took effect and he felt the ethereal rush. He began to hum an aimless song to himself and then to whistle very softly as he watched the blessed smoke twirl far up into the darkness above him. Around him, from the other cubicles, he saw the snakes of gray vapor rising too, like dozens of wispy cobras dancing to the tune of an invisible flute.

'Sloan?' The voice was familiar but seemed miles away.

Sloan sighed.

'You spend too much time on the pipe,' Tollie Fong's voice said. 'You have not been attending to business, as was our agreement.'

He stared up and refocused his eyes. Tollie Fong stood over him. There were three other Chins standing behind him. One of them was the new Red Pole, Billy Kot.

'You're ruining a perfectly good dream,' Sloan said softly, staring back up at the smoke.

'We need to talk.'

'Later.'

'You have broken a promise to me.'

'Later. I'm busy,' Sloan said dreamily.

'You stinking junkie,' Fong snarled back and hit Sloan in the mouth with a straight, hard right punch. Sloan went over backward, falling off the cot, his lips split and bleeding. He sat up, his eyes suddenly afire. *Control,* his opium-fogged mind thought. *Don't lose your control, Sloan.*

'That was a stupid thing to do,' he said through numbed lips.

'You made me a promise,' Fong hissed.

Sloan clambered off the floor. Only his eyes reflected his rage. 'You better pull it together, Fong, unless you're ready to take on the whole United States Army, because that's —'

Billy Kot hit him a sharp, hard rap on the back of the neck and Sloan fell abruptly to his knees. He turned painfully toward the short, wiry killer.

'This is the man who did your killing work for you,' Fong said contemptuously. 'His name is Billy Kot.'

Sloan slid onto the cot and wiped his mouth, staring down mutely at the blood on the back of his hand. The dope was beginning to wear off, chased by anger and pain.

'I'll give you one thing,' Sloan said quietly to Billy Kot. 'You're very good.'

414

The assassin nodded but said nothing.

'You don't know how good he really is – yet,' said Fong.

Sloan smiled up at his ally turned adversary. 'You scare me to death,' he said with resignation.

'You made me a promise, Sloan.'

'And so far I've kept my end of the bargain,' said Sloan.

'No! You said you would deliver Hatcher to me.'

'I said I'd have him find out if Cody was Thai Horse. If you weren't good enough to keep a finger on him, that's your problem.'

'You said he would kill Cody for us.'

Sloan shook his head. 'Never said that,' he said.

'You said he would kill Cody,' Fong insisted.

'I said he'd find him if he was alive,' Sloan said emphatically without raising his voice.

'Sloan, the deal was you would bring him in and he would find this Cody, if Cody indeed was Thai Horse, and he would kill him.'

'Well then, I was wrong about that,' Sloan said. The smile lingered on his swollen lips.

'You were wrong about a lot of things. This man of yours killed my number one in Hong Kong, tore up the Ts'e K'am Men Ti. He killed Batal and Billy Death – men we were training for you! And now he has vanished like clouds in the wind.'

'There's an old Swedish hymn that goes, "Nought is given 'neath the sun; nought is had that is not won."'

'I do not understand the meaning of that,' said Fong.

'Well, it is a little subtle for your pea brain,' Sloan said, wiping the blood from his split lips and staring numbly at it.

The pupils in Fong's eyes dilated with hate, his mouth remained a thin slash in his face. But he held his temper, his voice a whispered threat. 'We did our part of the bargain. Billy Kot killed the terrorist, took care of the bombing, killed the South American.'

Sloan looked up at the Chinese mobster, the usual smile on his face, his voice still soft as down.

'You idiot,' he said with a sneer.

The infuriated Fong pulled out his pistol. He held it an inch from the bridge of Sloan's nose. 'No *gwai-lo* talks to me like that.'

Sloan chuckled. He leaned his head forward until the muzzle of the gun rested against his forehead. 'Go ahead, shoot,' he said. '*Shoot,* you bastard!'

He stared past the gun, past Fong's arm and into his eyes.

415

'You need me,' Sloan said with an edge in his voice. 'You're sitting on dynamite. It's only a matter of time before the DEA tumbles on to your whole stash. They already know you got the stuff. They'll squash you like a bug. Without me, you'll be just another dumb Chinaman floating in the river.'

With a growl like an animal's, Fong slashed his pistol down on Sloan's skull, and the big man groaned and rolled over on his face.

'You are a dead soldier,' Fong hissed in his ear.

On the port side of the junk Hatcher worked his way up a pile of discarded produce and felt the surface of the boat, looking for chinks in its teakwood armor. He got a finger hold in a split in its side, pulled himself up and searched for another, then another, inching his way up the ancient side of the craft, split by split, chink by chink, like the old free-climbing days.

Unlike the regulars, he was too well known among the Chiu Chaos to walk brazenly aboard the produce boat. His face had been memorized by every one of Fong's assassins and he knew it. It was the way they operated. Like the FBI. Ten Most Wanted.

Earp, however, strolled the deck in a cowboy hat, a tan safari jacket tied loosely at the waist by a cloth belt. He lit a cigar, stared down through the latticework hatch into the hold below. He saw Billy Kot and two henchmen lounging in the booth, drinking. There was no sign of Fong.

Hatcher clung tenaciously to the side of the junk, his hand sliding quietly and expertly across its smooth teakwood hull. He felt a splinter, worked at it with his free hand, his sturdy fingers digging at the chink until he could get four fingertips into the slit. He pulled himself up slowly, let go with his other hand and groped for another slot.

On the deck of the junk, Earp thumped the watermelons, peeled back leaves of lettuce and smelled them, tried to look as if he knew what he was doing.

'Okay?' one of the Thai salesmen said.

'Yeah, not bad,' Earp answered. 'How much for the lot?' He swept his arm around the deck.

'All of it?' the astonished Thai answered.

'Yeah. What've you got below, any more stuff?'

'More of the same.'

'I'll just take a look.'

The Thai produce man, anxious to please Earp, led him toward the hatch that led belowdecks. Two Chinese gunmen leaned against the railing, watching them casually.

Sy swung a snaketail boat alongside and started chattering with one of the Thai off-loaders. Corkscrew, his shotgun tucked under his arm, pulled himself up on the lip of the boat and entered the hold. He saw Earp coming down the stairs.

Hatcher continued to inch his way up the side of the junk. Behind the guards he grasped the rail with one hand, then with the other, and then he peered over the side. He searched the people on deck for Potter but couldn't see him. Then he saw a stooped old Chinese walk over to one of the guards.

'A light, please?' the old man asked.

'No smoke.'

My God, it's Potter, Hatcher realized.

Potter stood in front of the other guard, who took out a Bic lighter and held it for him. Potter reached under his robe and grasped the handle of a K-Bar knife. Slowly he slid it out, and as Hatcher vaulted over the railing and pulled back the guard's head and slit his throat, Potter jammed the heavy assault knife, hilt deep, under the ribs of the second guard and up into his heart.

They both died without a sound.

Hatcher ran to the mainmast and quickly tied a rope around it, slipping one end through the ring in his belt.

Potter continued down the stairway toward the hold.

In the hatch a swaggering Earp walked over to the booth where Billy Kot and his two compatriots were sitting. Tollie Fong was nowhere to be seen.

'The name's Holliday, from Valdosta, Georgia, U.S. of A.,' Earp bellowed. 'I'm interested in buying up the rest of this cargo.'

'The whole thing?' Billy Kot asked with surprise.

'That's right. Allow me to give you my card.'

Earp stared into Billy Kot's eyes and, with a single, lightning move, reached under his jacket, hauled out his long-barreled .44, swung it out until it was six inches from Billy Kot's heart and fired. The gun roared, the shot ripped into Billy Kot's chest and exploded into his heart. He was lifted six inches off the floor and blown backward into the open hatch of the junk, where he landed spread-eagled on his back and slid to a stop.

Earp dived over the table and rolled away, he clawed loose one of the pipe bombs from his belt, lit it with his cigar and threw it over his shoulder toward the bulkhead.

On deck, Hatcher jumped up and, holding his legs together, came down feetfirst on the thin latticework hatch cover. It shattered and he dropped through. The floor below swept up

417

toward him. The Aug spat quietly in his hand, cutting down the other two Chinese gangsters in the alcove as Hatcher hit the floor.

The main room of the junk disintegrated into chaos.

Earp's bomb bounced with a ringing sound and exploded. Bits of wall and doors vanished in a white-hot blast, and a shower of dust and bits of wood clattered into the room. Flames licked the bulkhead of the junk.

Fong crouched in one of three small cells in the fore section of the junk adjacent to the cubicles of the opium den. Sloan sat on the floor leaning against the bulkhead. Fong leaned over so his face was inches from Sloan's. 'I will enjoy killing you, Harry,' he said softly.

Sloan laughed. It wasn't a big laugh, but it was sincere. 'You're stupid enough to do that,' Sloan said.

'I'm going to kill you a little bit at a time!' Fong said, his voice rising with his anger.

'Your smoke's been doing that for a long time,' Sloan said with a wave of his hand. He was staring at the floor, trying to get his bearings, trying to make his way through the hazy slow motion induced by drug and concussion.

'I'll wait until you come down,' Fong said. 'When it will hurt the most. I'm going to kill you and every *gwai-lo* that Yankee bastard Hatcher knows. I will kill the world out from under him. Then he will come to me.'

'I wouldn't look forward to that if I were you,' Sloan said.

A moment later, Earp's bomb went off.

Fong was knocked to his knees as the junk shuddered from the explosion. He whirled toward the sounds of gunfire, and Sloan slammed his foot into his back, sending him sprawling out of the cell. The gunman spun around and fired a shot at Sloan. The bullet ripped into his side.

'Ahh, damn!' Sloan bellowed and rolled into a tight ball against the bulkhead.

The stoned opium heads in the House of Dreams, awakened from their dreams by the explosion and the gunfire that followed, swarmed from their cubicles and rushed toward the main hold. Screaming, bumping into each other, babbling, tumbling down the narrow passage, they choked it from wall to wall, their vacant eyes suddenly alive with fear. The door to the House of Dreams burst open. Earp, Potter and Corkscrew were raking the interior of the junk with shotgun and rifle fire. A bullet smashed into Corkscrew's leg but he kept shooting. House of Dreams customers stumbled into gunfire, flames, smoke and destruction.

Faced with the insane nightmare, Fong forgot Sloan and dashed into the middle of the mad scramble, slashing his way with his gun through the crazed mob toward the exit. Then as he looked up he saw his deadliest enemy at the other end of the passageway. Hatcher, his eyes aglow with determination, was waiting for him at the exit to the main hatch.

Forgetting his own peril for the moment, Fong started firing at Hatcher. Hatcher ducked but did not back off. He charged into the screaming mob of Chinese, zigzagged directly toward Fong, his Aug chopping away at the wall as Fong ducked into the mass of fleeing men and then veered off into one of the opium cubicles.

A second bomb exploded, bursting another cache of produce to bits. The explosion sent Hatcher, Fong and the terrified dopers sprawling. More flames spewed from the side of the boat, and then from the center of the pile of shattered vegetables a geyser of white powder poured out. Tollie Fong's precious cargo of China White showered from its ruptured hiding place as flames roared up the side of the junk.

Hatcher fell against the wall as the turmoil intensified. Fong jumped into one of the cubicles of the House of Dreams and crouched there, waiting him out.

Hatcher started down the passageway, hugging the wall, his gun ready.

Behind him, Potter searched the bulkhead, saw the telltale bulge of the two hundred-gallon gas tanks. He cut loose with the AK-47. The 9 mm. slugs thunked into the tanks, rent them, blew off the nozzles. Gasoline sprayed out into the hold, hit the flames started by the two bombs.

Fire streaked up the streams of gas, burst into the tanks and exploded. Two tremendous swirling yellow balls of flame boiled out under the deck and swept through the hull. The blazing gas spilled out over the heroin and ignited it, melting it into black charcoal. The junk was transformed into an orange inferno.

Hatcher dived for the floor and covered his head with his hands. Fire roiled over his head and set the passage aflame.

A gas-fed fireball swept over Fong. His face was seared by the flames. His clothes burst into flames. Then the second tank blew, exploding the side of the junk, and the screaming Fong arced like a blazing skyrocket through the hole into the river.

The regulars rushed up the stairs and out of the roaring tomb, leaving behind Fong's dead or dying mobsters. Earp and Potter, dragging the wounded Corkscrew, rushed down the gangplank with the terrified Thai produce men into pure chaos on the wharf. A fire truck came through the crowd with its siren screaming. Behind it a police car appeared, then another. Riker spotted them and dropped the van into gear, pulling over beside his friends. Earp shoved Corkscrew in the side door before rolling in himself, and was followed by Potter, who slammed the door shut.

'Let's move it,' Earp said, and Riker turned the van away from the blazing junk, and headed away from Chinese Town.

'How'd it go?' Riker asked.

'We did the job,' Earp said.

'Three minutes, twenty-five seconds,' Potter said.

Earp checked the wounded Corkscrew. 'How's the leg?' he asked.

'Think it's broken,' he groaned.

'I got an old Purple Heart you can have,' said Potter, lying on his back gasping for breath.

'Already got one,' Corkscrew said and mustered as much of a laugh as the pain would allow.

Inside the burning passageway, Hatcher crawled quickly toward the bow of the junk. The fire roared around him, flames snatching at his clothes. He kicked open one of the small hatches, then the next, and saw Sloan crouched against the bulkhead clutching his bleeding side. Flames roared overhead like a furnace. Heat devoured oxygen. Hatcher dashed in, grabbed him by the collar and, dragging him to his feet, rushed toward the only open side hatch that wasn't consumed by fire.

'Can't do it!' Sloan cried out.

'Bullshit,' Hatcher answered.

'Hatch, over here!' Sy yelled, still in the snakeboat and hanging on to the side of the junk. Hatcher dragged Sloan through the flames and shoved him out of the open hatch and into the boat and tumbled in after him.

'Get the hell out of here,' he said, and Sy turned the slender boat and roared away from the inferno.

FINISHED BUSINESS

Sy eased the snakeboat up beside the wharf and Hatcher helped Sloan out. The wound in his side was still bleeding, despite a makeshift bandage Hatcher had fashioned from Sloan's shirttail.

420

'See you around sometime, Sy,' Hatcher said as he and Sloan struggled out of the boat and onto the wharf. Three blocks away the waterfront was pandemonium. The flaming junk cast a yellow glow over the river and the fire trucks, police cars and spectators on the pier.

'You be okay?' Sy asked.

'We're fine, pal. Head up one of the klongs and dump the boat. And stay away from the Longhorn for a couple of days.'

'You okay guy, Hatch,' the little Thai said.

'And you're a great fighter,' Hatcher answered.

He hoisted Sloan, helping him away from the wharf and across the street to an alley. It was deserted and quiet, the clamor from the fire scene barely discernible in the background. Finally Sloan fell against the wall and, sliding to the ground, squeezed his riddled side. Hatcher knelt beside him, pulled his hand away and inspected the wound.

'A beesting,' he said, 'you'll get over it.'

'It's killing me,' Sloan groaned, pressing his jacket against the wound.

'I should kill you. You're a menace. You lied to me, double-crossed me, set me up. If anybody deserved to die, it was you, not Cody.'

The customary smile played at Sloan's lips. 'No sympathy, huh, laddie?'

'I'd sooner have sympathy for the devil.'

'Hell, you couldn't kill me,' Sloan said wearily. 'I'm family.'

'Oh, I could kill you, Harry. But I'm not going to and it has nothing to do with family.'

'I did what I had to do, you did what you had to do,' said Sloan. 'I don't have to explain that to you.'

'There was no other way to deal with the problem,' Hatcher said.

'I've got the same trouble all over the world.'

'No, Harry. This was survival. Your job is political expediency.'

'Whatever you call it, you do it and forget it.'

'No, *you* do it and forget about it. *I* think about it.'

'Ah bullshit. You're a soldier. You did what soldiers do.'

'You've been telling me that for years. I didn't do what soldiers do, I did what *you* told me to do.'

'Why the hell did you come over here anyway?' Sloan asked.

'I thought I was doing something decent for a change, a sense of responsibility to an old friend. I'm talking about Cody, not you.'

421

Sloan said, 'Ahh,' and waved the remark off with his hand. There was a moment of awkward silence and then Sloan said, 'You were the best, the best I ever had. The perfect shadow warrior.'

'Trouble is, you ran out of soldiers, didn't you, Harry. One double cross too many, one lie too often, and one morning you woke up and you didn't have any warriors left. They were either dead, crippled or had quit. That's why you made your deal with Fong.'

Sloan leaned over and pressed his side harder and groaned with the pain that was burning deep in his side. 'Just tell me one thing,' he asked. 'Is Cody alive?'

'No, he's dead,' Hatcher whispered. 'He died a long time ago.'

'I'll be damned,' said Sloan. 'All this fuss for nothing.'

'It wasn't for nothing. It was a payoff trip.'

'Payoff? To who?'

'You were paying off Tollie Fong.'

'You're crazy. Why would I owe Tollie Fong anything. Because I smoked a little of his pipe?'

'No. Because he took our place. When you ran out of soldiers, you had an execution squad made to order – Fong and his Chiu Chao assassins. He got rid of Campon for you in Atlanta because Campon was too independent, too corrupt. Sooner or later it would have come out and the boys in the State Department would've had fits dealing with that. On the other hand, Cosomil was nice and safe.'

'And he didn't have half of Madrango's treasury in bank accounts in Switzerland,' Sloan added.

'And Cosomil would be a good little boy and take his orders from the White House,' said Hatcher.

Behind them, two dozen yards away, Tollie Fong swam out of the darkness and grabbed a ladder on the dock. His arm was burned and his face was scorched. He started up the ladder and heard the voices. He cautiously peeked over the lip of the wharf. Hatcher and Sloan were fifty yards away.

'I know you too well,' Hatcher was saying. 'I've done the same things for you too many times. In Paris you were in real top form. You not only got rid of three ambassadors that were giving us a bad time about our bases in Europe, you laid it off on the Hyena and got rid of him too. You always were resourceful. Always looking to cover two or three bases at a time.'

'Well, that's the mission, isn't it?'

'That's a matter of interpretation.'

422

'Call it whatever you want. The enemy never sleeps, pal, don't forget it. You want to turn namby-pamby, go right ahead, but let me tell you, if I can get rid of a piece of shit like Hadif and I have to bend the rules a little, you bet your ass I'll do it. It's my *job*. Sure, I made a deal with Fong. He was on the same side we're on.'

'He may have been on your side, Harry. He sure as hell wasn't on mine.'

'I had that under control.'

Fong clung to the ladder and sneered as he listened to Sloan's confident explanation.

'He raped and murdered Daphne Chien in cold blood just to get even with me,' Hatcher said hoarsely. 'He was about to hand you your brains. He was training antiterrorists upriver, that's what ex-SAVAKs and Tontons were doing up there.'

'He was training them for me,' Sloan said bluntly.

Hatcher shook his head. 'And what was the big payoff, Harry? Were you going to set him up so he could smuggle a thousand keys of 999 past customs?'

'What the hell, if it wasn't him it'd be somebody else. It's good for the economy.'

'Fifteen years ago you sent me upriver to get rid of the Chiu Chao dope smugglers. Now you're in bed with them.'

'Water under the bridge, laddie,' said Sloan. 'You've got Paris, New York, Chicago, your buddy in the insurance company. I've got Thailand. What the hell's the diff?'

Hatcher stood up.

'For years I thought you had turned me into a judge, jury and executioner. It finally got to me in Los Boxes, when I had nothing else to think about. Now I know I was never judge and jury – that was your job. I was just the executioner. Anyhow, somebody else will have to judge you. I'm through with all of that.'

'Where are you going?'

'Home.'

'What about me?'

'Tell Buffalo Bill his son died honorably on the field of battle. He can die in peace. See you, Harry.'

Hatcher turned and walked away.

'Wait a minute, damn it!' Sloan called after him.

But Hatcher vanished into the swirling black smoky mist.

'The world is divided into the shit-throwers and the shit-throwees, Hatcher,' Sloan yelled after him. 'Remember that. The throwees have damn little to recommend them.'

Sloan leaned back against the wall. The pain in his side burned deeper, but he turned his mind away from it as he worked up a story for the Thai major, the Mongoose, when he showed up.

He didn't hear Tollie Fong drag himself painfully out of the river behind him, didn't hear him creep across the dock, his feet squishing under him. Fong was almost on top of him before he became aware of his presence and turned – just in time to see the deadly dagger drop silently through the air and feel its awful point pierce his throat.

FISHING

Hatcher lay flat on his back staring at the ceiling. The boat rocked gently in the evening breeze, occasionally bumping the dock. He felt safe here and secure. It was good to be back home. After twelve hours of sleep his furnaces were beginning to fire up again. He watched a sliver of sunlight move slowly across the ceiling and vanish as the sun set. The mantle of darkness brought with it the night birds, who started calling to one another. He heard the car cruise slowly into the parking lot, its wheels crushing the oyster shells under them, and then the familiar footsteps. He felt the boat rock ever so gently. His eyes closed, and a moment later he felt her sit on the edge of the bed.

'You're late,' he said without opening his eyes.

'I went by the Crab Trap. Got us some shrimp and clam chowder,' she said. 'I didn't think either of us felt like cooking tonight.'

He reached up, pulled her gently down beside him, and she nuzzled his neck with her face.

'I was thinking,' he said. 'Why don't we crank up the old scow and take a run out to the reef, eat out there, maybe even go for a moonlight swim.'

'The ocean's getting cold,' she said.

'Sure, I'll bet it's a freezing seventy-five degrees out there.'

There was a difference in their metabolism. She was always cold and he was always warm. What was comfortable to him raised goose bumps on her arms. In the heat of summer, air conditioning drove her crazy, while it was his salvation. But he had learned to compromise, something that had been alien to his experience before he met her. Ceiling fans and fast runs through the sound to the open sea worked for both of them.

She lay close to him, stroking his hard arms and hard stomach and wrapping one leg over his, pressing against him, drawing his strength to her.

'Are you all right?' she asked. It was the first thing she had asked him since his return the night before.

'Tired,' he answered. 'It's been a rough two weeks.'

'Was the trip successful?'

'Yes.'

She did not ask why he had gone or what had happened on the trip; she was grateful that he had returned as quickly as he had.

As he lay there she noticed that the hair on his arm was singed and his fingernails were cracked and damaged. But she put her curiosity aside. She knew eventually he would tell her what he wanted her to know. The rest was part of the secretness she had come to accept.

'I had some bad times on this trip,' he said suddenly, surprising her.

'Bad in what way?'

'The Chinese have a saying, "Killing the past scars the soul." I put a lot of scars on my soul this trip.'

'Are you sure you want to talk about this?'

'No, I think it would be better to forget it, but I want you to know there were chapters in my life that needed closing and now they're closed. There's nothing more to be gained by looking back or talking about them.'

'Oh, I don't know. We learn from the past.'

'There's nothing I want to learn from mine.'

Unconsciously she rubbed the stubble on his arm as he spoke.

'I put a lot of ghosts to rest.' He sighed.

'Is that why you went?'

He hesitated for a moment before answering. 'That was part of it. I also felt an obligation to an old friend.'

'Did all this have to do with that man who came here?'

'He was part of it. He was the catalyst. It's much too complicated to explain. But I'm glad I went. I had to deal with some things I've been ignoring for a long time.'

'What kind of things?'

'The dark side of my nature.'

'Ah, so there is a dark side after all.'

'Yes. There sure is.'

'I've never seen that side of you.'

'You see only what people let you see, Ginia.'

'Is this going to be some kind of confession?'

'No. I'd like to forget it now.'

'Then I'll forget it,' she said. 'I only know I missed you. I missed you every day. I'd come by the boat and sit up there and wonder where you were and what you were doing and whether you were well. I had this awful feeling you weren't coming back.'

Close, he thought, your instincts are pretty damn good.

'I thought a lot about you, too,' he said.

'I realized how little I know about you in those two weeks,' she said. 'I don't know anything about you before you came to the island. You could be married, for all I know.'

He laughed. 'No, no wife. No children. No ugly surprises like that.'

'I didn't know you went to Annapolis, although I suppose I should have guessed, you're so good with boats.'

'Where did you learn that?'

'From Jim Cirillo. I was over one day cleaning the boat and he came by. He really loves you, you know, I don't think I ever realized that before. You're like a son to him. He worries about you.'

'And do you?'

She smiled, nuzzling harder. 'Not when you're here.'

'I don't think I'll be going anywhere for a long time now.'

'That's good news.'

'It is?'

'I've become too accustomed to being with you, Hatcher. It's screwed up my life-style.'

'Screwed it up?'

'Well, not in a bad sense. I suppose that was the wrong way of putting it. I've become – dependent on you for certain things. I was always radically independent before you. That kind of thing can be, uh, uncomfortable.'

He rose on his elbows and stared down at her. The lights from the wharf reflected off the water and danced on the ceiling of the cabin. She turned her eyes away from his and rolled over, swinging her legs to the floor.

'Why don't I get our dinner ready,' she said. 'You must be starved.'

He reached out and pulled her back across his lap.

'Not for food,' he said.

'See,' she said, 'that's what I mean –'

'Listen to me,' he said. 'I'm attracted to you like I've never been attracted to any other woman. It's not just sex, it's everything. It's this island that you're part of. It's the way you

426

think, your independence, your sense of humor. The mystery of you.'

'Mystery?'

'We both have dark times in our past – everybody does.'

'And you think that's good?'

'I think it's interesting. There are some things that don't need to be shared.'

'Well, I think your mysteries are probably one hell of a lot more interesting than mine.'

'What I did on this trip, it was like cleaning out the attic, throwing away things that don't really matter anymore. The friends I said good-bye to will always be friends. It's just that our wavelengths have changed. My life is here, not there.'

He leaned over and kissed her softly on the mouth. Her lips, soft and yielding at first, became demanding. Her hand moved up the back of his neck, pressed his face harder against hers. Then suddenly she broke away and sat up. 'Going to the reef is a wonderful idea,' she said. 'Besides, some of your fishing pals are liable to drop by if we stay here.'

'I'll put out the "Do not disturb" sign.'

She stood up and shook her clothes back in place.

'No. Get some clothes on and crank this thing up.'

'Done, mate,' he whispered. He slipped on a pair of gray jogging pants, a T-shirt and sneakers and went up on deck. A southeasterly wind blew in off the ocean, carrying with it a hint of rain. The sky was dark, moonless and cloud-cluttered.

'It tastes like rain,' he said.

'Good. I like to make love in the rain.'

'It could get choppy out there.'

'Are you backing out?' she demanded.

'Oh hell no, just making observations.'

A hundred feet away in the darkness of the parking lot, a skulking figure watched the boat, saw Hatcher and the woman come out on deck, heard their laughter, watched them kiss each other.

Tollie Fong leered in the darkness. Perfect, he thought. Two *gwai-lo* for the price of one.

Hatcher put the key in the ignition, primed the engine and cranked it up. In the stern the two big engines rumbled to life and muttered cantankerously for a minute or two before settling into a low, steady growl. Ginia went up on the wharf and loosened the bowline, coiling it over elbow and hand before dropping it on deck. Then she went to the rear and did the same, dropping the coiled line near the stern.

427

Hatcher was a formidable foe, but this time surprise would be on Fong's side. He moved closer through the shadows, focusing on Hatcher. He could tell he was unarmed. And there did not appear to be any weapons secreted in the cockpit.

Safe and secure, they thought. Focused on each other.

That would make it all the sweeter and easier. Fong thought.

Hatcher was busy turning on radar and sonar and radio and other switches. He completed his usual check of engines and rpm's and fuel.

'How about a beer for the captain?' he said.

'Aye, aye,' she said, vanishing into the cabin for a minute.

As she appeared back in the hatchway with a beer in each hand, he felt the boat dip ever so slightly to port. But before he could turn he saw her eyes widen, heard her gasp, then heard the voice.

'Hatcher,' it hissed.

He turned quickly. Fong was twenty feet away, standing in the bow of the boat, a pistol pointed at Hatcher's head. Fear streaked through him for a moment, a lightning flash dispelled instantly by the thought of Ginia. He moved to his left in front of her.

'What —' she began and Hatcher said, softly, 'Shh.'

'Always the hero, eh?' Fong snarled, his yellow eyes eager with anticipation. 'You think standing in front of her will help? What a futile little gesture. I will kill her first, Hatcher, before I skin you alive.'

'My God,' Ginia whispered behind Hatcher.

There was a twisted ugly patch of skin on one side of Fong's face, the result of a burn that would be a perpetual scar. His eye was half closed. The hair on one side of his head had been scorched to within an inch of his scalp. One hand was bandaged. Fong had avoided painkillers to stay alert as he followed Hatcher halfway across the world. Now hatred, mixed with the pain, oozed out of him, fired his eyes, distorted what was left of his ruined face.

'How appropriate,' Fong said in a voice that was soft but trembling with fury. 'First my boat, then yours.'

Hatcher still did not respond. He was standing squarely in front of Ginia now. He knew where she was standing, knew he could make a backward tumble and knock her back into the cabin. But then what? He was unarmed. The closest weapon was a knife in the galley. His weapons were locked away in the hold.

The thought flashed in Hatcher's mind that he was going to die, and he accepted that as a reality. But he also knew Fong would kill Ginia. And probably first.

428

Fong stood in the bow of the boat, his automatic aimed at Hatcher's head.

'Surprised?' Fong said.

Hatcher still did not answer. Within his peripheral vision he could see Fong step closer to the coil of rope on the deck. But the throttles were just out of reach and to go for them, to try to throw him off-balance, would leave Ginia exposed.

The gleaming blade of Fong's stiletto appeared at Fong's sleeve. His fingers clutched the hilt. He held the knife up, twisting it slightly so its evil blade glittered in the light from the dock.

'Just for you,' Fong said. 'I used it on Sloan, too. Just after you left him there – alone.'

Hatcher still did not respond.

'What's the matter, Hatcher, can't you talk anymore?'

'You're going to die too, you know,' he said finally.

'Don't you wish. I'll be back in Hong Kong before they even find you.'

Fong took another step closer. Hatcher's muscles tensed. He spread his feet a little farther apart.

'Why don't you beg for the lady's life at least,' Fong sneered. 'Why don't you get down on your knees and do that.'

He took another step. His foot was inside the ring of rope on the deck.

'You'd really like that, wouldn't you,' Hatcher whispered.

Fong smiled, an ugly leer, bubbling over with satisfaction.

'Yes,' he hissed, 'I would like that a lot.'

'Forget it,' Hatcher snapped. He shoved backward, knocking Ginia back down the stairs into the cabin, dodged to his left and then just as quickly jumped to the right. Fong's eyes widened. He fired once. The bullet sighed past Hatcher's ear and arced off the corner of the windscreen as Hatcher's hand found the throttles.

A second shot rang out. But it did not come from Fong's gun; it came from up the pier somewhere in the dark, hitting Fong squarely in the chest. His shirt burst open and blood splashed from his heart. He shrieked with pain.

Hatcher dived forward, grabbing the coil of rope and pulling it so it snapped around Fong's ankle. The Chinese flew backward off the boat and hit the water with a flat, hard splash. Hatcher wrapped the other end of the line around a rail hitch. He turned and crawled back to the cabin.

Ginia was sitting flat on the lower deck, her eyes wide with shock. Hatcher grabbed her hand and pulled her up and wrapped his arms around her. 'It's okay, it's all over,' he said.

'Am I gonna be getting you out of trouble for the rest of eternity?' Cirillo said, stepping out of the shadows. He held his weapon in the crook of his arm.

Ginia sagged into Hatcher's arms.

'Where did you come from?' Hatcher said with a sigh.

'Saw Old Bob Hill up at the Big T. He saw this Oriental gentleman follow you in last night, so I decided to check him out. Pretty smart guy. He came in to Jacksonville on the plane *ahead* of you, rented a car, then waited until you arrived and followed you up here. You're getting awful reckless in your old age,' Cirillo said.

'I thought he was dead,' Hatcher said simply.

'He is now,' Cirillo answered, looking down at Fong's body, which had rolled over facedown in the water. 'Can I assume this is one of the bad guys?'

'The worst.'

'So how do we explain this to the rest of the world?' Cirillo asked.

Hatcher pulled in the line until Fong's lifeless body was a foot or so off the stern and tightened it around the rail hitch.

'We don't,' Hatcher answered.

'I don't understand.'

'Trust me on this, Jimmy. This guy doesn't even deserve six feet of earth. I'm going to make a run out to the reef and feed the fish.'

Cirillo stared at his friend for a long time, perhaps a full minute. He reached in his pocket and took out a set of car keys and held them up.

'He was planning a fast getaway,' said Cirillo. 'Left the keys in the car. Rental papers are in the glove compartment. It was prepaid by credit card. I think maybe I'll just drive it down the Jax airport and drop the keys on the desk.'

'Thanks, Jimmy. Believe me, you did the world a favor putting a bullet in him.'

Cirillo stared down at the soggy form floating facedown behind the big boat. He lit a cigarette with a match, which he flicked into the water. 'Gimme a call when you get back.'

'I'll do that,' Hatcher said. He stepped into the cockpit, and eased the throttles forward.

Hatcher put his arm around Ginia and drew her close to him. 'You okay?'

430

'I . . . think . . . so.'

'Good.'

'I think maybe we need to talk about this one,' she said.

He smiled and said, 'I think maybe you're right,' and pulling her closer to him, he shoved the throttles forward and the big boat streaked out into the sound with its ugly cargo dragging through the water behind it, past the now empty pier, past the friendly finger of light from the lighthouse, out to the open sea toward the reef.